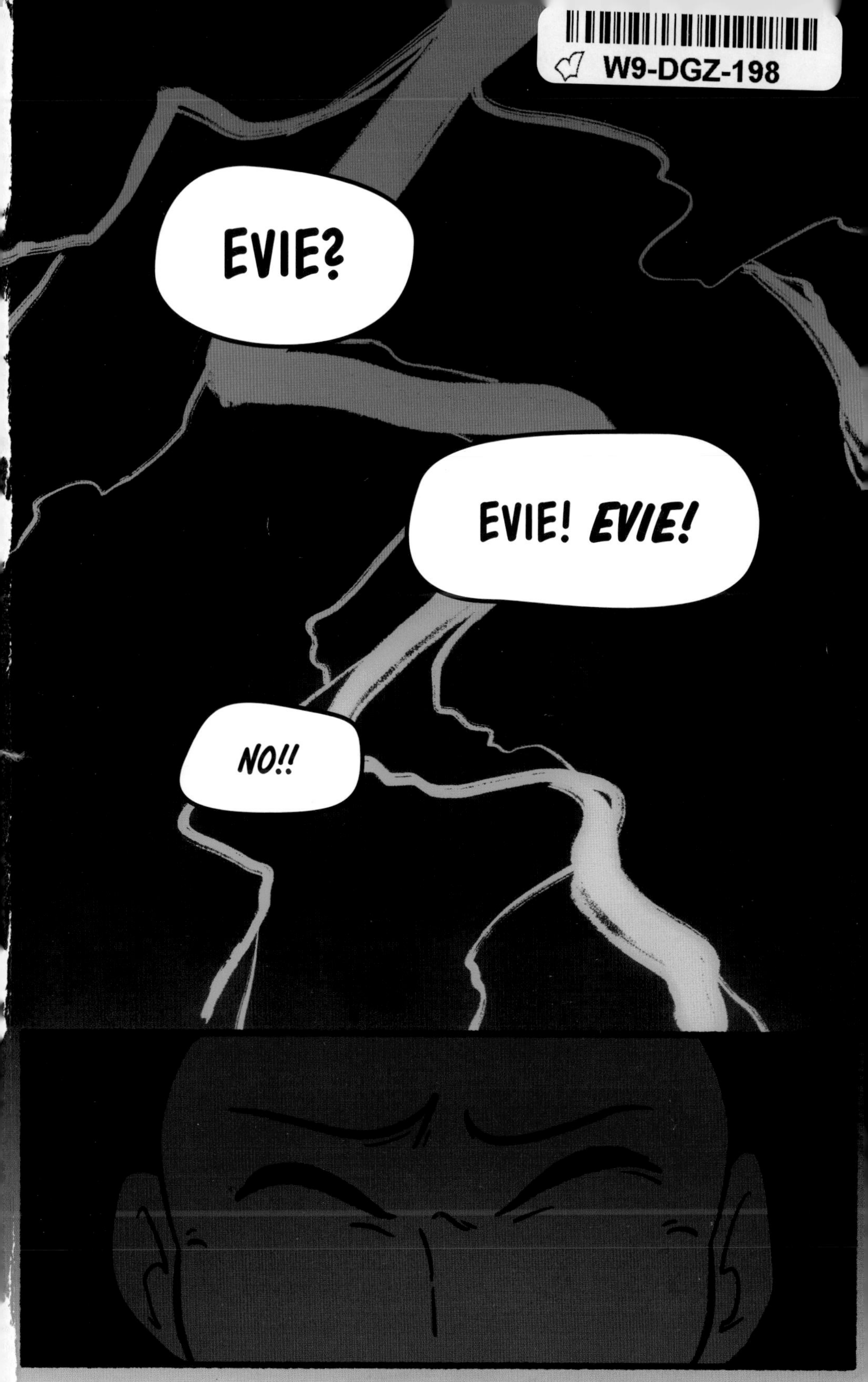
EVIE?
EVIE! EVIE!
NO!!

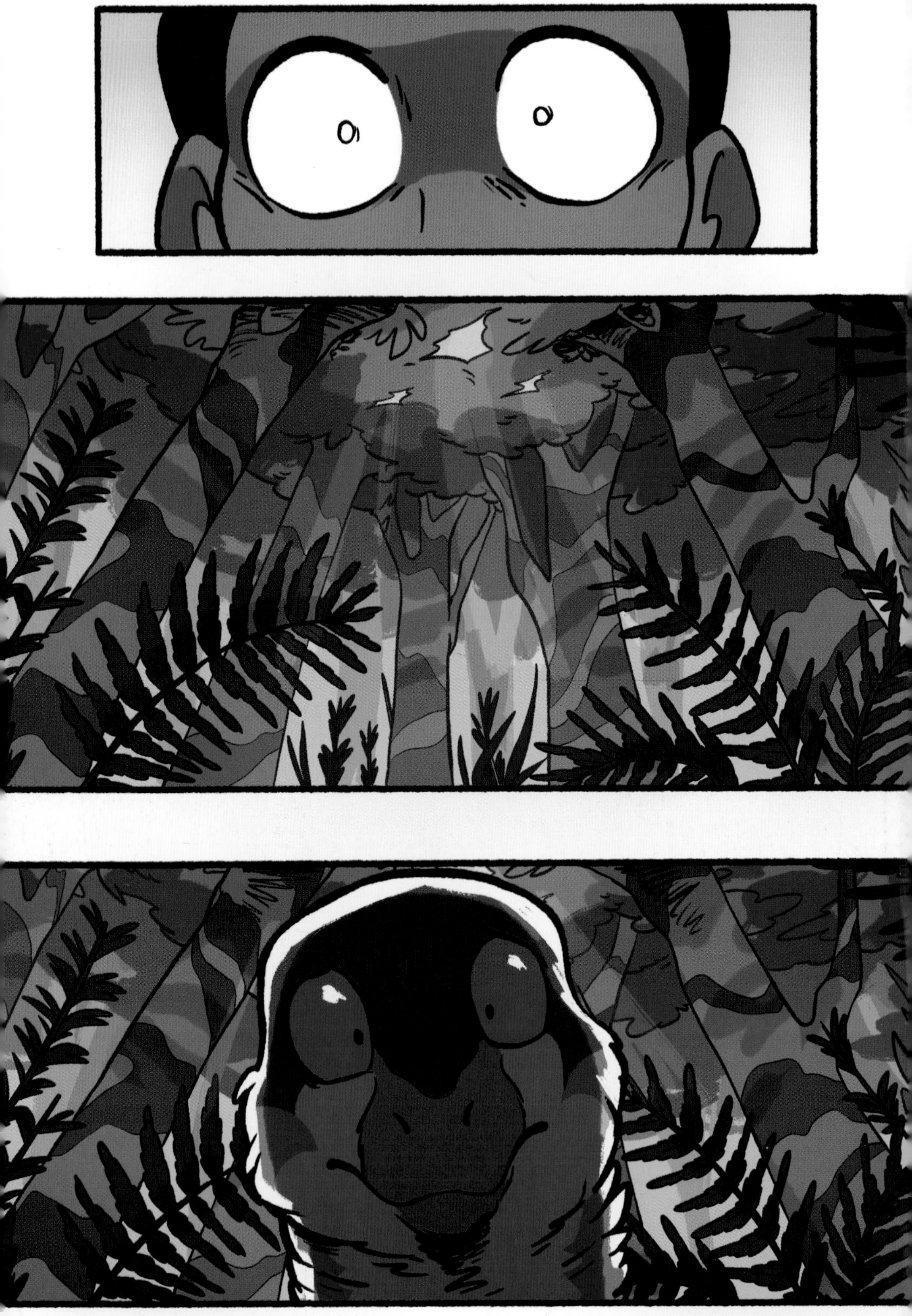

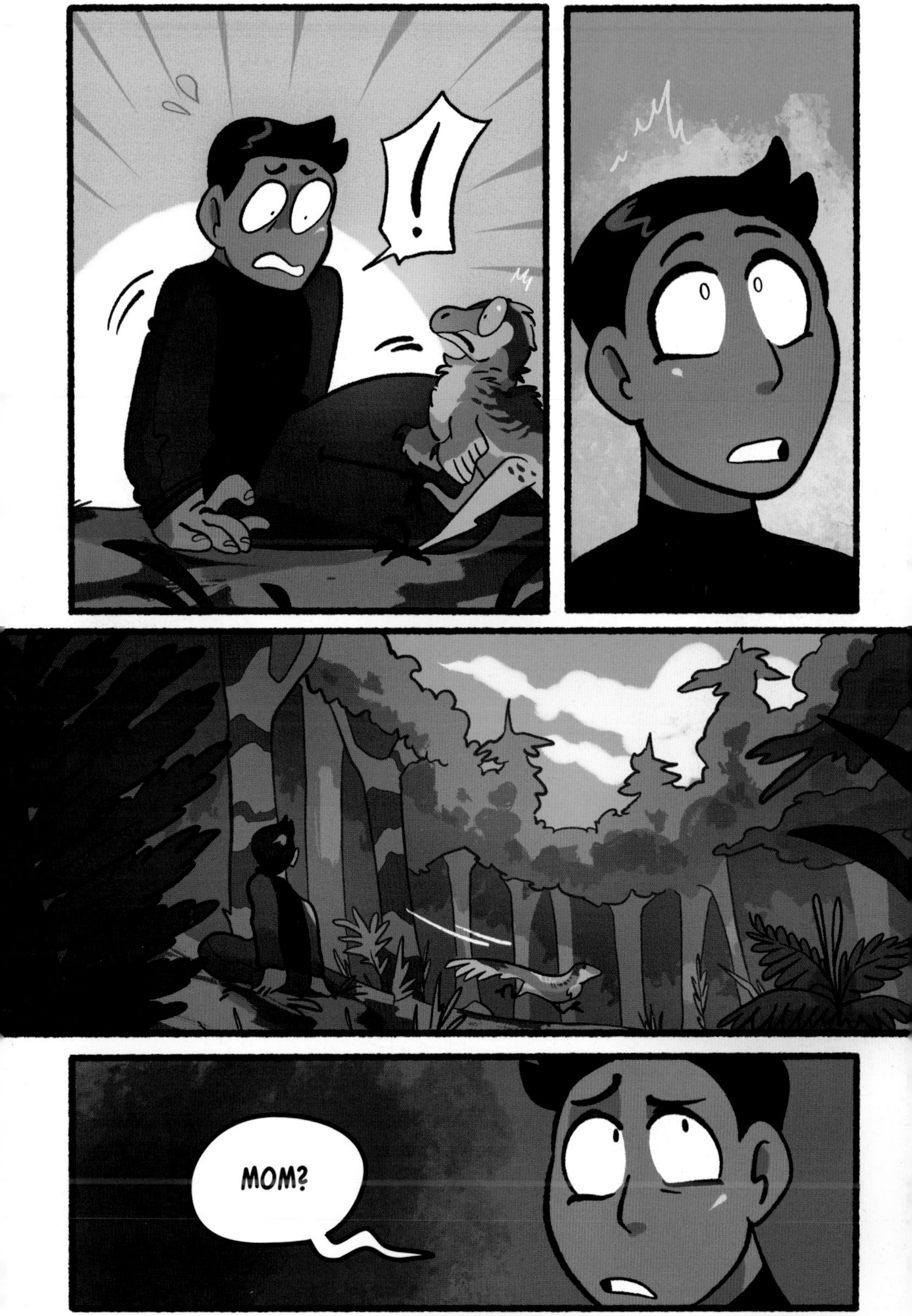
!
MOM?

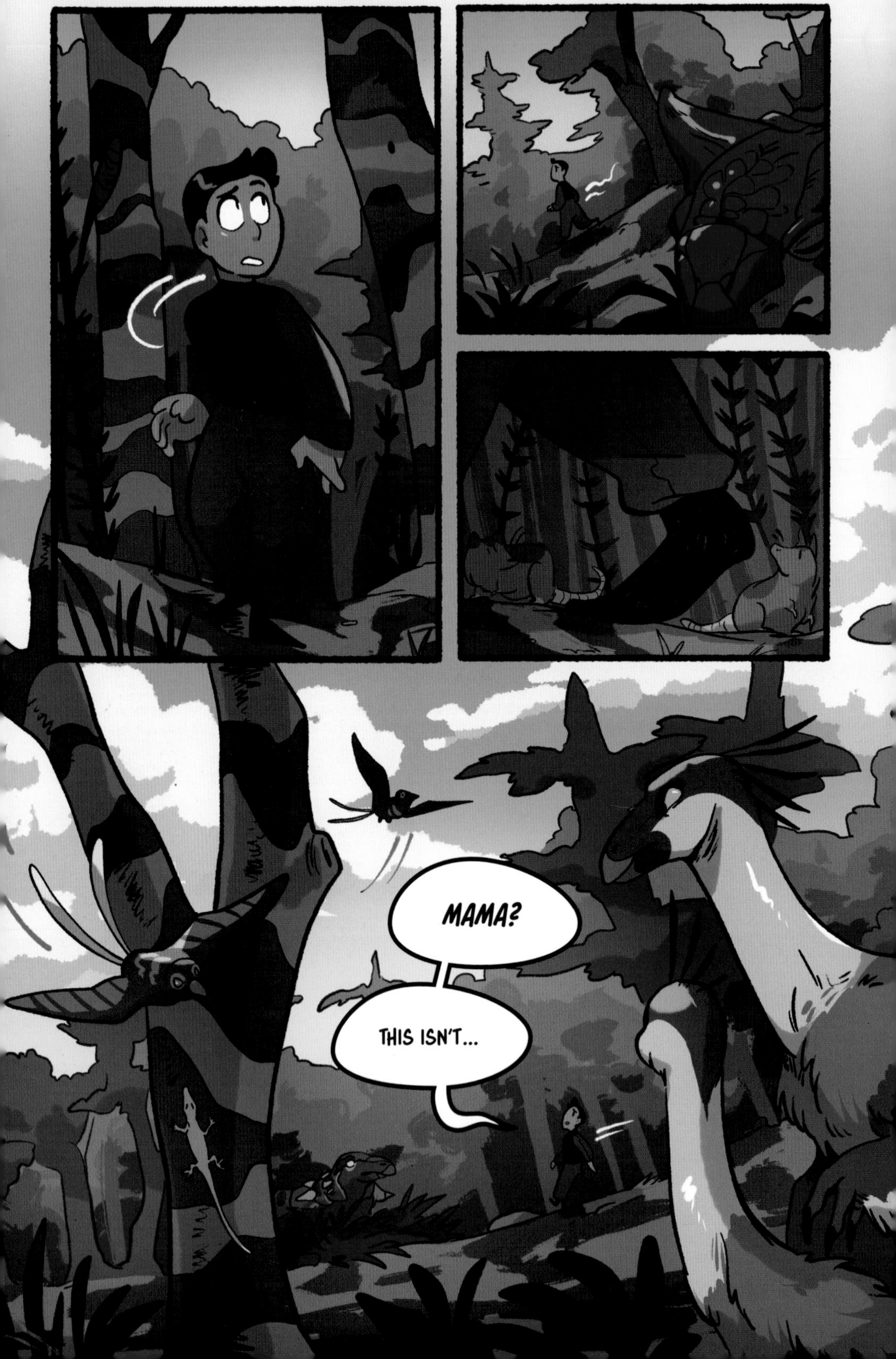
MAMA?
THIS ISN'T...

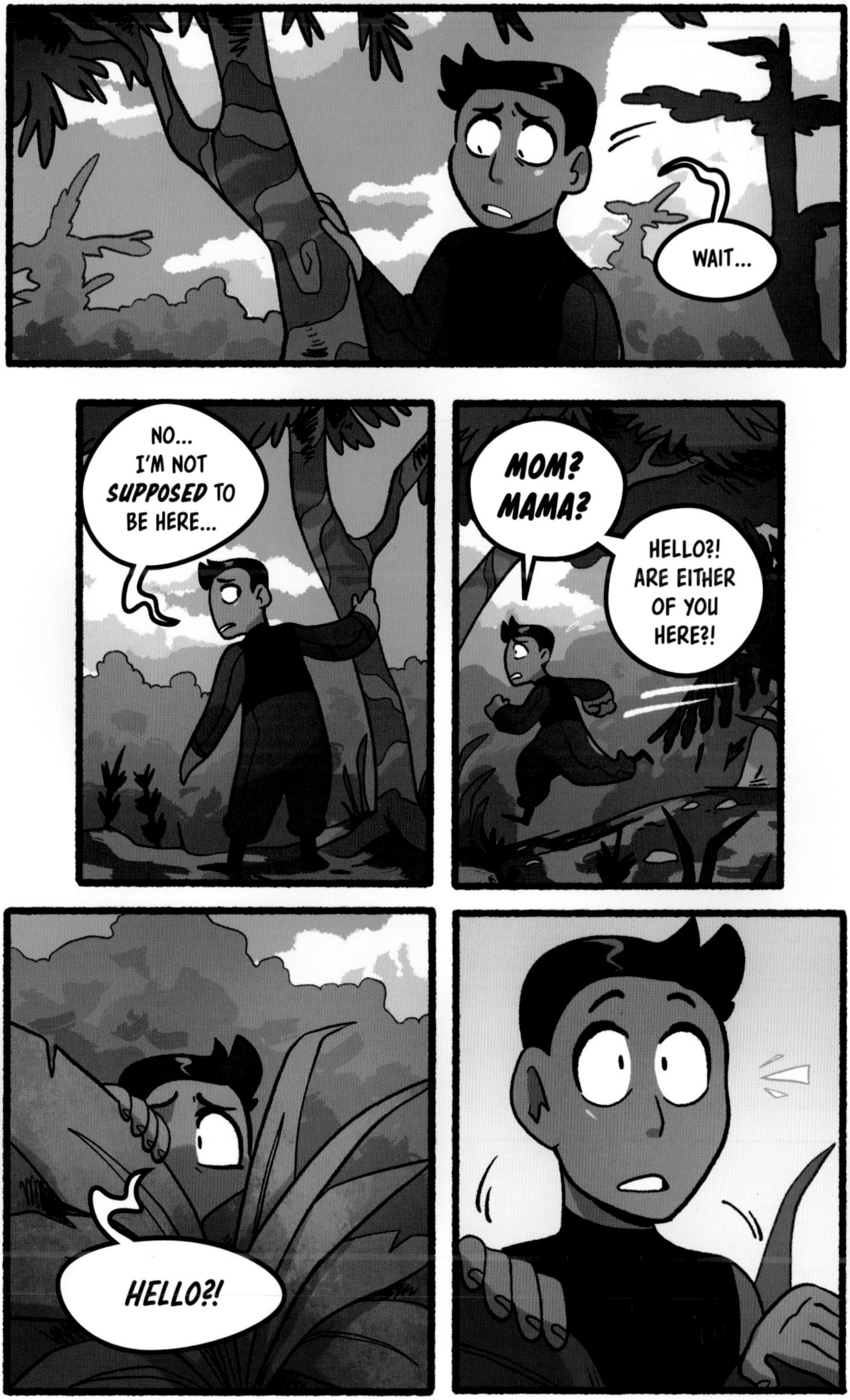
WAIT...
NO... I'M NOT *SUPPOSED* TO BE HERE...
MOM? MAMA?
HELLO?! ARE EITHER OF YOU HERE?!
HELLO?!

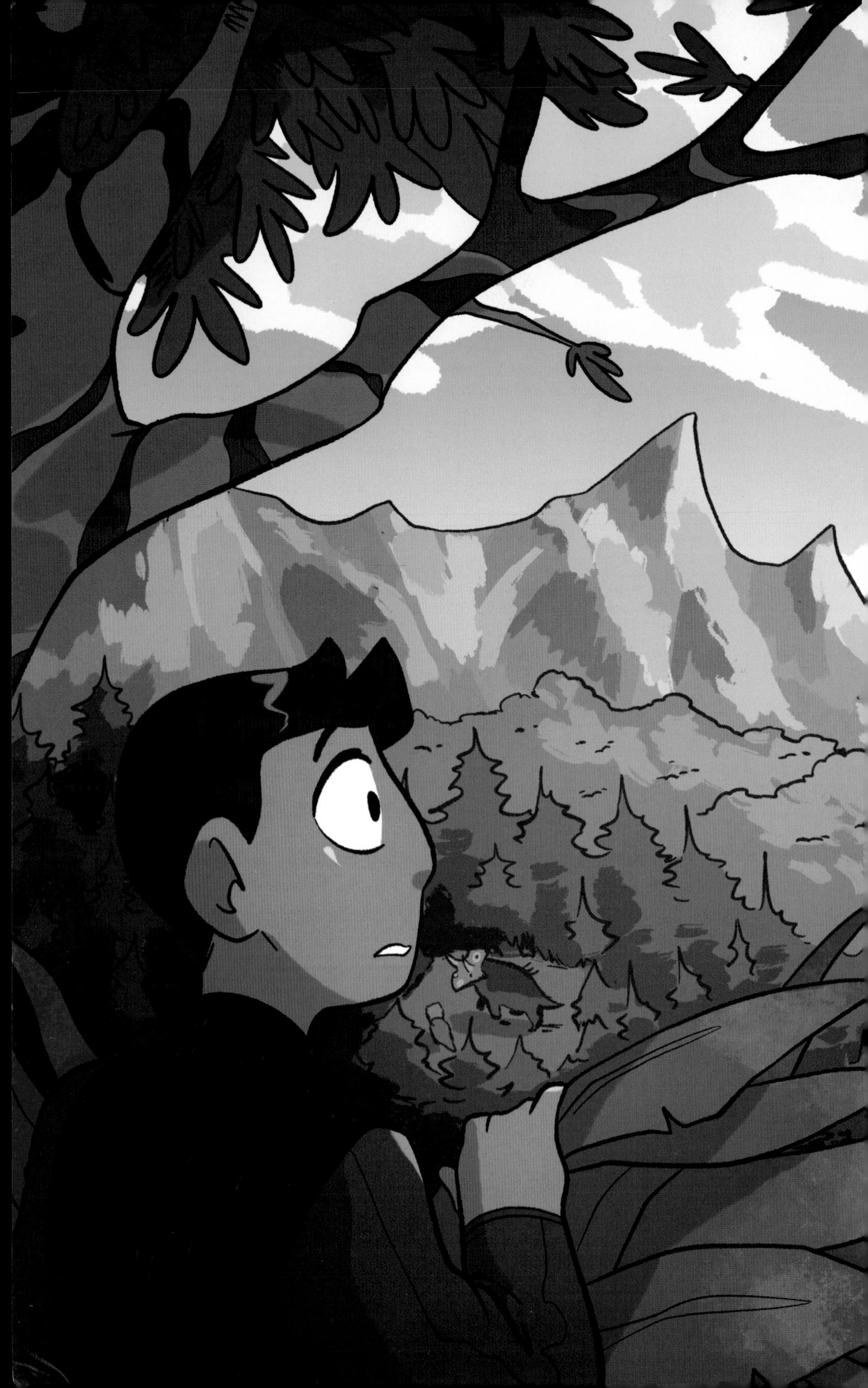

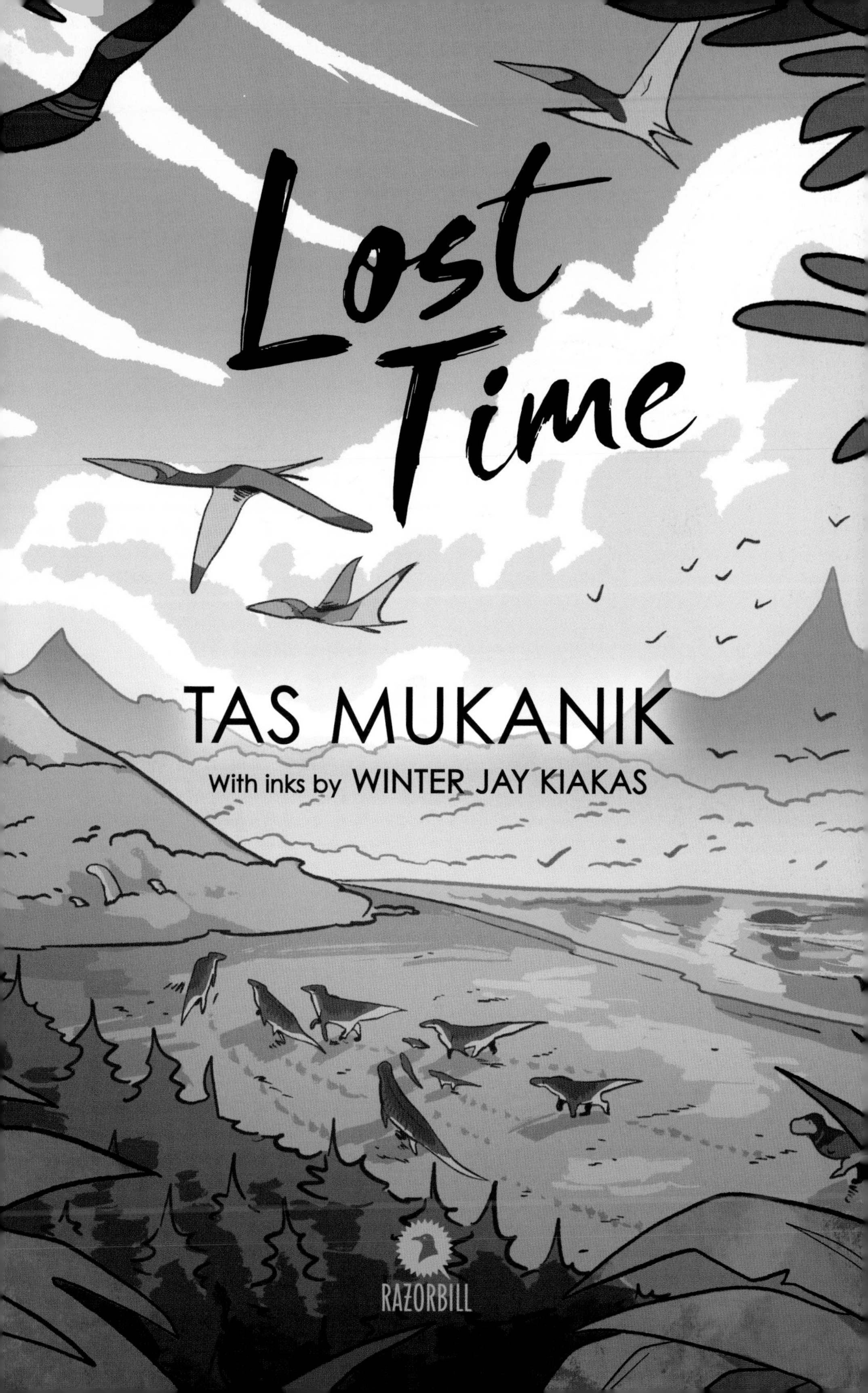

Lost Time

TAS MUKANIK

With inks by WINTER JAY KIAKAS

RAZORBILL

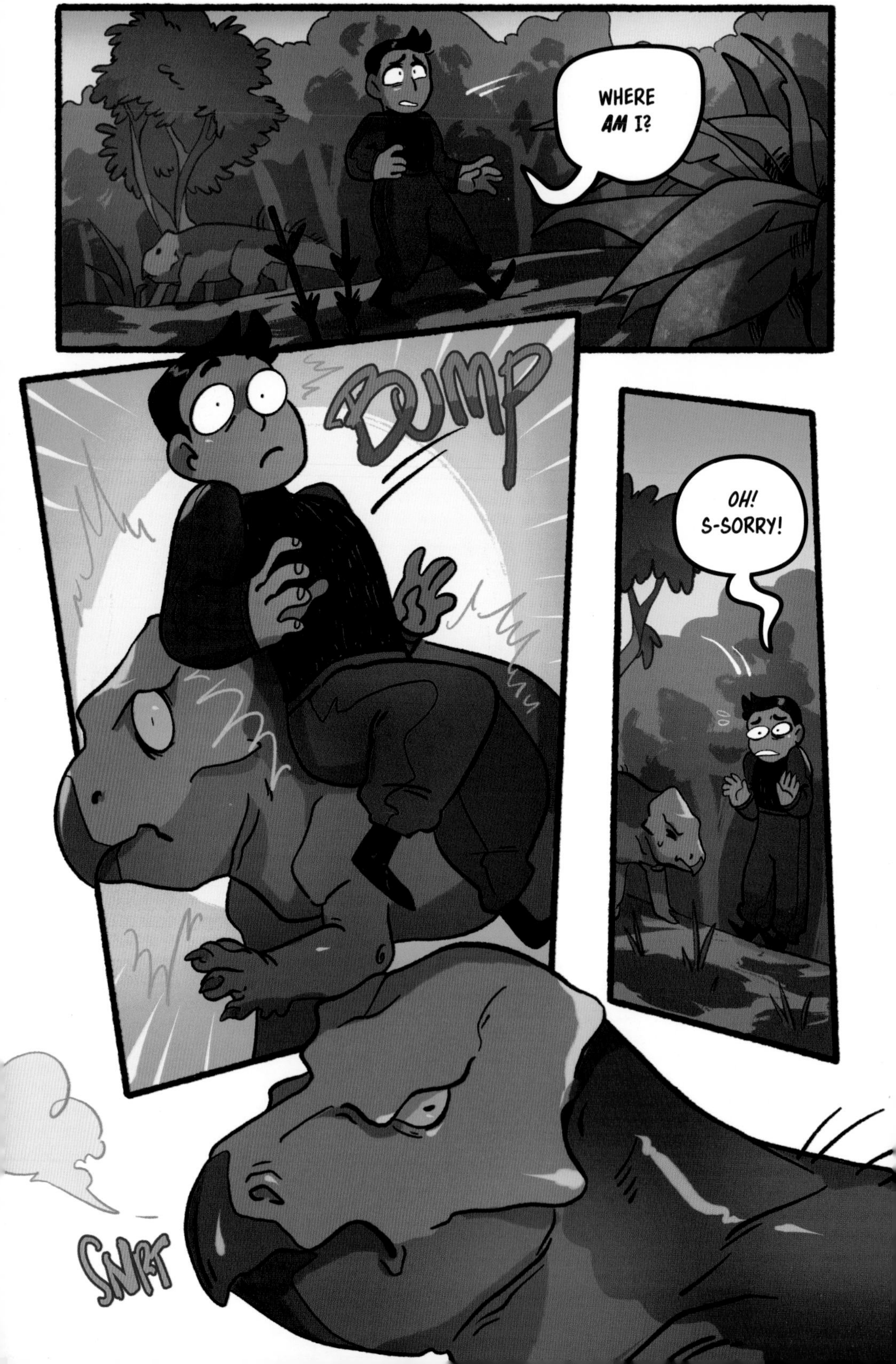
WHERE AM I?
DUMP
OH! S-SORRY!
SNRT

P-PLEASE DON'T EAT ME!

SNAP

AAAAAAAAAAAAA

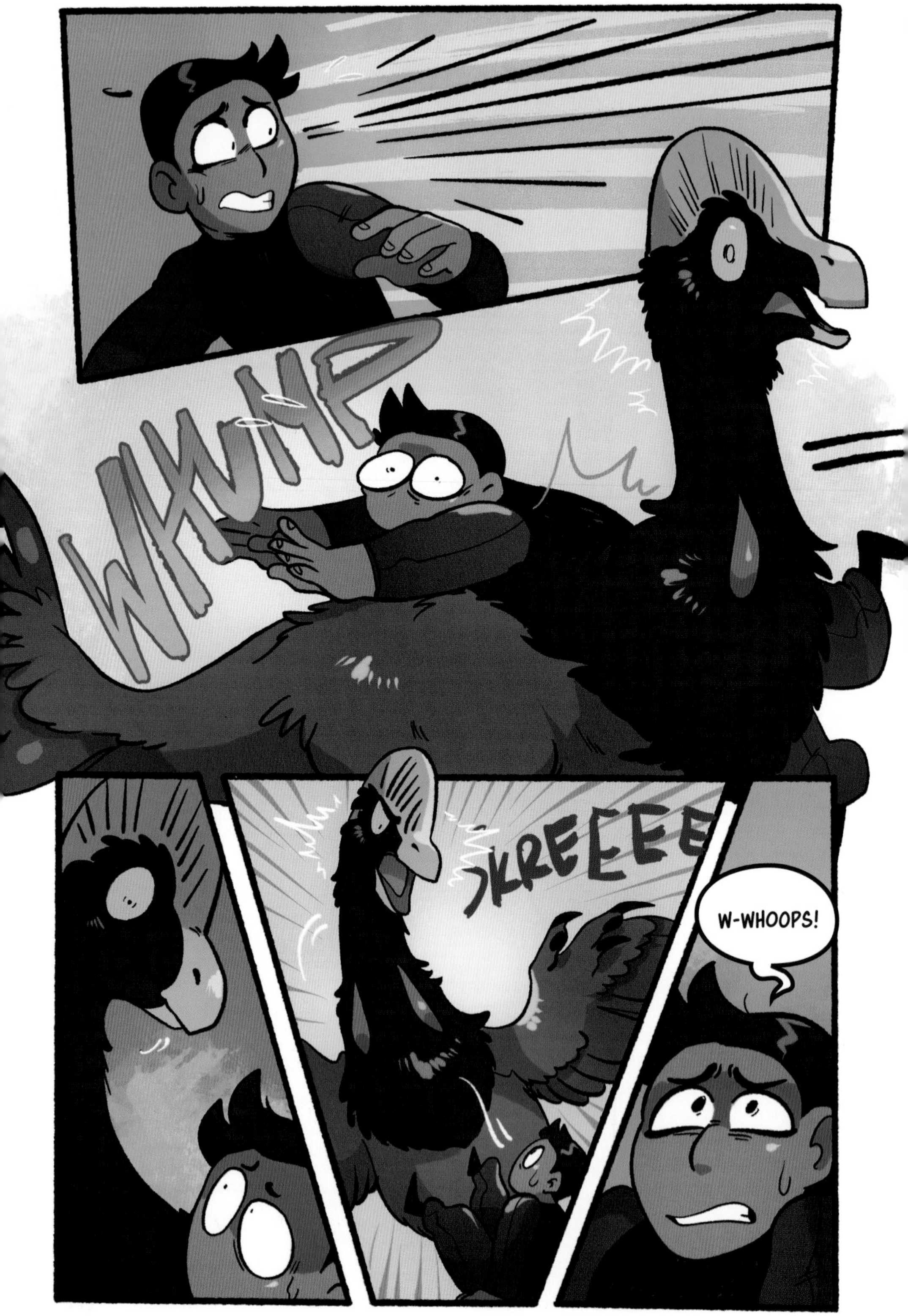
WHUMP
SKREEEEE
W-WHOOPS!

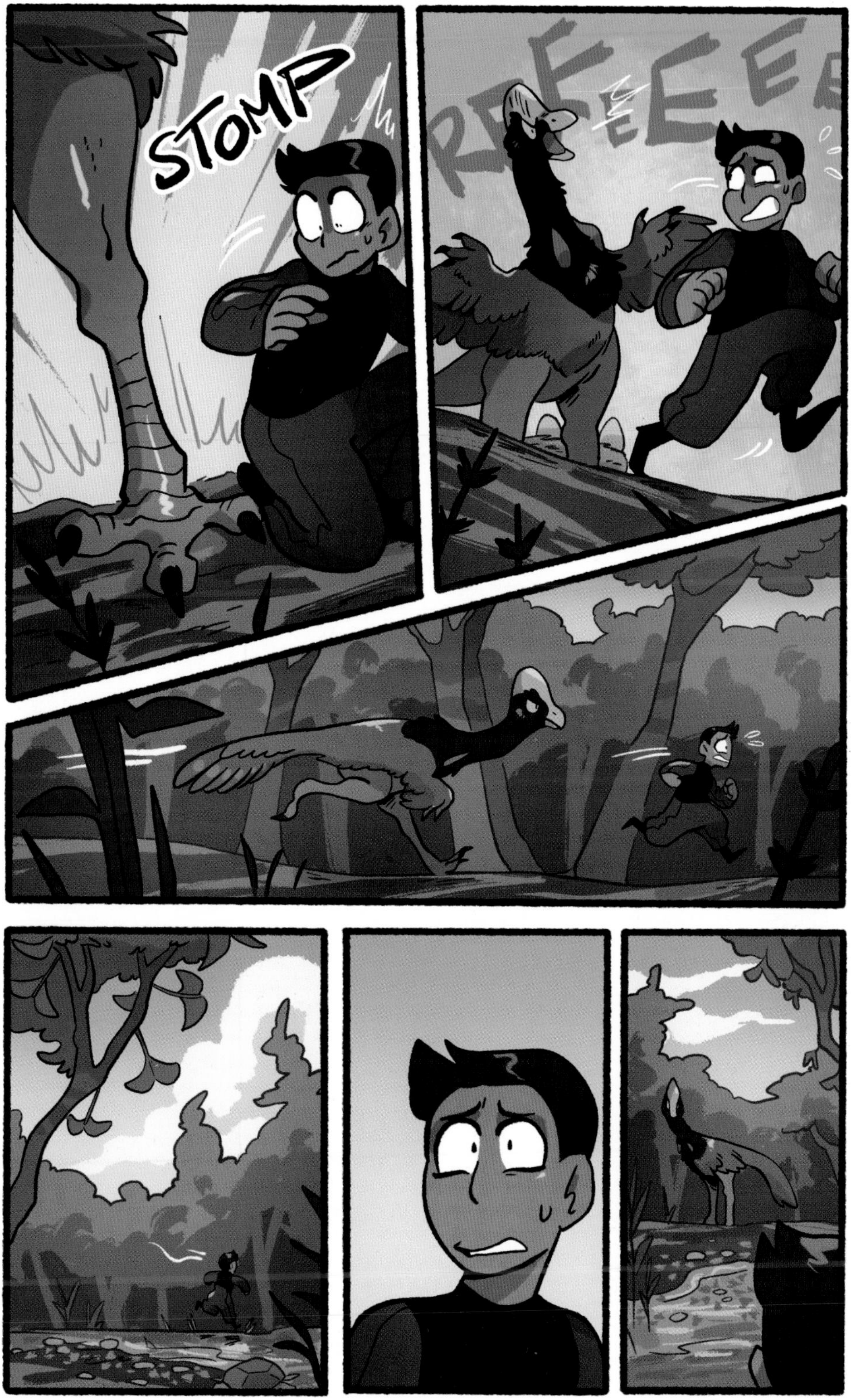
STOMP
REEEEEE

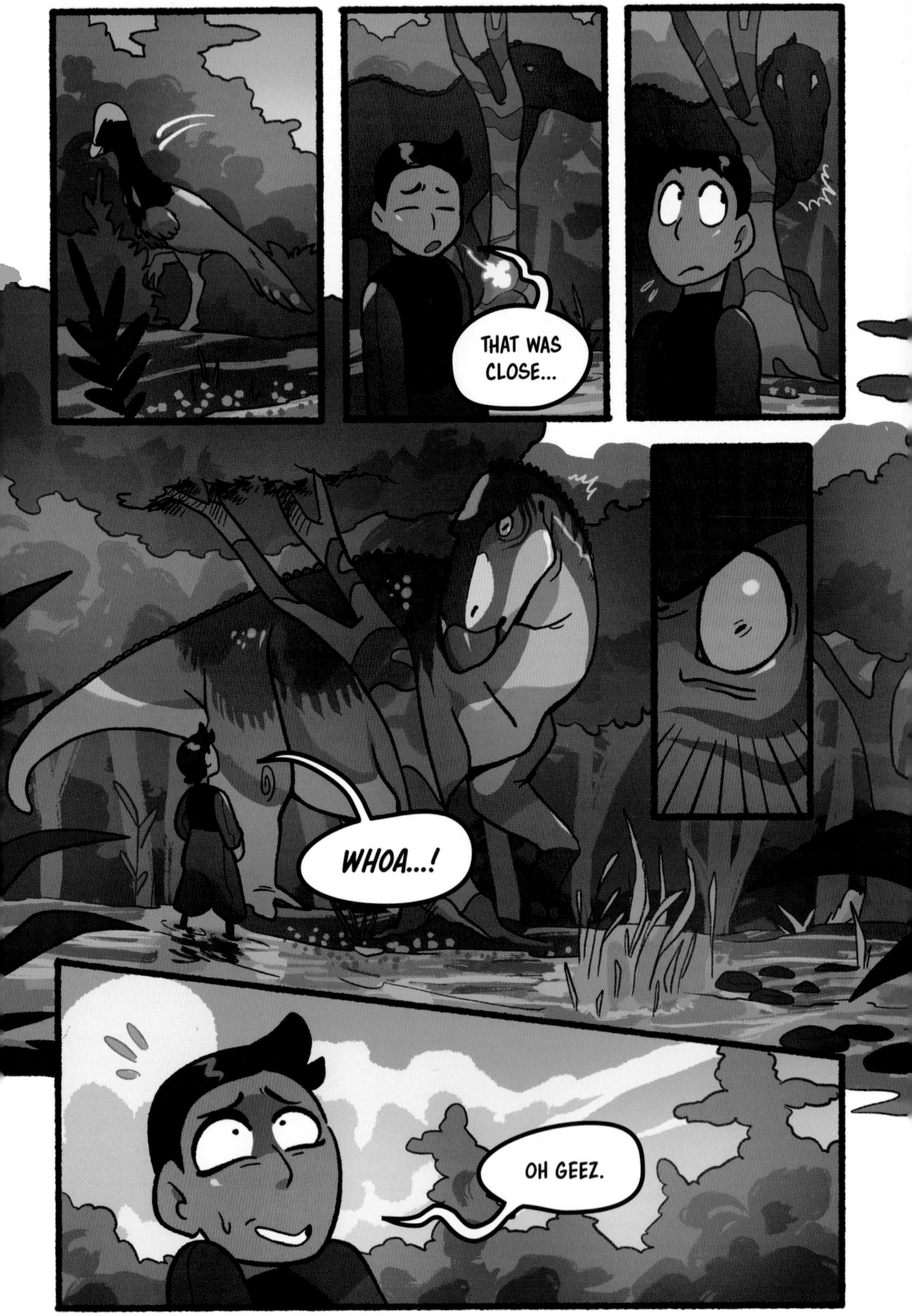
THAT WAS CLOSE...
WHOA...!
OH GEEZ.

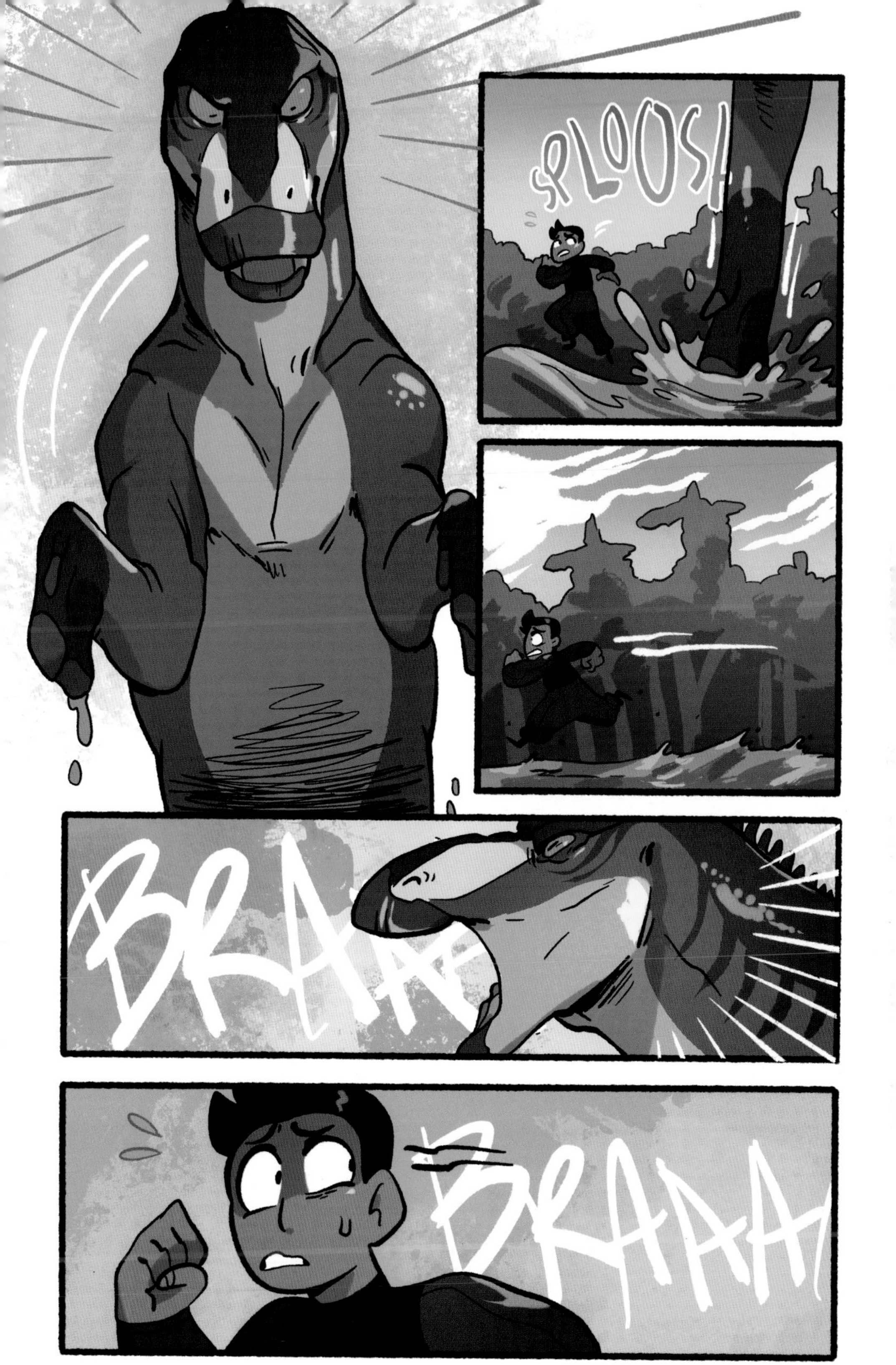
SPLOOSH
BRAA
BRAAA

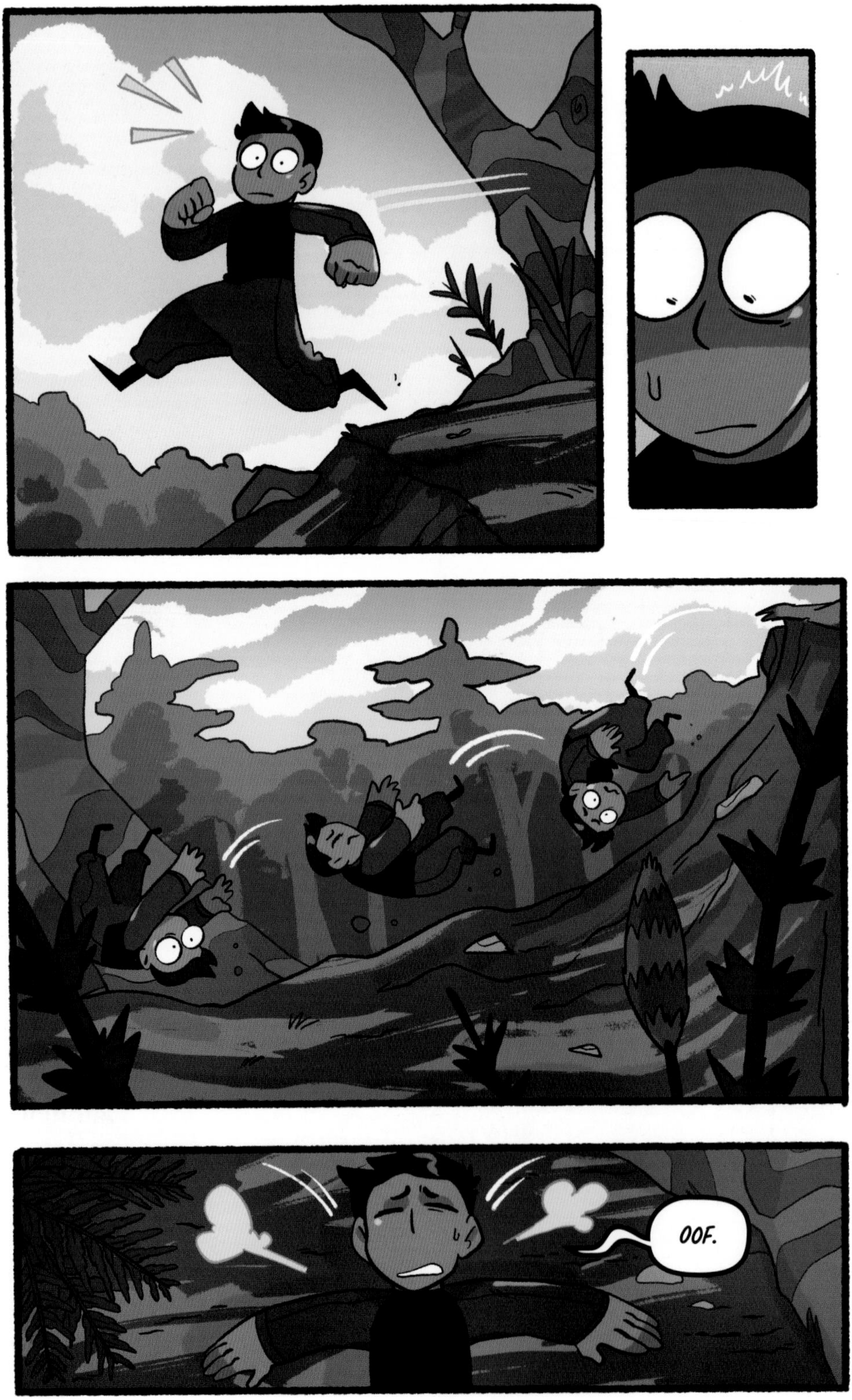
OOF.

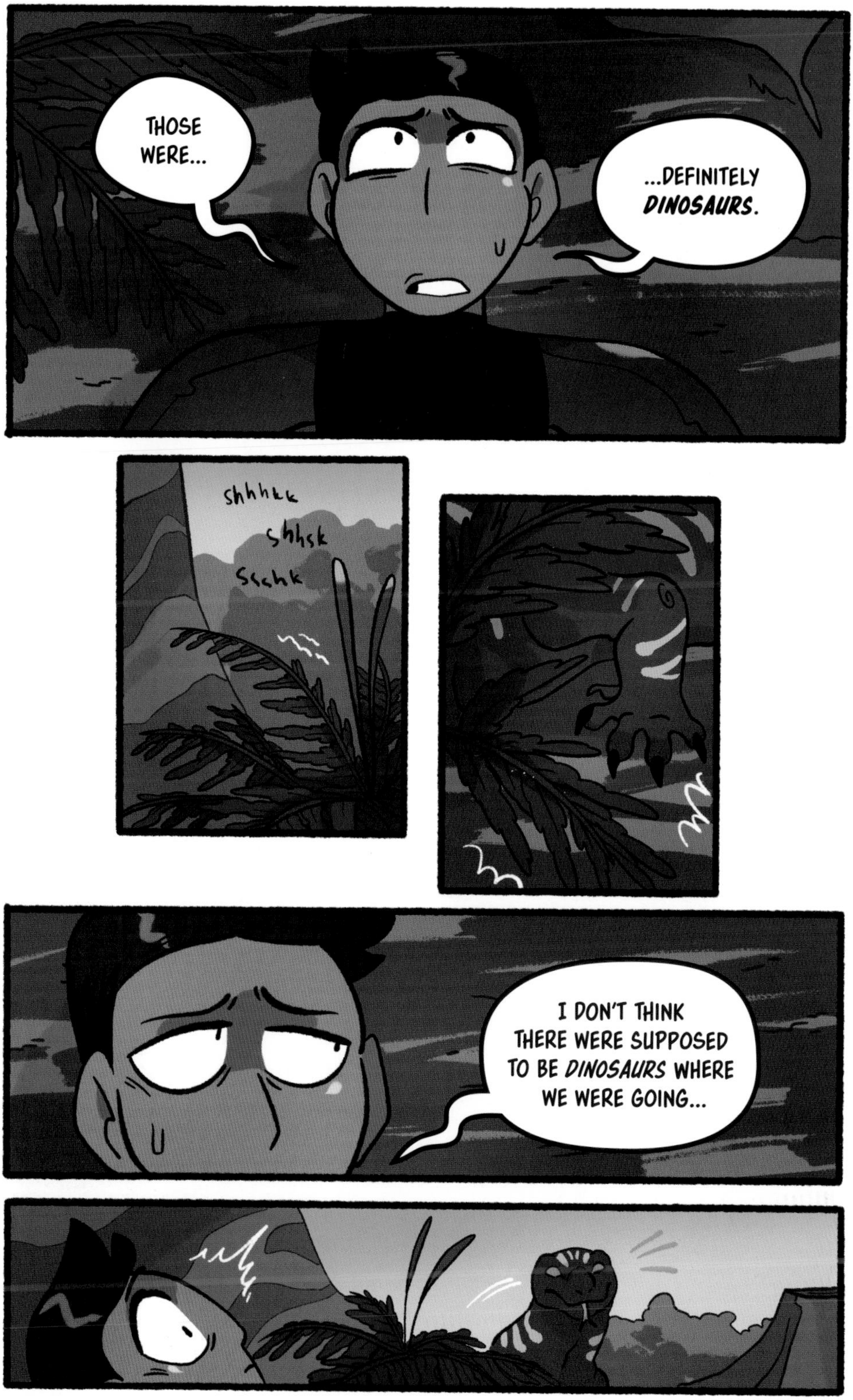
THOSE WERE...
...DEFINITELY *DINOSAURS*.
shhhkk
shhsk
Sschk
I DON'T THINK THERE WERE SUPPOSED TO BE *DINOSAURS* WHERE WE WERE GOING...

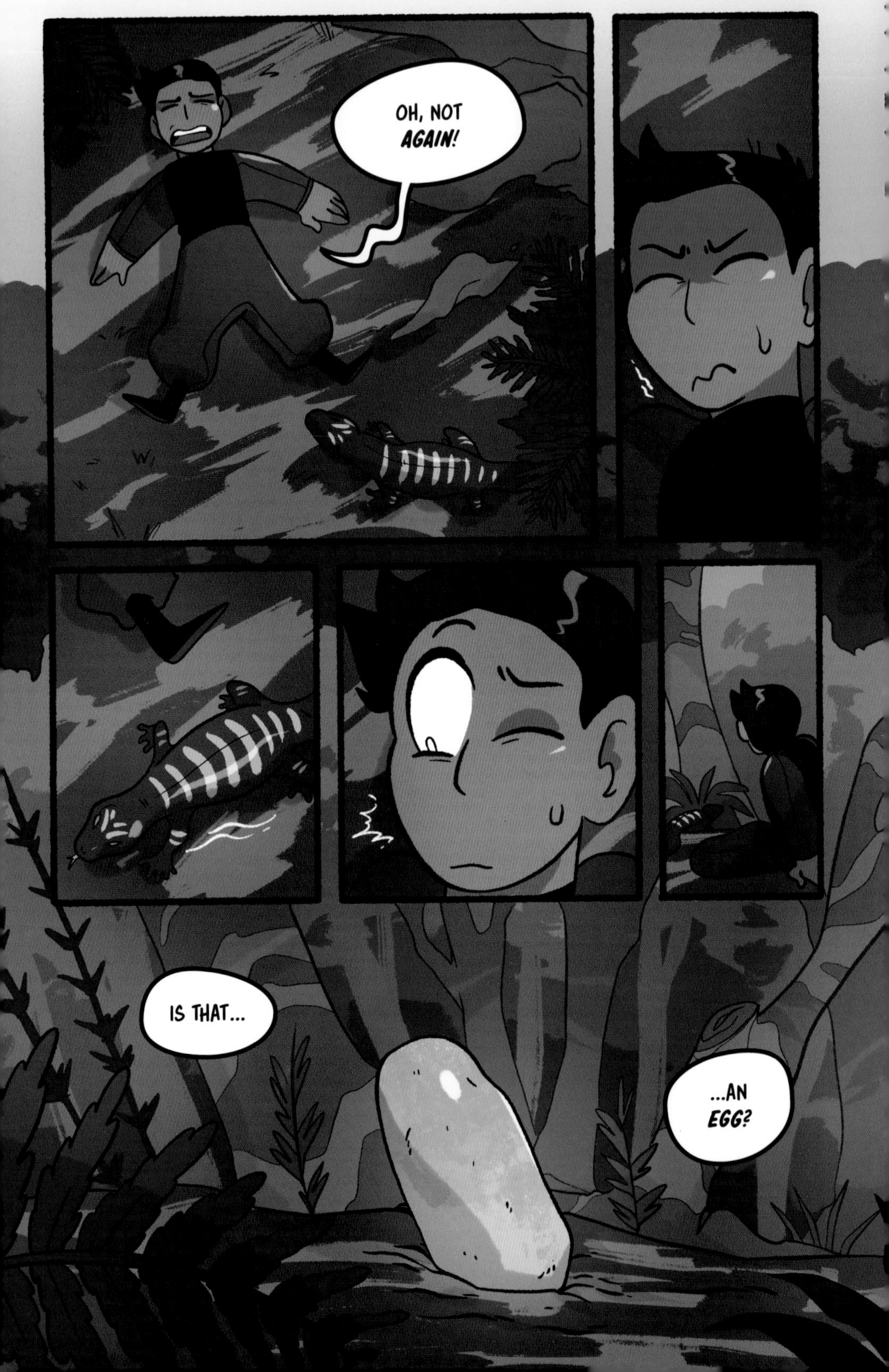
OH, NOT AGAIN!
IS THAT...
...AN EGG?

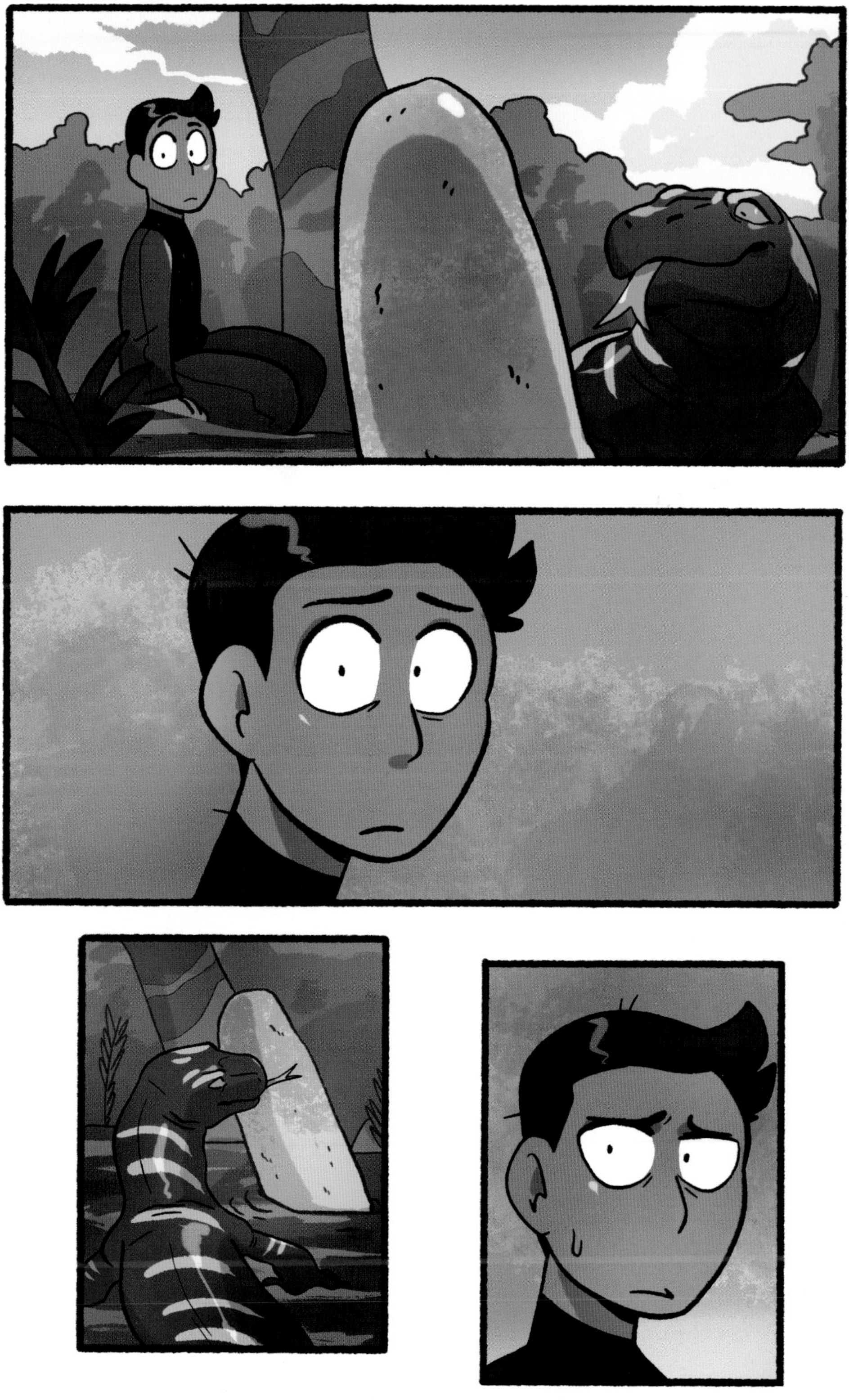

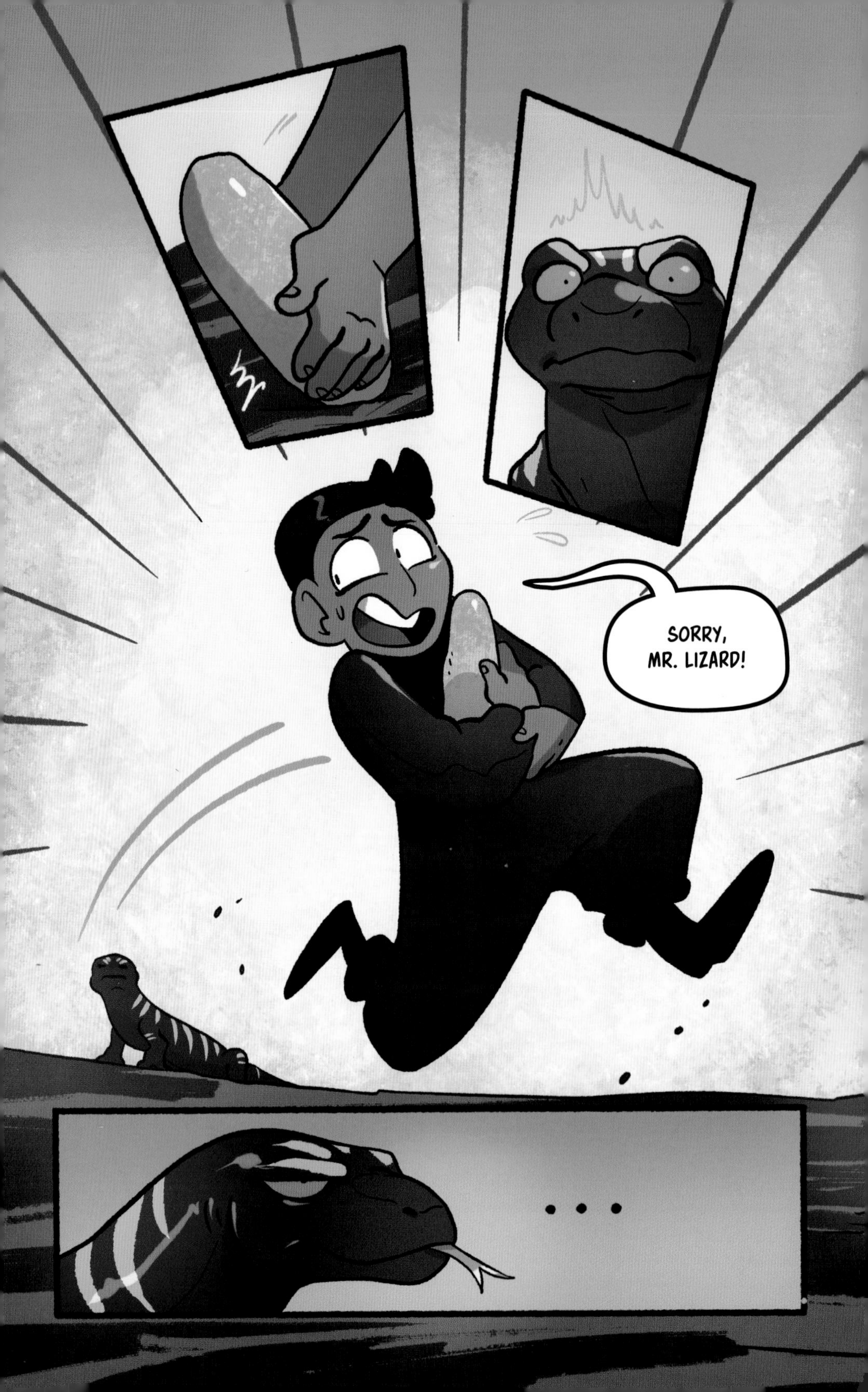
SORRY, MR. LIZARD!
. . .

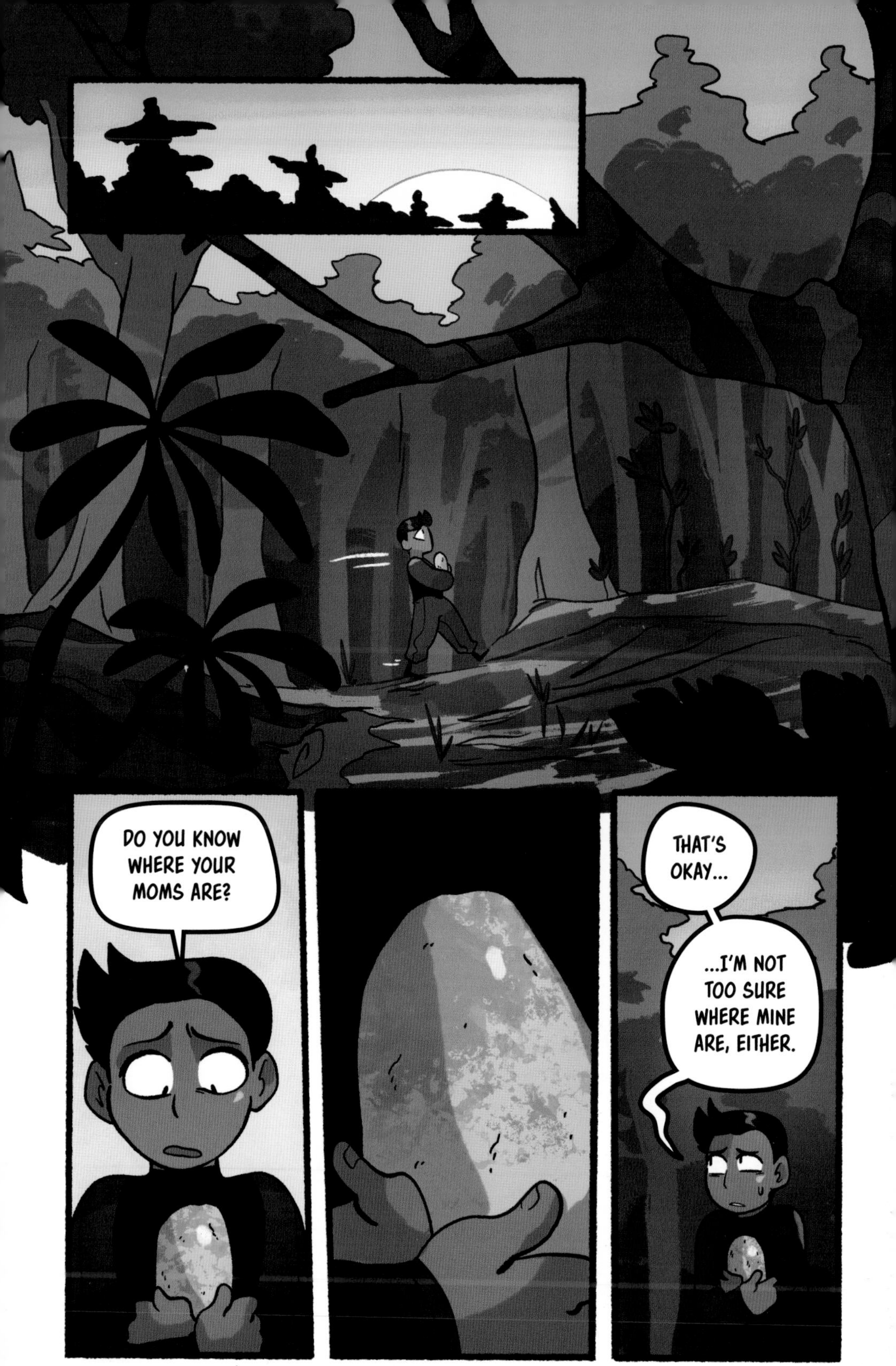
DO YOU KNOW WHERE YOUR MOMS ARE?
THAT'S OKAY...
...I'M NOT TOO SURE WHERE MINE ARE, EITHER.

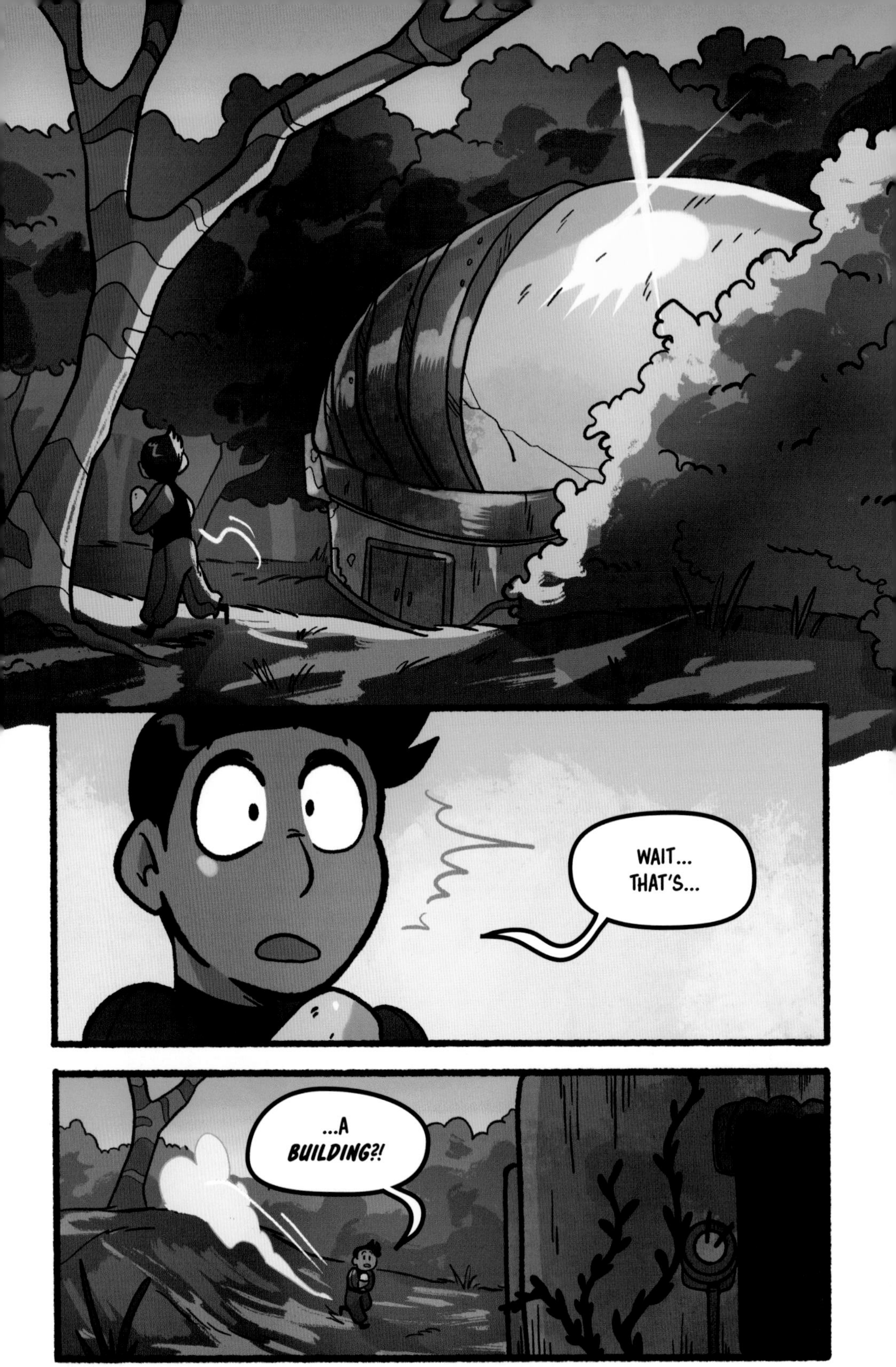
WAIT... THAT'S...
...A *BUILDING?!*

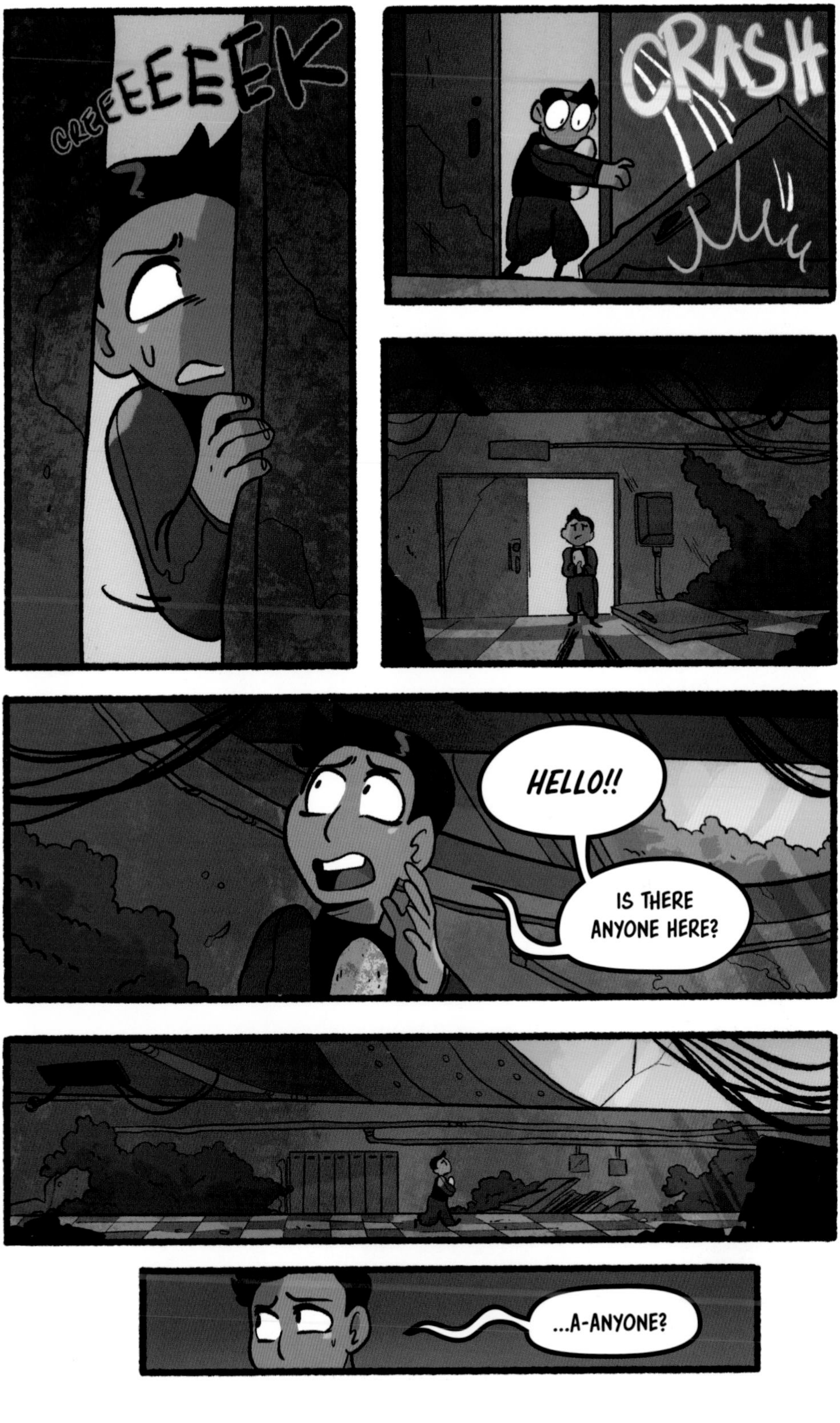
CREEEEEEEK
CRASH
HELLO!!
IS THERE ANYONE HERE?
...A-ANYONE?

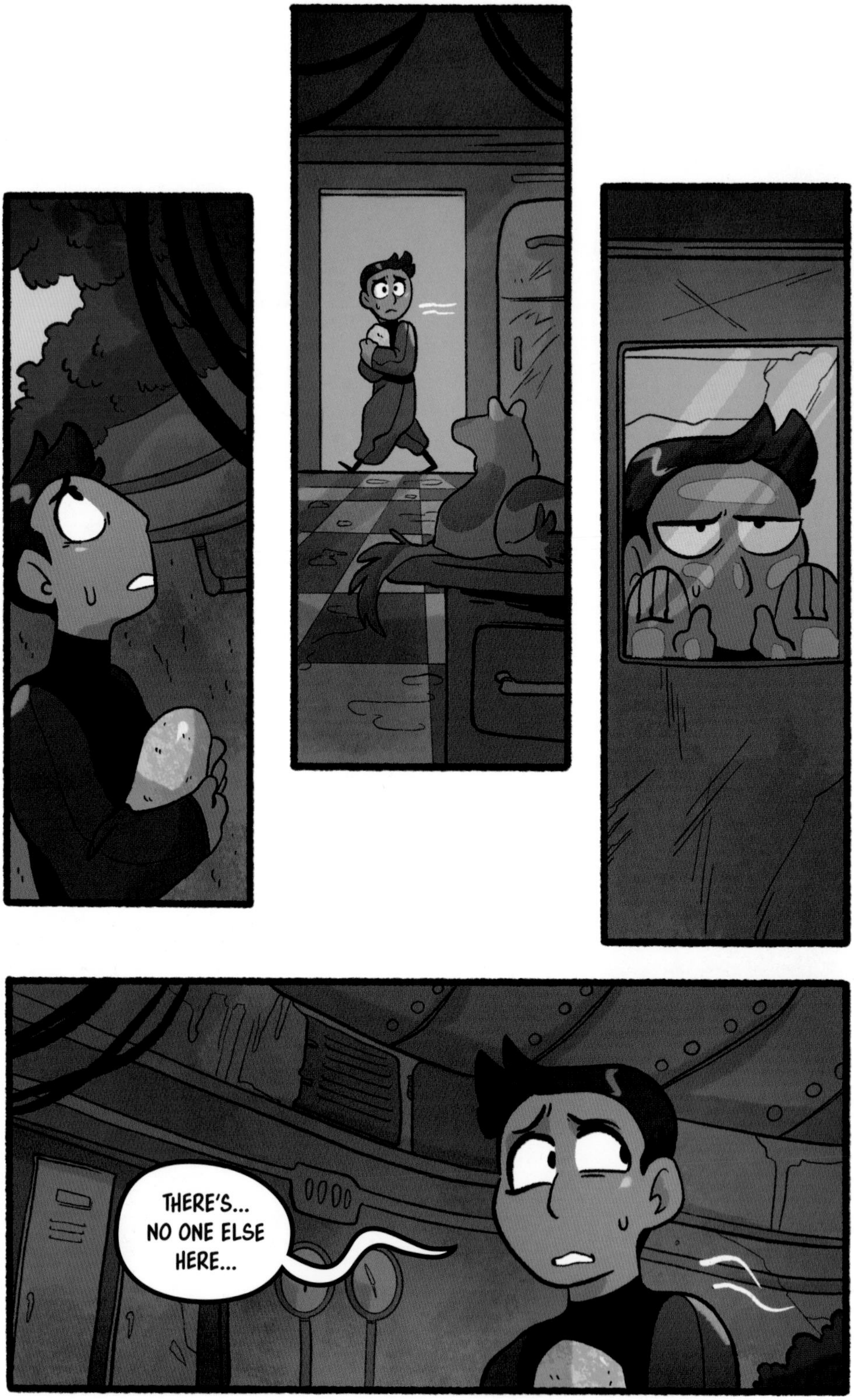
THERE'S... NO ONE ELSE HERE...

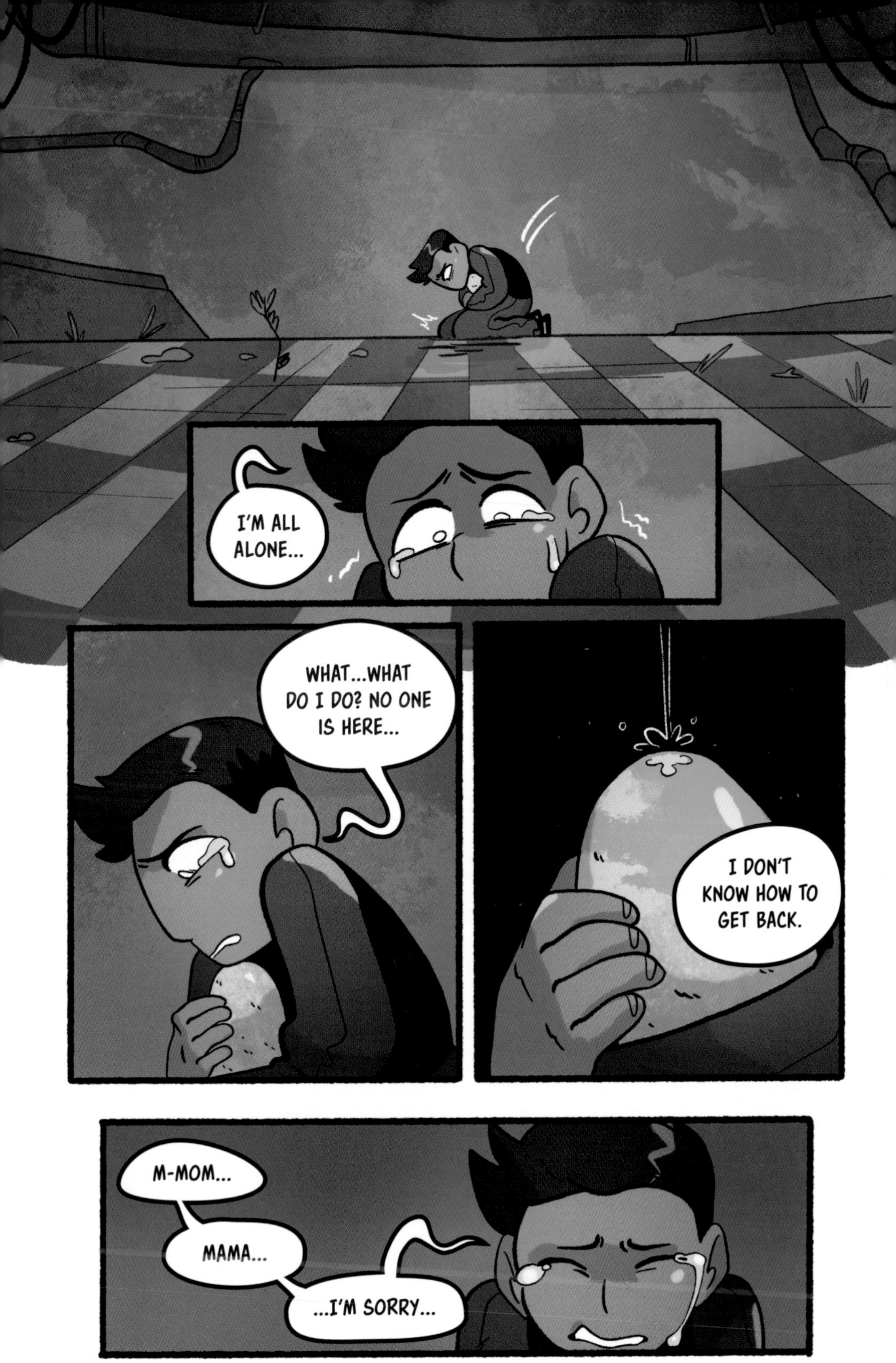
I'M ALL ALONE...
WHAT...WHAT DO I DO? NO ONE IS HERE...
I DON'T KNOW HOW TO GET BACK.
M-MOM...
MAMA...
...I'M SORRY...

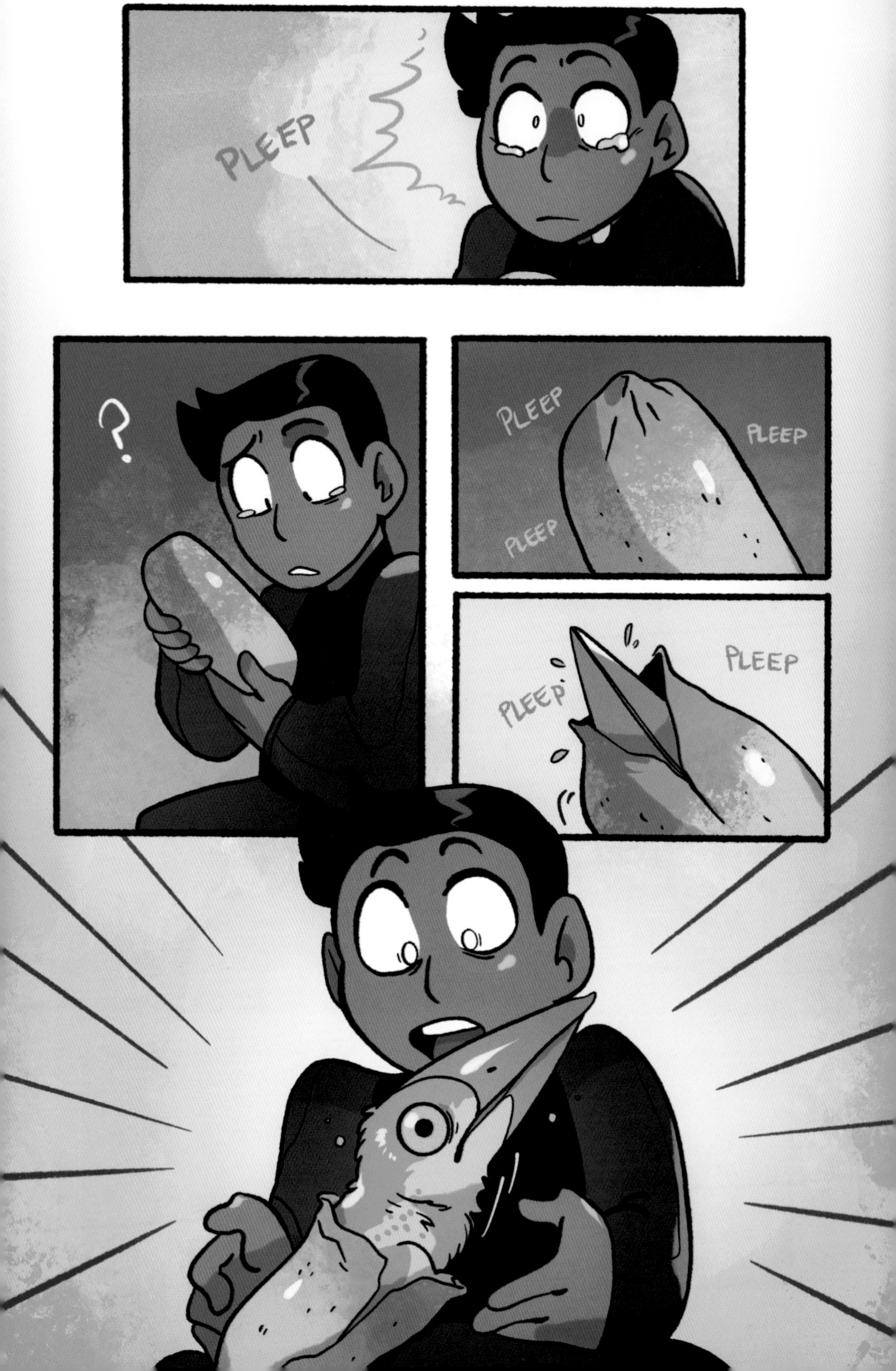
PLEEP
?
PLEEP
PLEEP
PLEEP
PLEEP
PLEEP

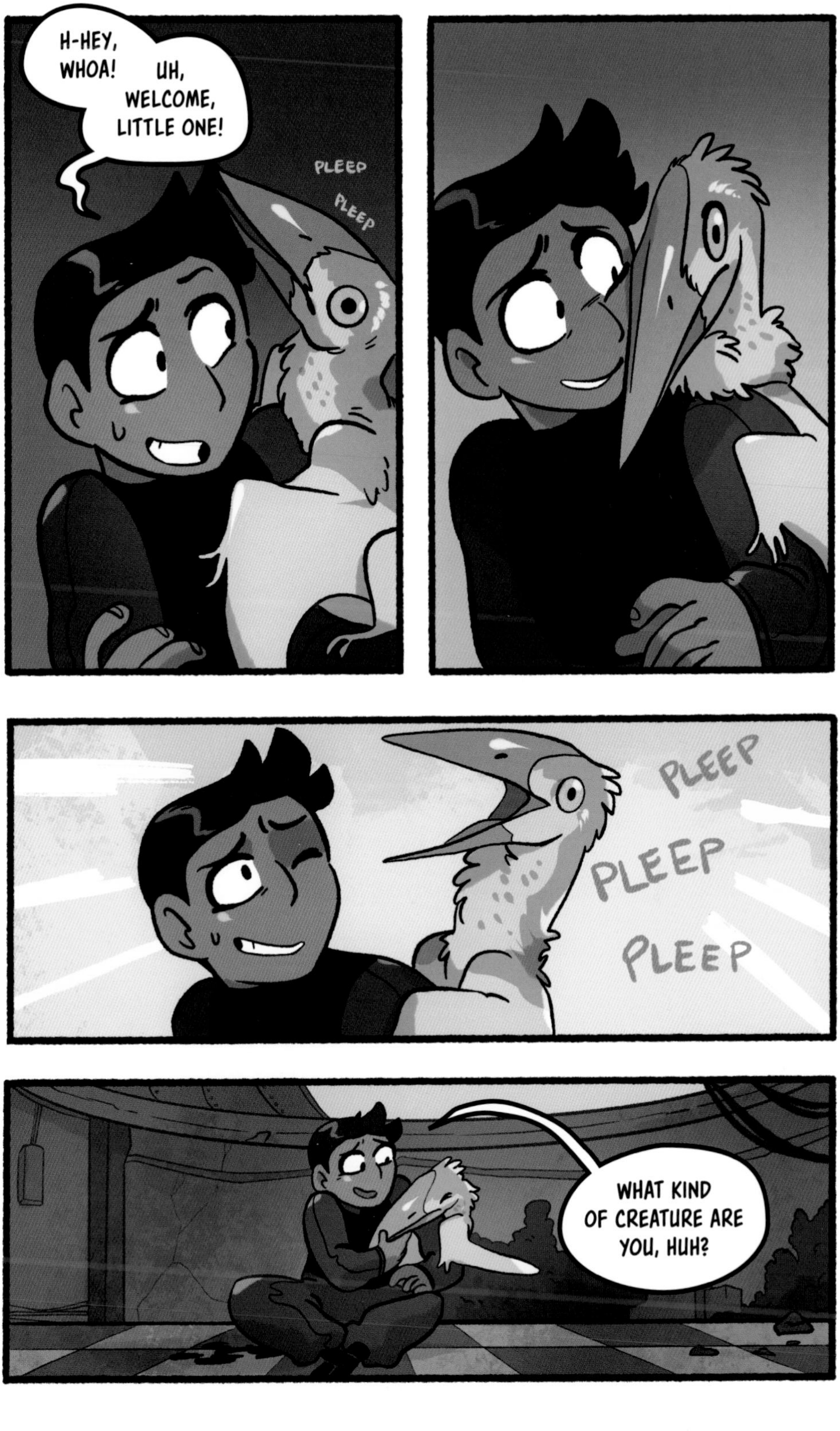
H-HEY, WHOA!
UH, WELCOME, LITTLE ONE!
PLEEP
PLEEP
PLEEP
PLEEP
PLEEP
WHAT KIND OF CREATURE ARE YOU, HUH?

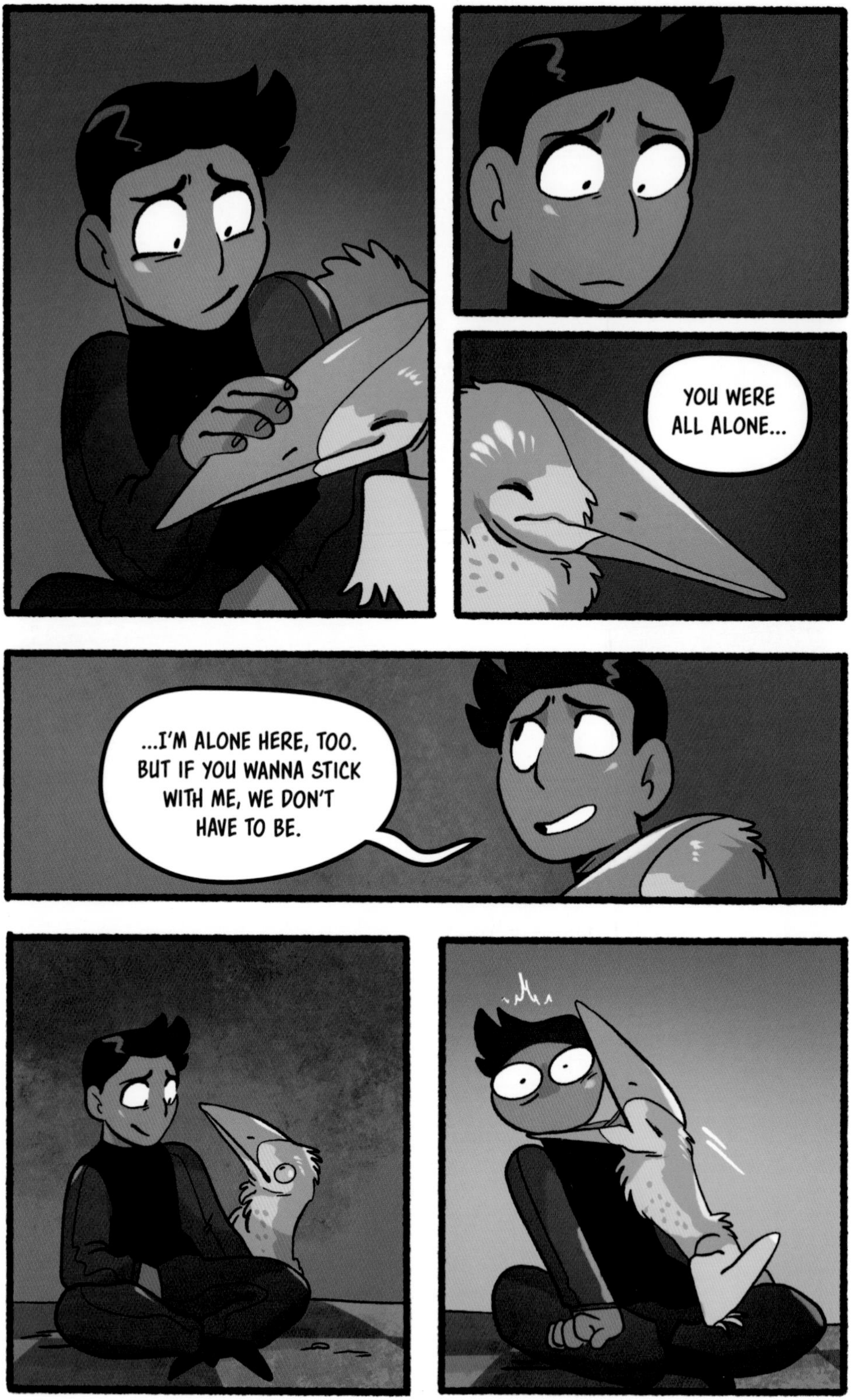
YOU WERE ALL ALONE...
...I'M ALONE HERE, TOO. BUT IF YOU WANNA STICK WITH ME, WE DON'T HAVE TO BE.

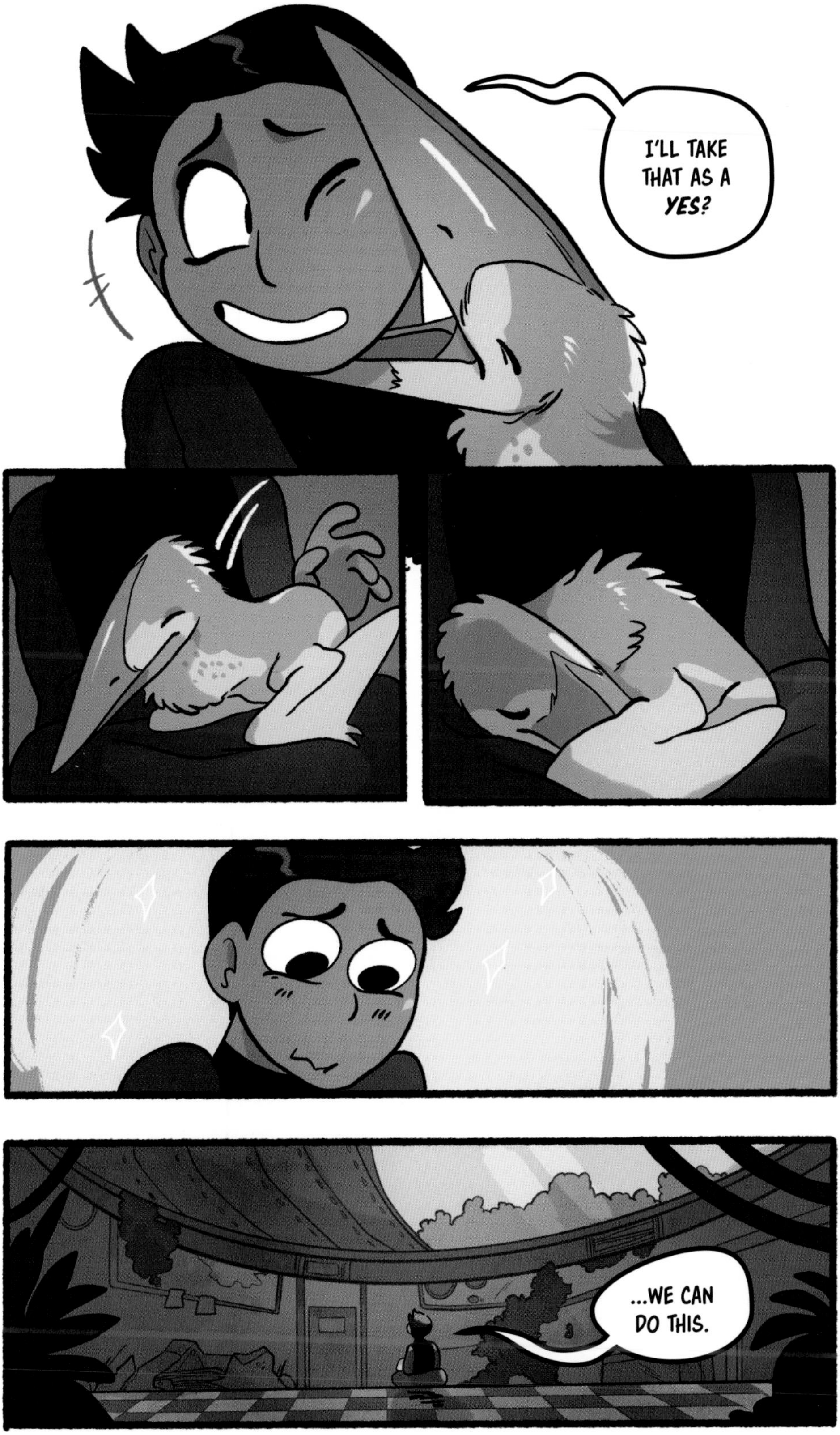
I'LL TAKE THAT AS A *YES?*
...WE CAN DO THIS.

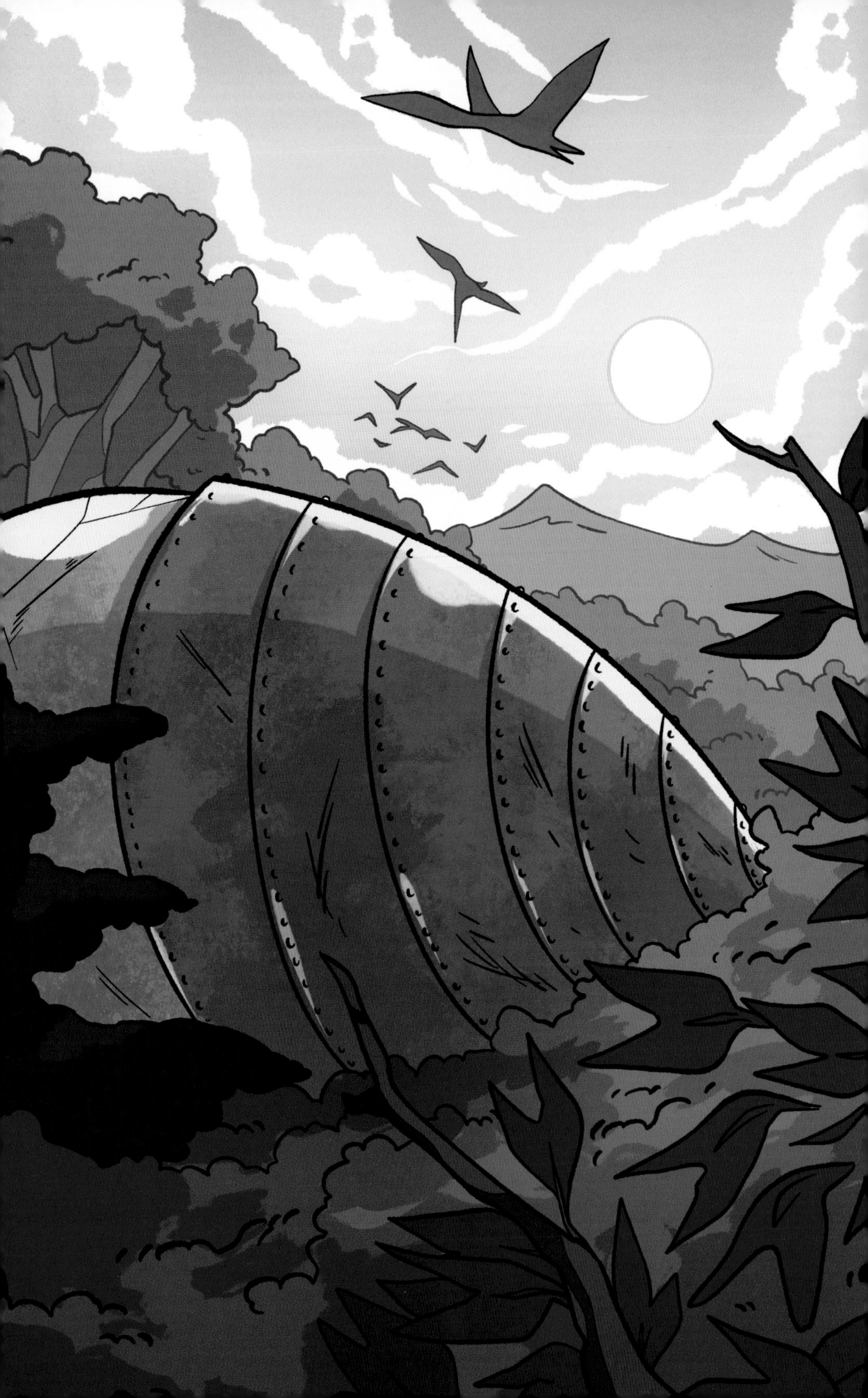

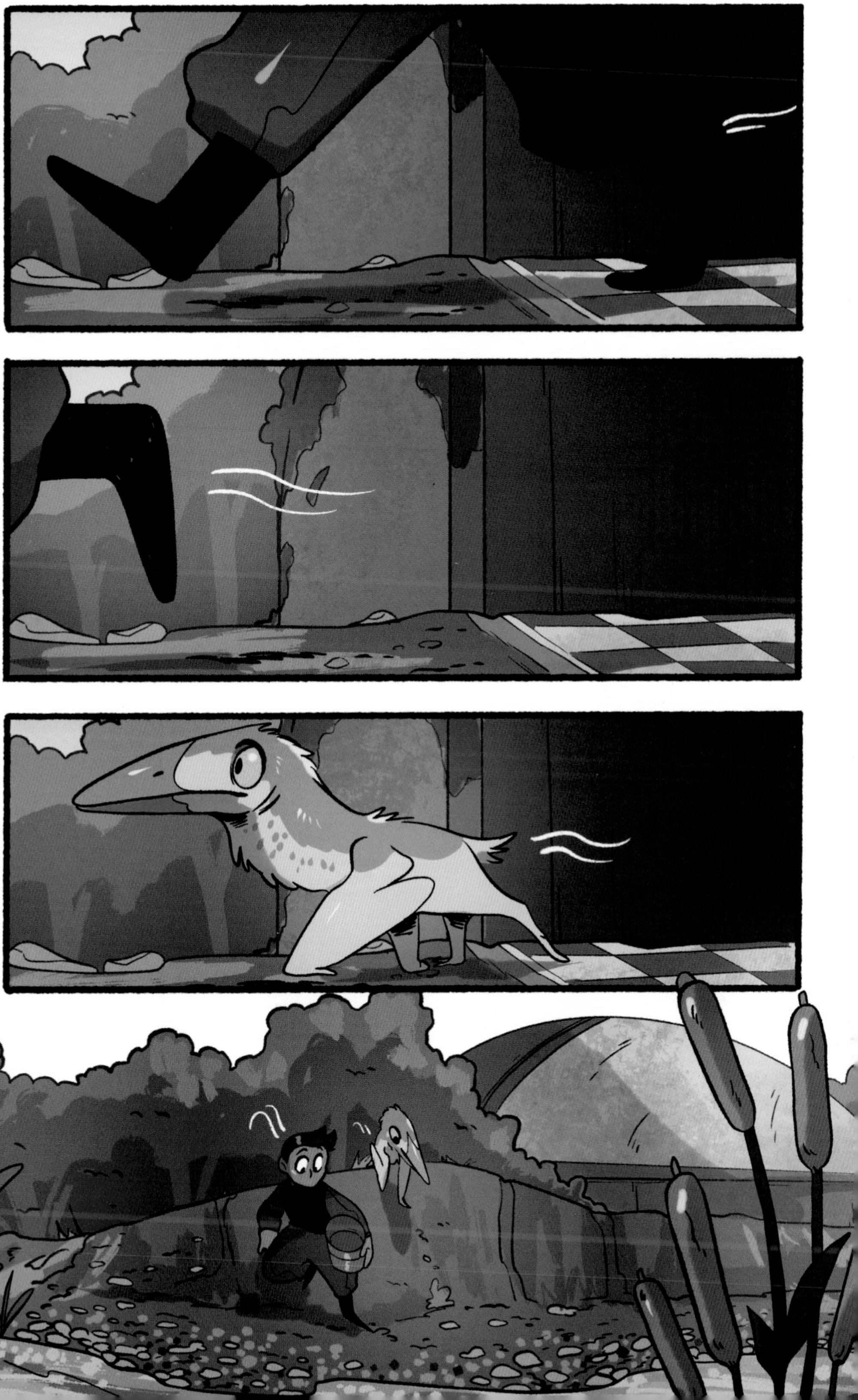

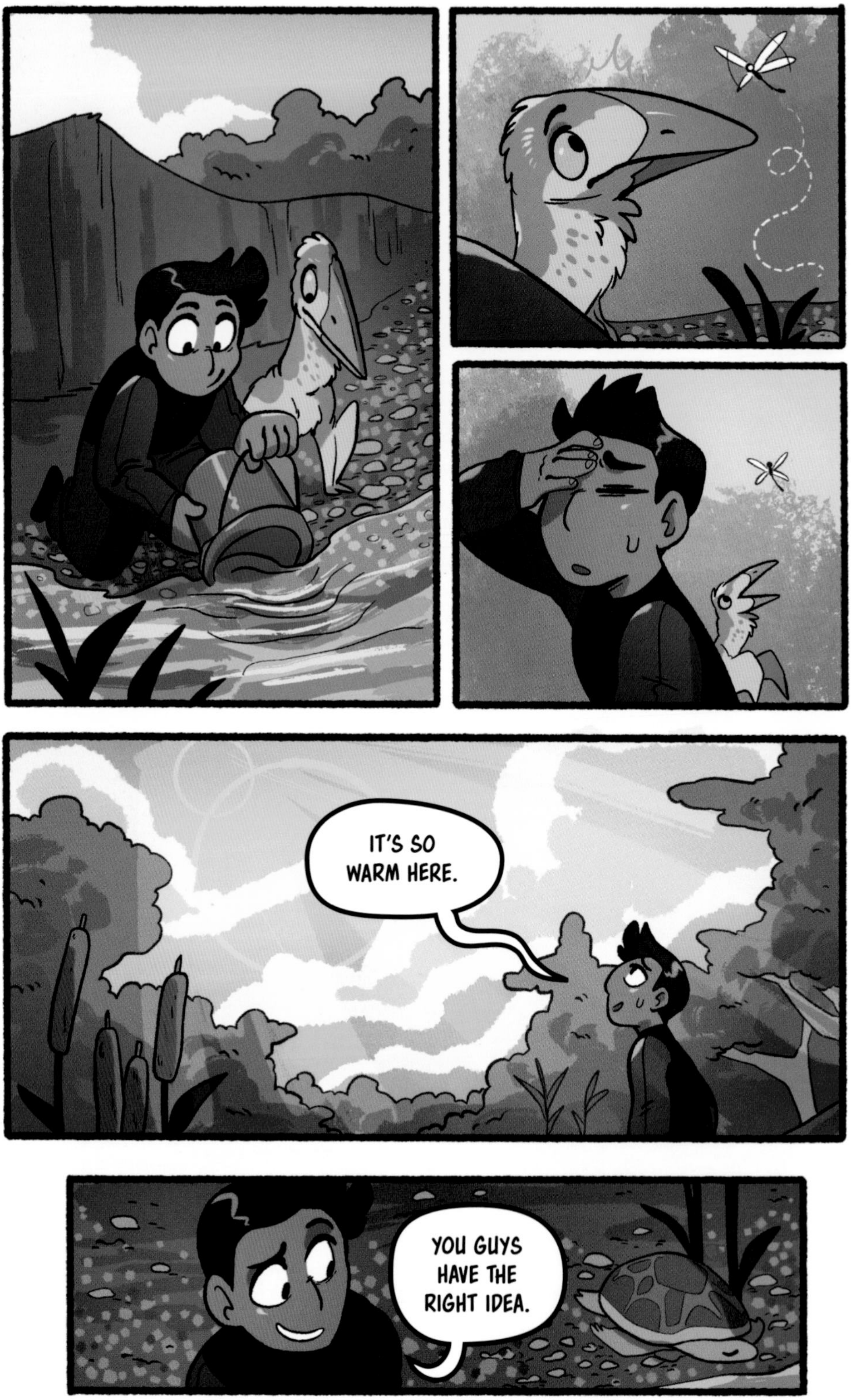
IT'S SO WARM HERE.
YOU GUYS HAVE THE RIGHT IDEA.

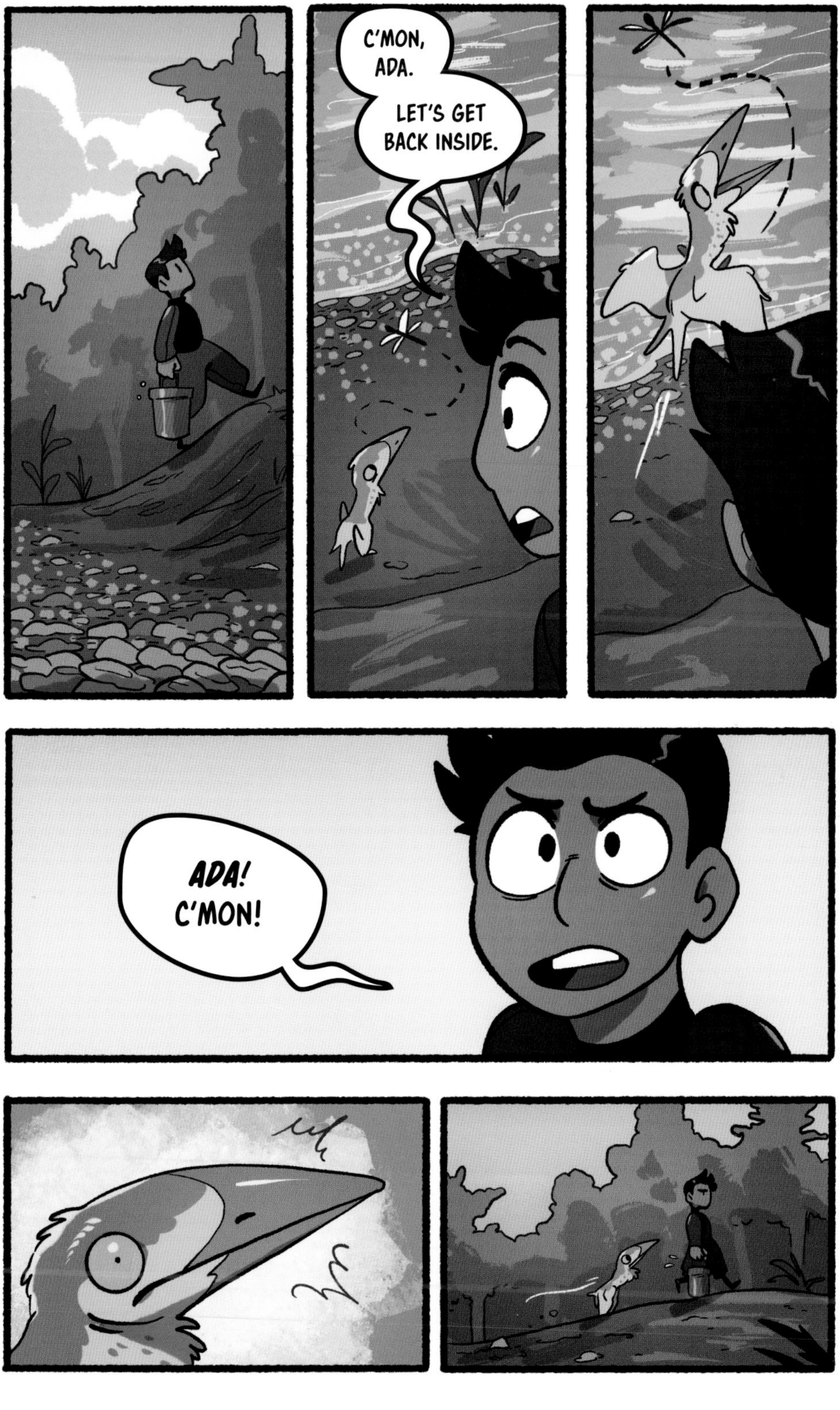
C'MON, ADA.
LET'S GET BACK INSIDE.
ADA! C'MON!

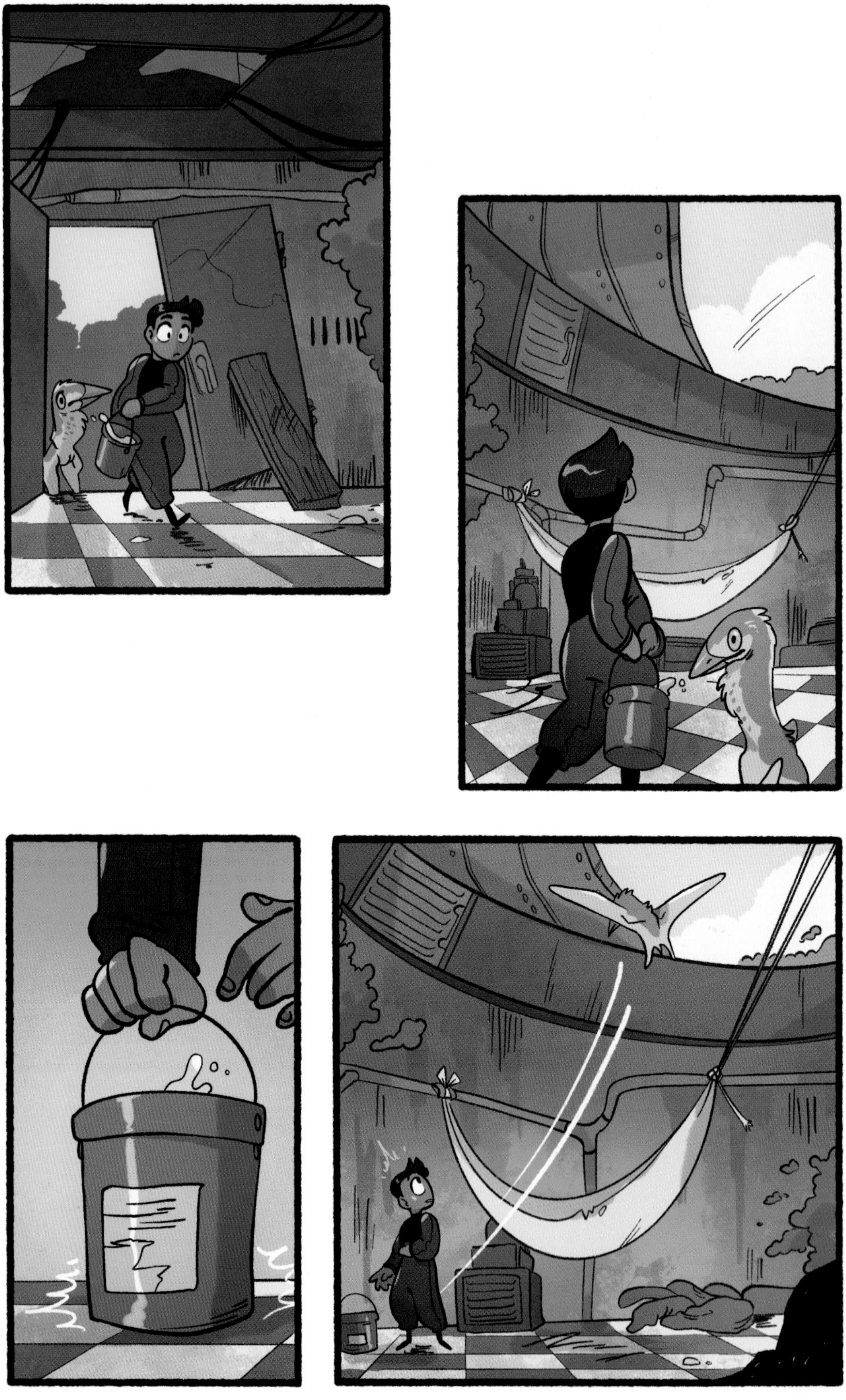

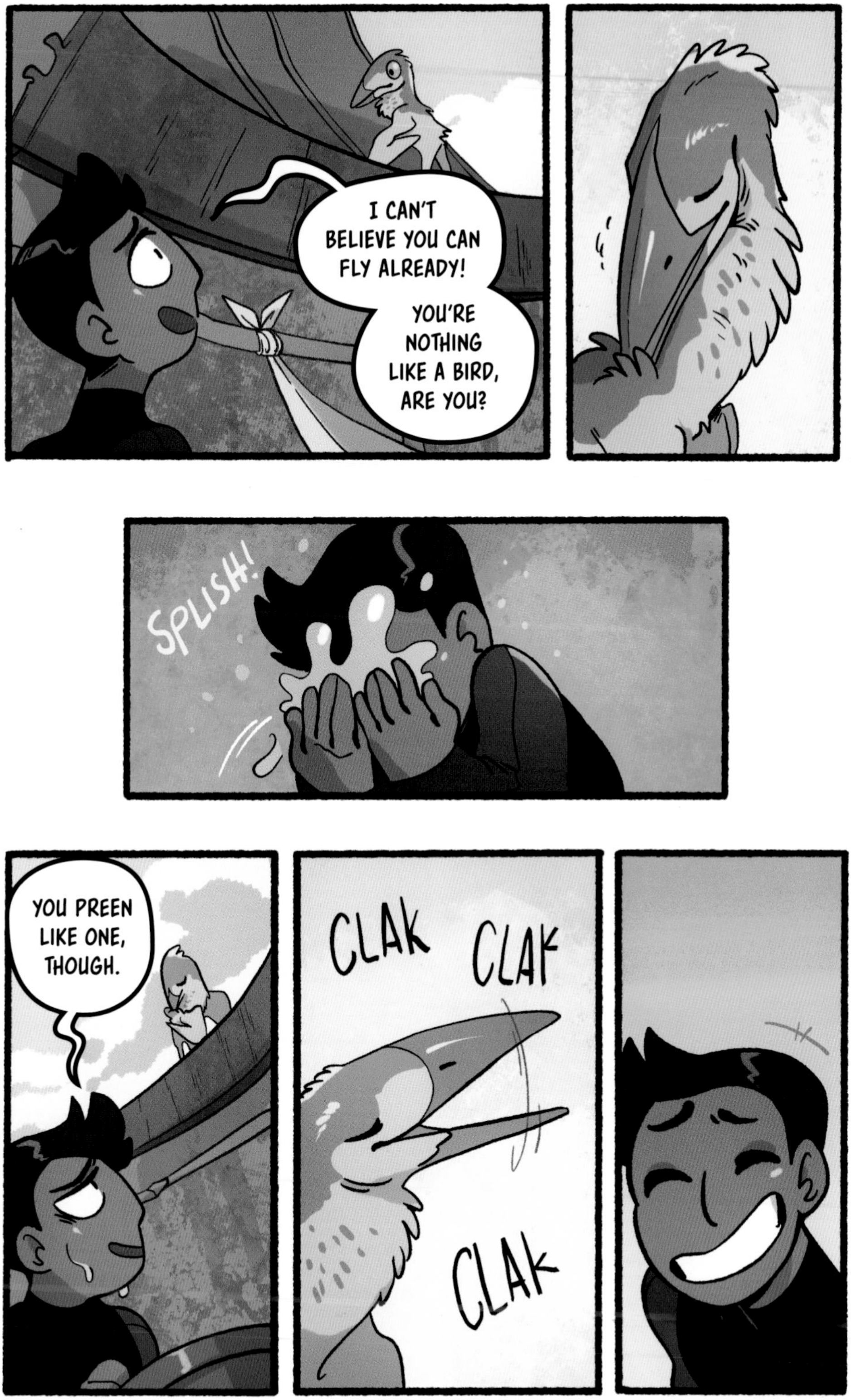
I CAN'T BELIEVE YOU CAN FLY ALREADY!
YOU'RE NOTHING LIKE A BIRD, ARE YOU?
SPLISH!
YOU PREEN LIKE ONE, THOUGH.
CLAK
CLAK
CLAK

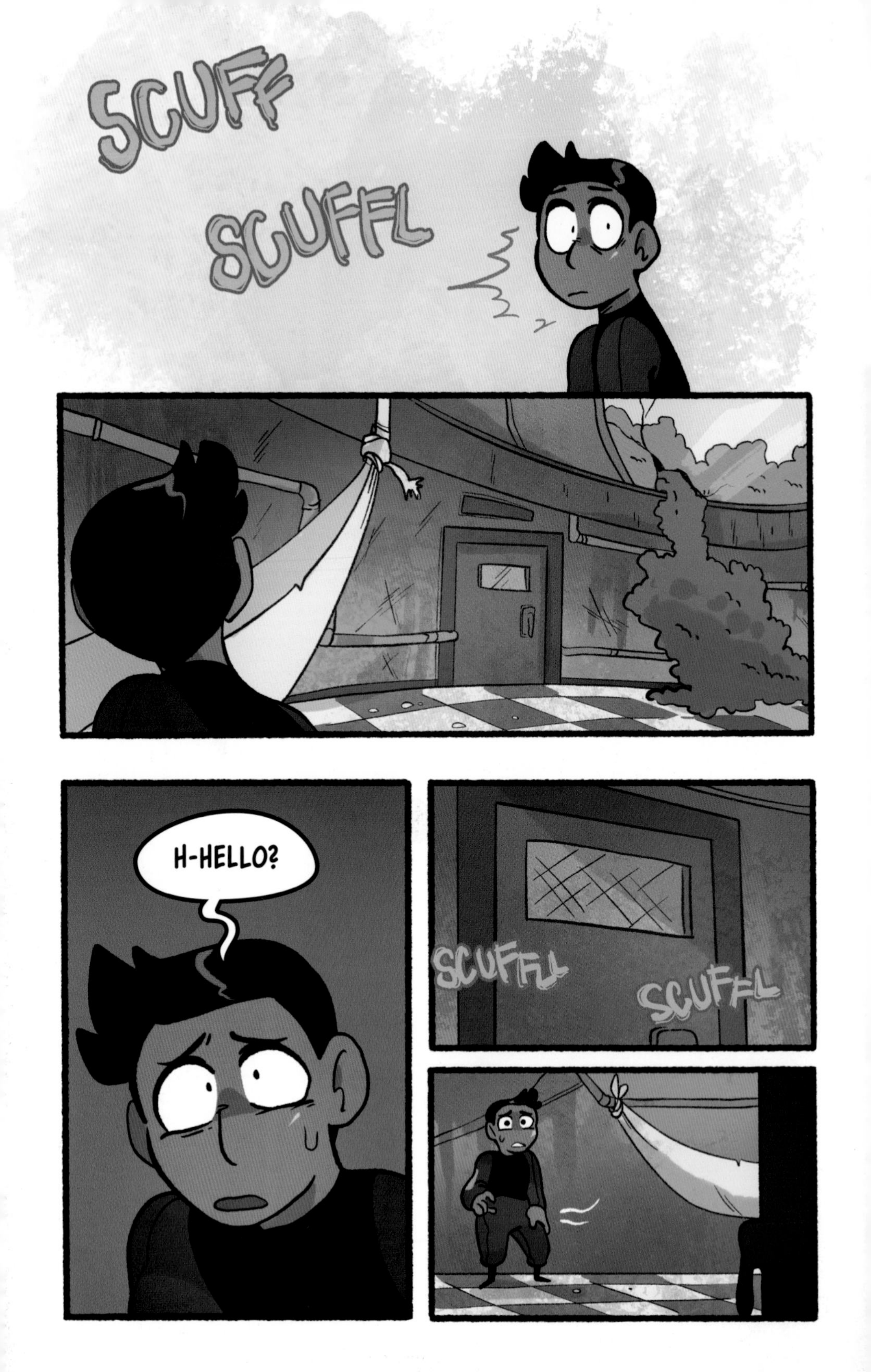
SCUFF
SCUFFL
H-HELLO?
SCUFFL
SCUFFL

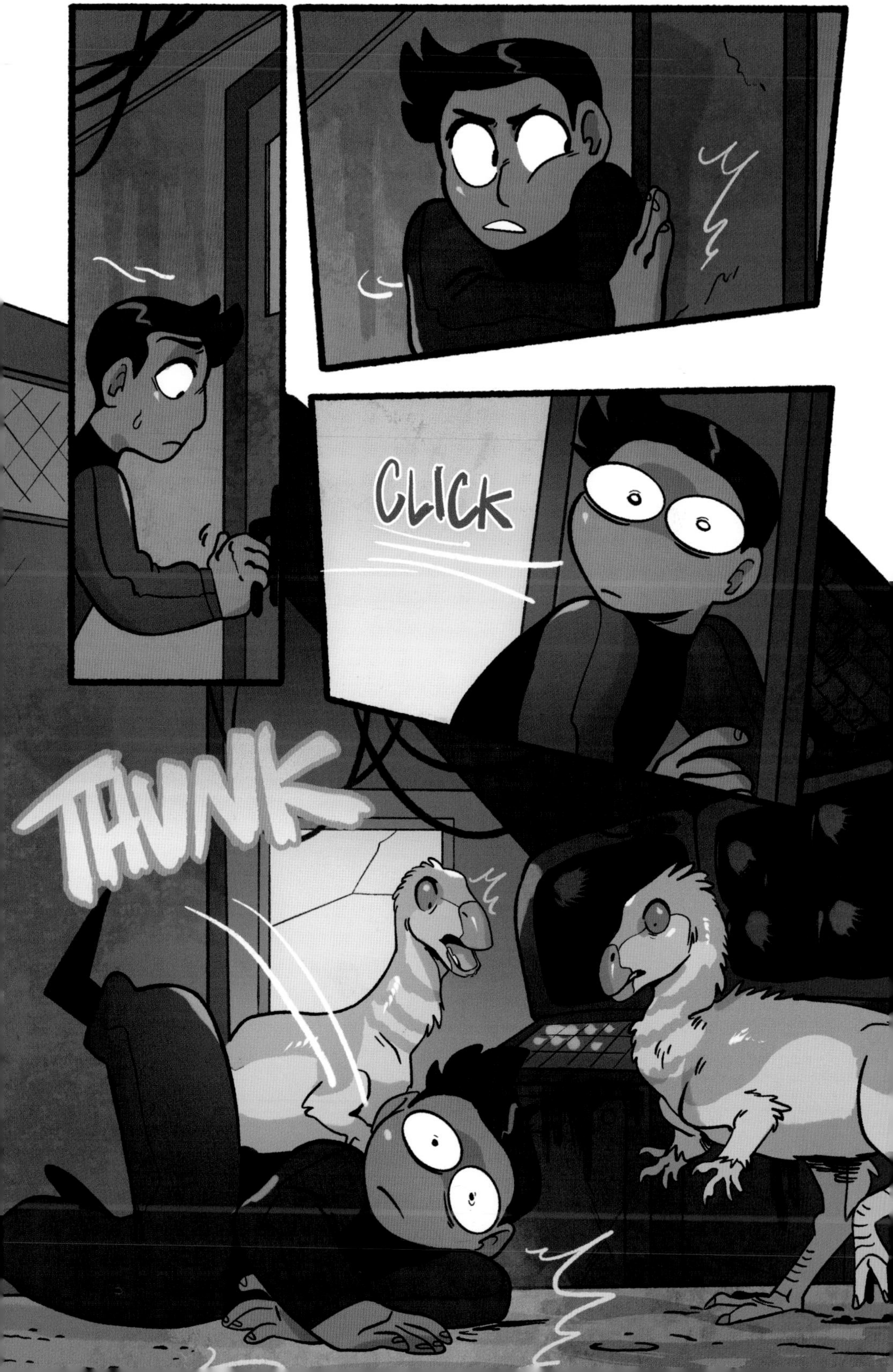
CLICK
THUNK

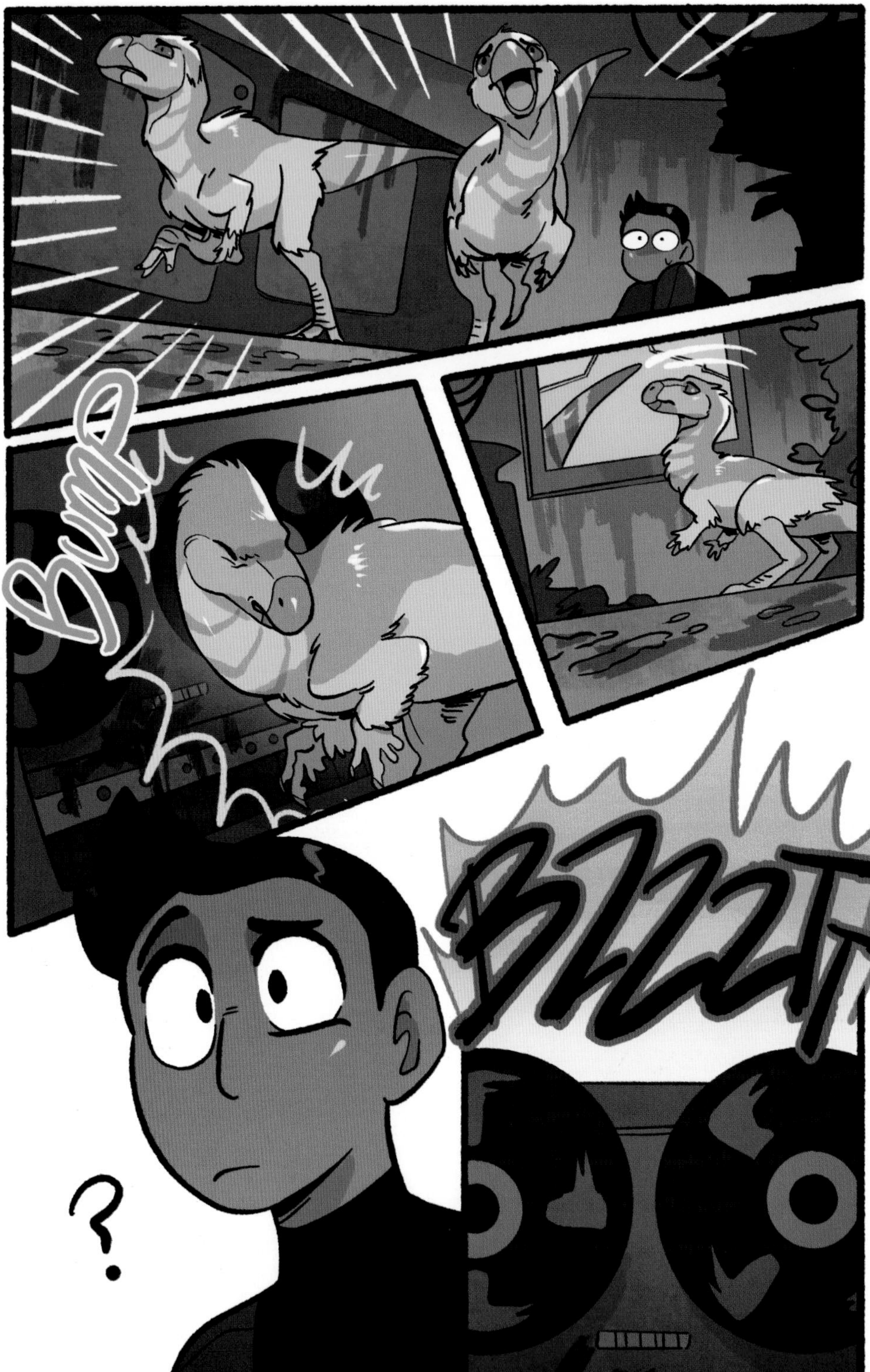
BUMP
BZZZT
?

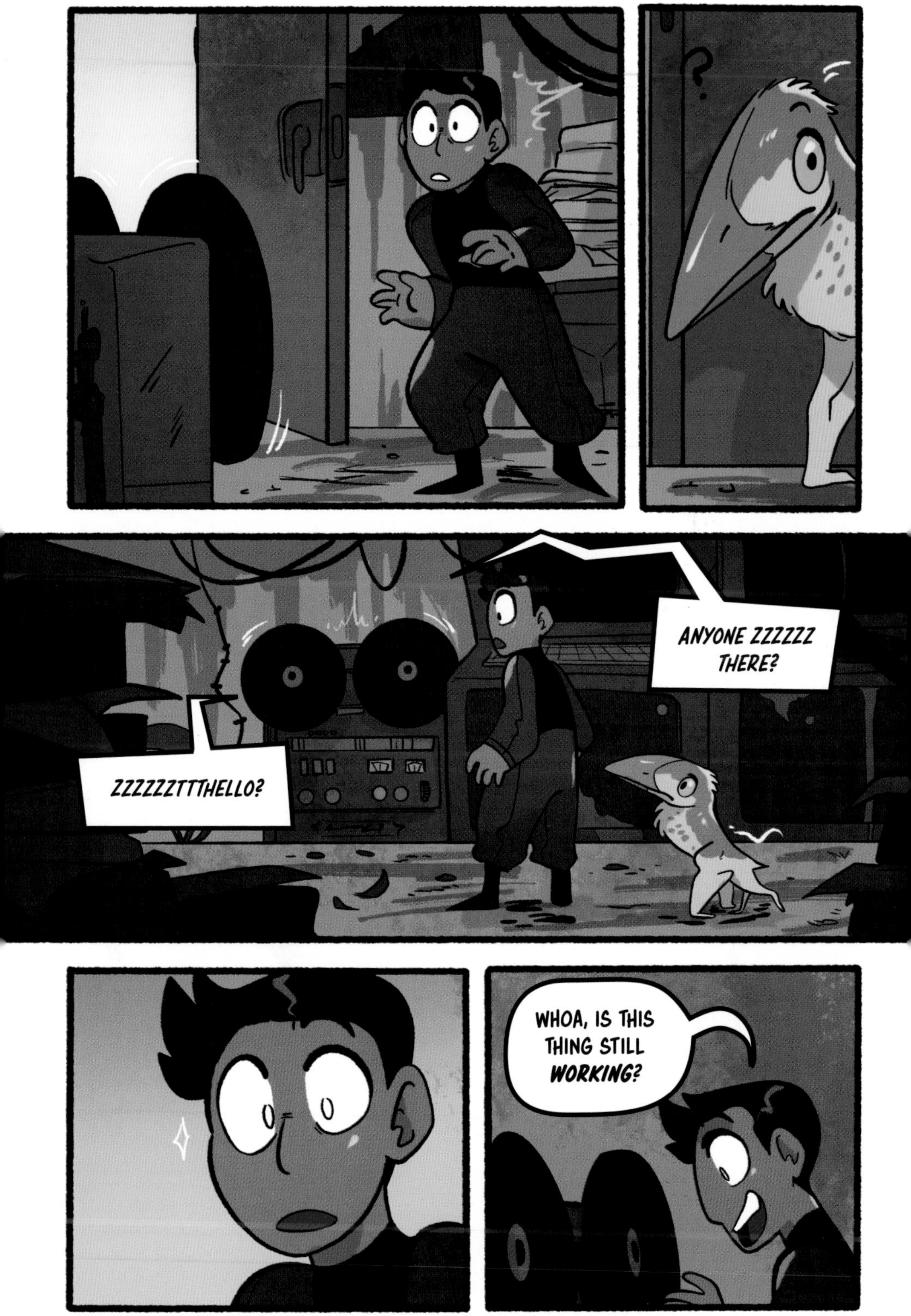
ANYONE ZZZZZZ THERE?
ZZZZZZTTTHELLO?
WHOA, IS THIS THING STILL WORKING?

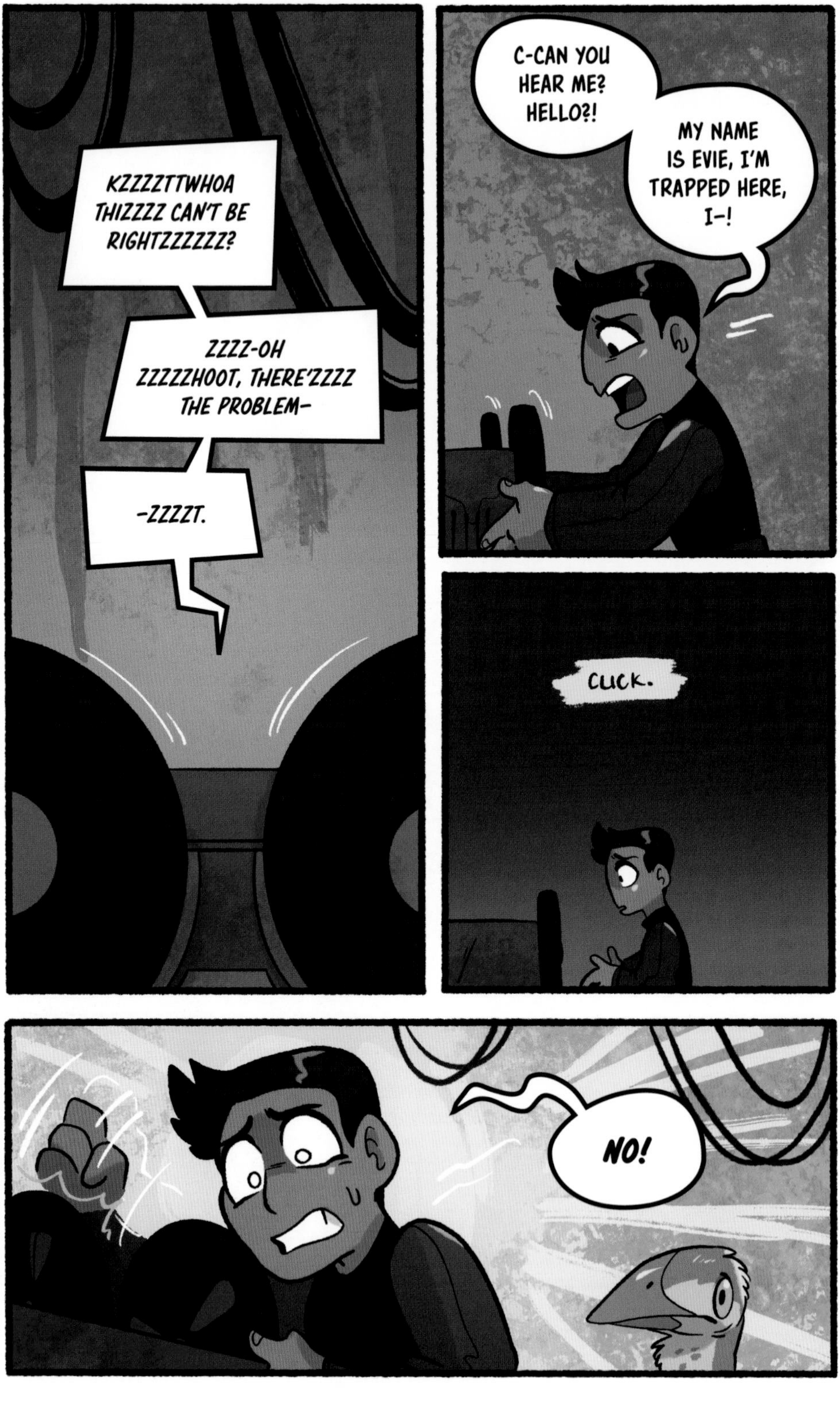
KZZZZTTWHOA THIZZZZ CAN'T BE RIGHTZZZZZZZ?
ZZZZ-OH ZZZZZHOOT, THERE'ZZZZ THE PROBLEM-
-ZZZZT.
C-CAN YOU HEAR ME? HELLO?!
MY NAME IS EVIE, I'M TRAPPED HERE, I-!
CLICK.
NO!

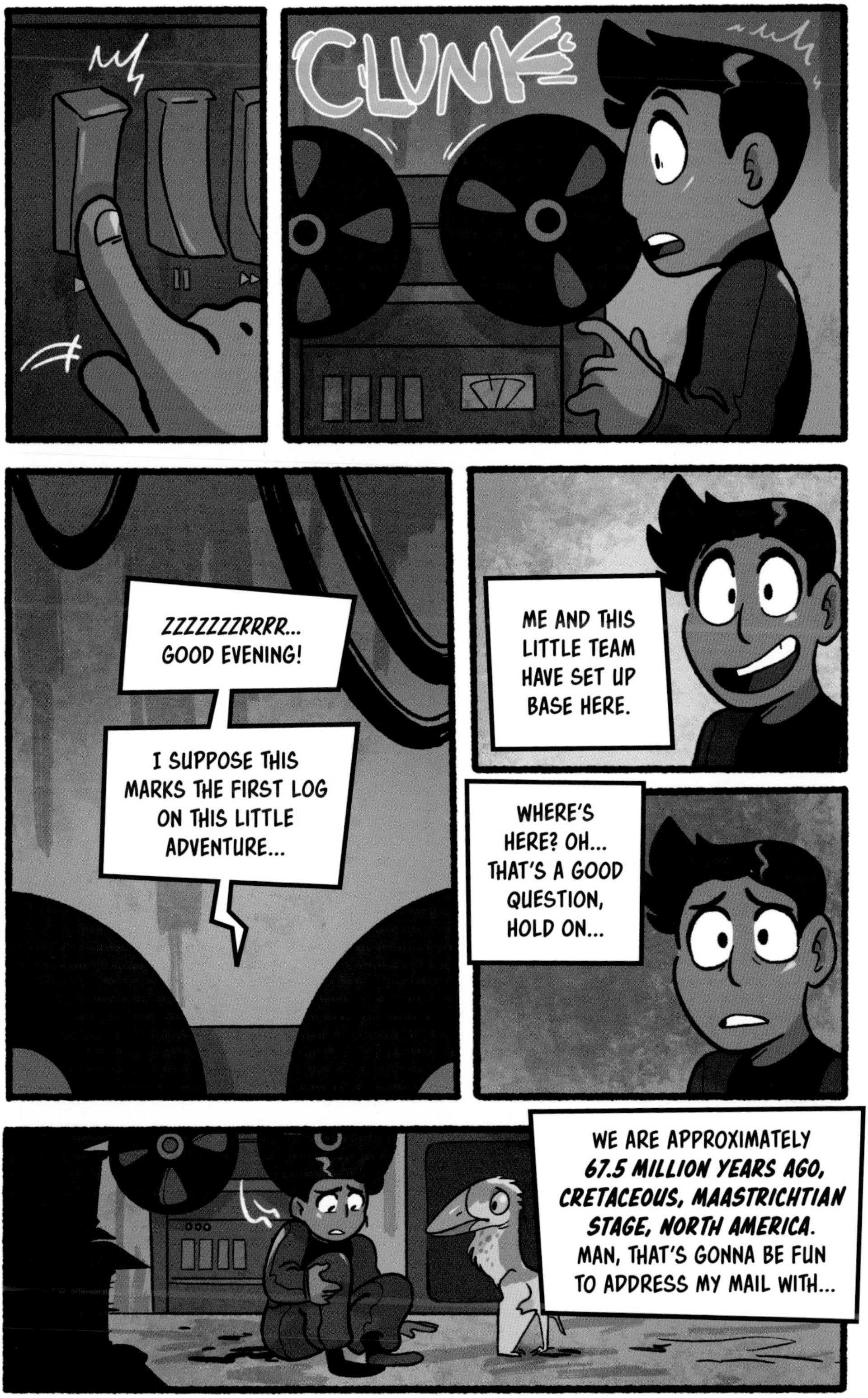
CLUNK
ZZZZZZZRRRR... GOOD EVENING!
I SUPPOSE THIS MARKS THE FIRST LOG ON THIS LITTLE ADVENTURE...
ME AND THIS LITTLE TEAM HAVE SET UP BASE HERE.
WHERE'S HERE? OH... THAT'S A GOOD QUESTION, HOLD ON...
WE ARE APPROXIMATELY 67.5 MILLION YEARS AGO, CRETACEOUS, MAASTRICHTIAN STAGE, NORTH AMERICA. MAN, THAT'S GONNA BE FUN TO ADDRESS MY MAIL WITH...

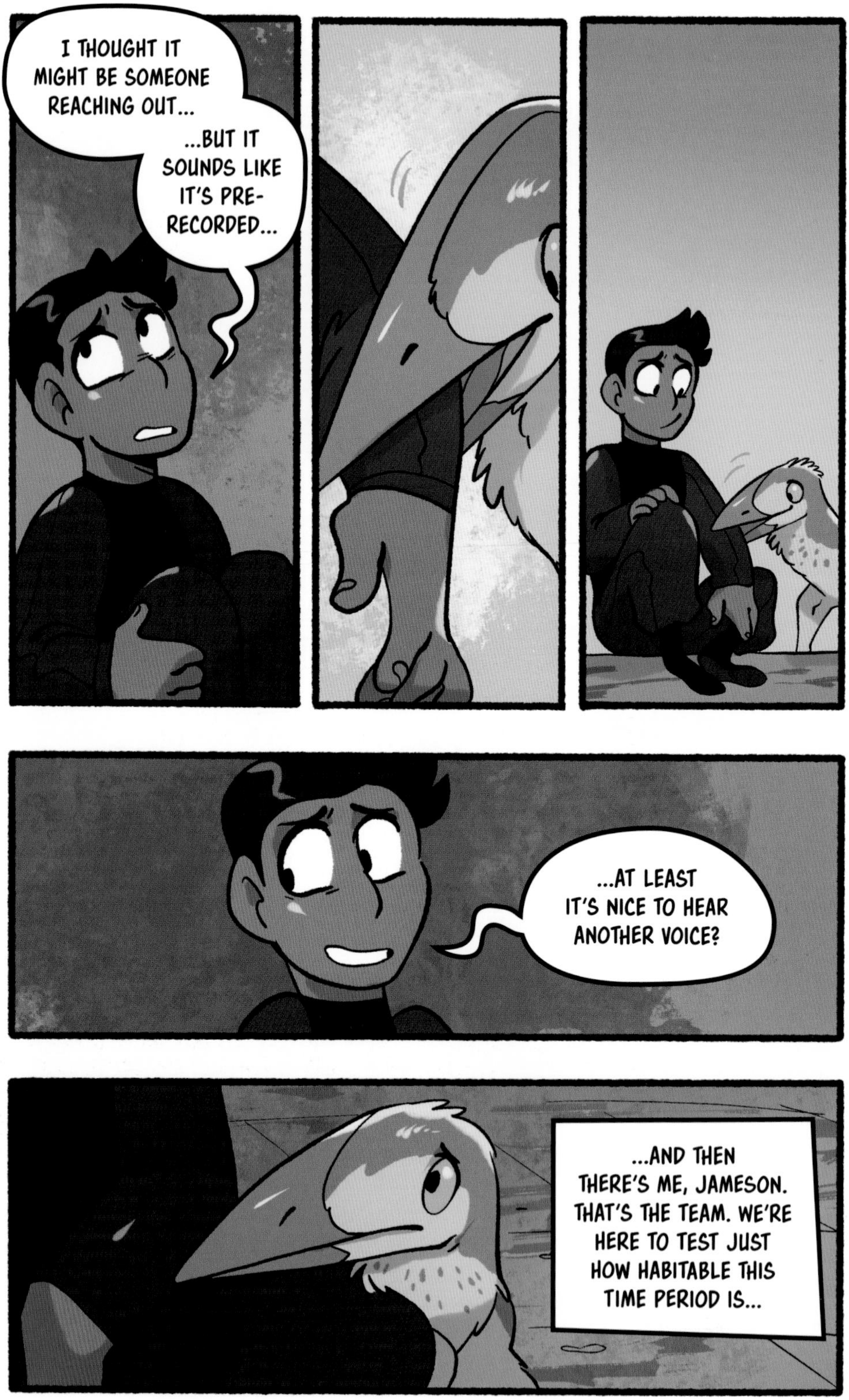
I THOUGHT IT MIGHT BE SOMEONE REACHING OUT...
...BUT IT SOUNDS LIKE IT'S PRE-RECORDED...
...AT LEAST IT'S NICE TO HEAR ANOTHER VOICE?
...AND THEN THERE'S ME, JAMESON. THAT'S THE TEAM. WE'RE HERE TO TEST JUST HOW HABITABLE THIS TIME PERIOD IS...

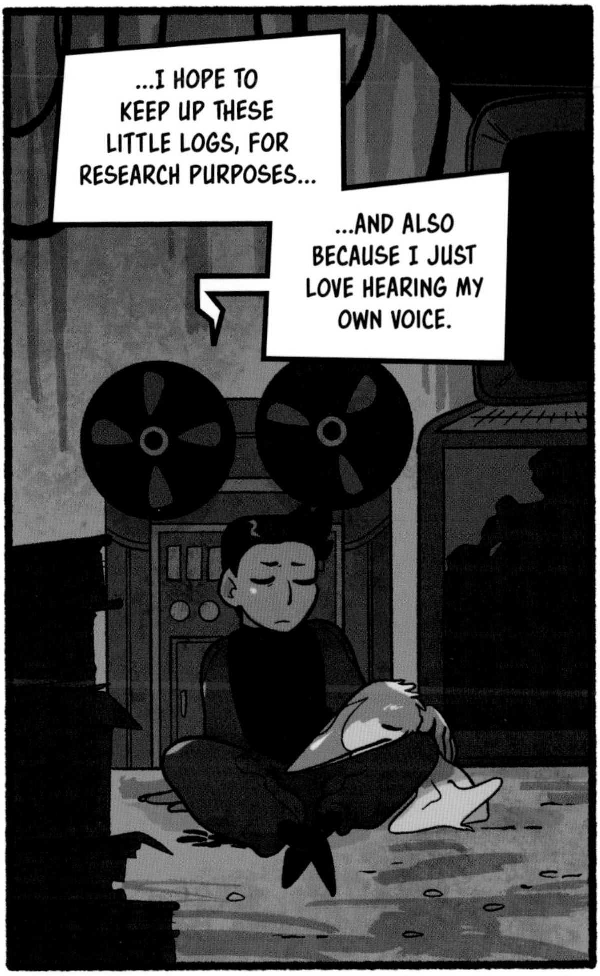
...I HOPE TO KEEP UP THESE LITTLE LOGS, FOR RESEARCH PURPOSES...
...AND ALSO BECAUSE I JUST LOVE HEARING MY OWN VOICE.

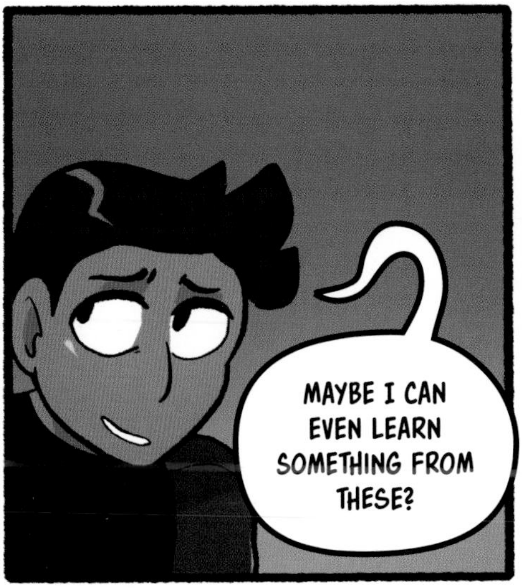
MAYBE I CAN EVEN LEARN SOMETHING FROM THESE?

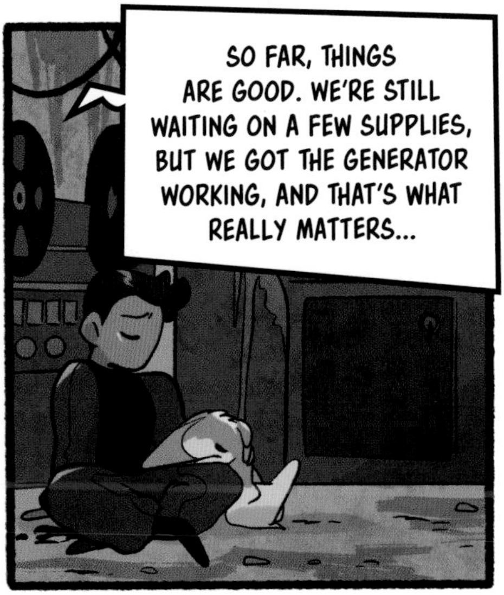
SO FAR, THINGS ARE GOOD. WE'RE STILL WAITING ON A FEW SUPPLIES, BUT WE GOT THE GENERATOR WORKING, AND THAT'S WHAT REALLY MATTERS...

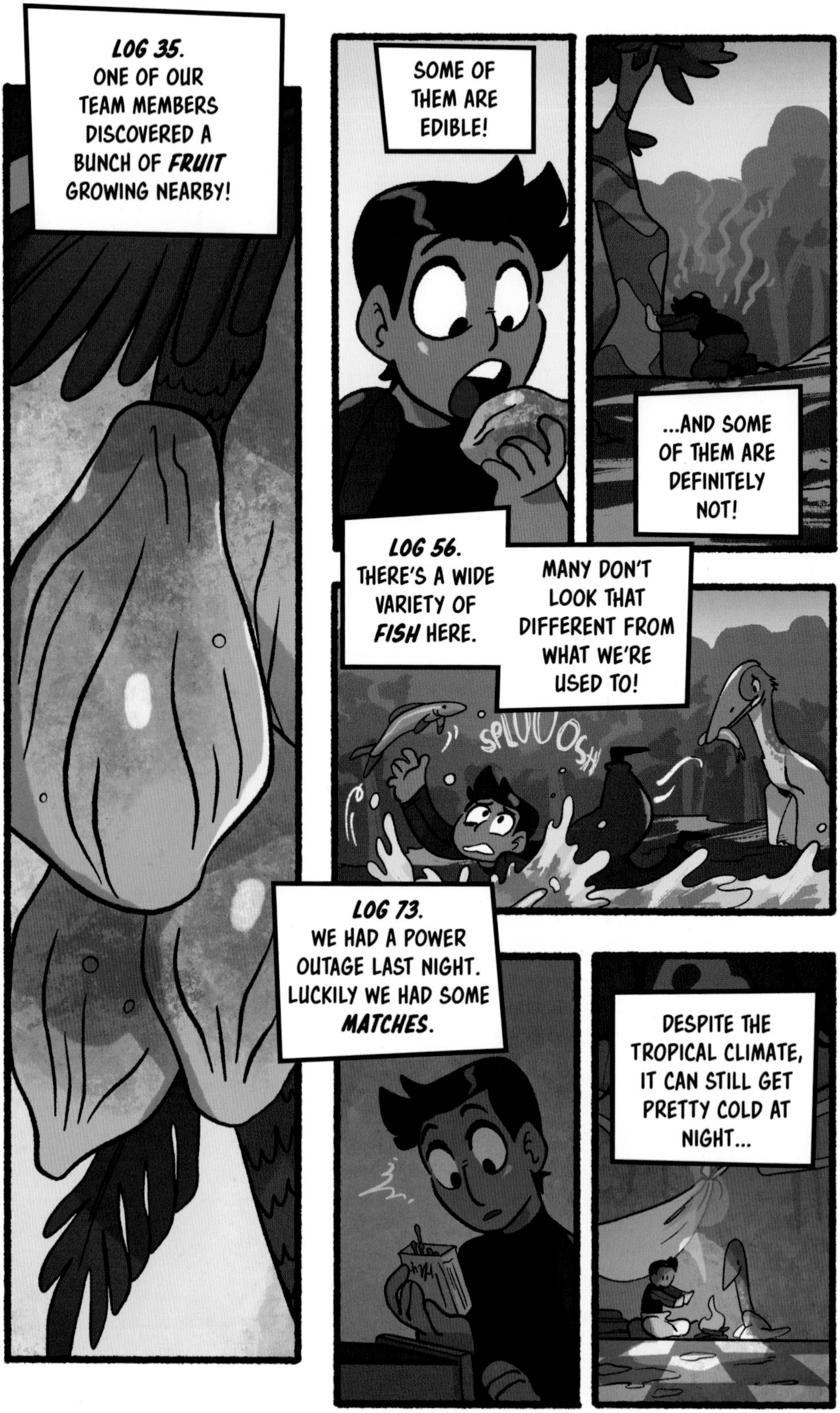

LOG 35.
ONE OF OUR TEAM MEMBERS DISCOVERED A BUNCH OF ***FRUIT*** GROWING NEARBY!
SOME OF THEM ARE EDIBLE!
...AND SOME OF THEM ARE DEFINITELY NOT!
LOG 56.
THERE'S A WIDE VARIETY OF ***FISH*** HERE.
MANY DON'T LOOK THAT DIFFERENT FROM WHAT WE'RE USED TO!
SPLOOOSH
LOG 73.
WE HAD A POWER OUTAGE LAST NIGHT. LUCKILY WE HAD SOME ***MATCHES***.
DESPITE THE TROPICAL CLIMATE, IT CAN STILL GET PRETTY COLD AT NIGHT...

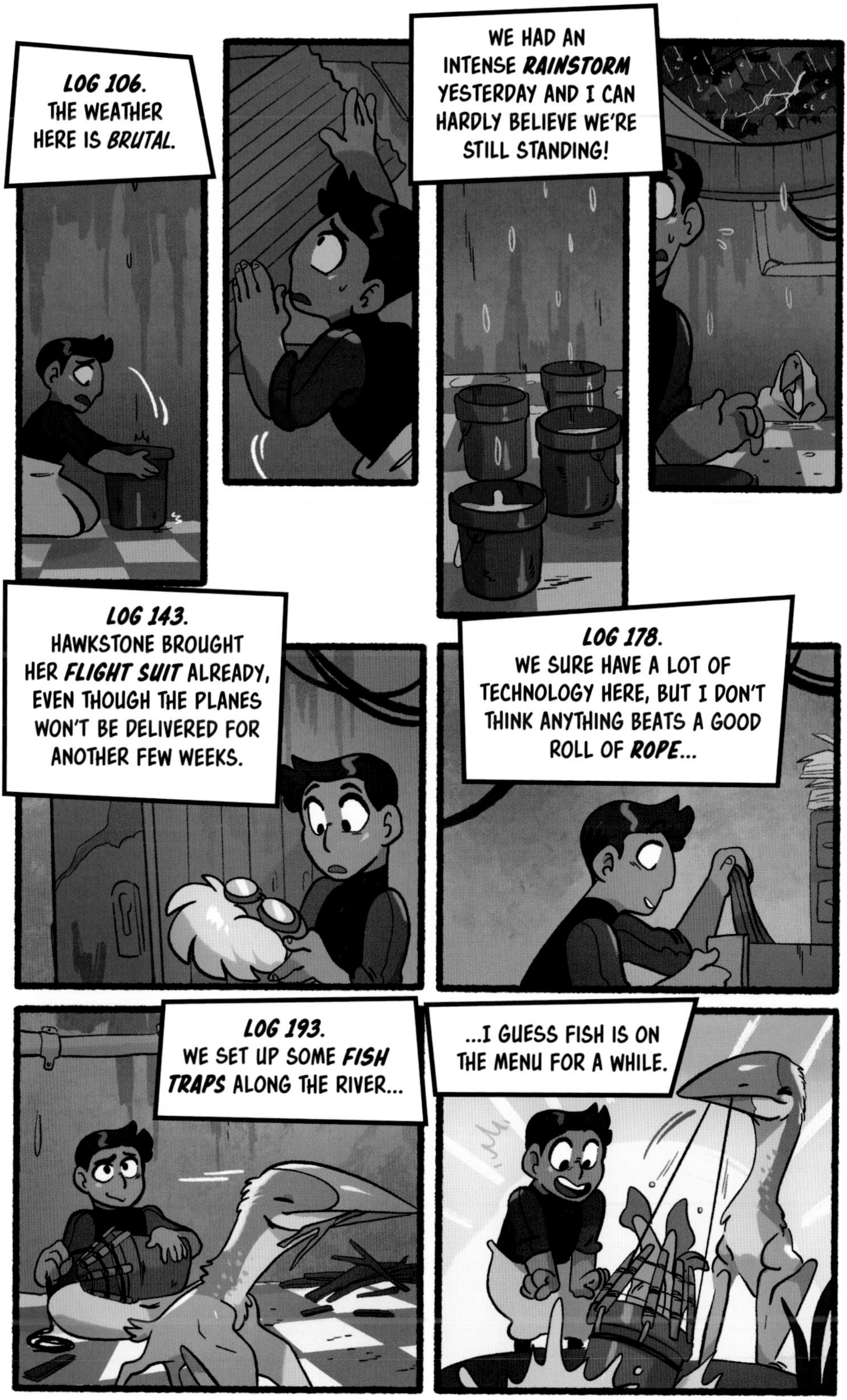
LOG 106.
THE WEATHER HERE IS BRUTAL.
WE HAD AN INTENSE RAINSTORM YESTERDAY AND I CAN HARDLY BELIEVE WE'RE STILL STANDING!
LOG 143.
HAWKSTONE BROUGHT HER FLIGHT SUIT ALREADY, EVEN THOUGH THE PLANES WON'T BE DELIVERED FOR ANOTHER FEW WEEKS.
LOG 178.
WE SURE HAVE A LOT OF TECHNOLOGY HERE, BUT I DON'T THINK ANYTHING BEATS A GOOD ROLL OF ROPE...
LOG 193.
WE SET UP SOME FISH TRAPS ALONG THE RIVER...
...I GUESS FISH IS ON THE MENU FOR A WHILE.

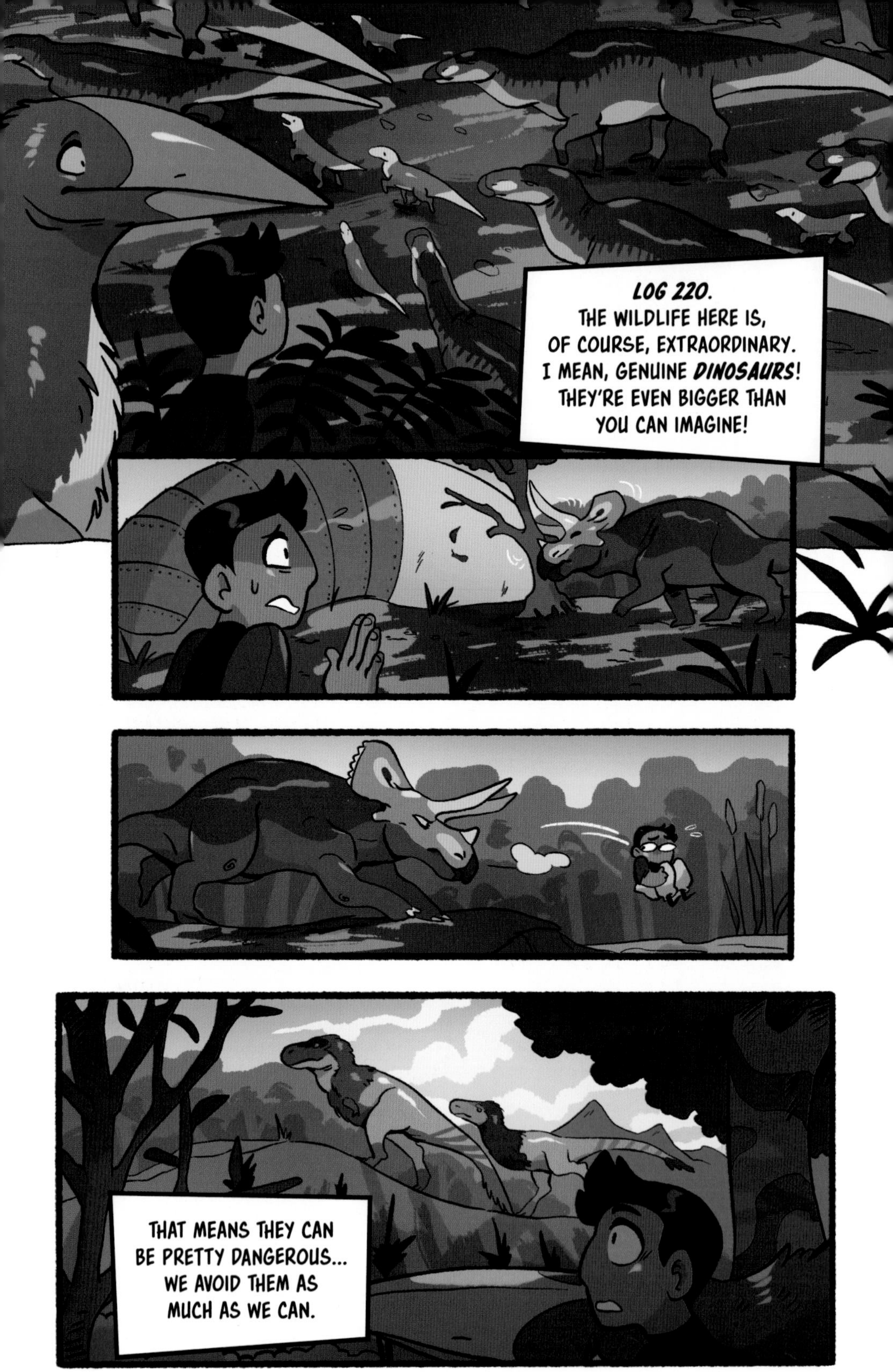
LOG 220. THE WILDLIFE HERE IS, OF COURSE, EXTRAORDINARY. I MEAN, GENUINE DINOSAURS! THEY'RE EVEN BIGGER THAN YOU CAN IMAGINE!
THAT MEANS THEY CAN BE PRETTY DANGEROUS... WE AVOID THEM AS MUCH AS WE CAN.

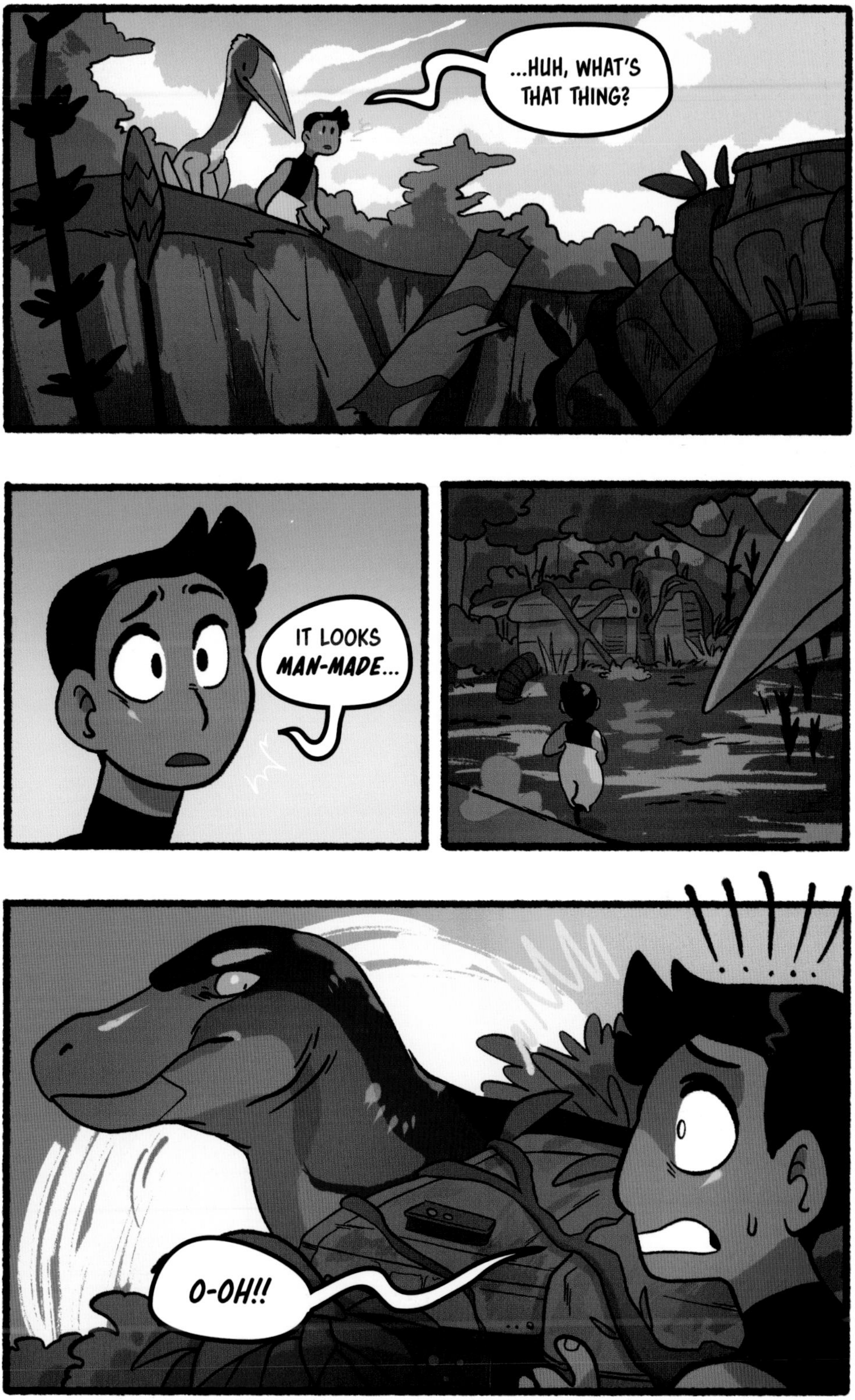
...HUH, WHAT'S THAT THING?
IT LOOKS MAN-MADE...
O-OH!!

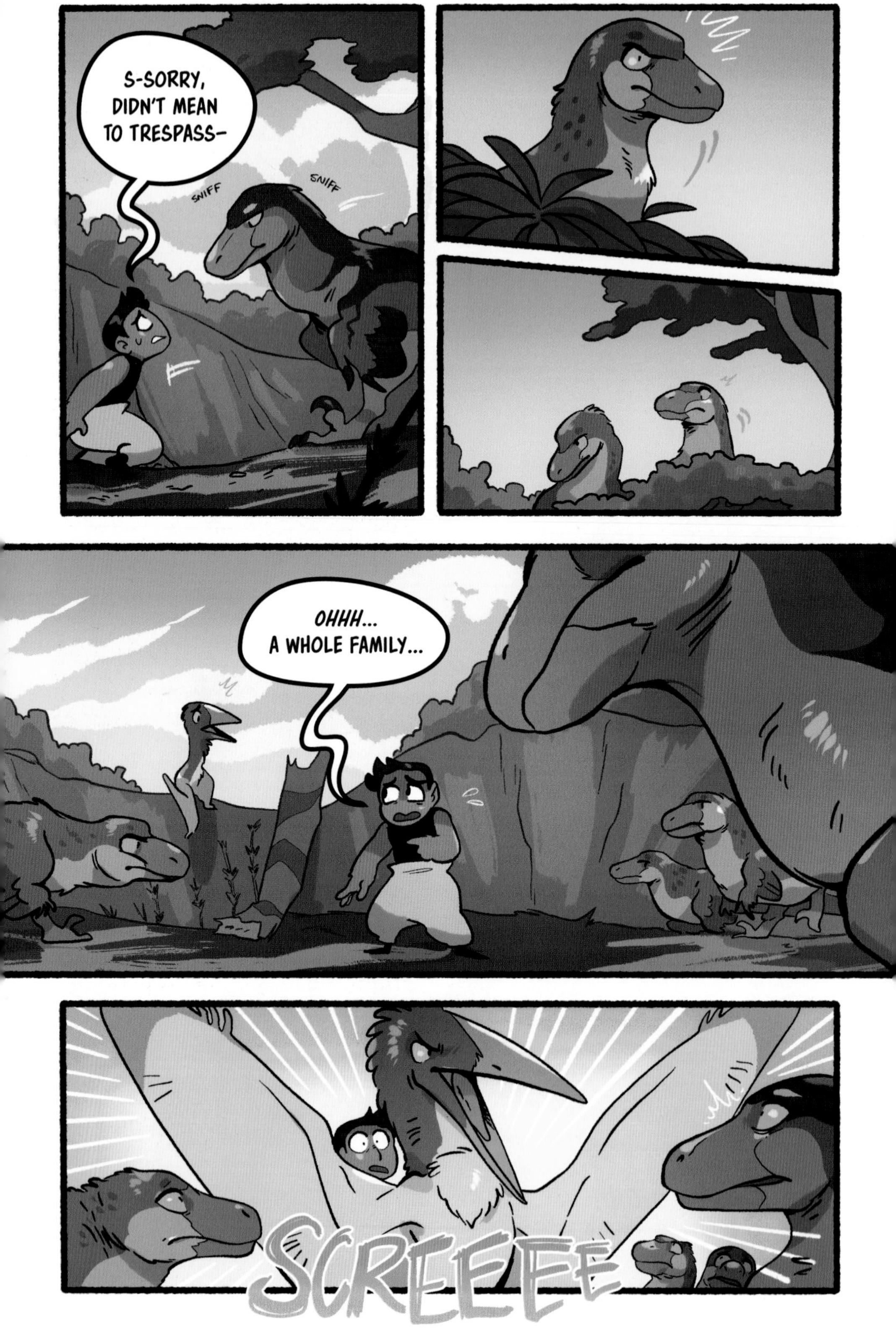
S-SORRY, DIDN'T MEAN TO TRESPASS-
SNIFF
SNIFF
OHHH... A WHOLE FAMILY...
SCREEEE

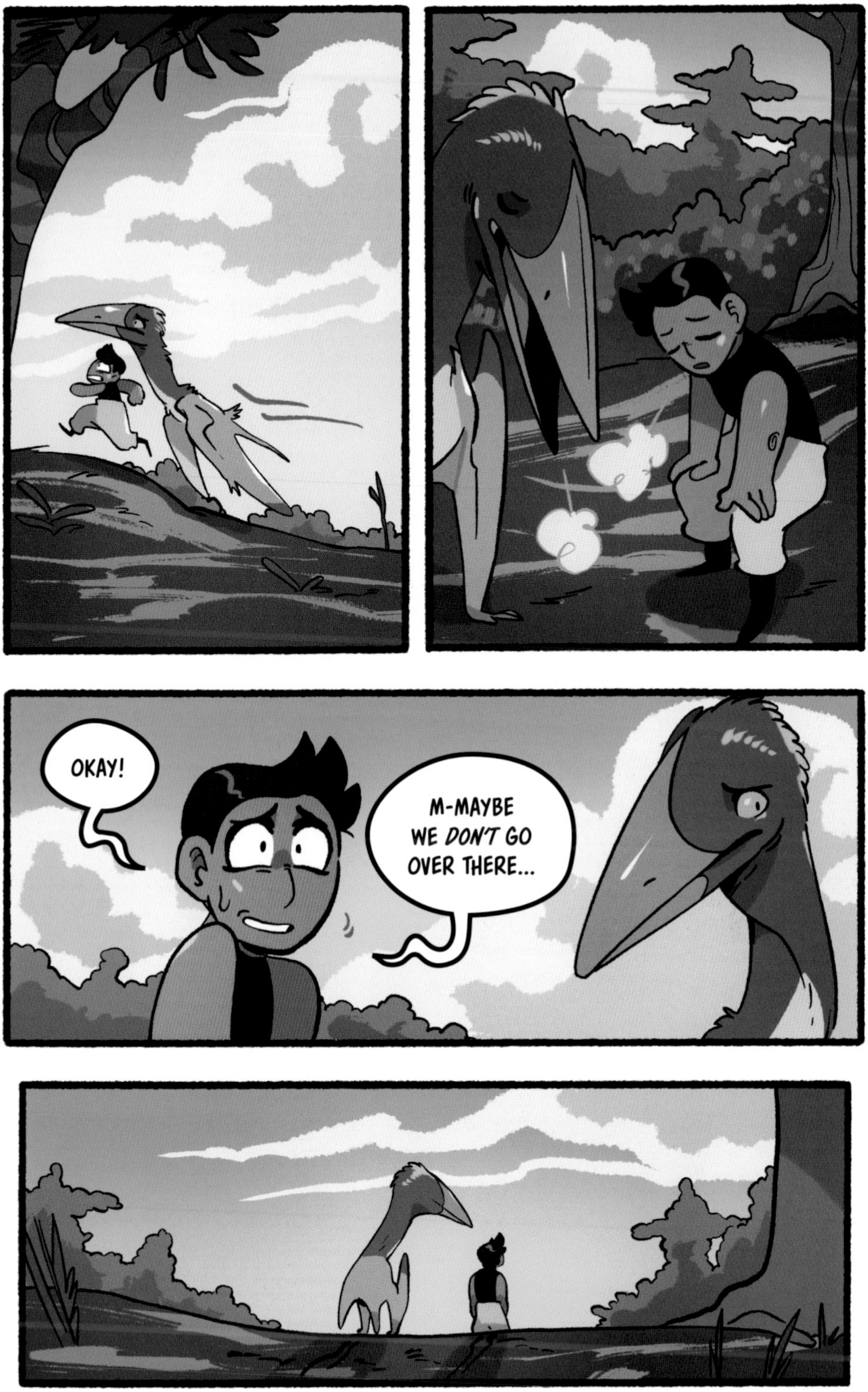
OKAY!
M-MAYBE WE DON'T GO OVER THERE...

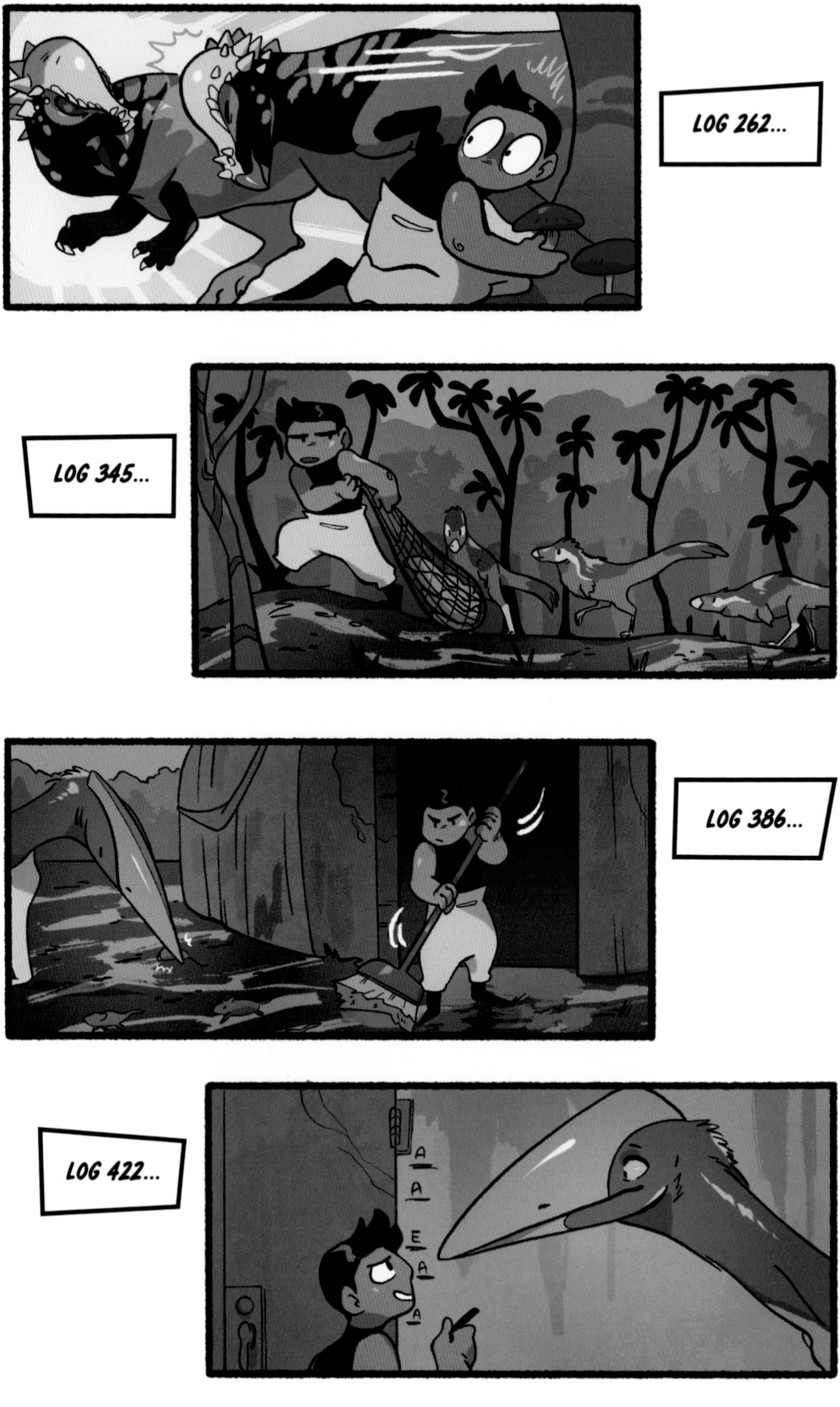
LOG 262...
LOG 345...
LOG 386...
LOG 422...

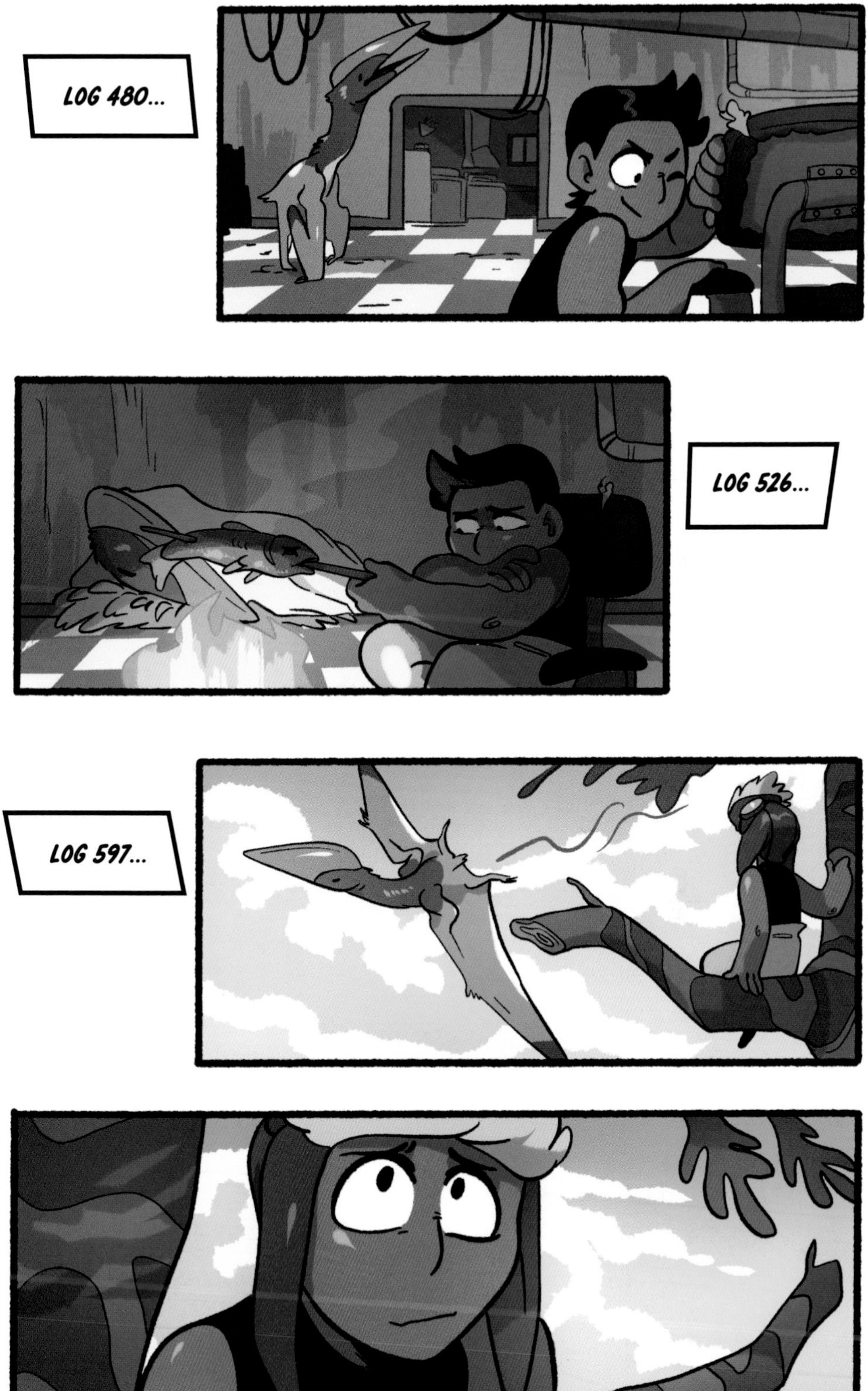
LOG 480...
LOG 526...
LOG 597...

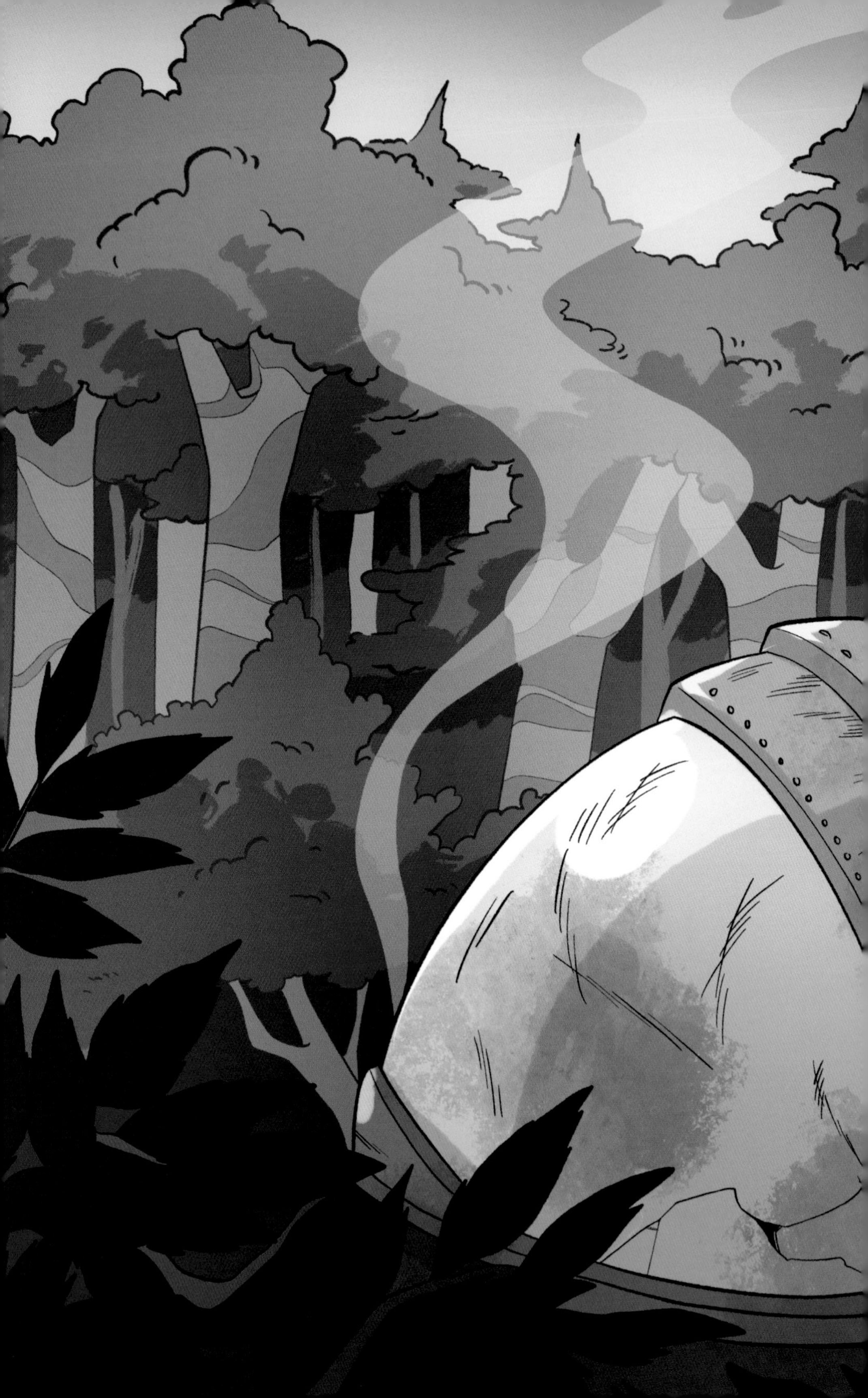

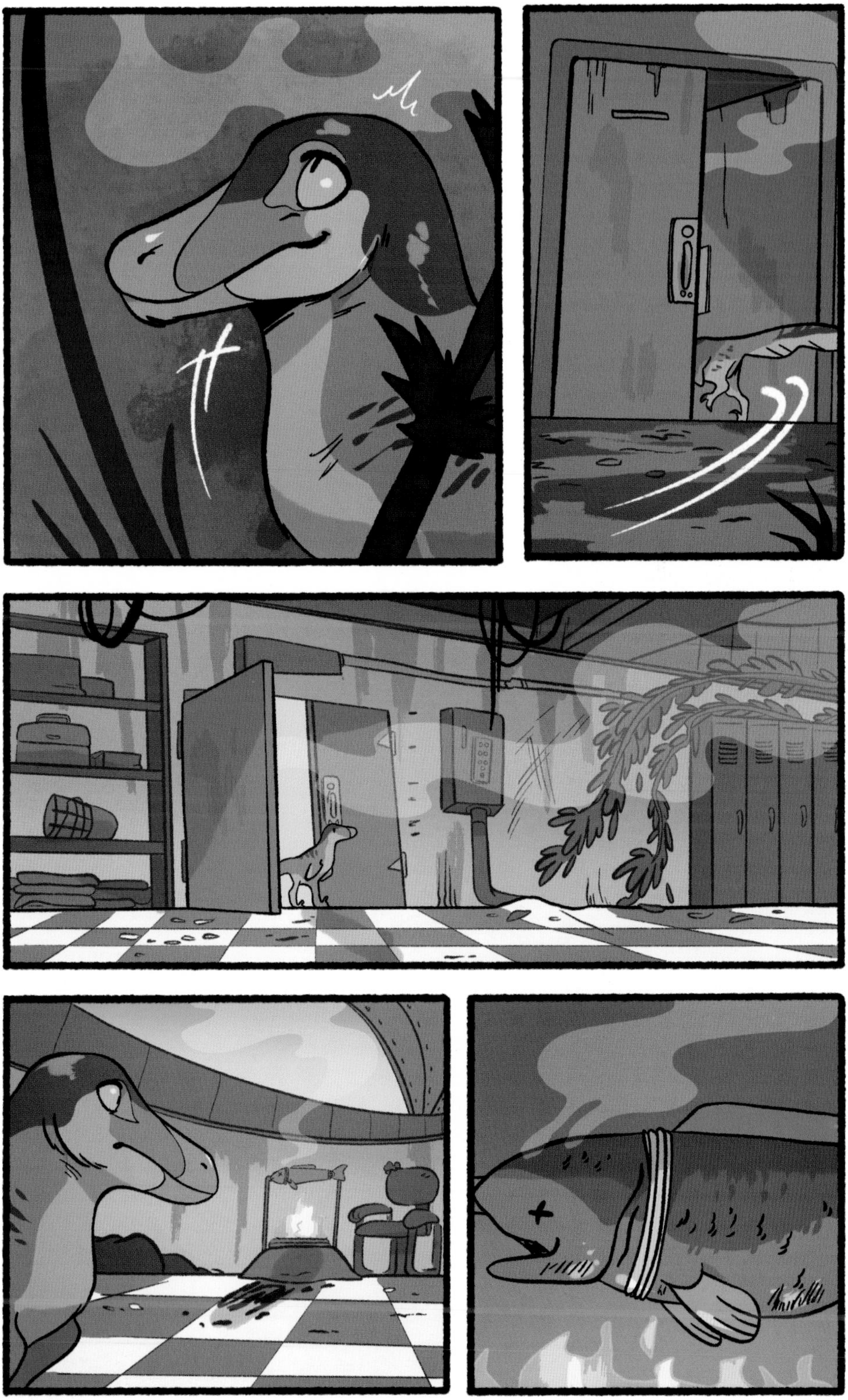

HEY!

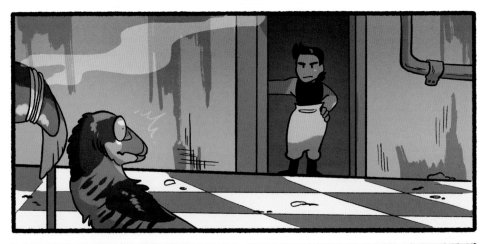

THAT'S
MINE,
THANK
YOU.

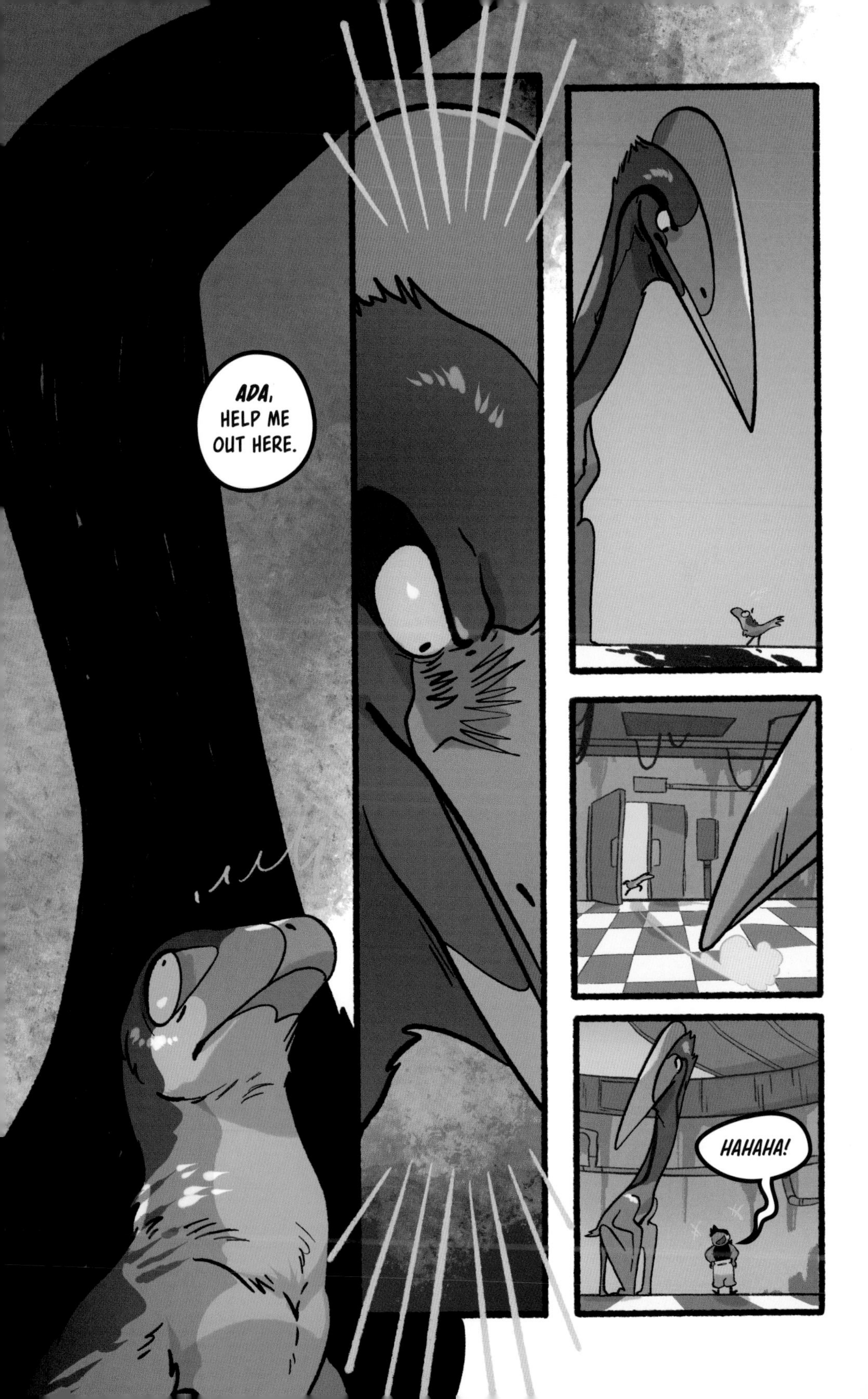
ADA,
HELP ME
OUT HERE.
HAHAHA!

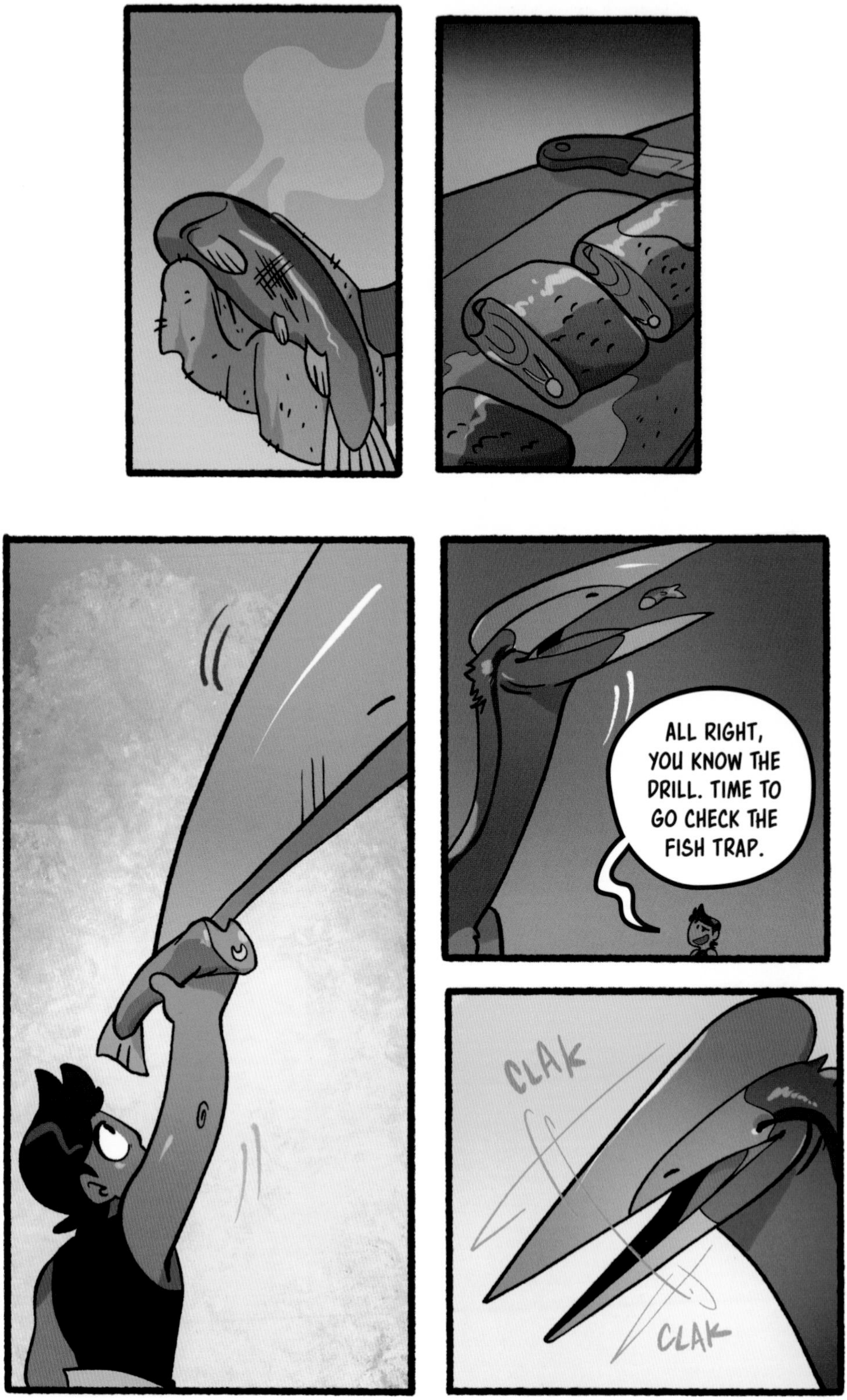
ALL RIGHT, YOU KNOW THE DRILL. TIME TO GO CHECK THE FISH TRAP.
CLAK
CLAK

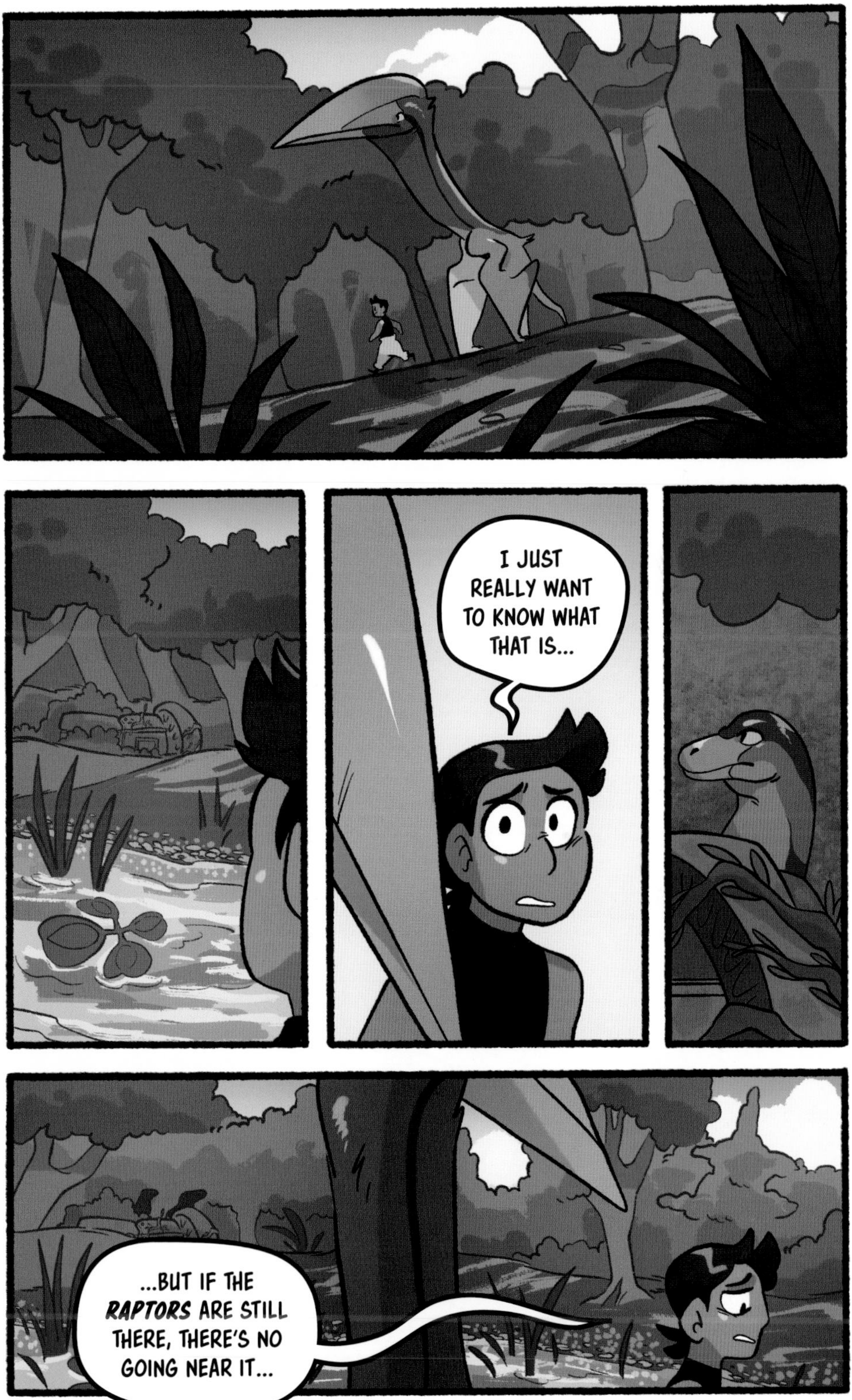
I JUST REALLY WANT TO KNOW WHAT THAT IS...
...BUT IF THE *RAPTORS* ARE STILL THERE, THERE'S NO GOING NEAR IT...

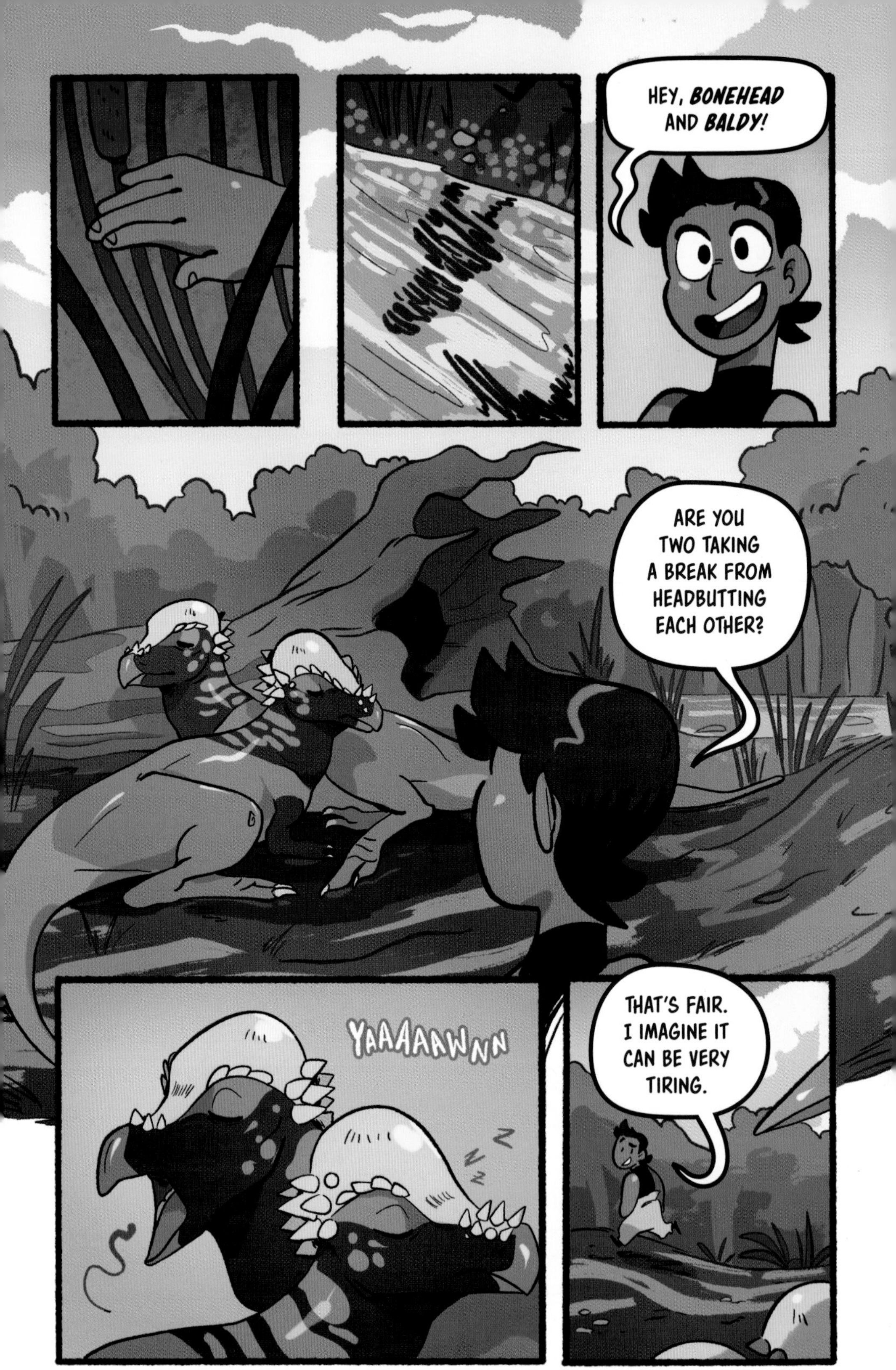
HEY, ***BONEHEAD*** AND ***BALDY!***
ARE YOU TWO TAKING A BREAK FROM HEADBUTTING EACH OTHER?
YAAAAAWNN
THAT'S FAIR. I IMAGINE IT CAN BE VERY TIRING.

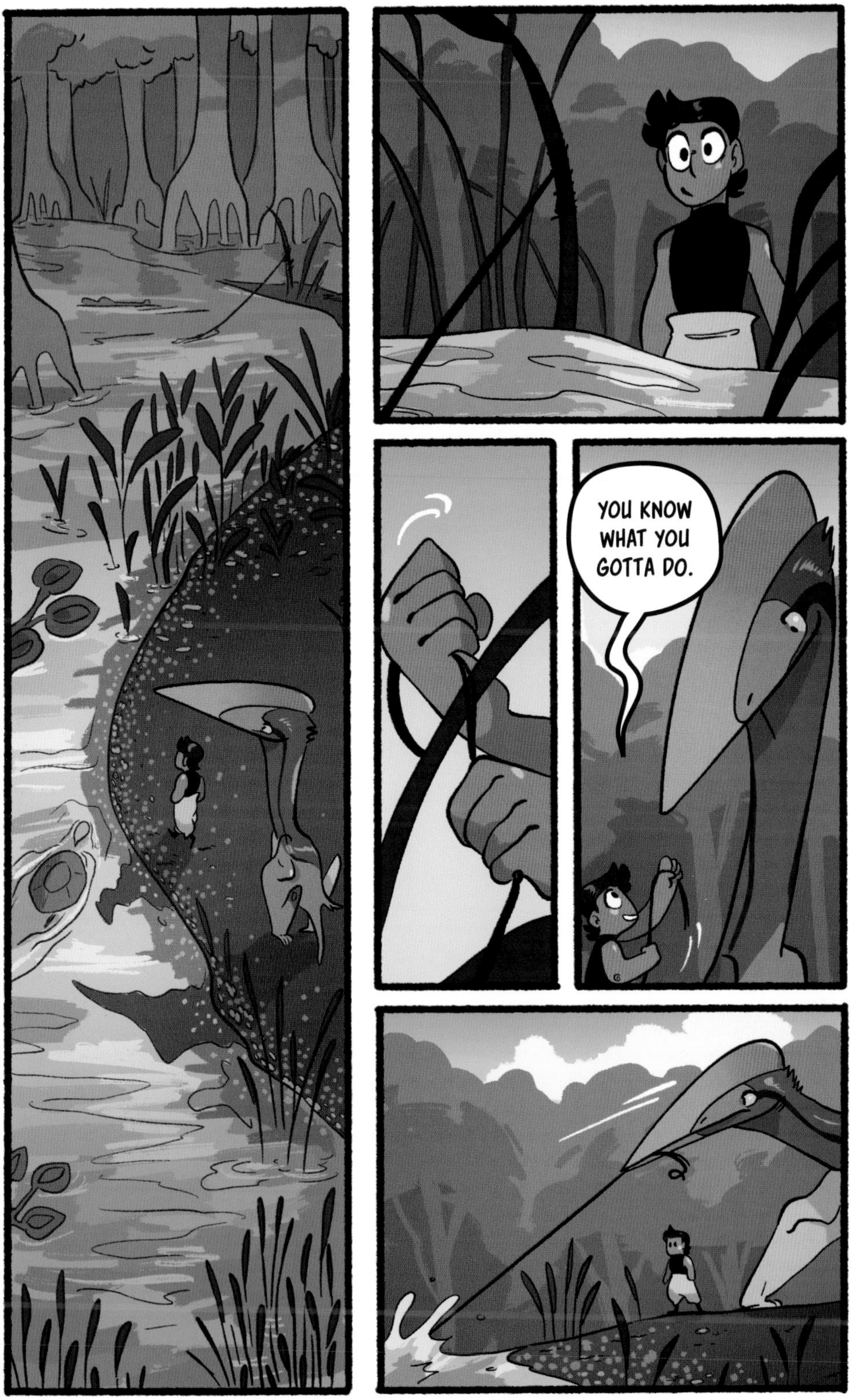
YOU KNOW WHAT YOU GOTTA DO.

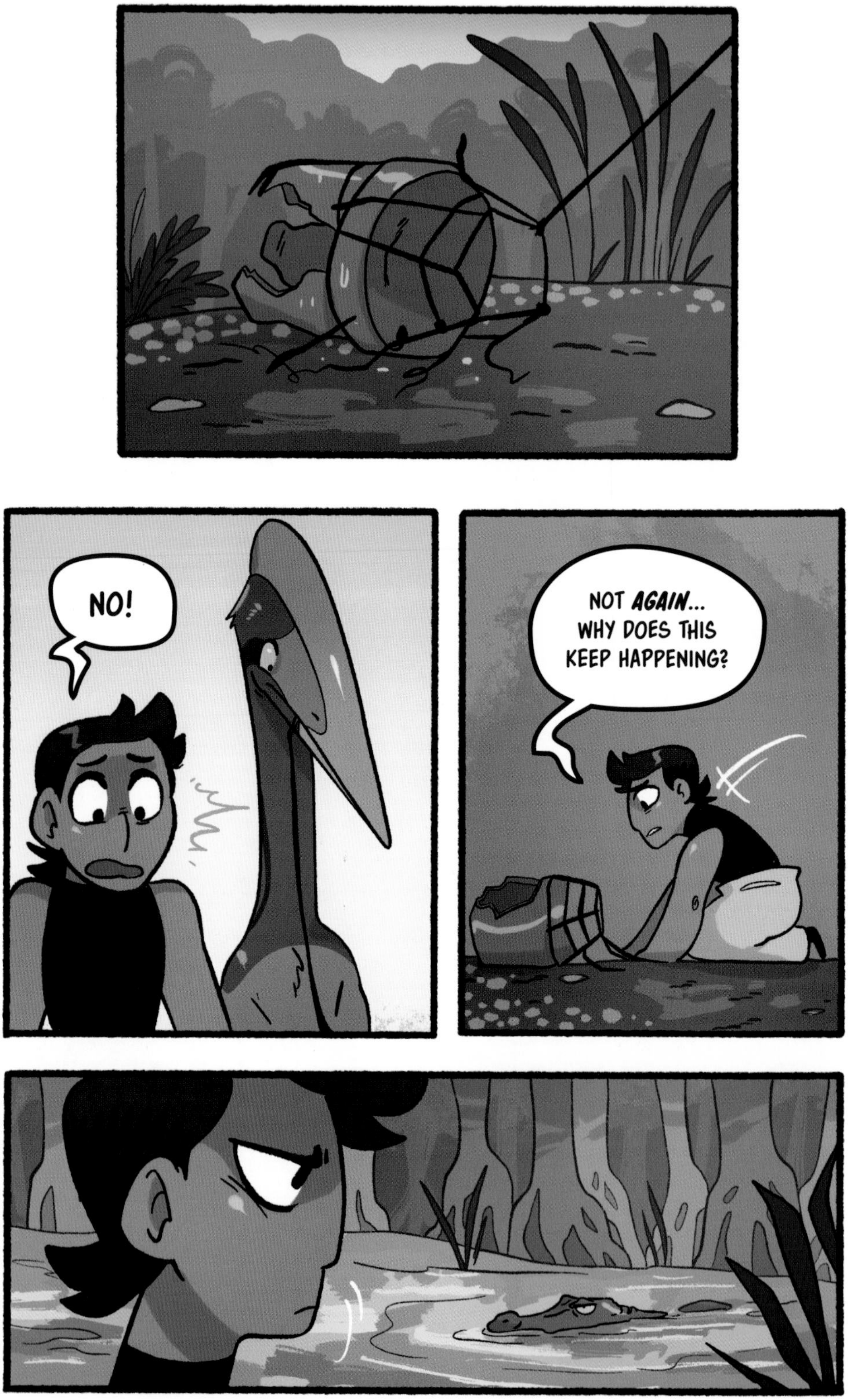
NO!
NOT **AGAIN**... WHY DOES THIS KEEP HAPPENING?

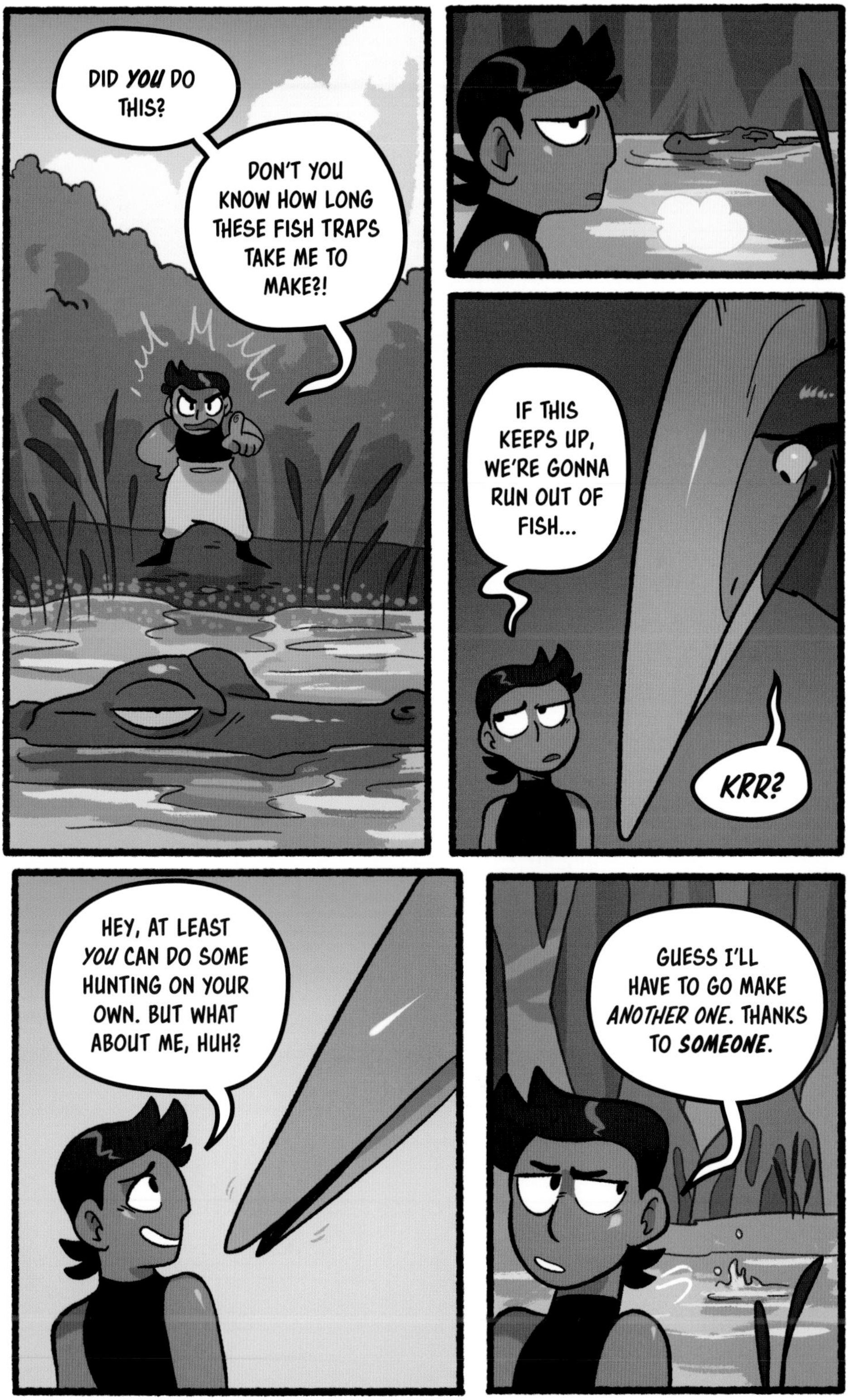
DID *YOU* DO THIS?
DON'T YOU KNOW HOW LONG THESE FISH TRAPS TAKE ME TO MAKE?!
IF THIS KEEPS UP, WE'RE GONNA RUN OUT OF FISH...
KRR?
HEY, AT LEAST *YOU* CAN DO SOME HUNTING ON YOUR OWN. BUT WHAT ABOUT ME, HUH?
GUESS I'LL HAVE TO GO MAKE *ANOTHER ONE*. THANKS TO ***SOMEONE***.

ZZZT—
WELL THAT'S THE LAST TIME I TRY TO WALK ANYWHERE CLOSE TO A *DENVERSAURUS.*

I THINK I SAW MY LIFE FLASH BEFORE MY EYES.

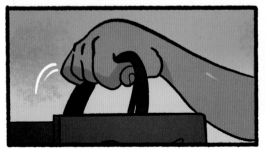

I GUESS I'M MAKING A NEW FISH TRAP TODAY.

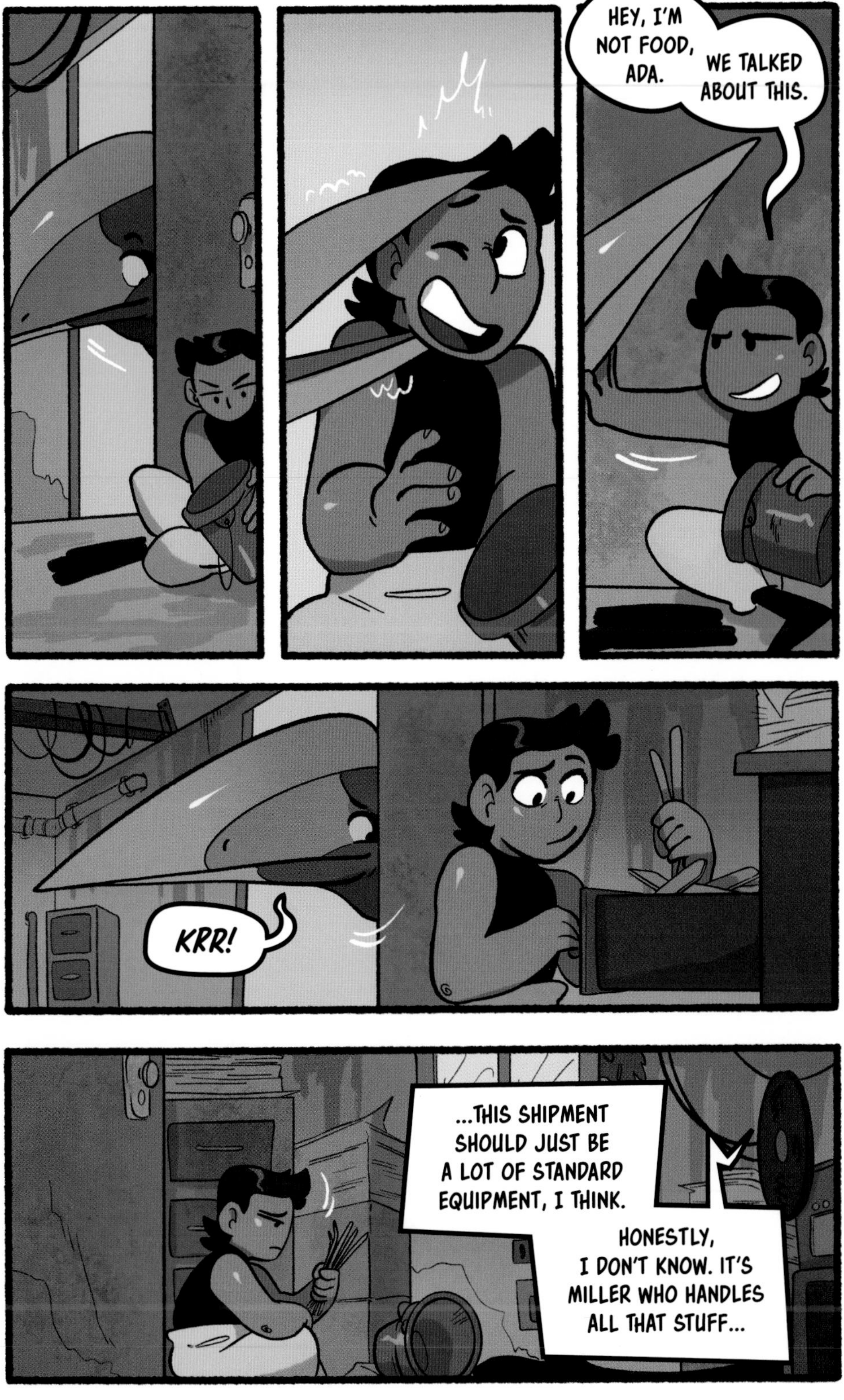
HEY, I'M NOT FOOD, ADA.
WE TALKED ABOUT THIS.
KRR!
...THIS SHIPMENT SHOULD JUST BE A LOT OF STANDARD EQUIPMENT, I THINK.
HONESTLY, I DON'T KNOW. IT'S MILLER WHO HANDLES ALL THAT STUFF...

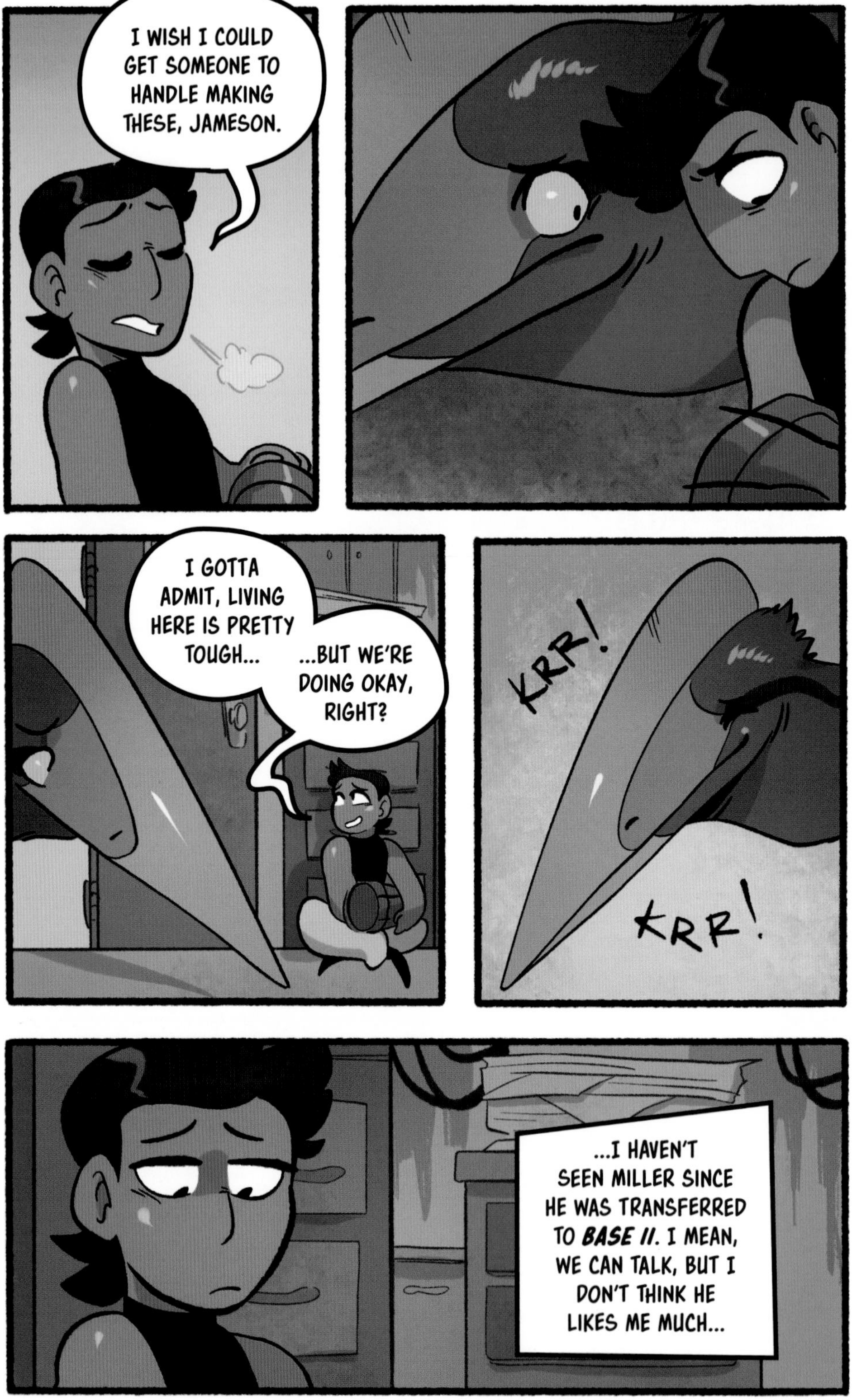
I WISH I COULD GET SOMEONE TO HANDLE MAKING THESE, JAMESON.
I GOTTA ADMIT, LIVING HERE IS PRETTY TOUGH...
...BUT WE'RE DOING OKAY, RIGHT?
KRR!
KRR!
...I HAVEN'T SEEN MILLER SINCE HE WAS TRANSFERRED TO BASE II. I MEAN, WE CAN TALK, BUT I DON'T THINK HE LIKES ME MUCH...

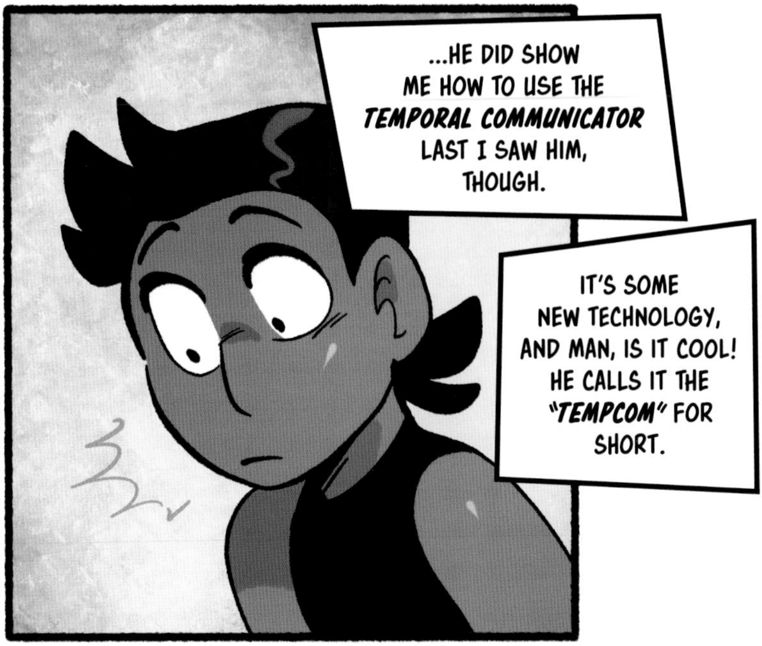
...HE DID SHOW ME HOW TO USE THE *TEMPORAL COMMUNICATOR* LAST I SAW HIM, THOUGH.
IT'S SOME NEW TECHNOLOGY, AND MAN, IS IT COOL! HE CALLS IT THE *"TEMPCOM"* FOR SHORT.

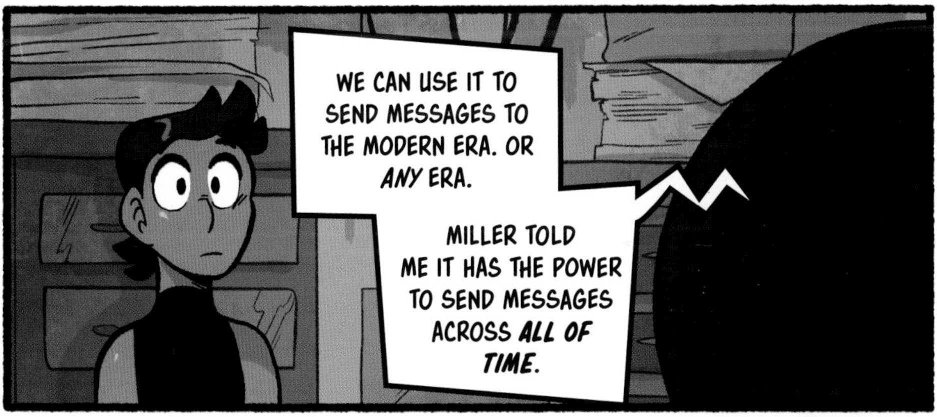
WE CAN USE IT TO SEND MESSAGES TO THE MODERN ERA. OR *ANY* ERA.
MILLER TOLD ME IT HAS THE POWER TO SEND MESSAGES ACROSS *ALL OF TIME*.

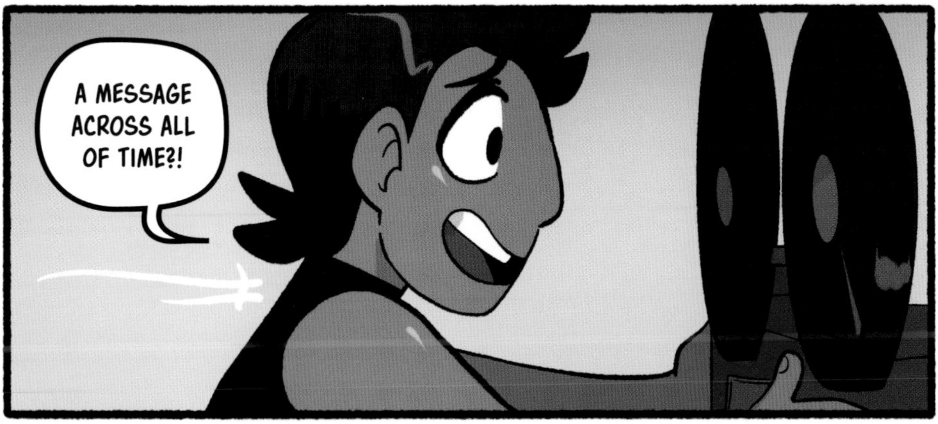
A MESSAGE ACROSS ALL OF TIME?!

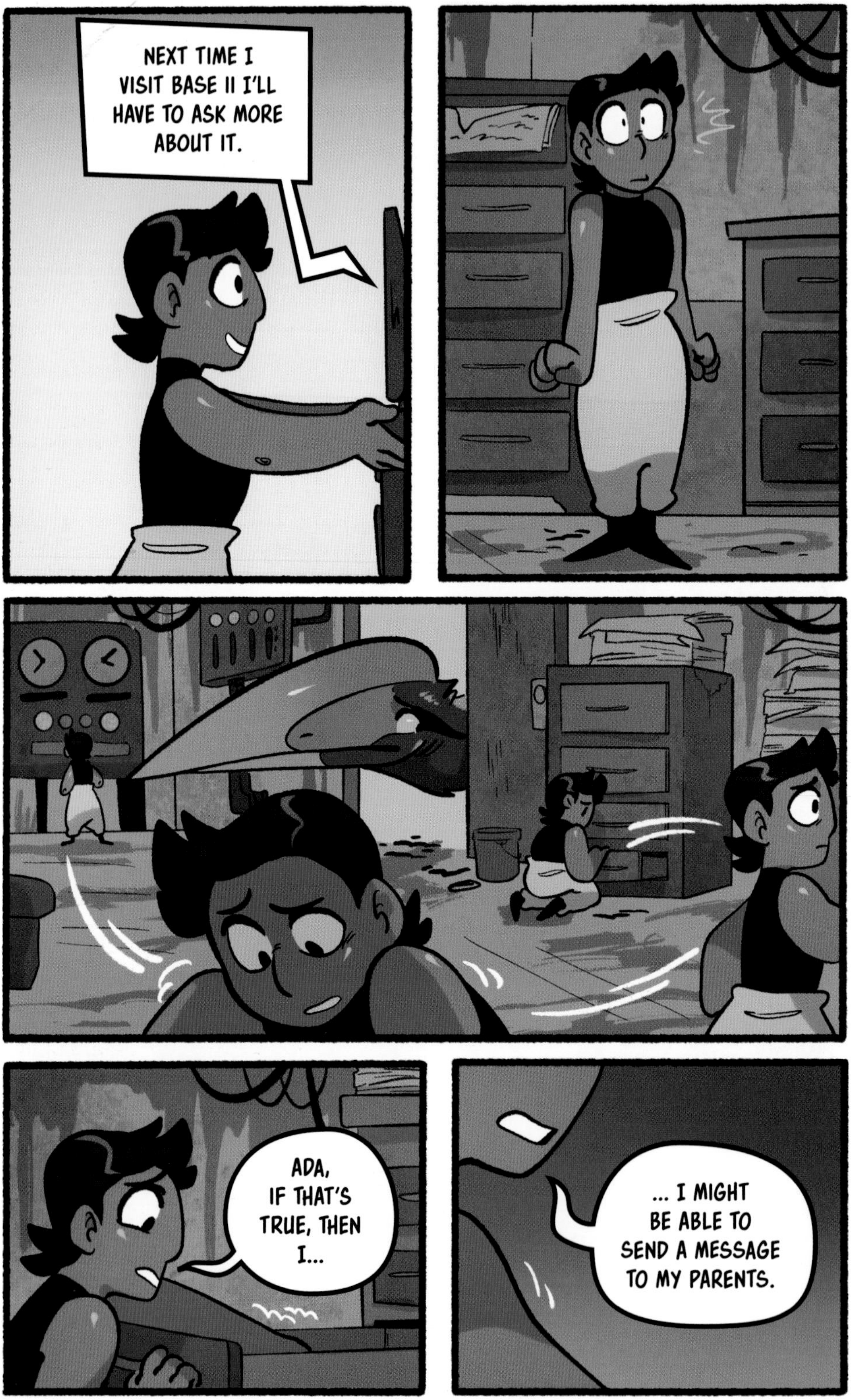
NEXT TIME I VISIT BASE II I'LL HAVE TO ASK MORE ABOUT IT.
ADA, IF THAT'S TRUE, THEN I...
... I MIGHT BE ABLE TO SEND A MESSAGE TO MY PARENTS.

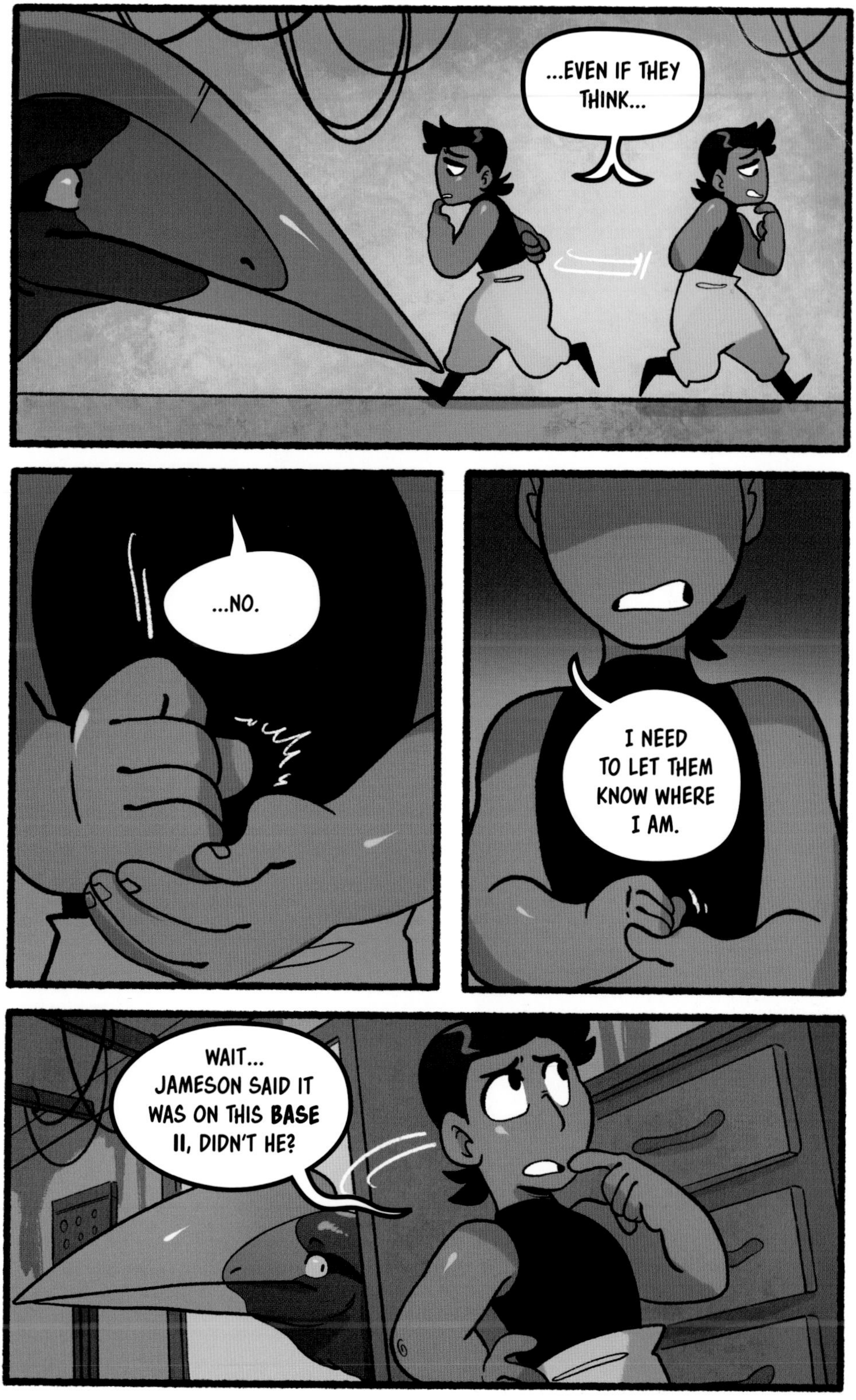
...EVEN IF THEY THINK...
...NO.
I NEED TO LET THEM KNOW WHERE I AM.
WAIT... JAMESON SAID IT WAS ON THIS BASE II, DIDN'T HE?

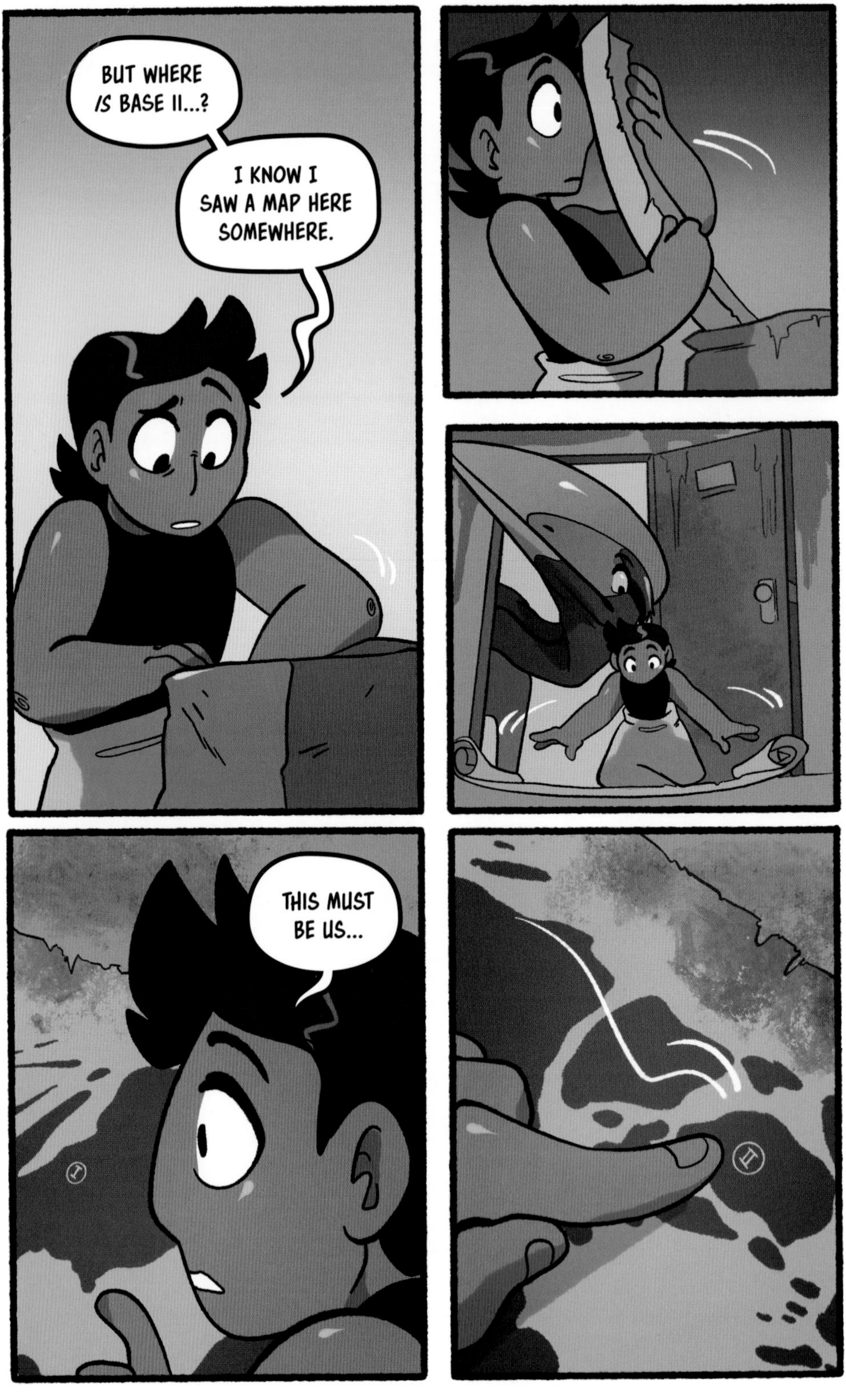
BUT WHERE IS BASE II...?
I KNOW I SAW A MAP HERE SOMEWHERE.
THIS MUST BE US...

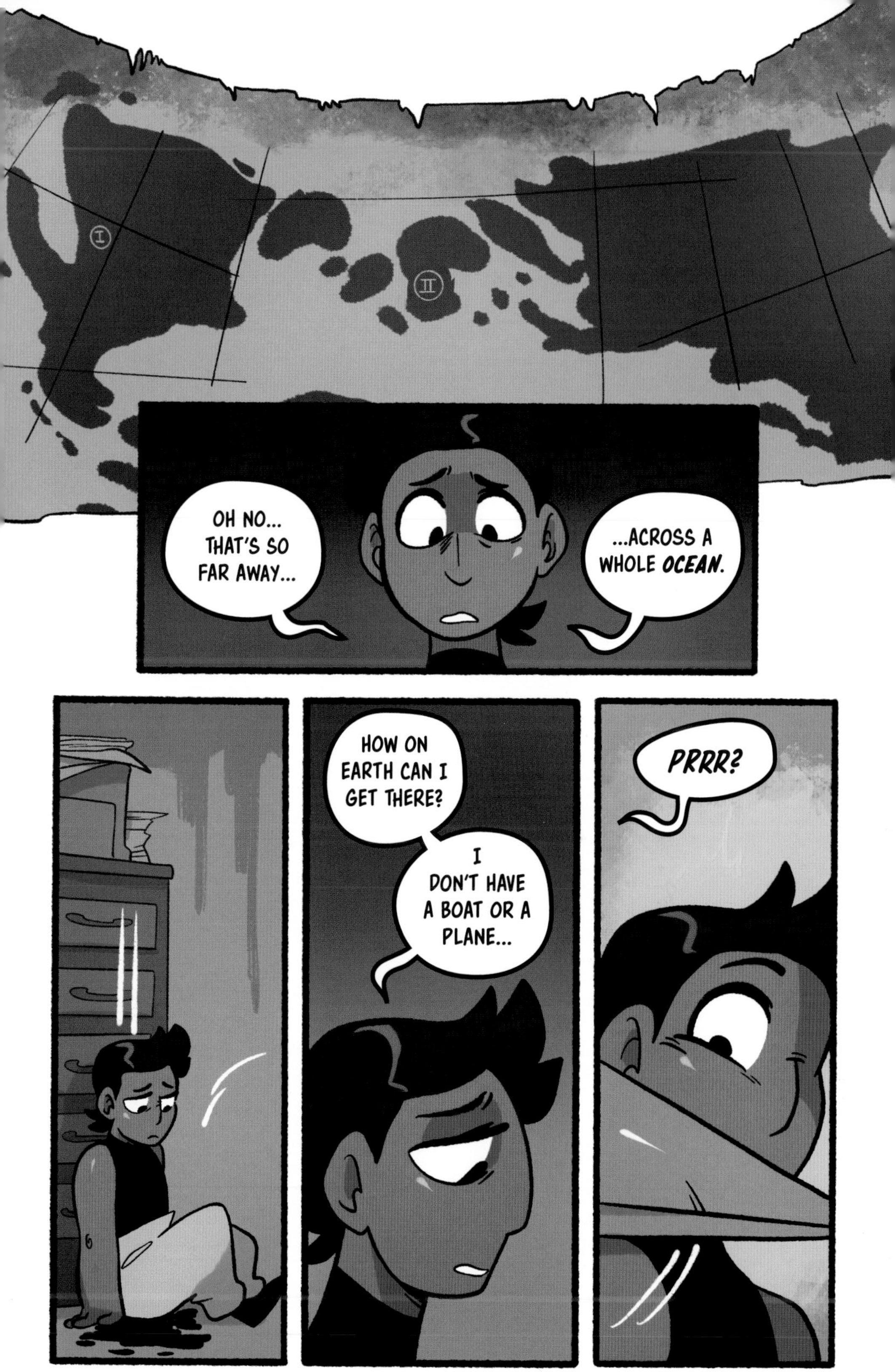
I
II
OH NO... THAT'S SO FAR AWAY...
...ACROSS A WHOLE OCEAN.
HOW ON EARTH CAN I GET THERE?
I DON'T HAVE A BOAT OR A PLANE...
PRRR?

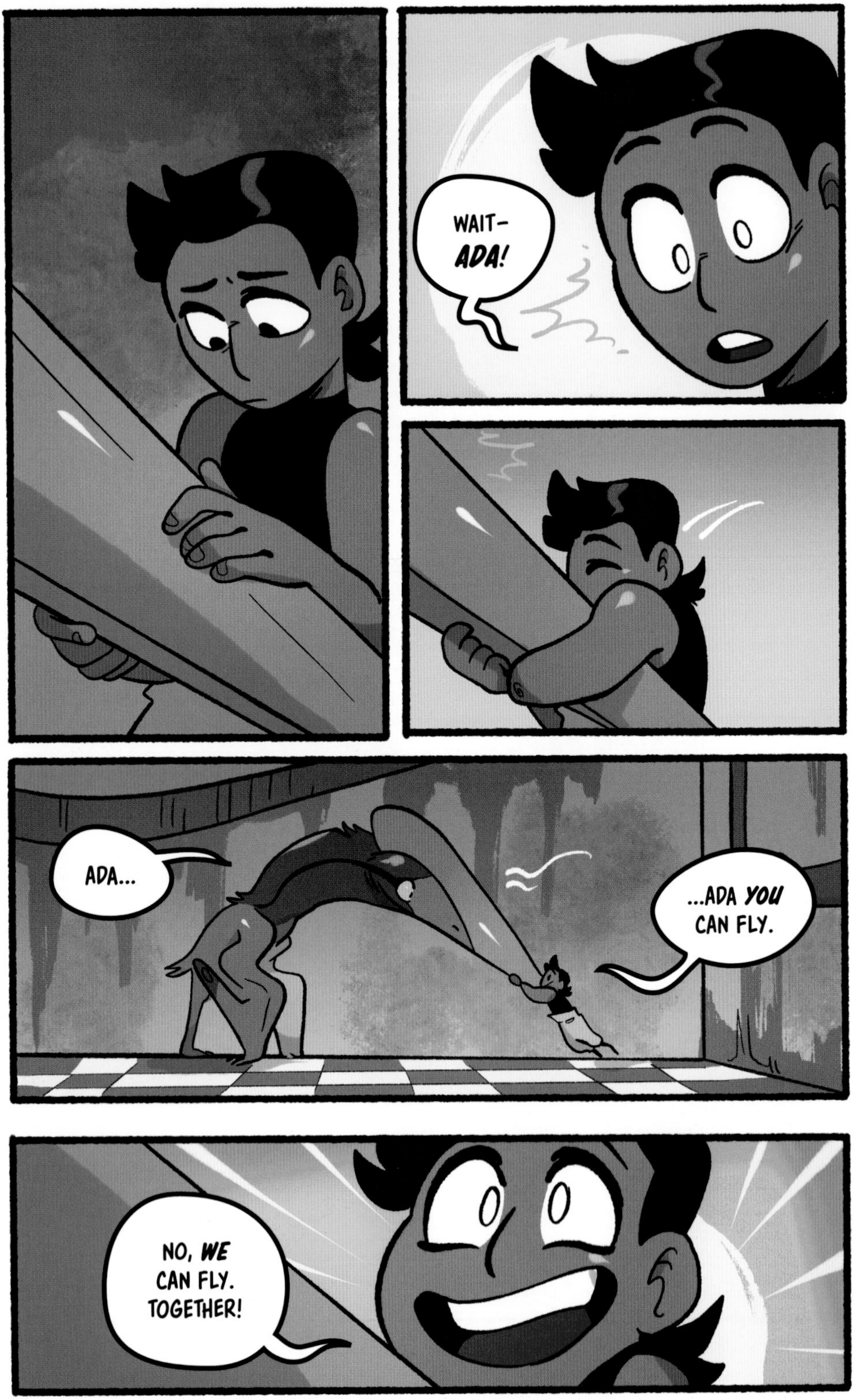
WAIT-
ADA!
ADA...
...ADA YOU CAN FLY.
NO, WE CAN FLY. TOGETHER!

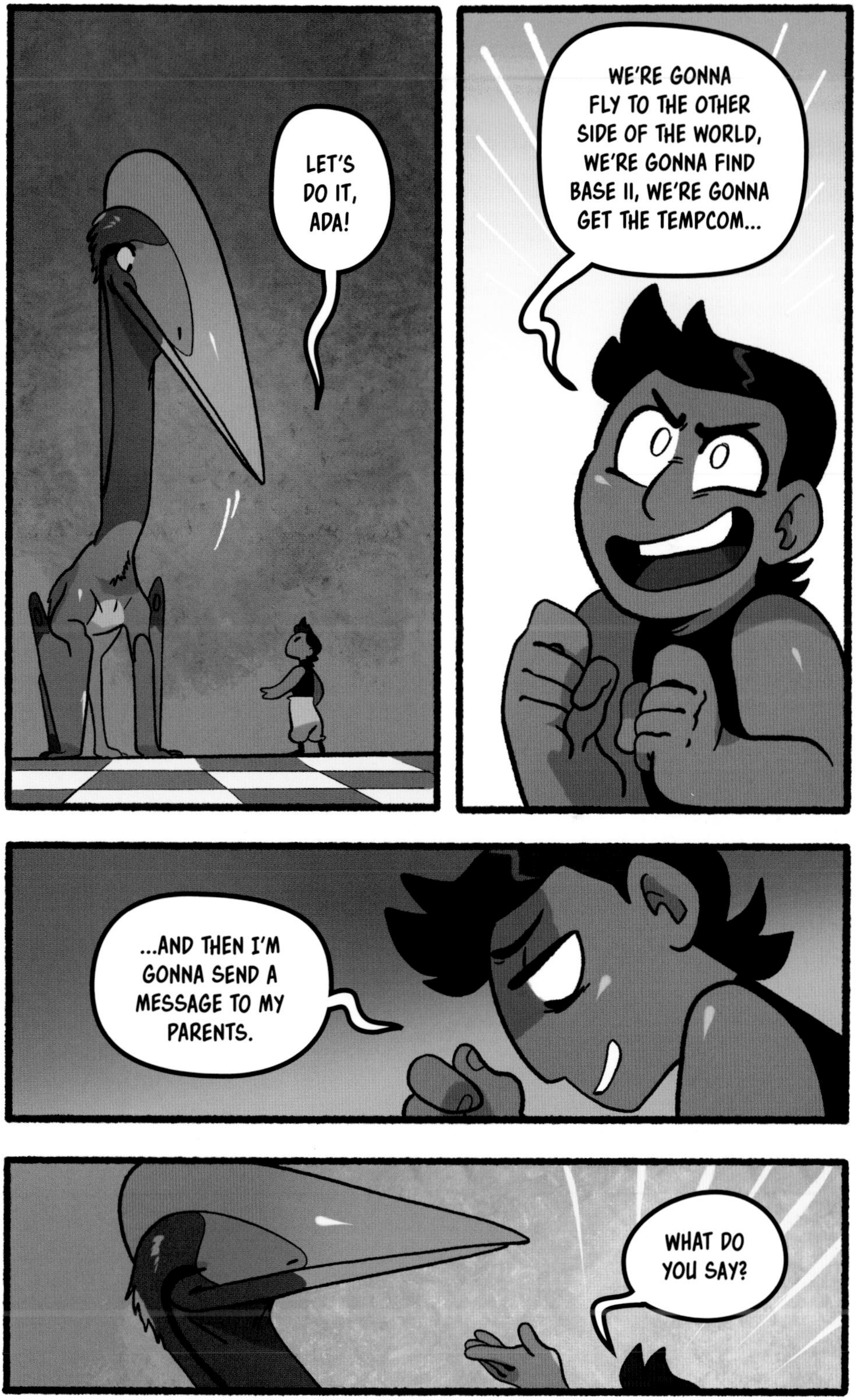
LET'S DO IT, ADA!
WE'RE GONNA FLY TO THE OTHER SIDE OF THE WORLD, WE'RE GONNA FIND BASE II, WE'RE GONNA GET THE TEMPCOM...
...AND THEN I'M GONNA SEND A MESSAGE TO MY PARENTS.
WHAT DO YOU SAY?

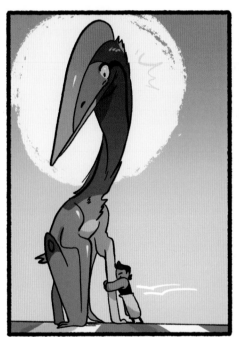

THANK YOU, ADA.

WE CAN START TRAINING TOMORROW.

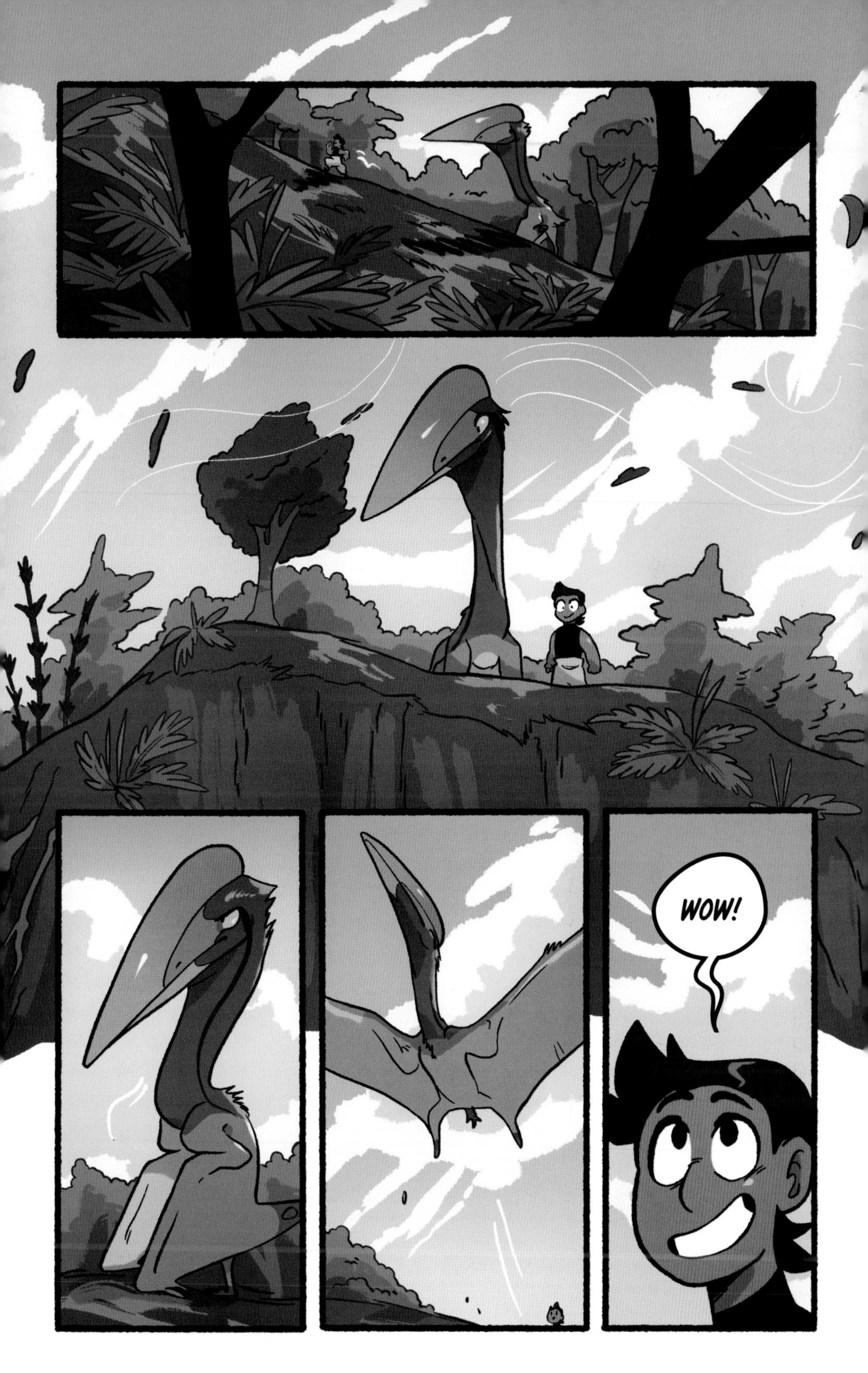
WOW!

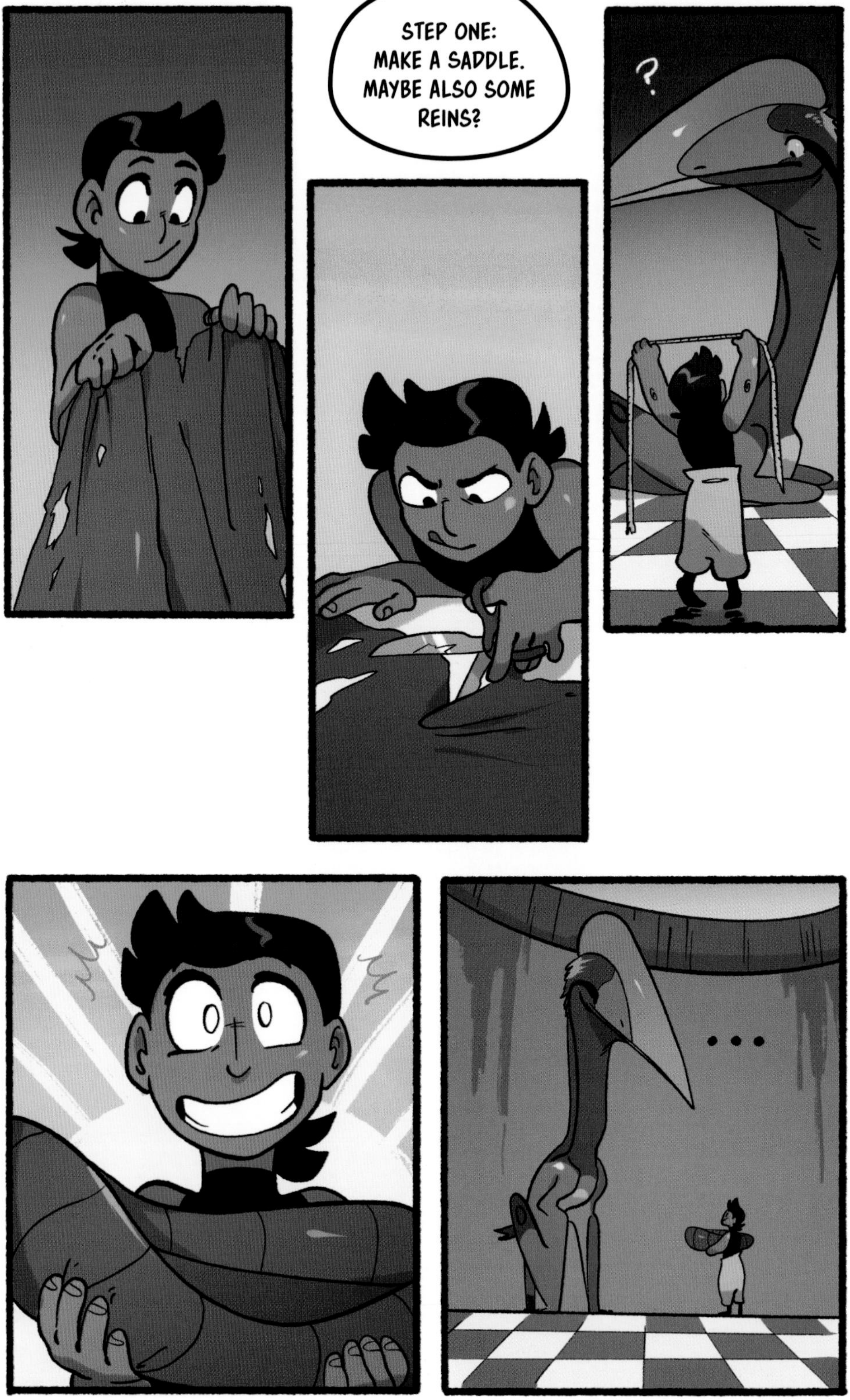
STEP ONE:
MAKE A SADDLE.
MAYBE ALSO SOME
REINS?
?
...

STEP TWO:
...GET THEM ON ADA.

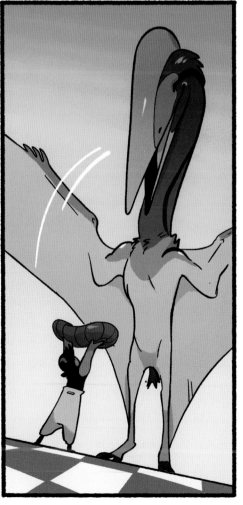

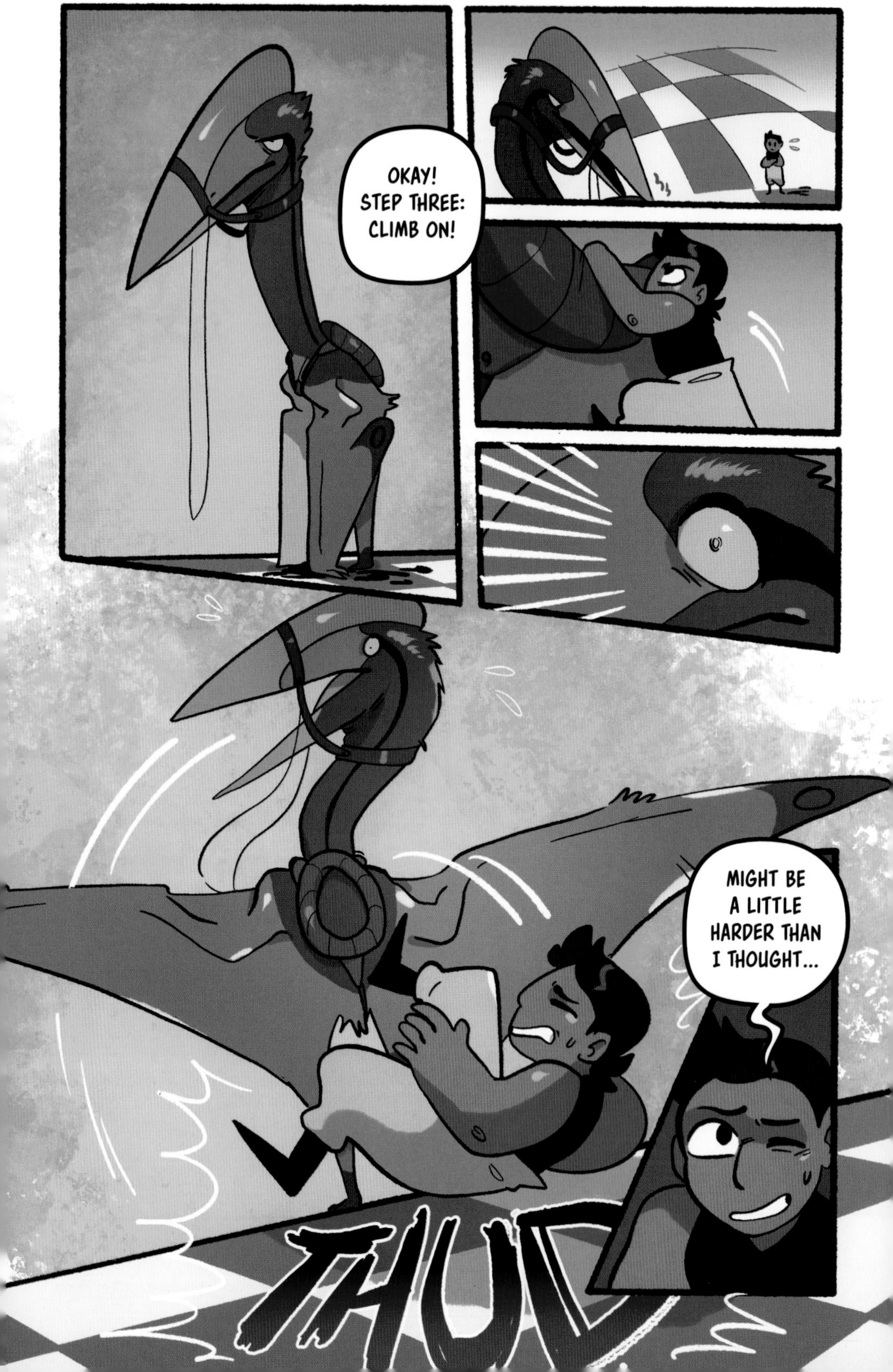
OKAY! STEP THREE: CLIMB ON!
MIGHT BE A LITTLE HARDER THAN I THOUGHT...
THUD

I'M SURE I'LL GET IT IN NO TIME.

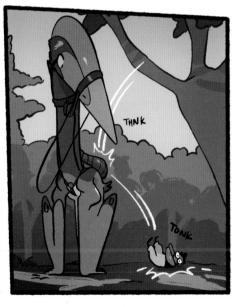

THNK

TONK

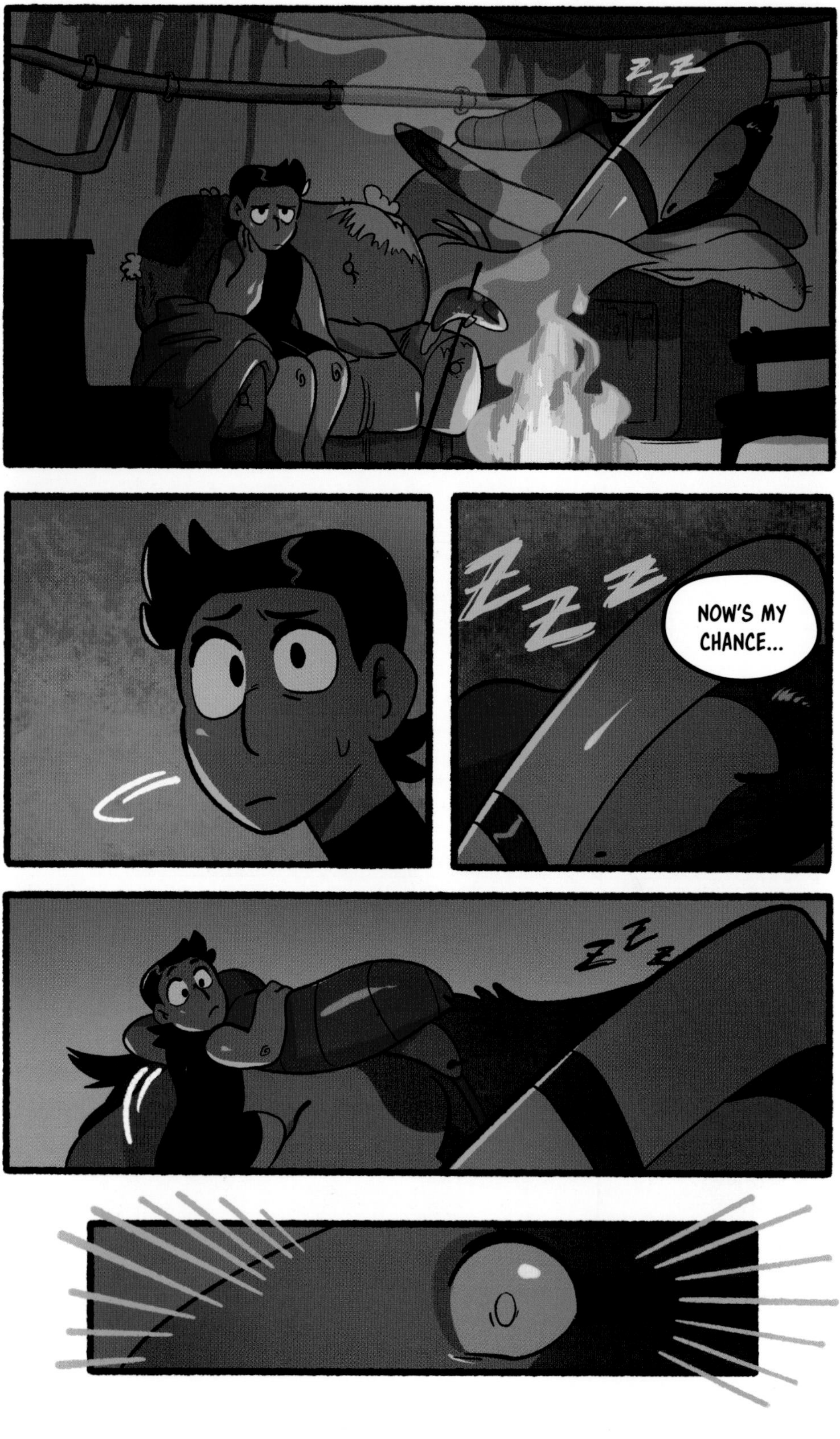
ZZZ
ZZZ
NOW'S MY CHANCE...
ZZZ

IT'S OKAY, IT'S OKAY! IT'S JUST ME, ADA.

YOU'RE DOING GREAT.

WE'LL TAKE IT SLOW, OKAY?

LET'S JUST GO FOR A LITTLE WALK.

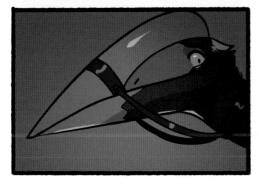

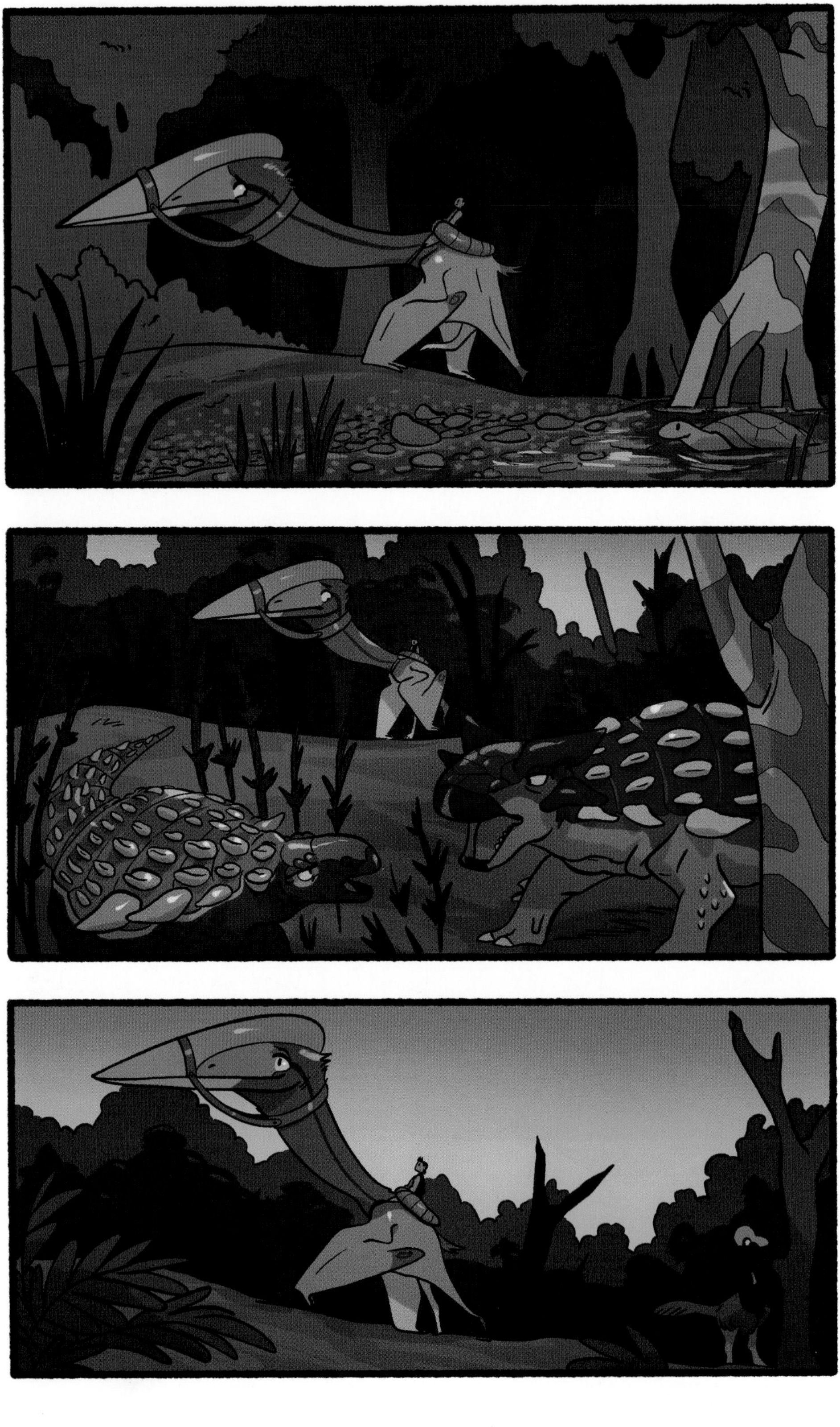

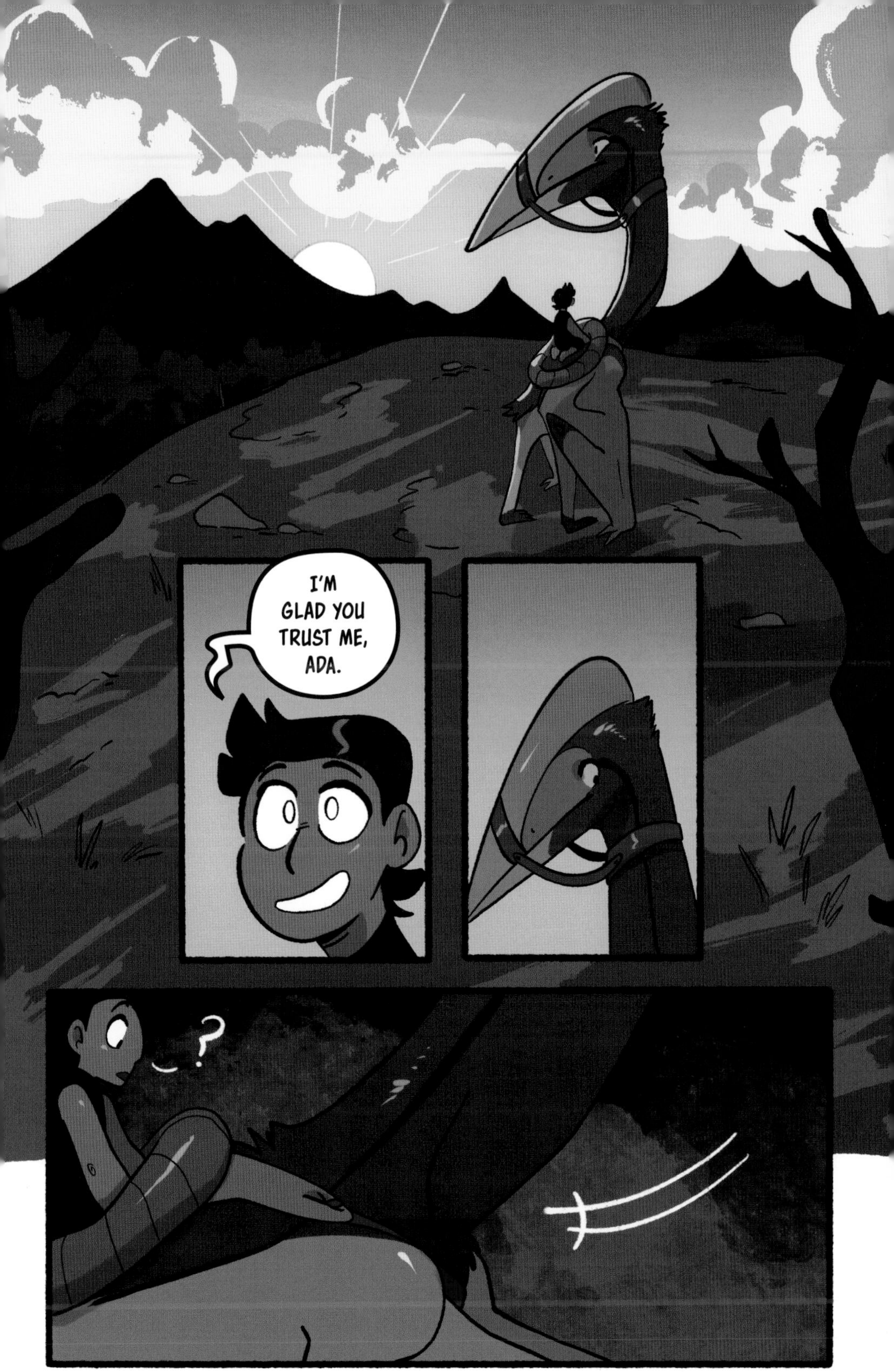
I'M GLAD YOU TRUST ME, ADA.
?

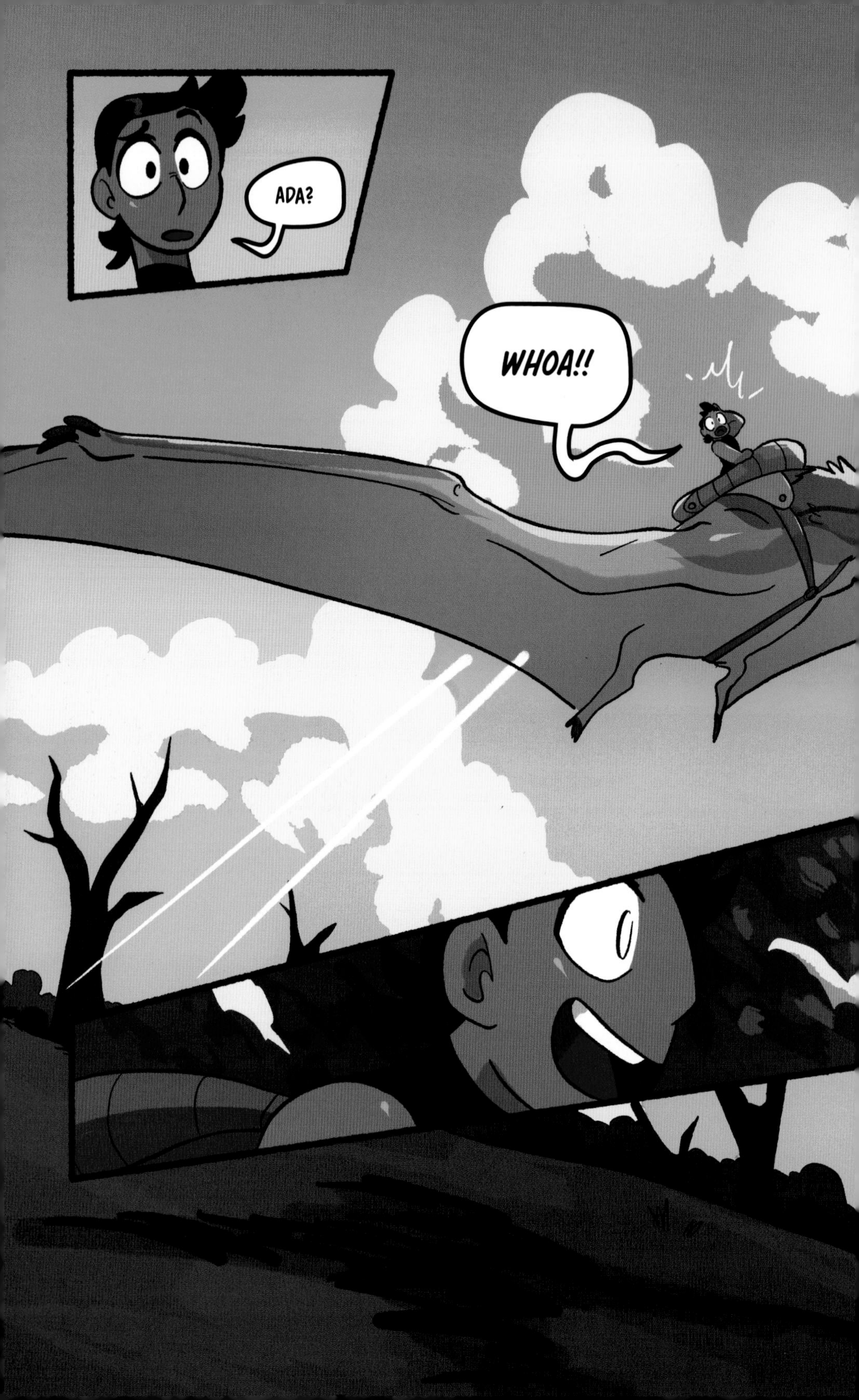
ADA?
WHOA!!

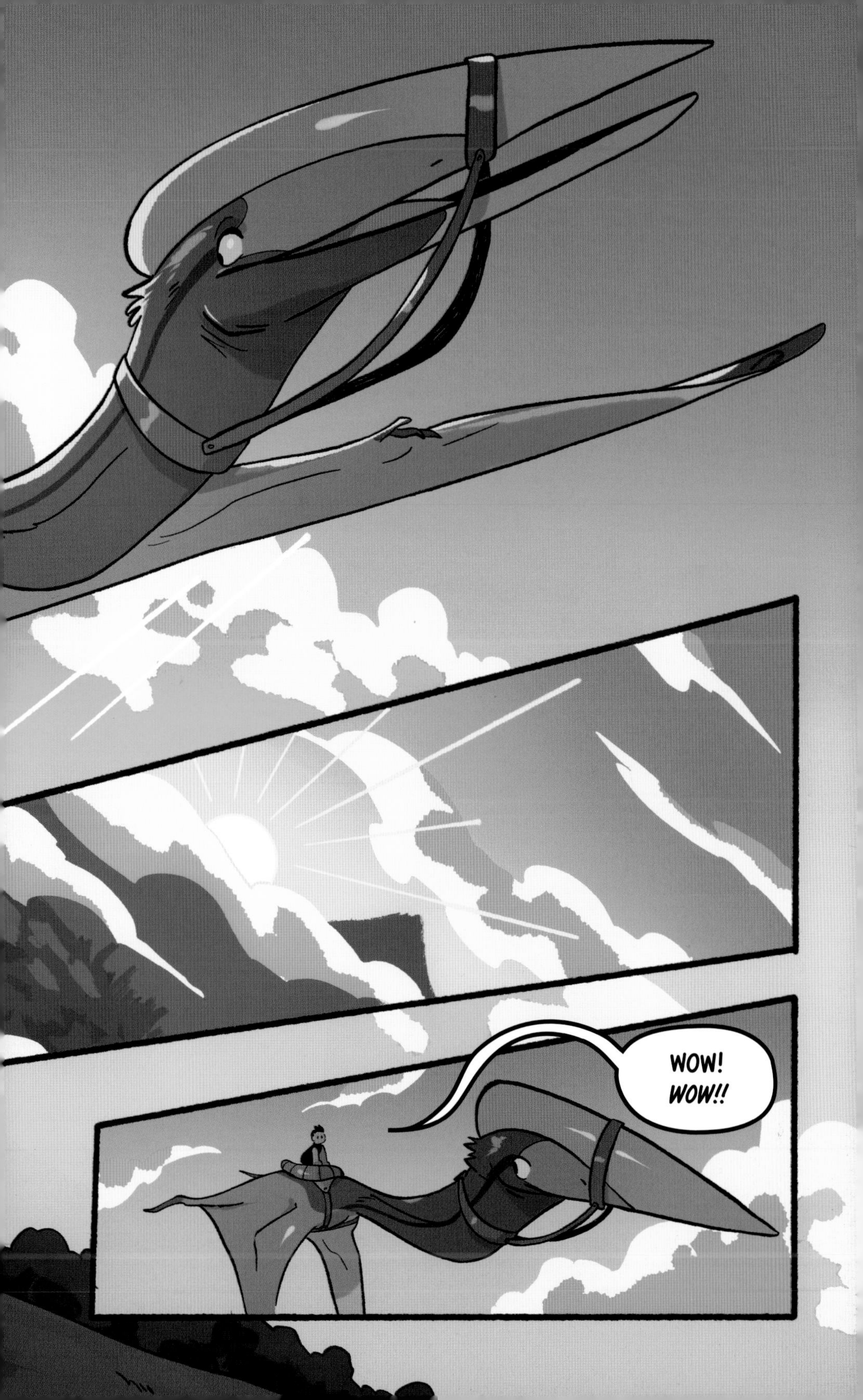
WOW!
WOW!!

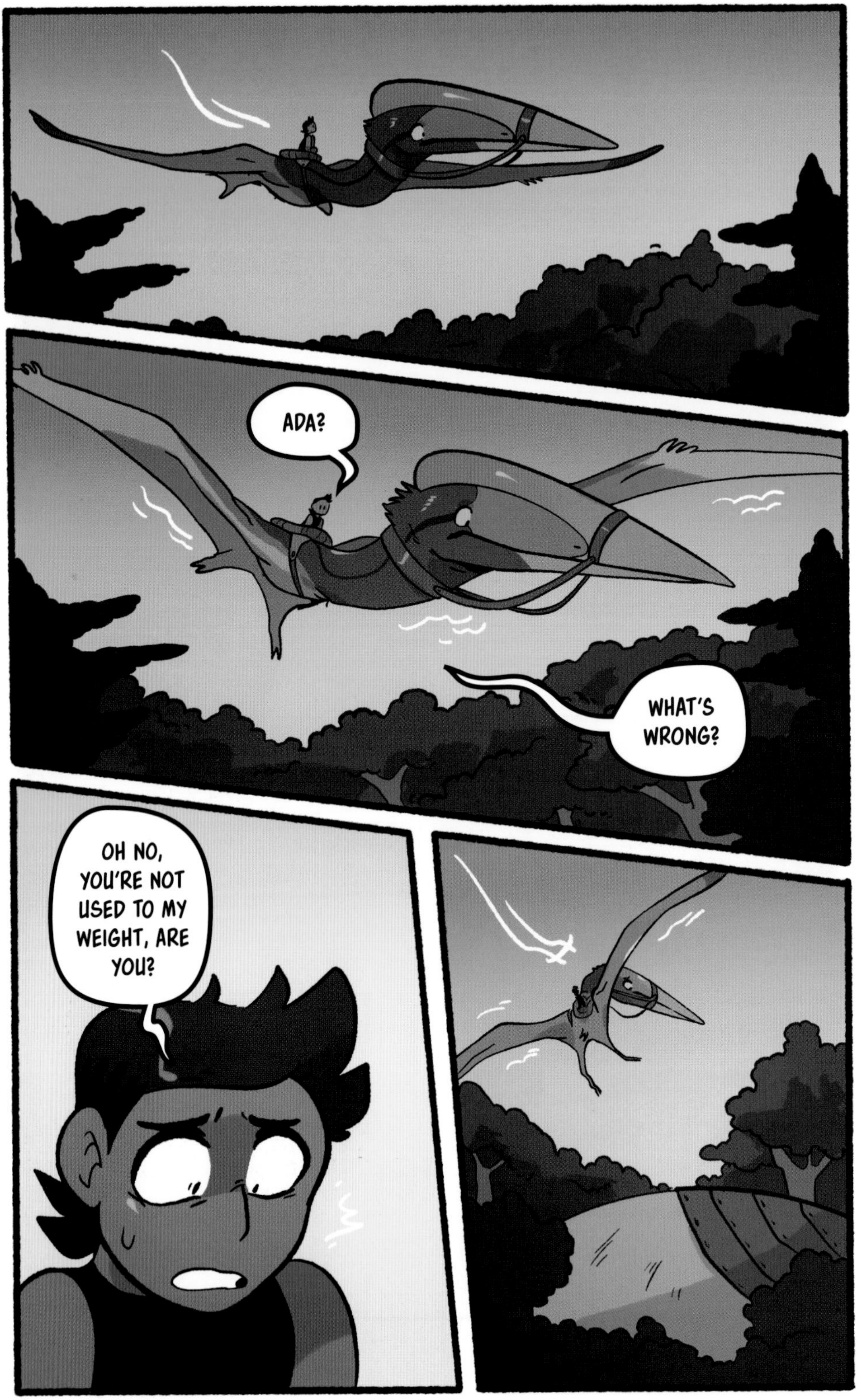
ADA?
WHAT'S WRONG?
OH NO, YOU'RE NOT USED TO MY WEIGHT, ARE YOU?

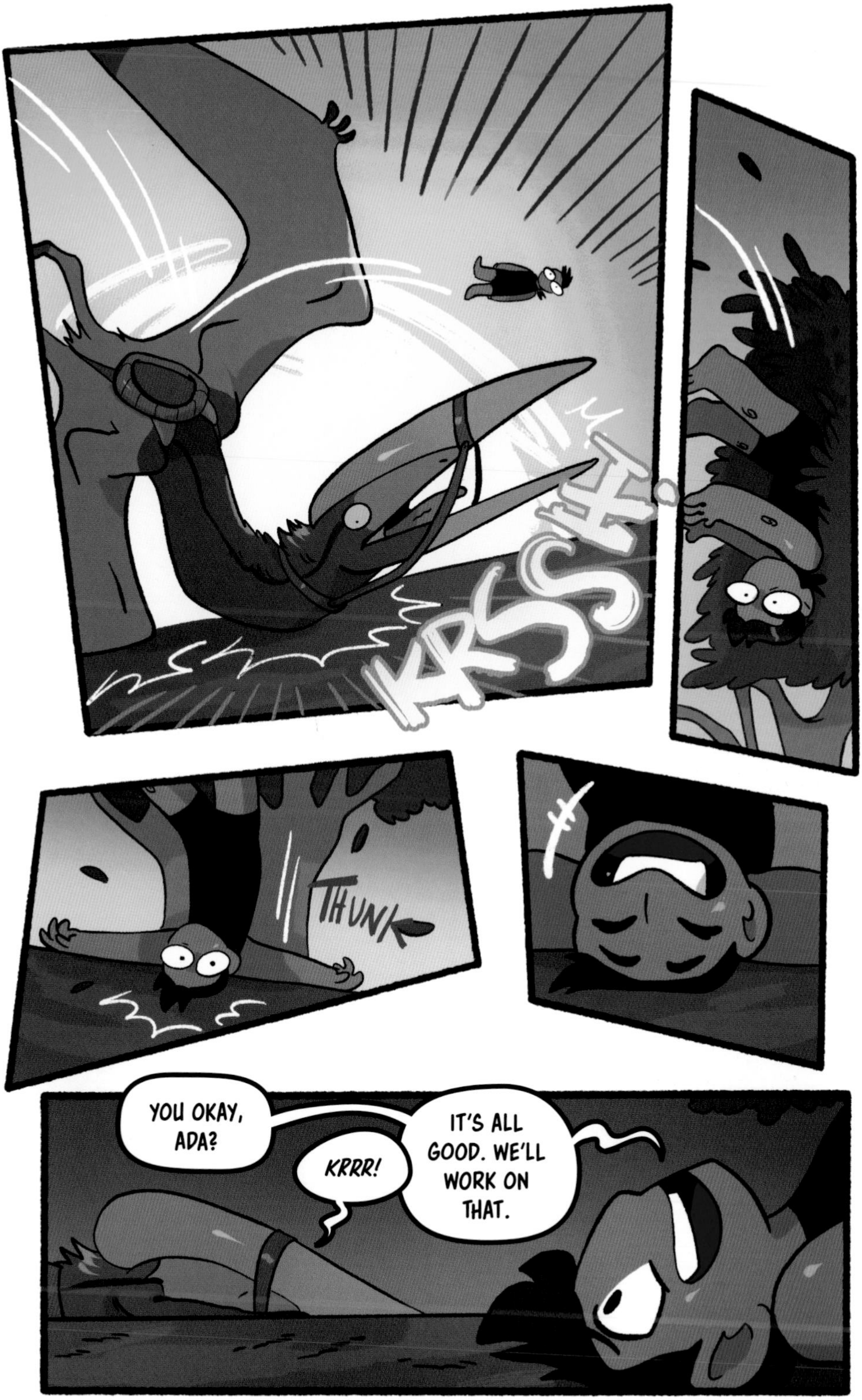
KRSSH!
THUNK
YOU OKAY, ADA?
KRRR!
IT'S ALL GOOD. WE'LL WORK ON THAT.

WE'LL FIX WHAT WE NEED TO.

CLICK

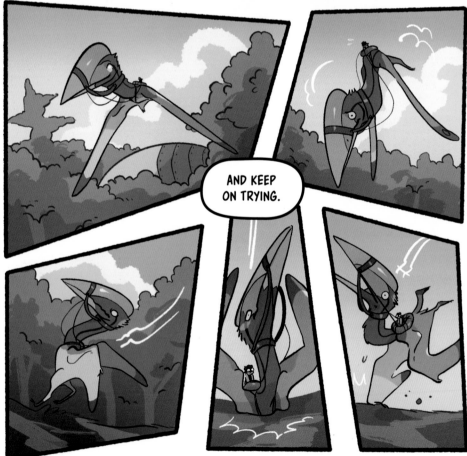

AND KEEP ON TRYING.

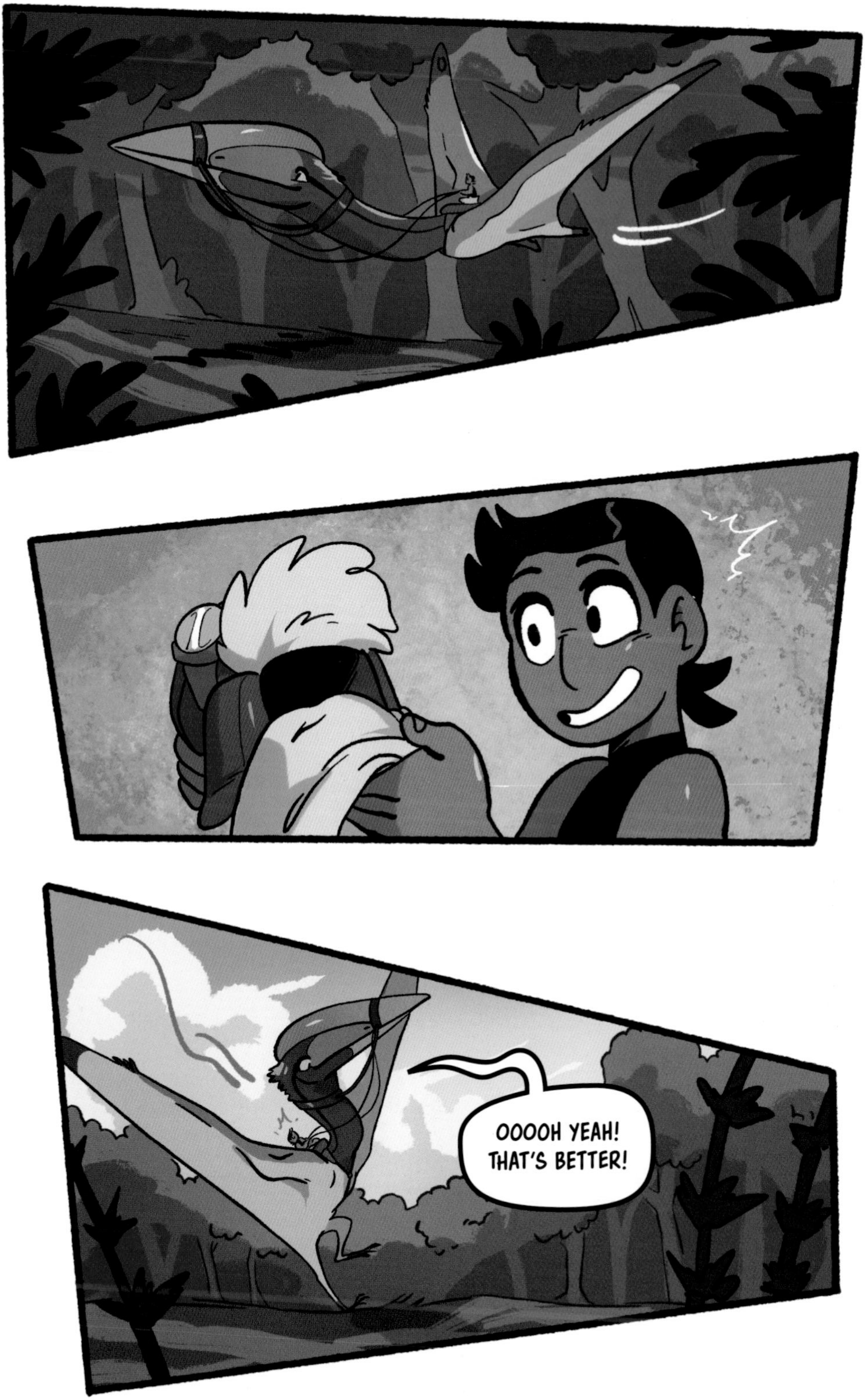
OOOOH YEAH! THAT'S BETTER!

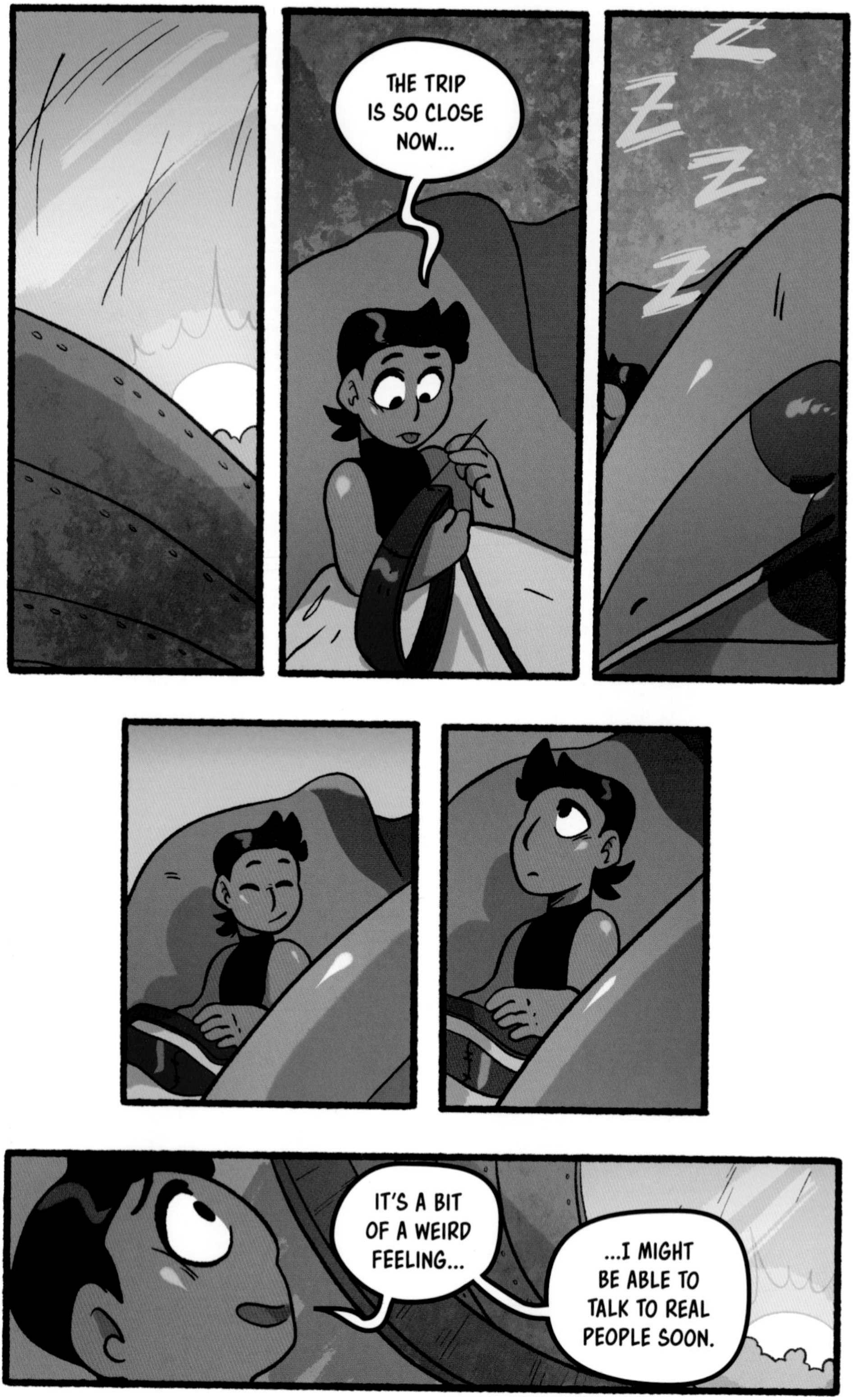
THE TRIP IS SO CLOSE NOW...
Z Z Z Z
IT'S A BIT OF A WEIRD FEELING...
...I MIGHT BE ABLE TO TALK TO REAL PEOPLE SOON.

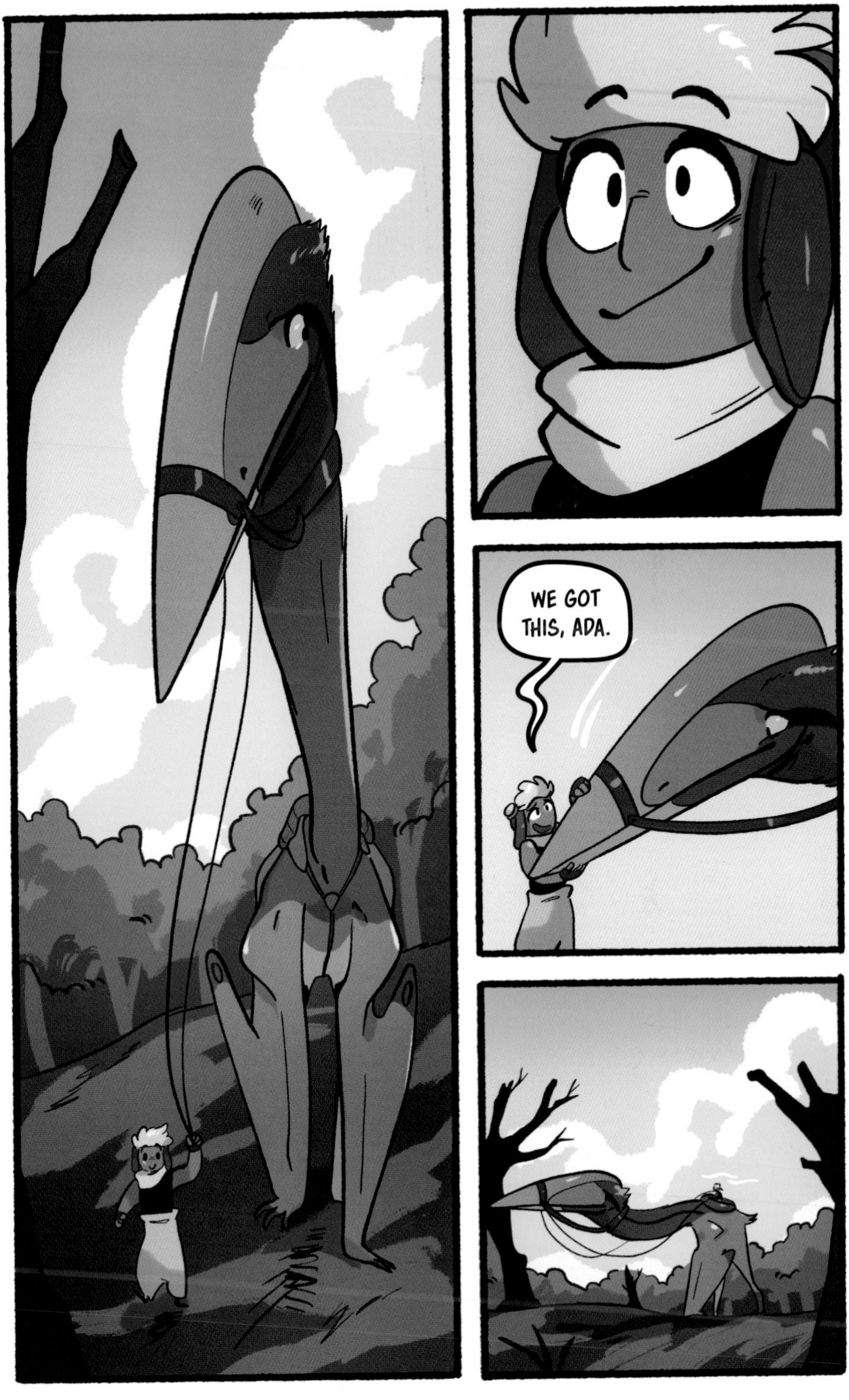
WE GOT THIS, ADA.

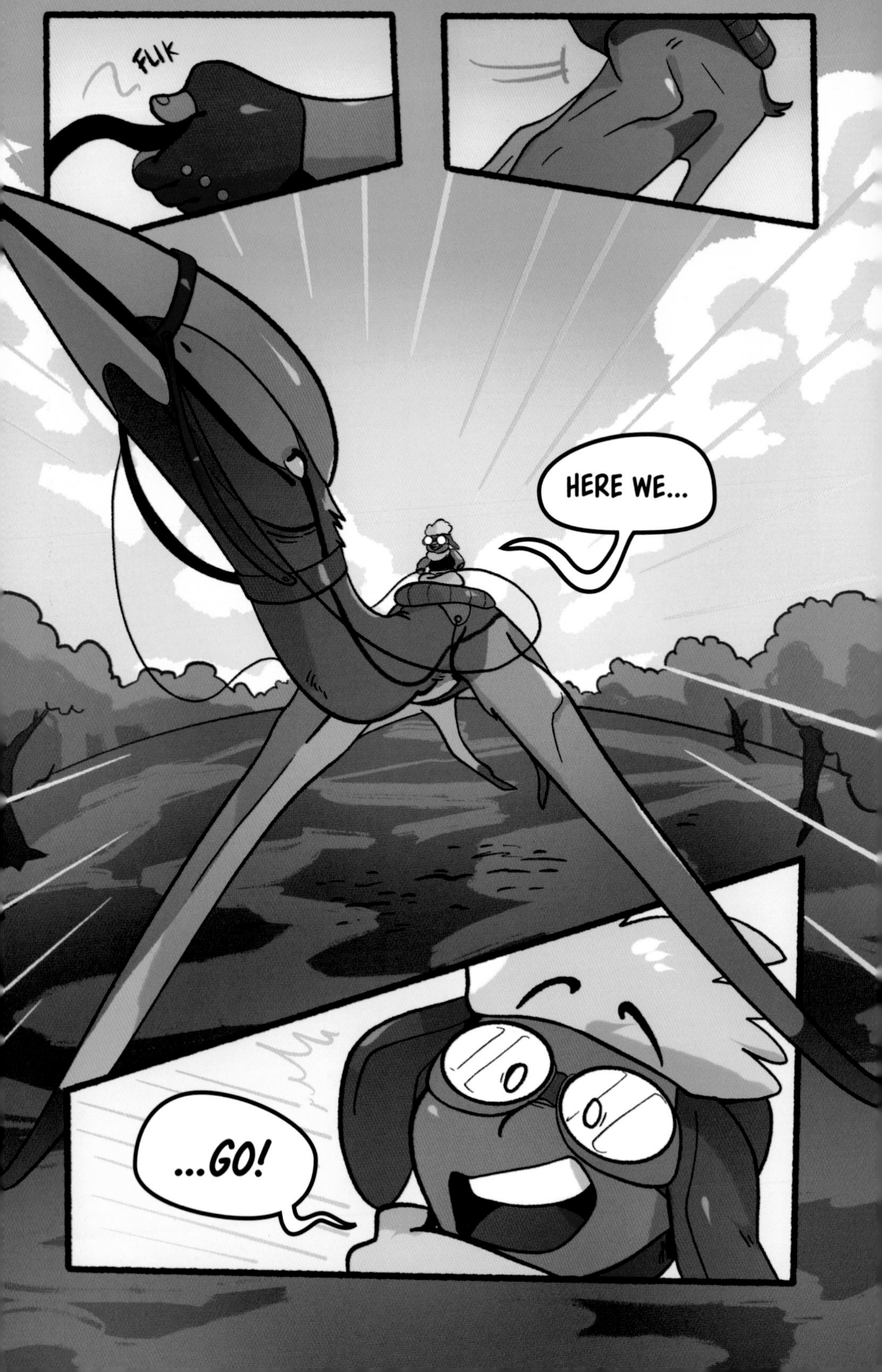
FLIK
HERE WE...
...GO!

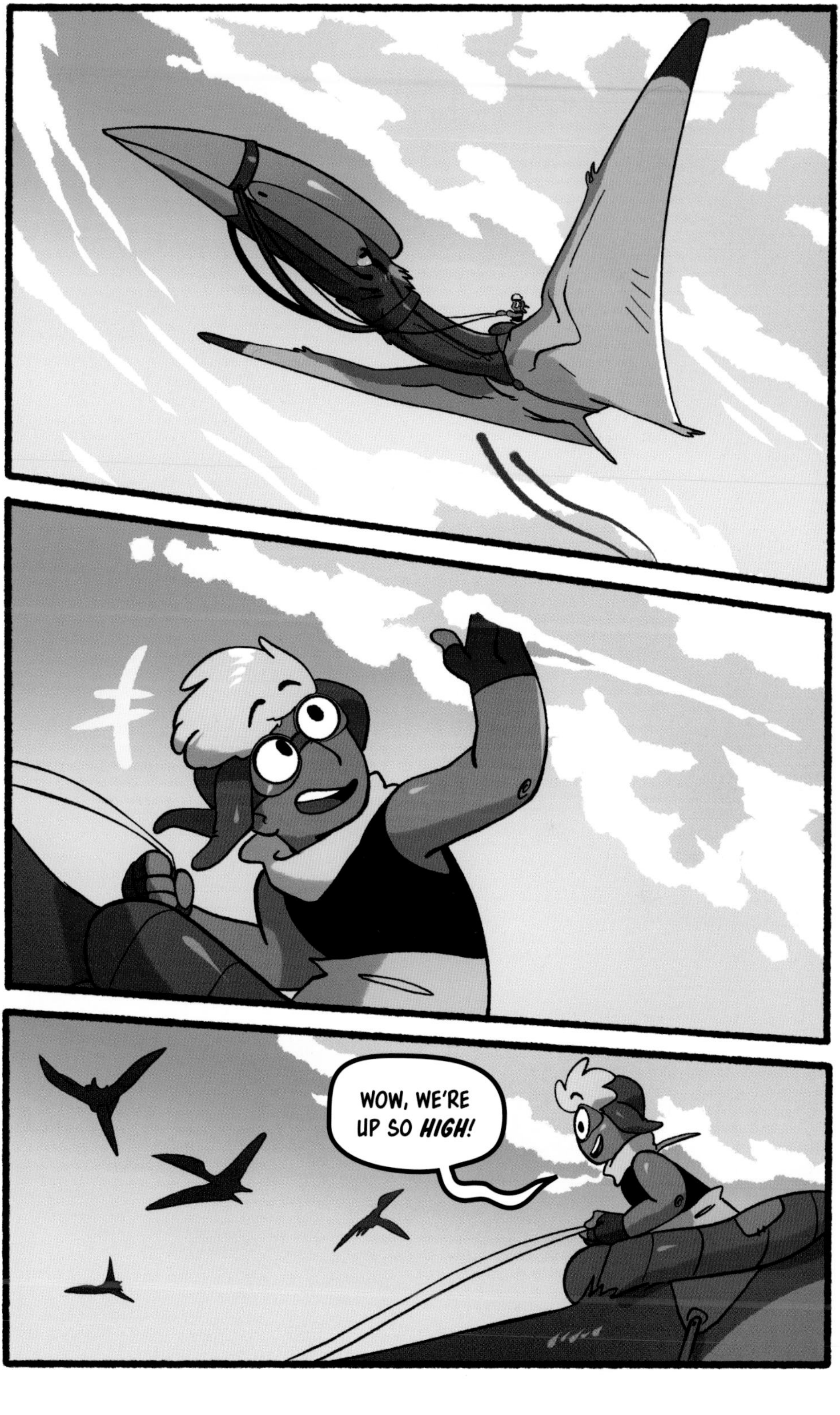
WOW, WE'RE UP SO HIGH!

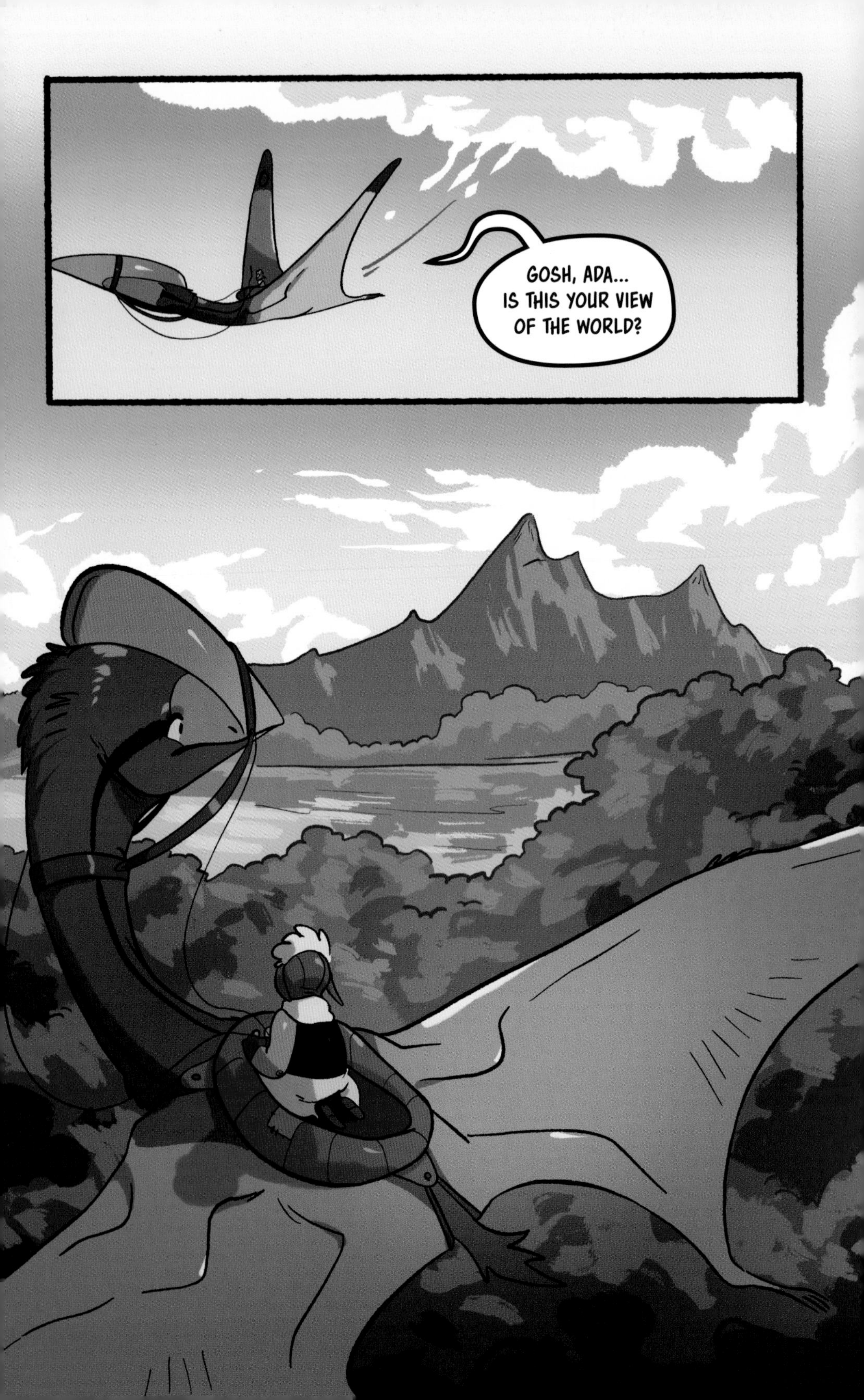
GOSH, ADA... IS THIS YOUR VIEW OF THE WORLD?

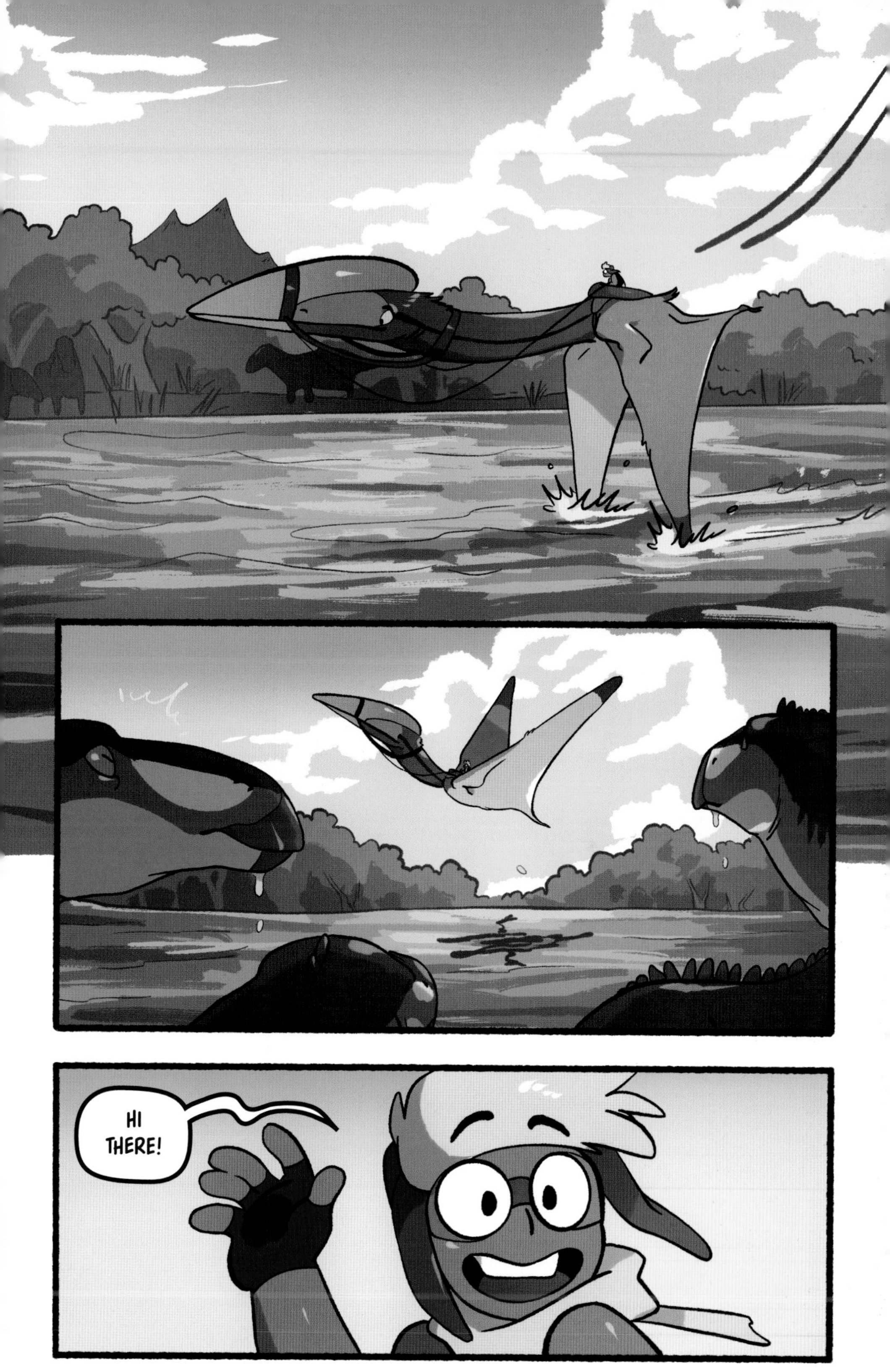
HI
THERE!

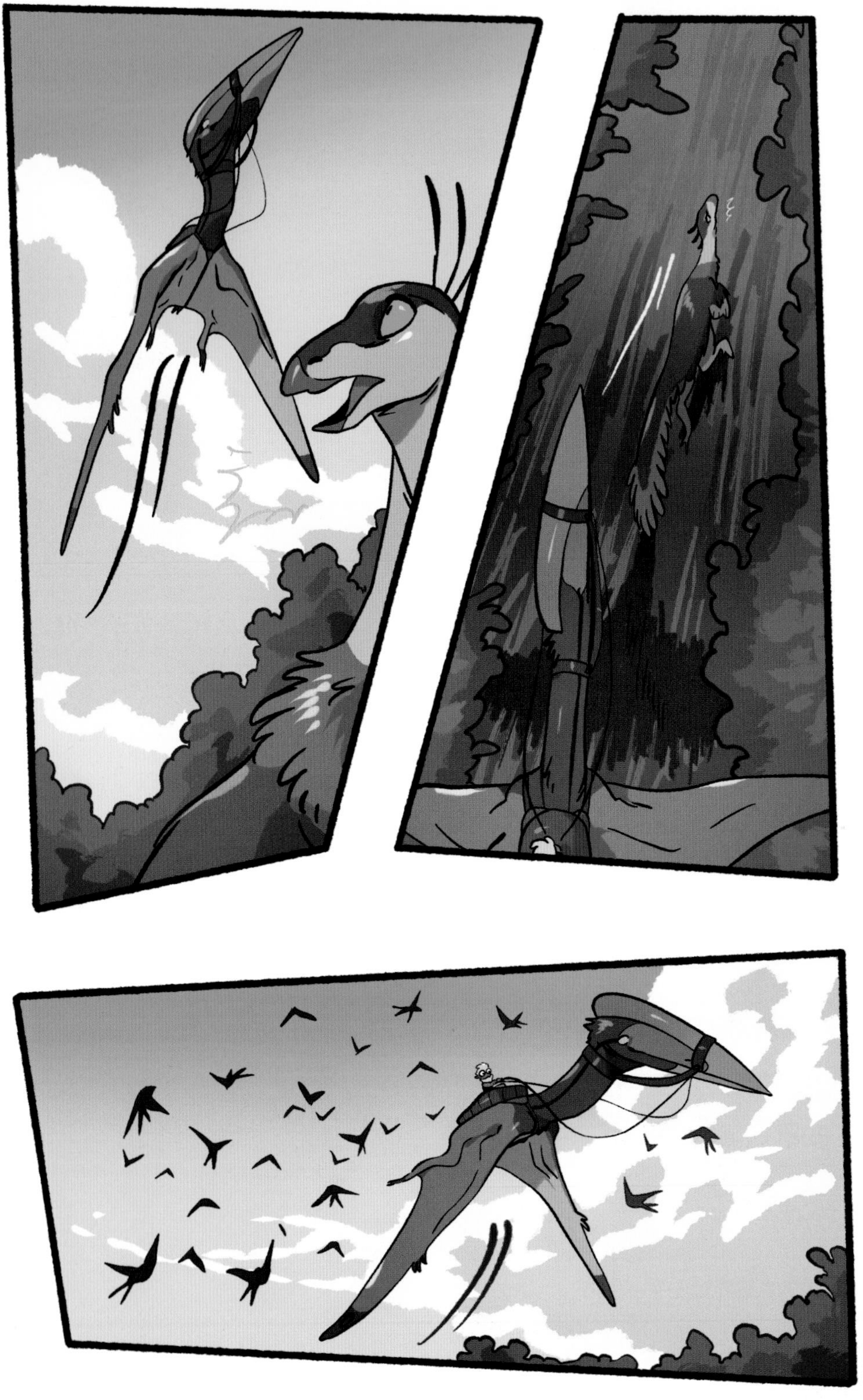

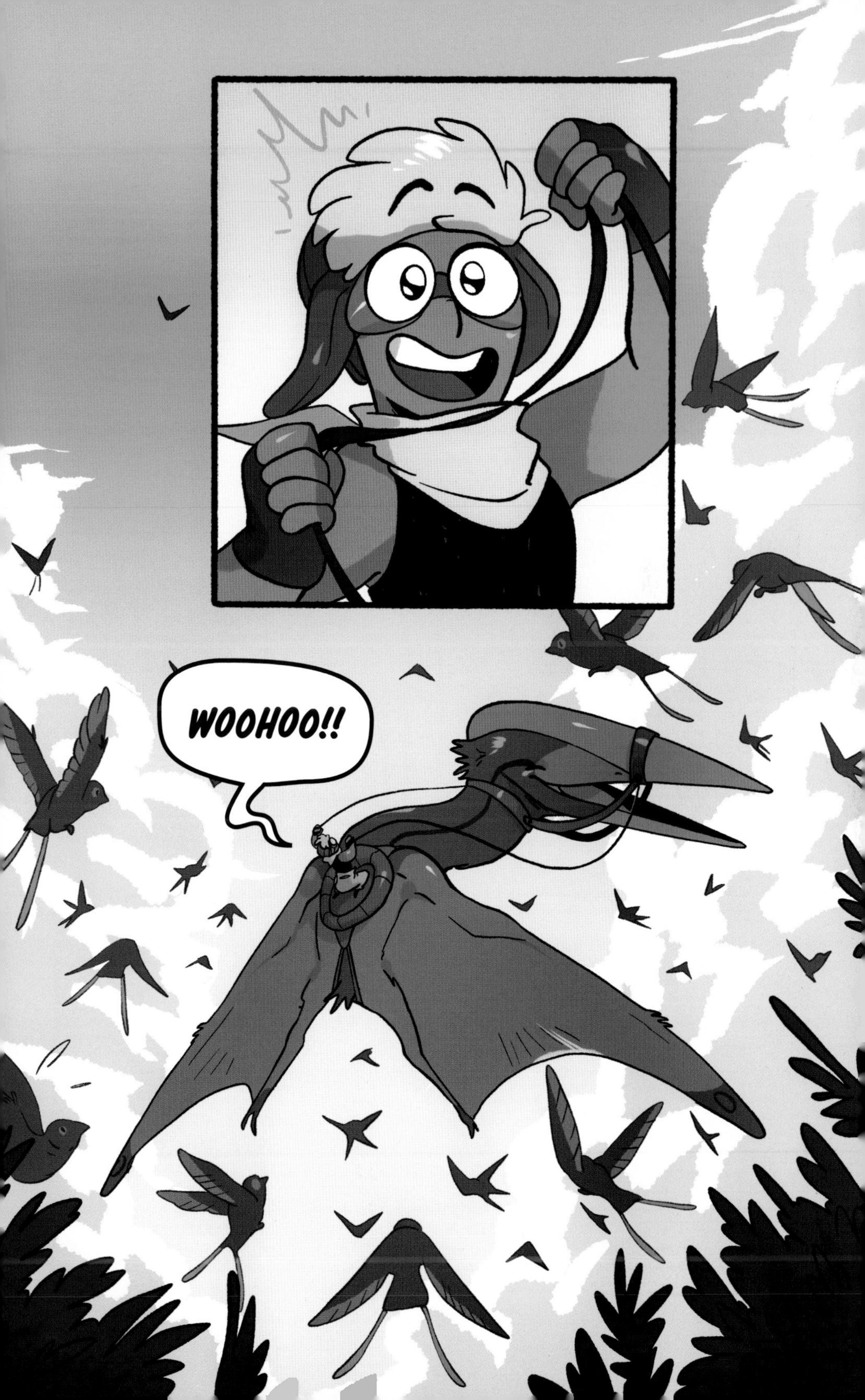
WOOHOO!!

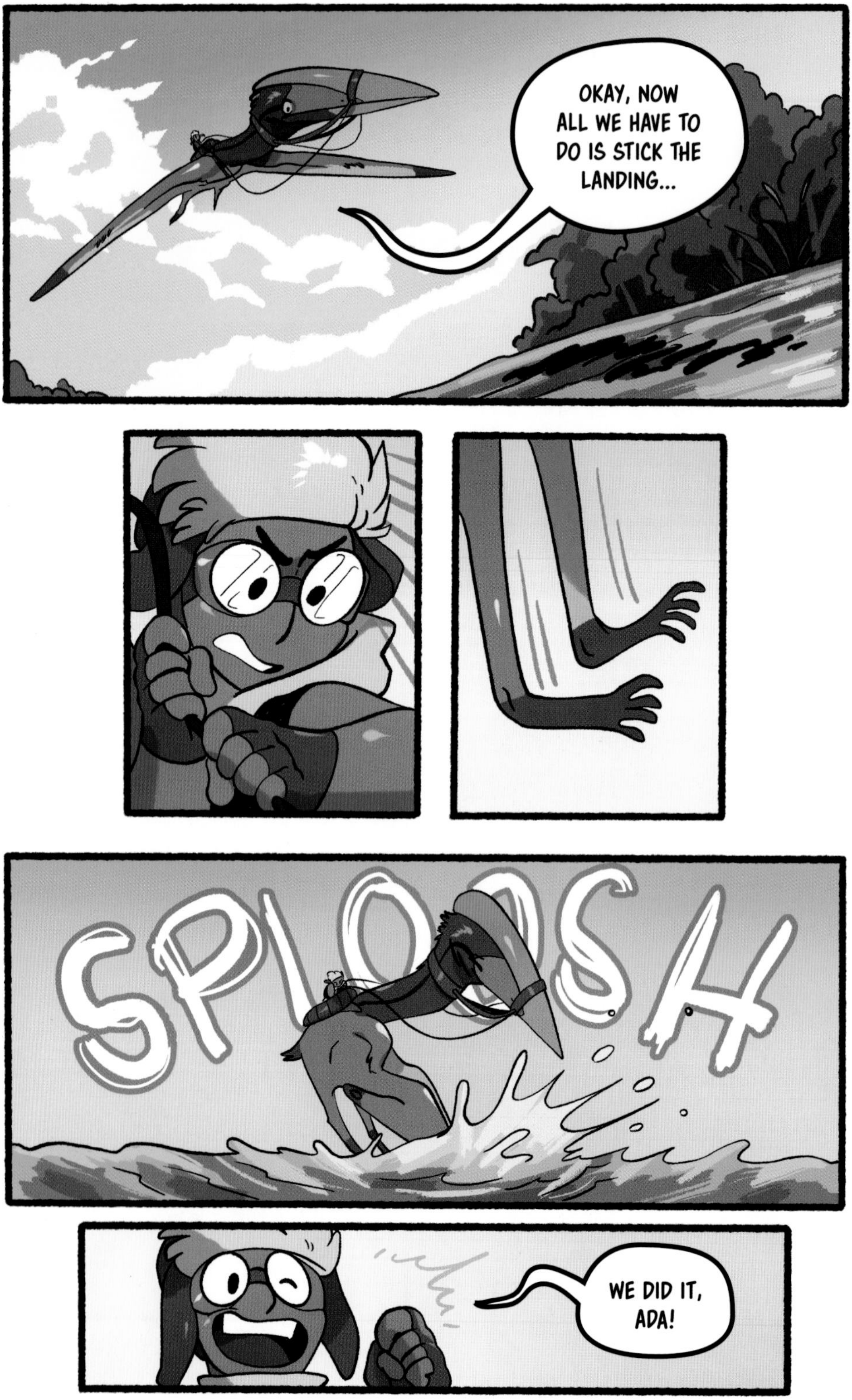
OKAY, NOW ALL WE HAVE TO DO IS STICK THE LANDING...
SPLOOSH
WE DID IT, ADA!

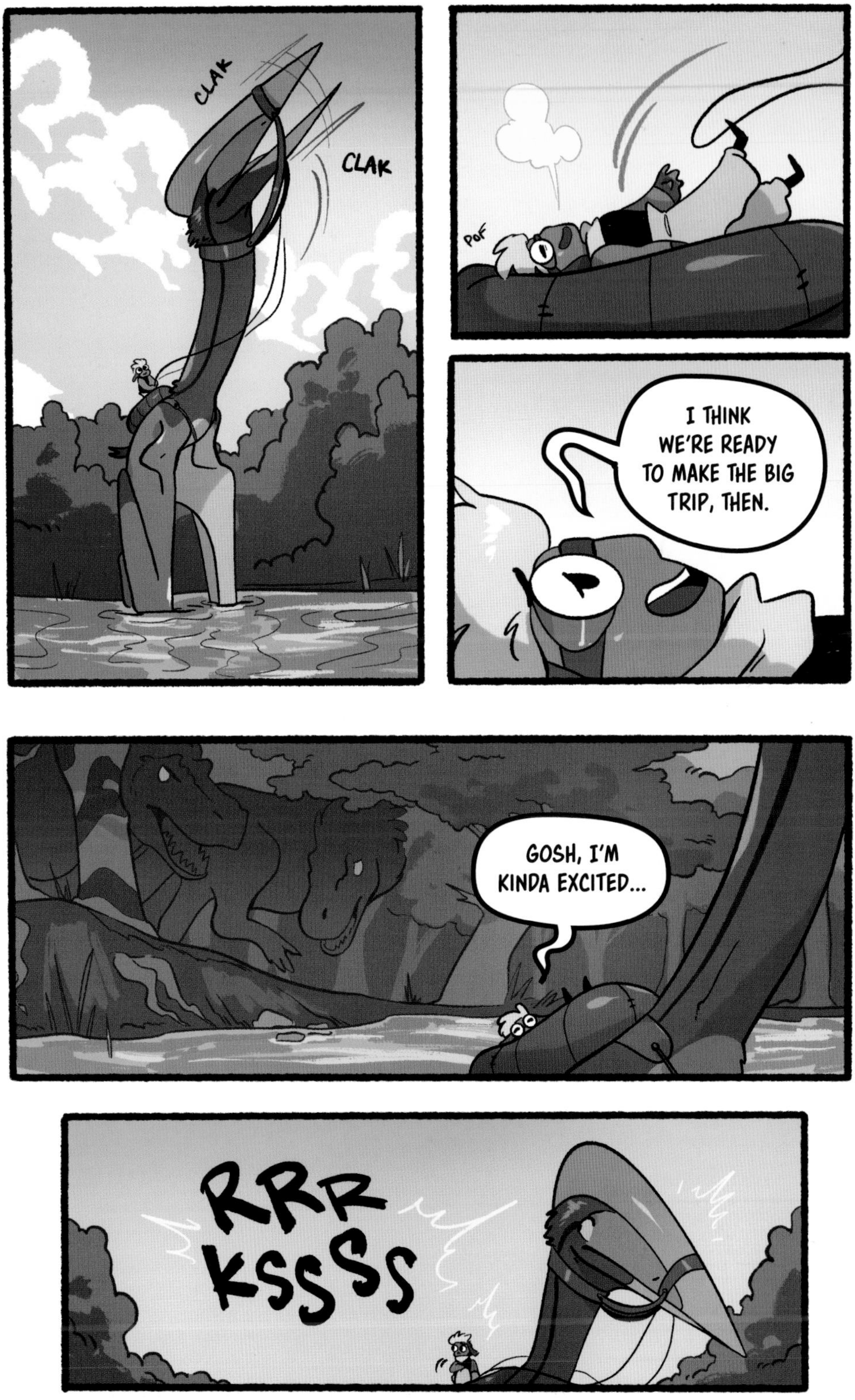
CLAK
CLAK
POF
I THINK WE'RE READY TO MAKE THE BIG TRIP, THEN.
GOSH, I'M KINDA EXCITED...
RRR KSSSS

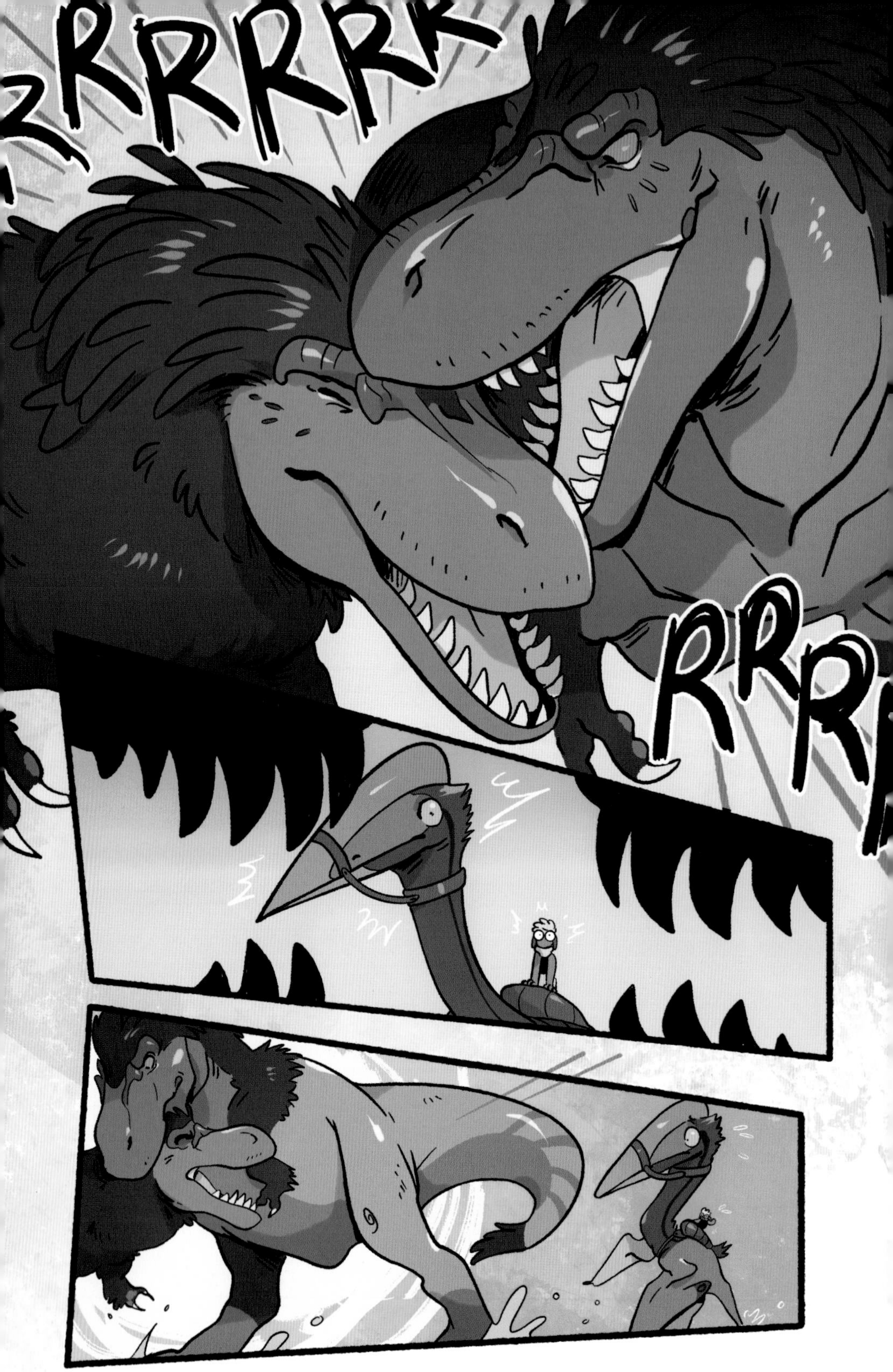
RRRRRRK
RRRR

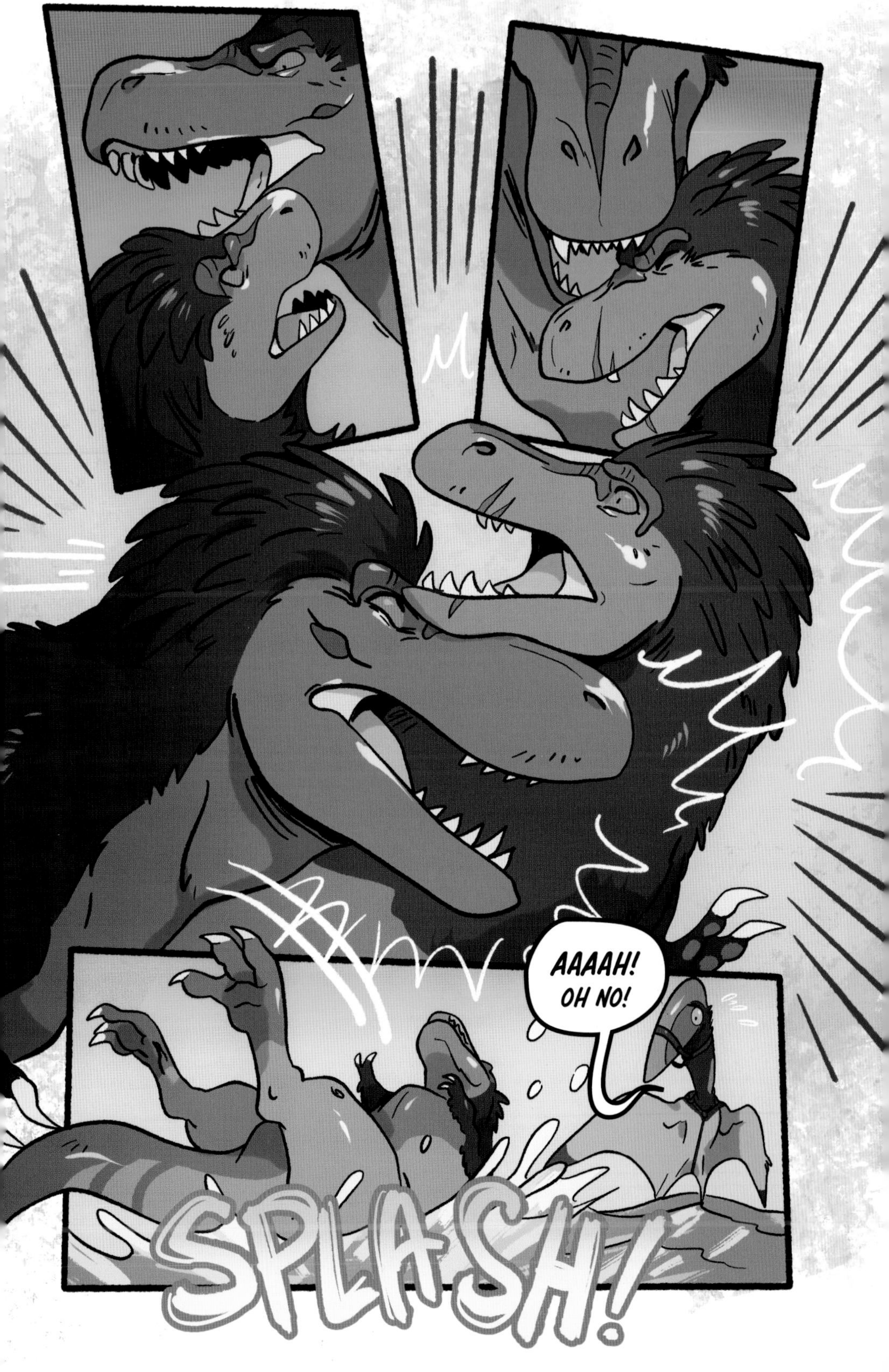
AAAAH!
OH NO!
SPLASH!

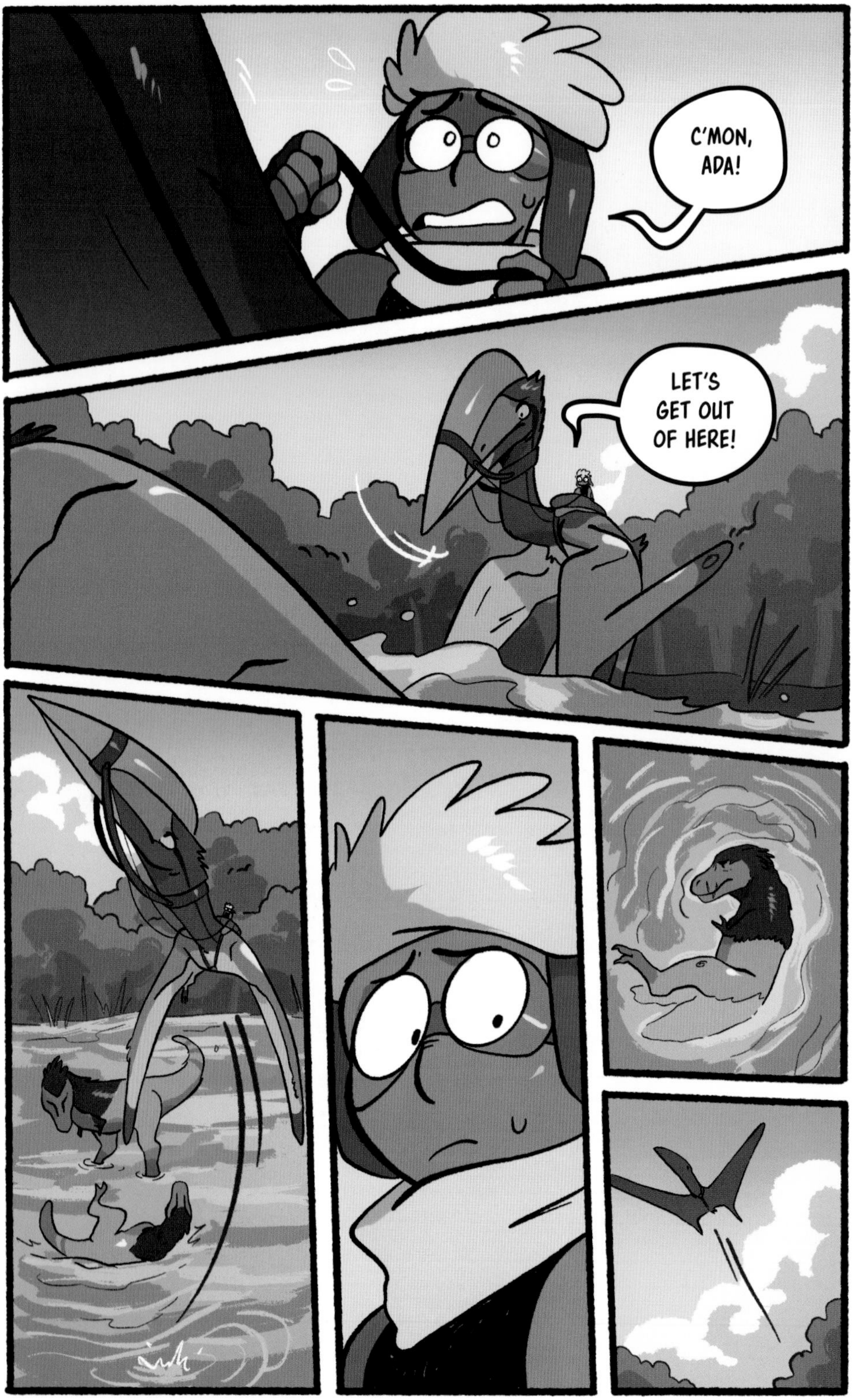
C'MON, ADA!
LET'S GET OUT OF HERE!

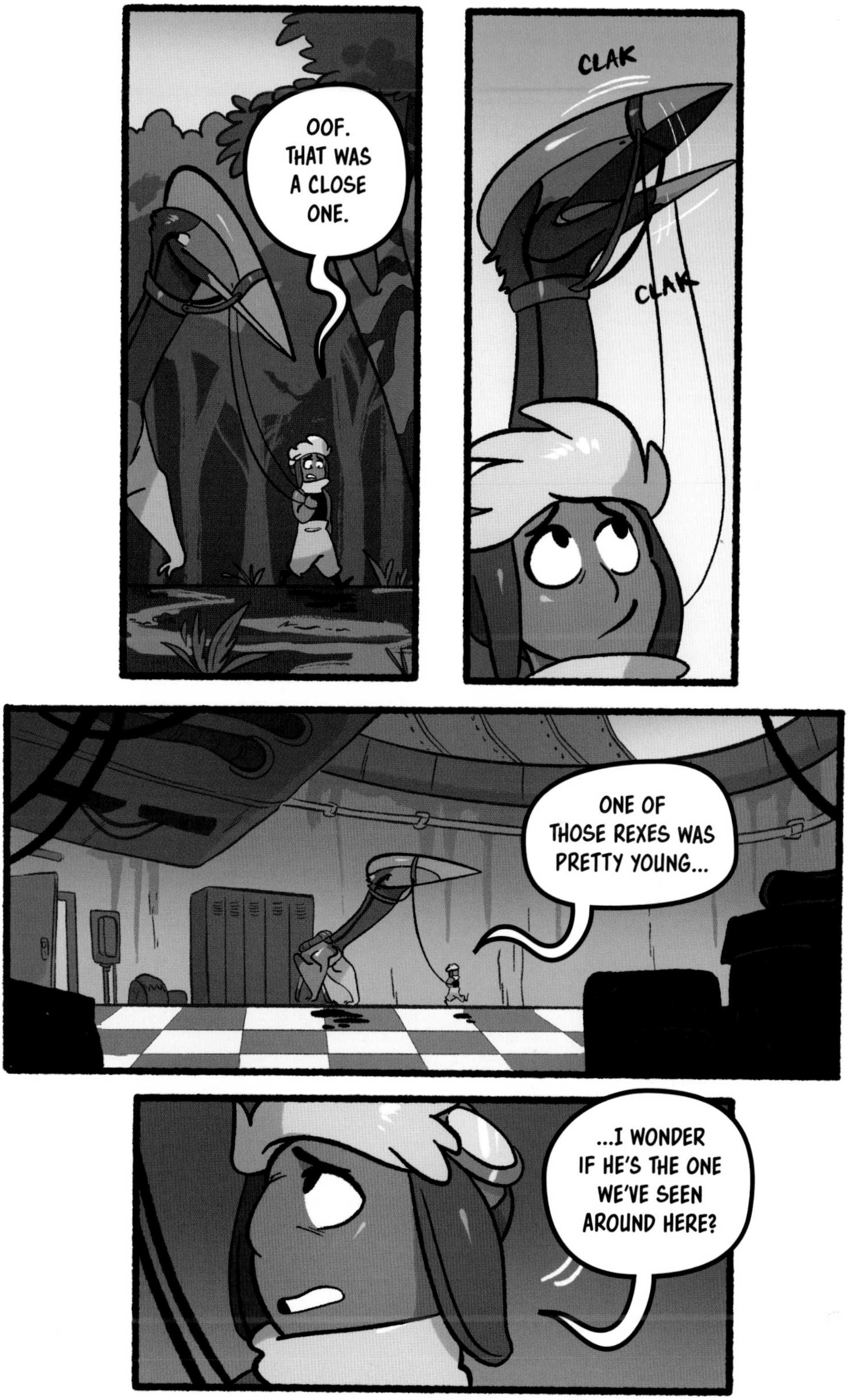
OOF. THAT WAS A CLOSE ONE.
CLAK
CLAK
ONE OF THOSE REXES WAS PRETTY YOUNG...
...I WONDER IF HE'S THE ONE WE'VE SEEN AROUND HERE?

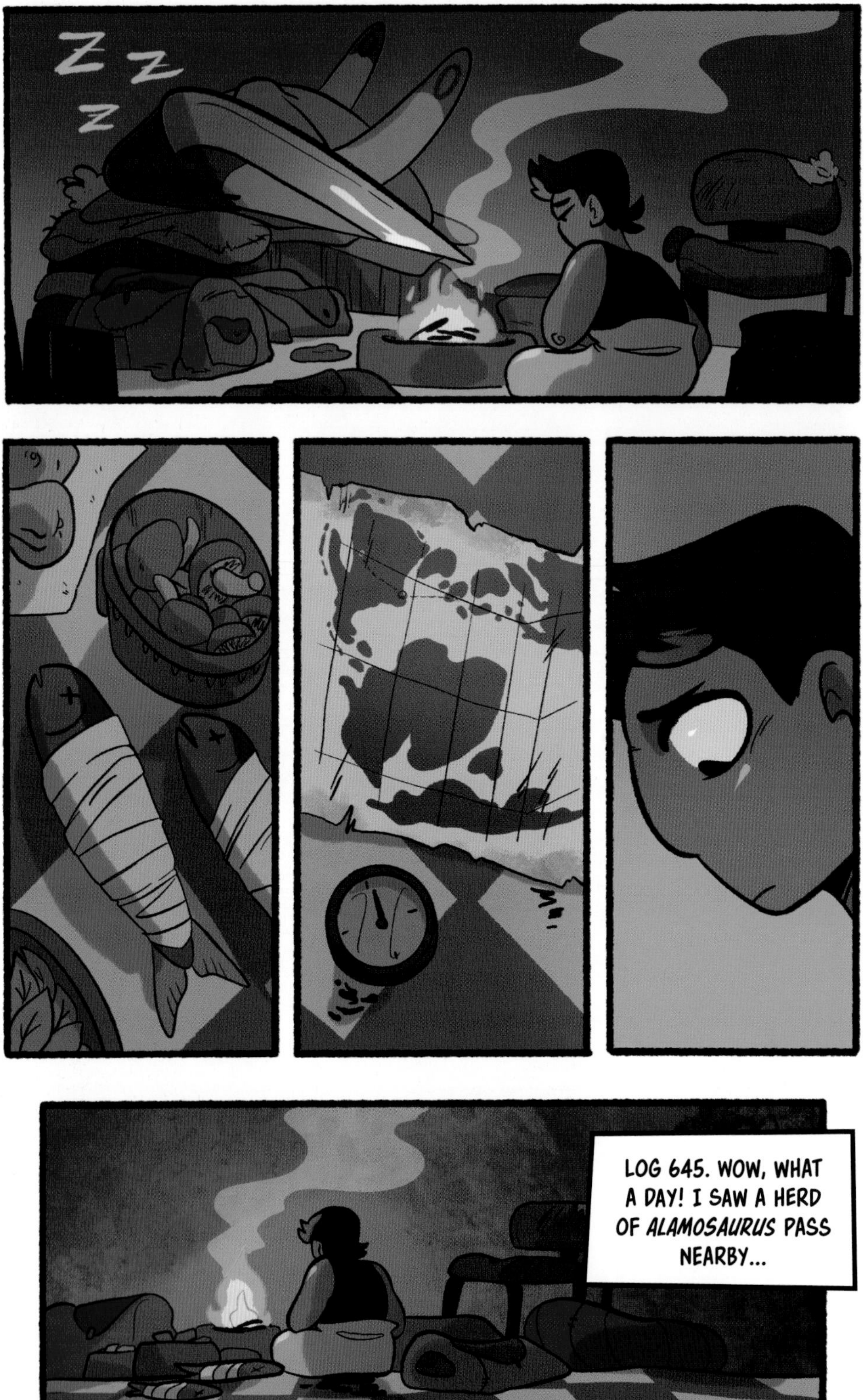
Z Z Z
LOG 645. WOW, WHAT A DAY! I SAW A HERD OF *ALAMOSAURUS* PASS NEARBY...

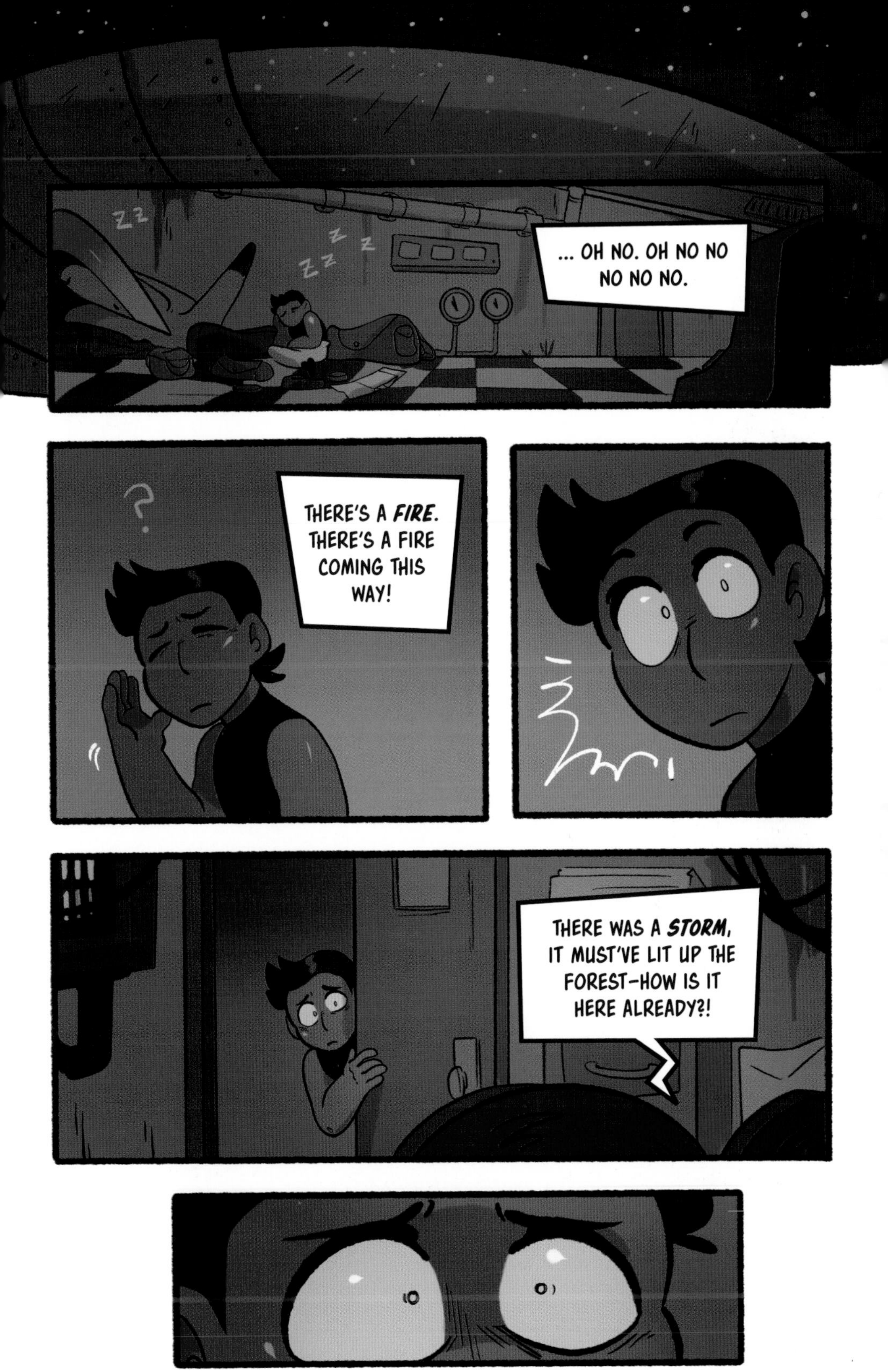
... OH NO. OH NO NO NO NO NO.
THERE'S A *FIRE*. THERE'S A FIRE COMING THIS WAY!
THERE WAS A *STORM*, IT MUST'VE LIT UP THE FOREST–HOW IS IT HERE ALREADY?!

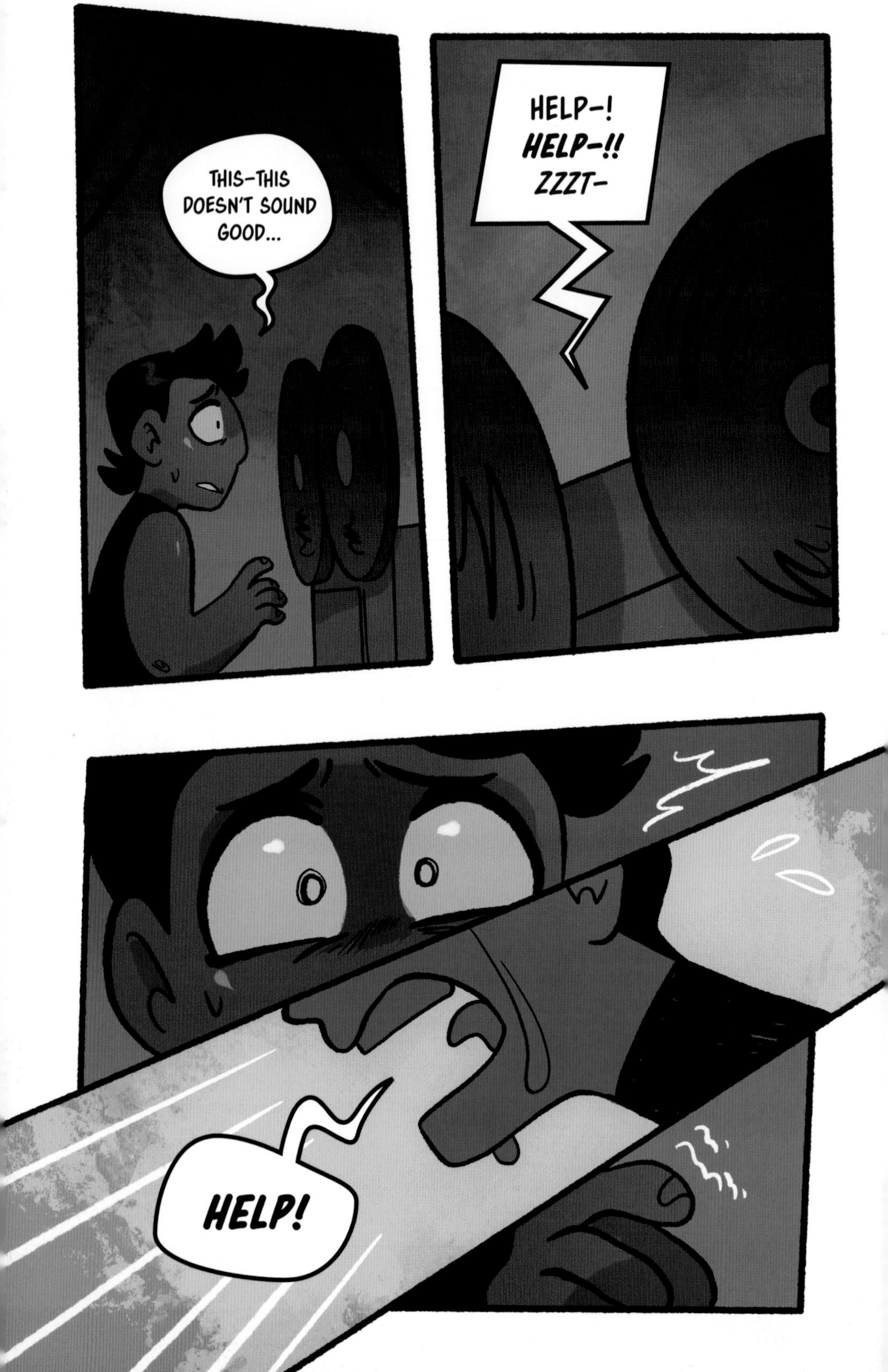
THIS-THIS DOESN'T SOUND GOOD...
HELP-! HELP-!! ZZZT-
HELP!

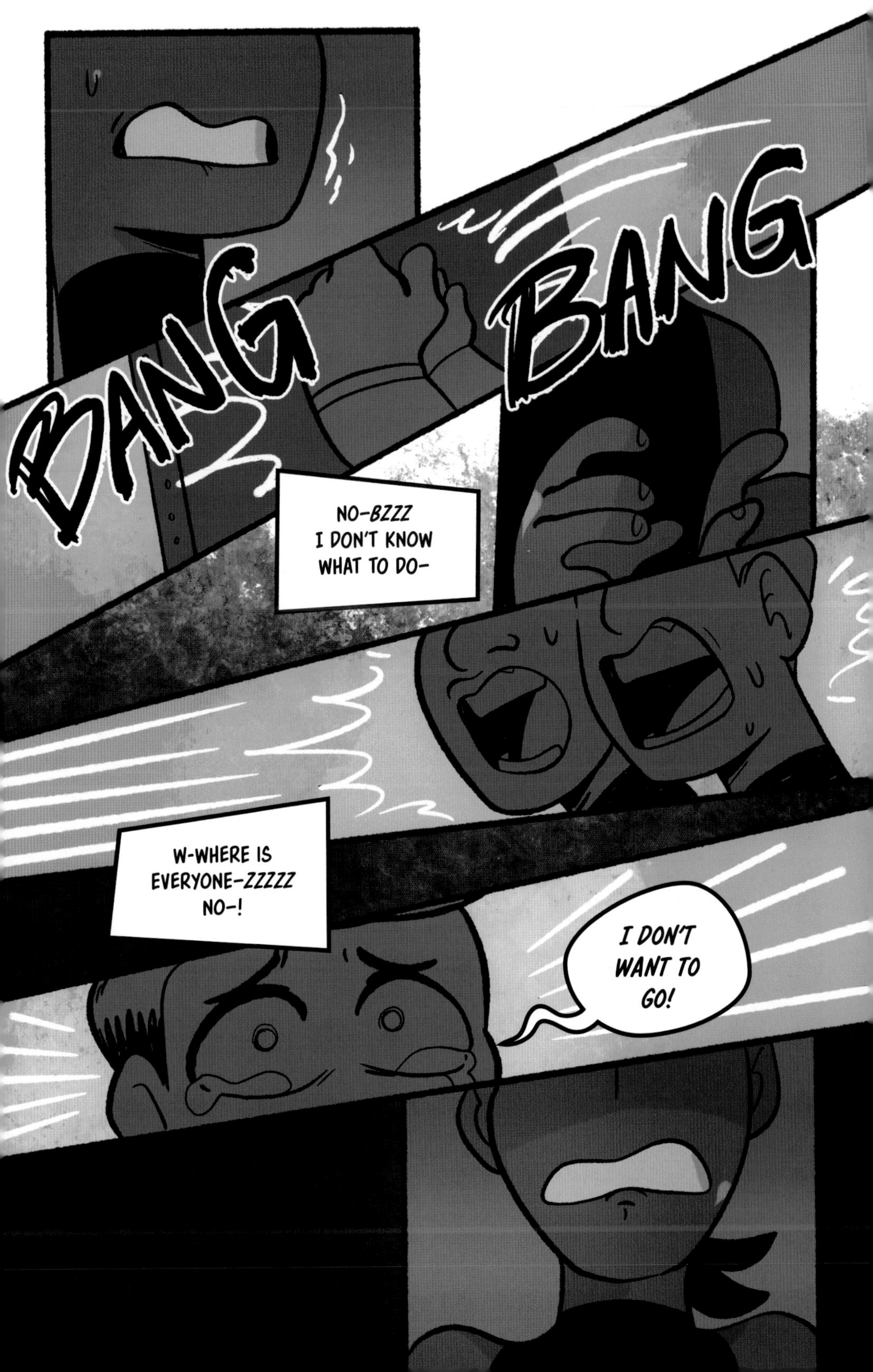
BANG
BANG
NO-BZZZ I DON'T KNOW WHAT TO DO-
W-WHERE IS EVERYONE-ZZZZZ NO-!
I DON'T WANT TO GO!

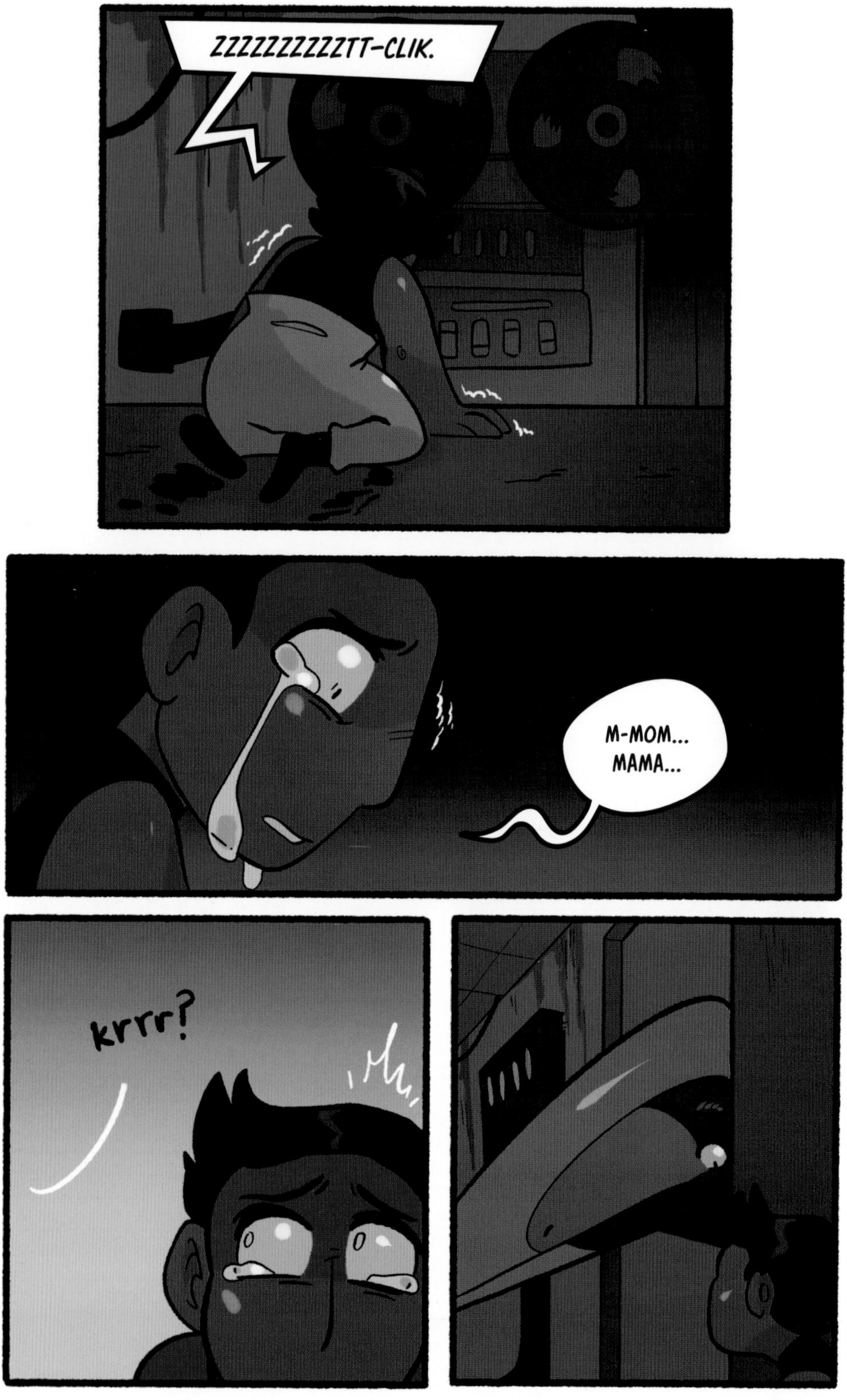
ZZZZZZZZZZZTT-CLIK.
M-MOM...
MAMA...
krrr?

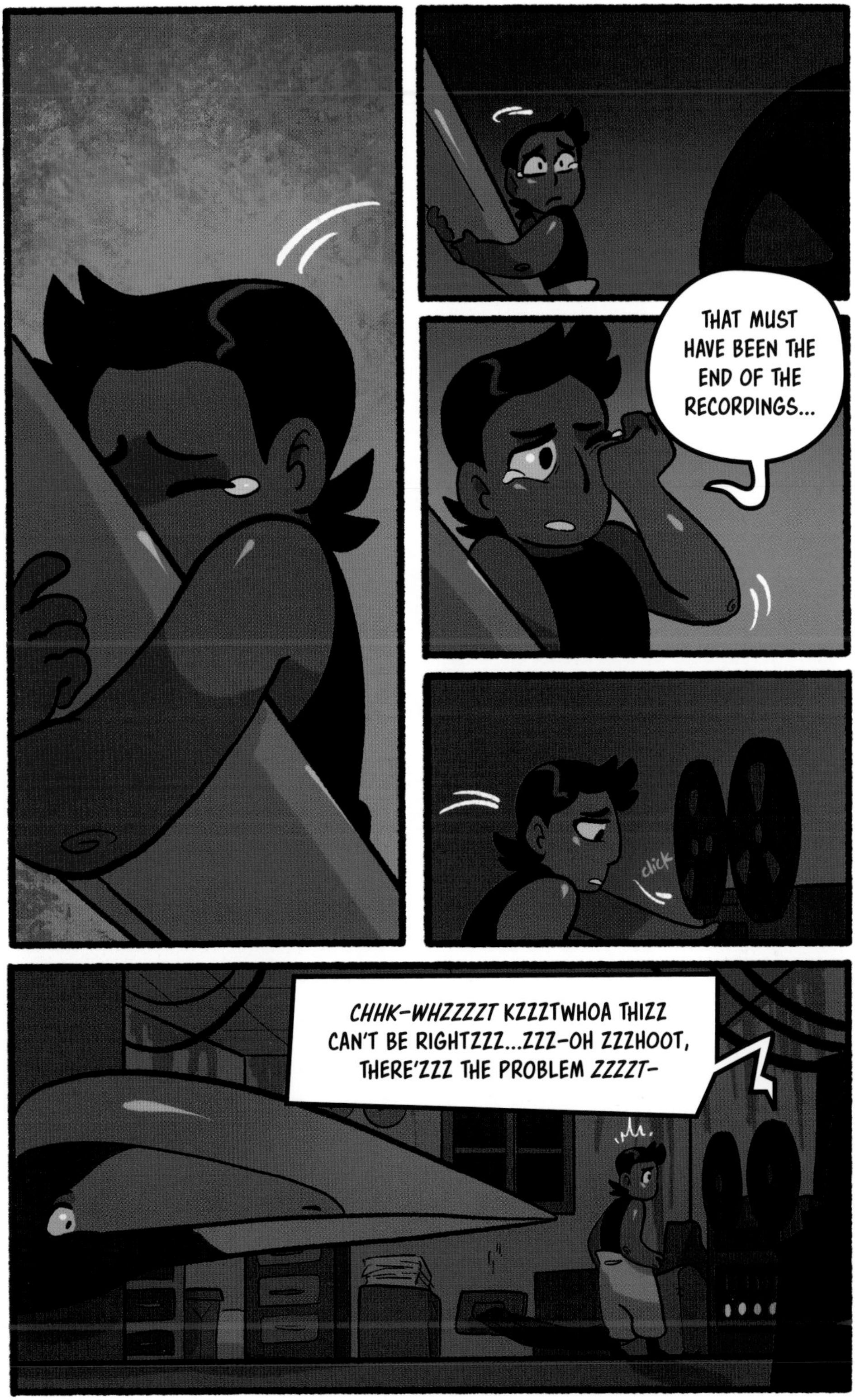
THAT MUST HAVE BEEN THE END OF THE RECORDINGS...
click
CHHK-WHZZZZT KZZZTWHOA THIZZ CAN'T BE RIGHTZZZ...ZZZ-OH ZZZHOOT, THERE'ZZZ THE PROBLEM ZZZZT-

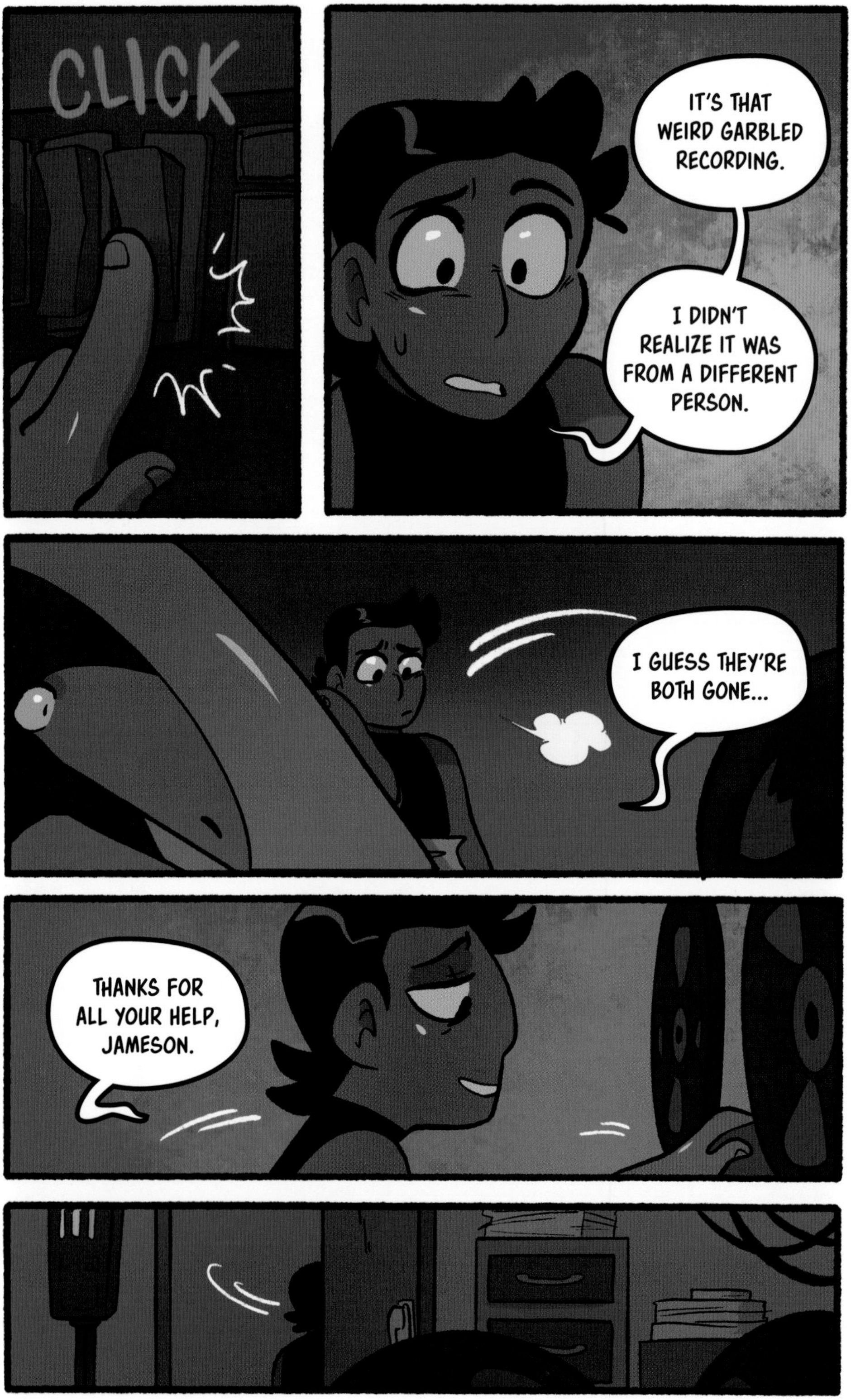
CLICK
IT'S THAT WEIRD GARBLED RECORDING.
I DIDN'T REALIZE IT WAS FROM A DIFFERENT PERSON.
I GUESS THEY'RE BOTH GONE...
THANKS FOR ALL YOUR HELP, JAMESON.

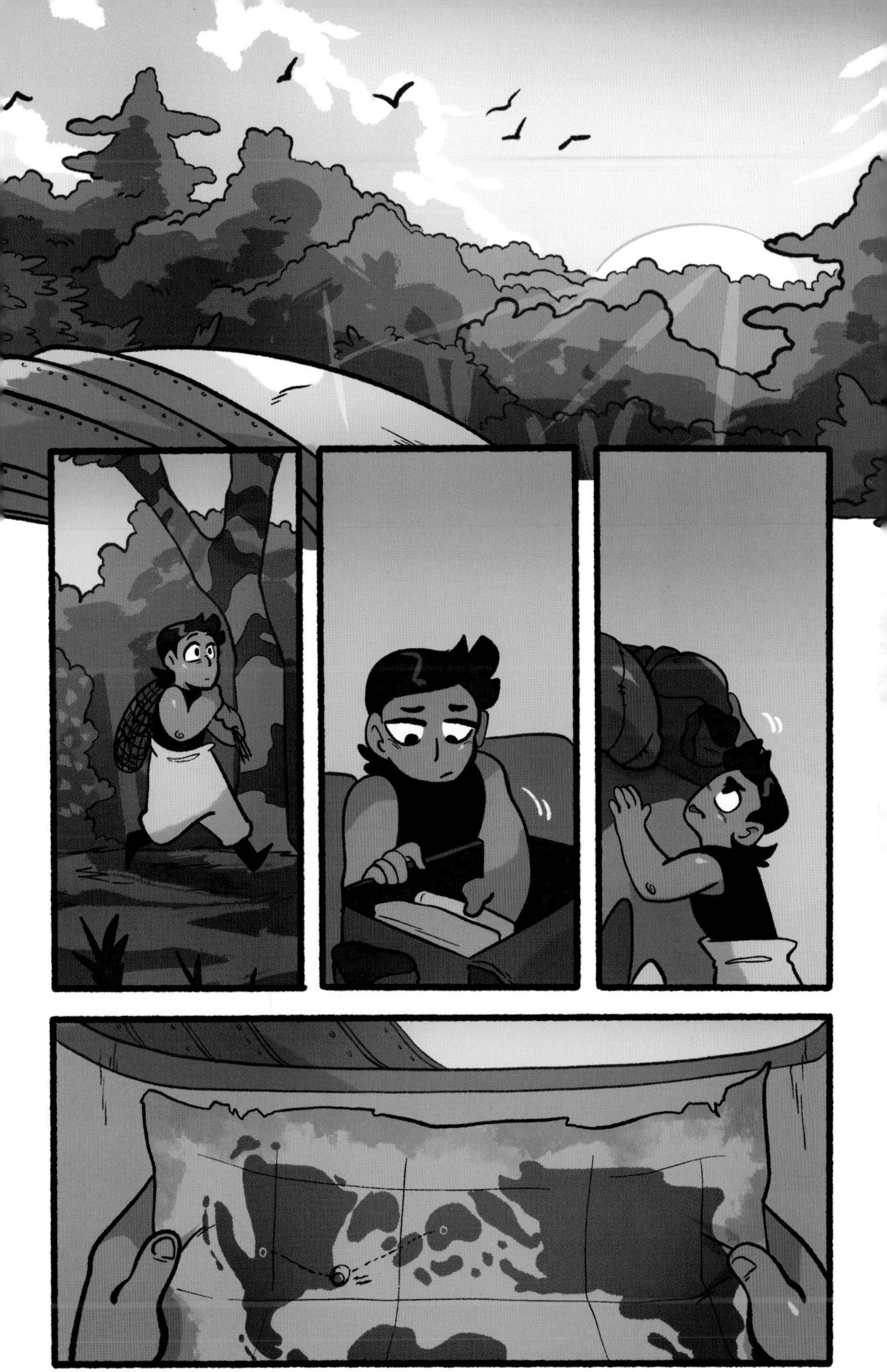

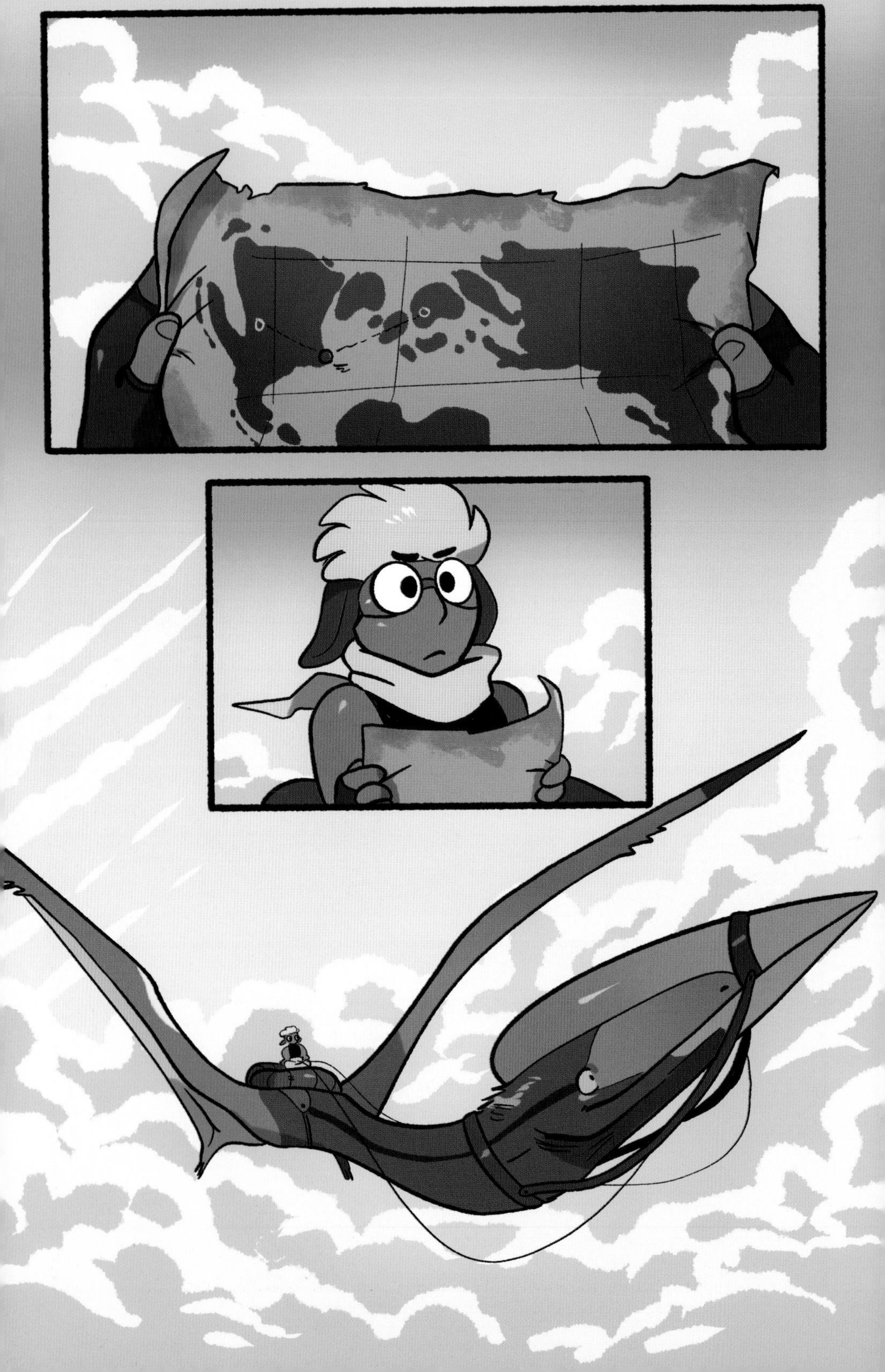

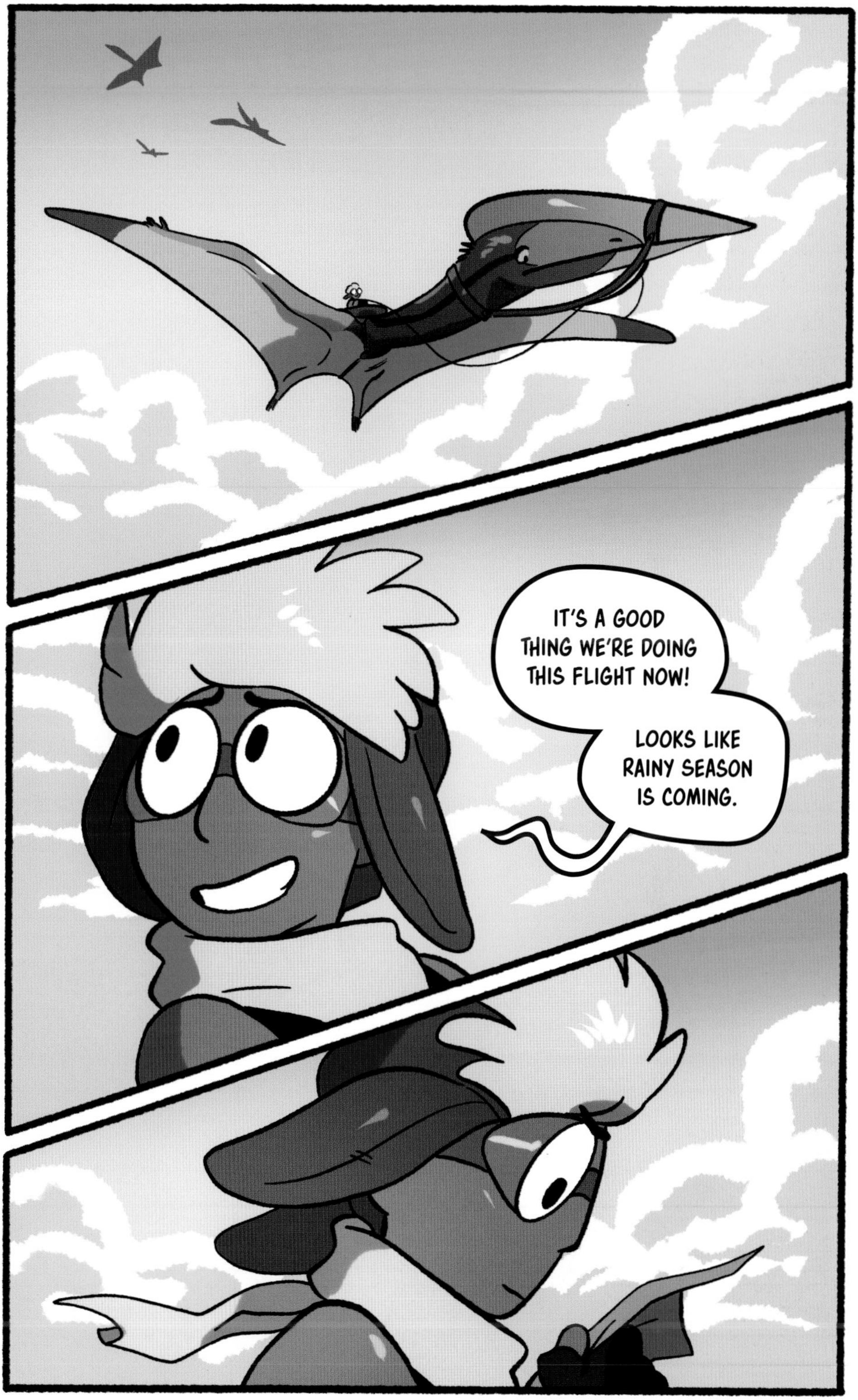
IT'S A GOOD THING WE'RE DOING THIS FLIGHT NOW!
LOOKS LIKE RAINY SEASON IS COMING.

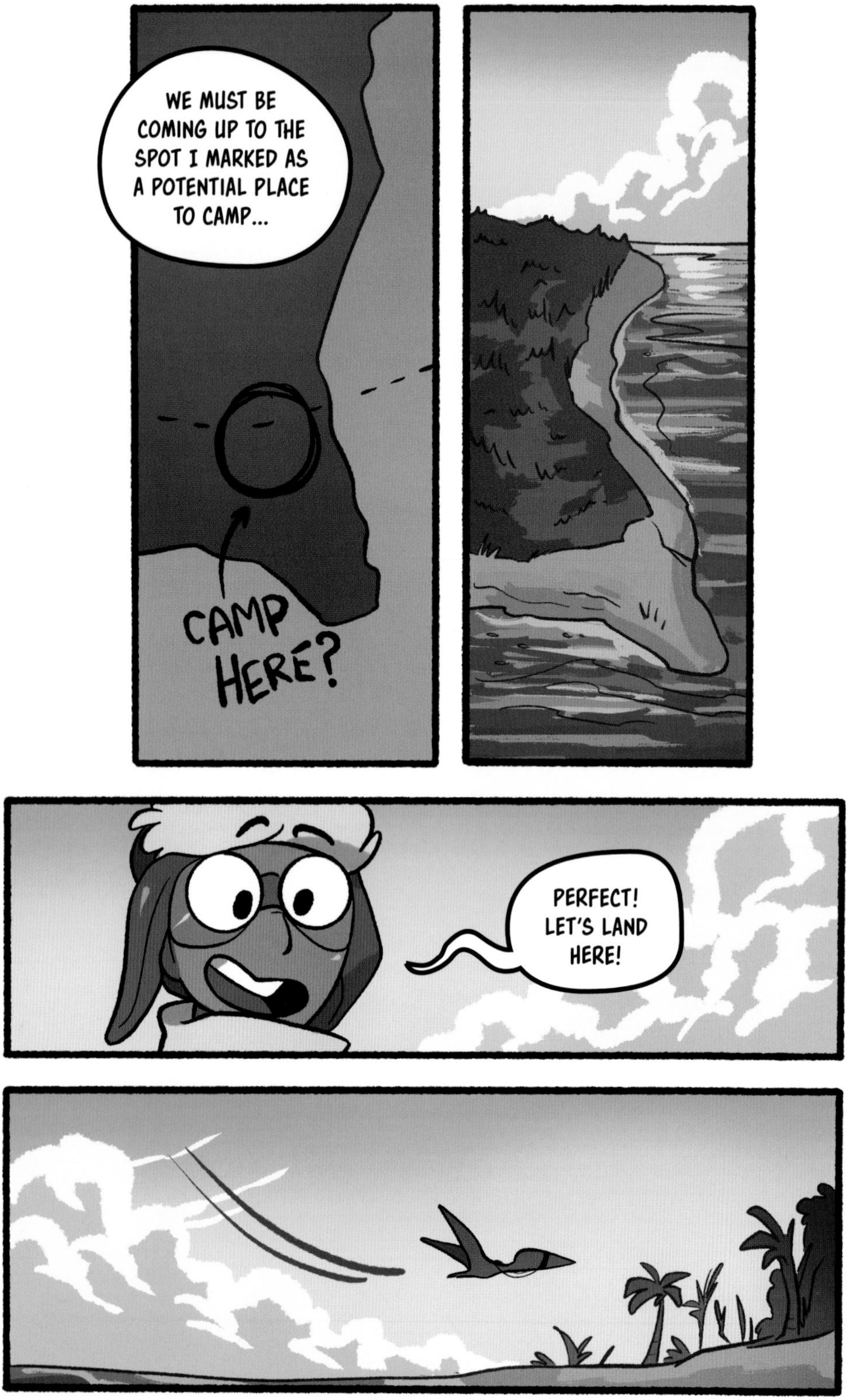
WE MUST BE COMING UP TO THE SPOT I MARKED AS A POTENTIAL PLACE TO CAMP...
CAMP HERE?
PERFECT! LET'S LAND HERE!

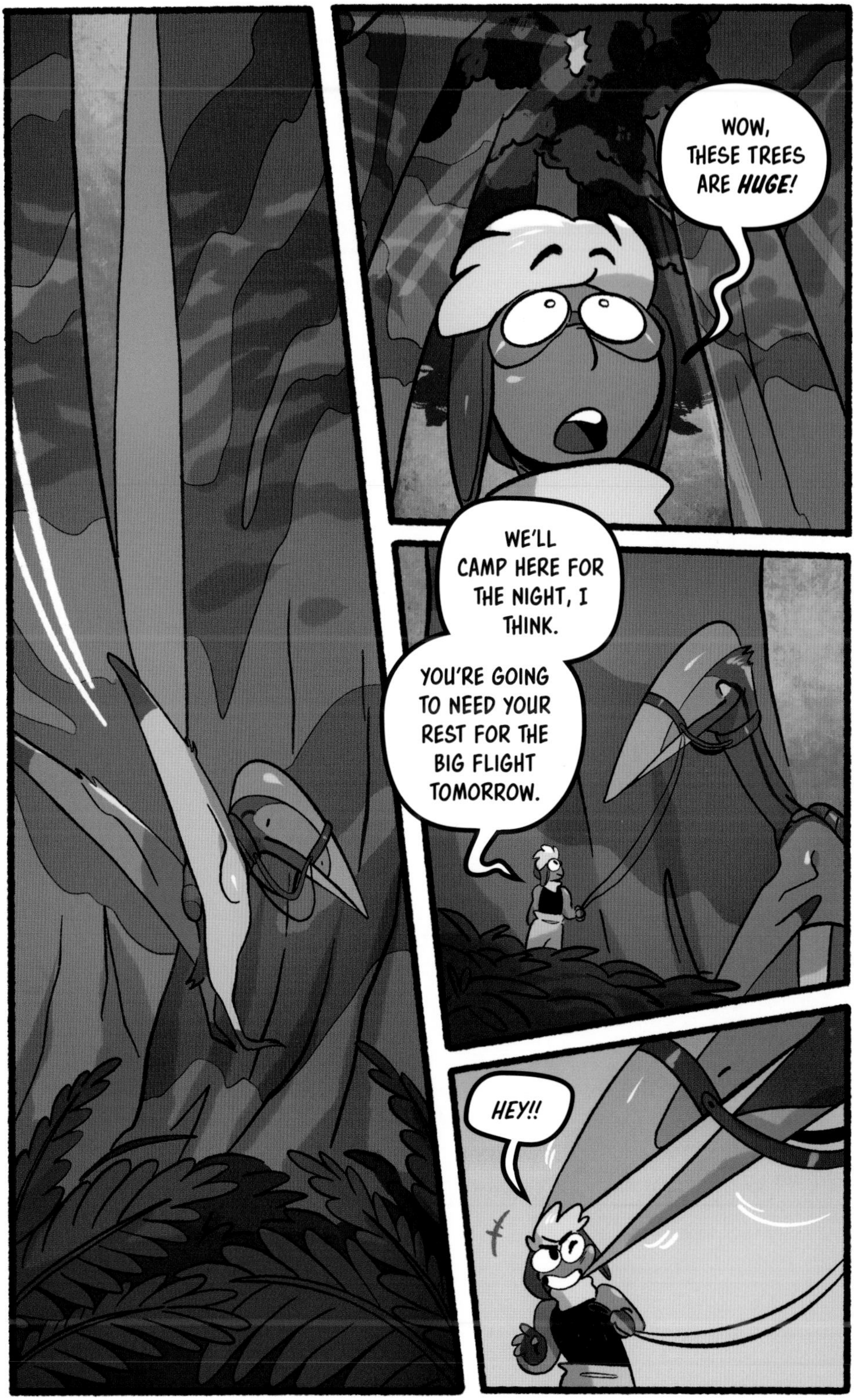
WOW, THESE TREES ARE *HUGE!*
WE'LL CAMP HERE FOR THE NIGHT, I THINK.
YOU'RE GOING TO NEED YOUR REST FOR THE BIG FLIGHT TOMORROW.
HEY!!

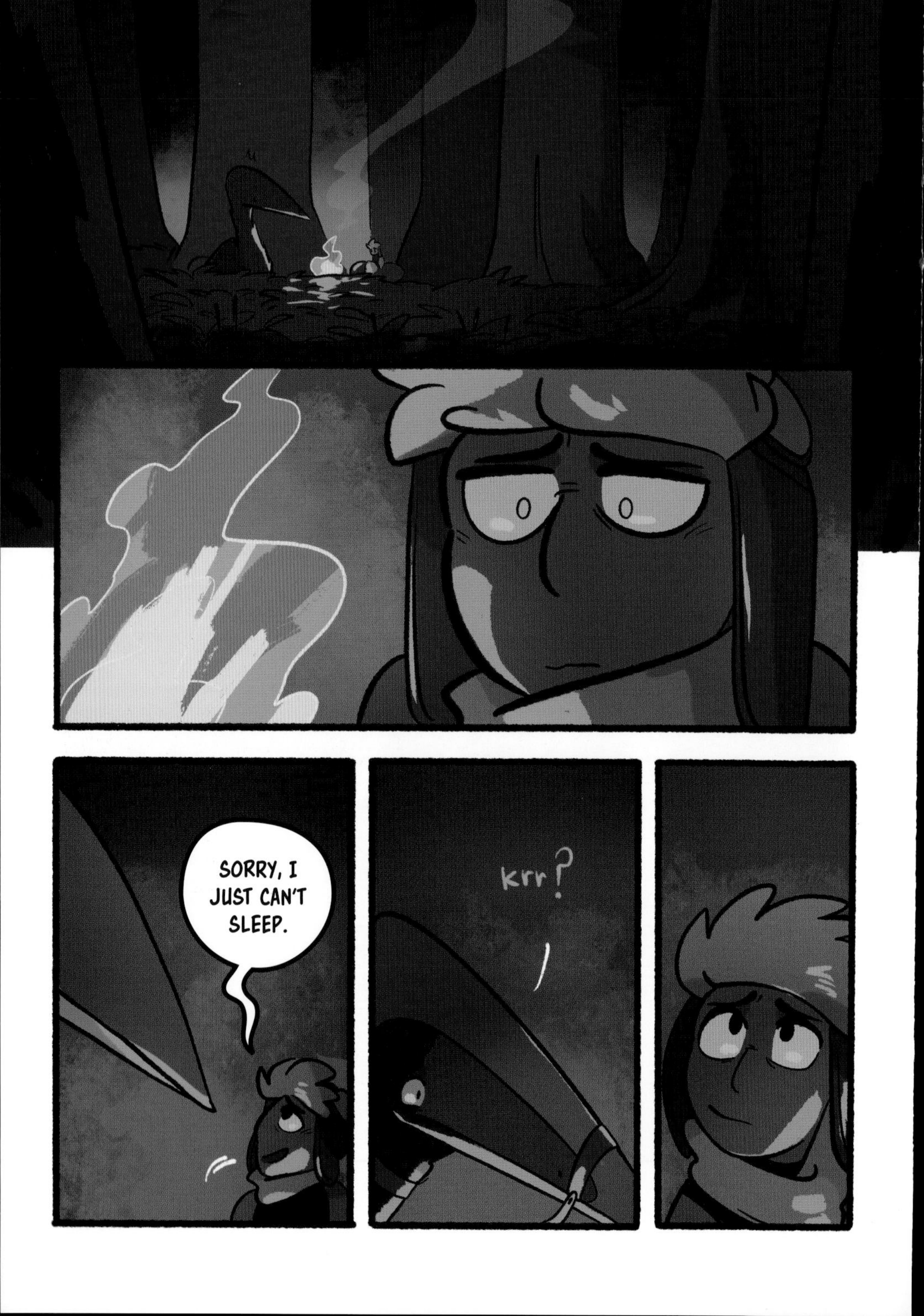
SORRY, I JUST CAN'T SLEEP.
krr?

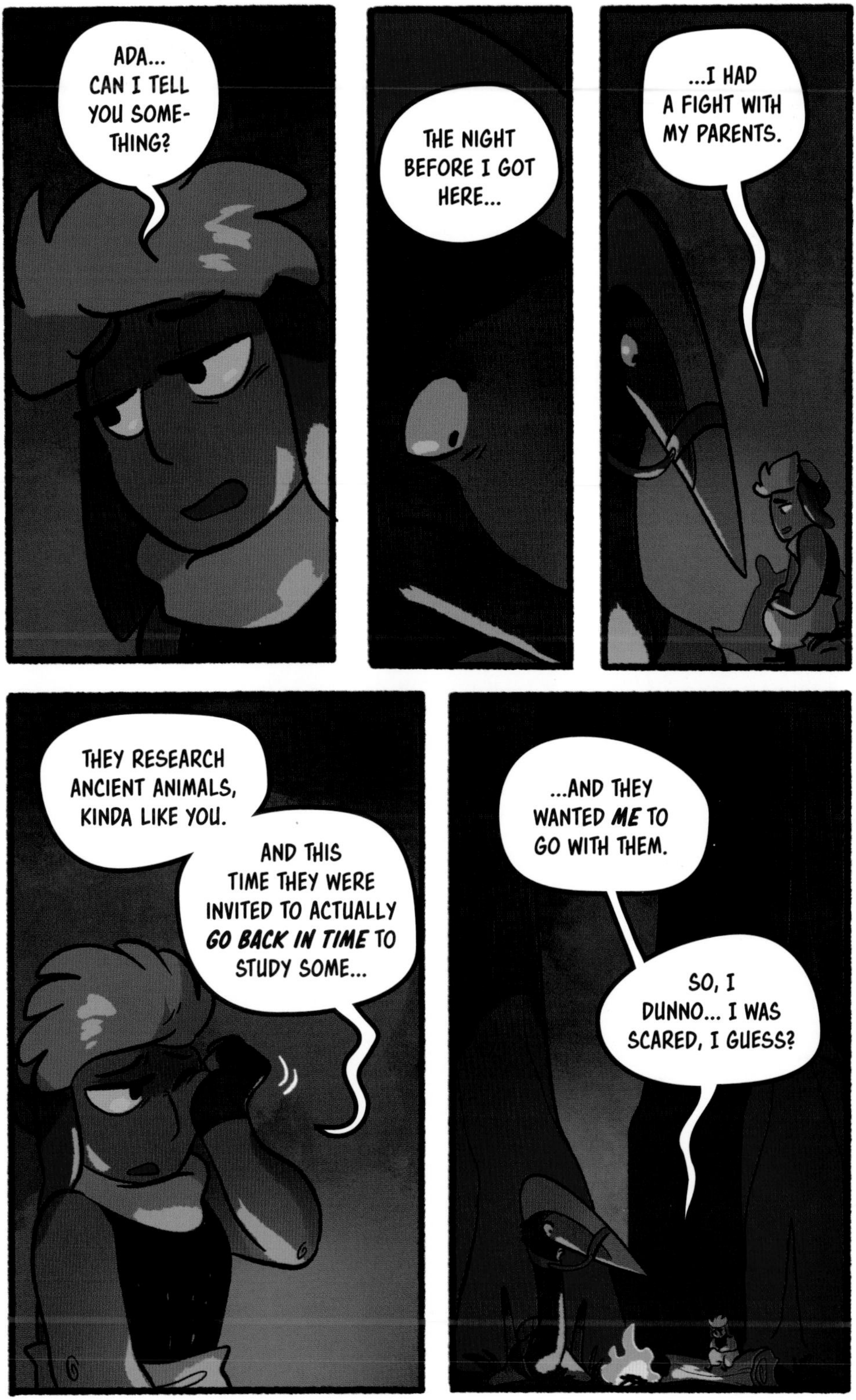
ADA... CAN I TELL YOU SOME-THING?
THE NIGHT BEFORE I GOT HERE...
...I HAD A FIGHT WITH MY PARENTS.
THEY RESEARCH ANCIENT ANIMALS, KINDA LIKE YOU.
AND THIS TIME THEY WERE INVITED TO ACTUALLY *GO BACK IN TIME* TO STUDY SOME...
...AND THEY WANTED *ME* TO GO WITH THEM.
SO, I DUNNO... I WAS SCARED, I GUESS?

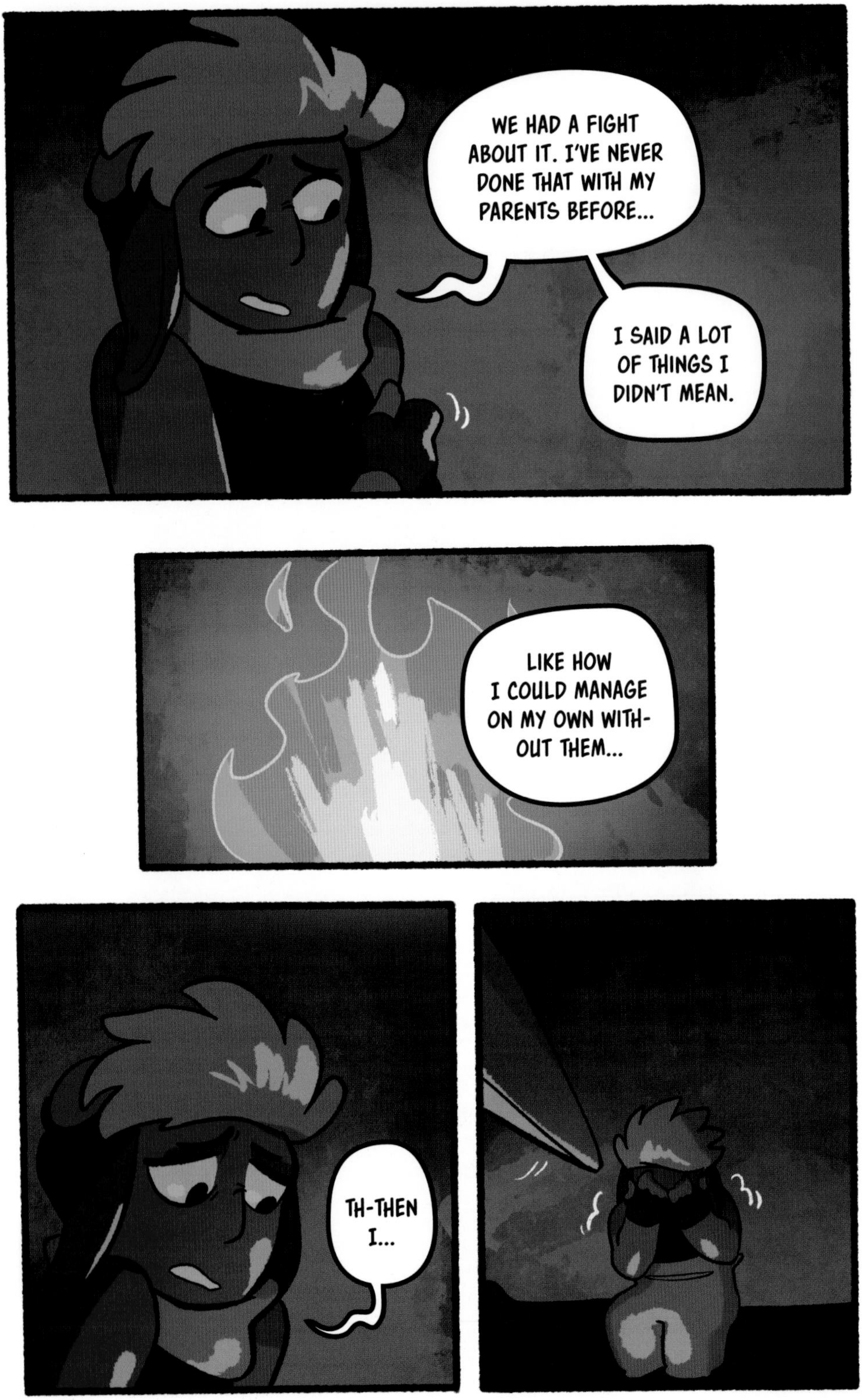
WE HAD A FIGHT ABOUT IT. I'VE NEVER DONE THAT WITH MY PARENTS BEFORE...
I SAID A LOT OF THINGS I DIDN'T MEAN.
LIKE HOW I COULD MANAGE ON MY OWN WITH-OUT THEM...
TH-THEN I...

I'M WORRIED THEY MIGHT STILL BE MAD AT ME.

MAYBE THAT'S WHY THEY HAVEN'T FOUND ME YET. I JUST GOT WHAT I ASKED FOR.

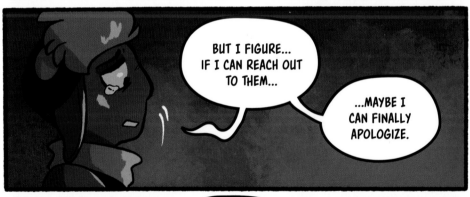

BUT I FIGURE... IF I CAN REACH OUT TO THEM...

...MAYBE I CAN FINALLY APOLOGIZE.

GOSH, IS IT A LITTLE WEIRD BARING YOUR FEELINGS TO A GIANT REPTILE?

HA HA HA

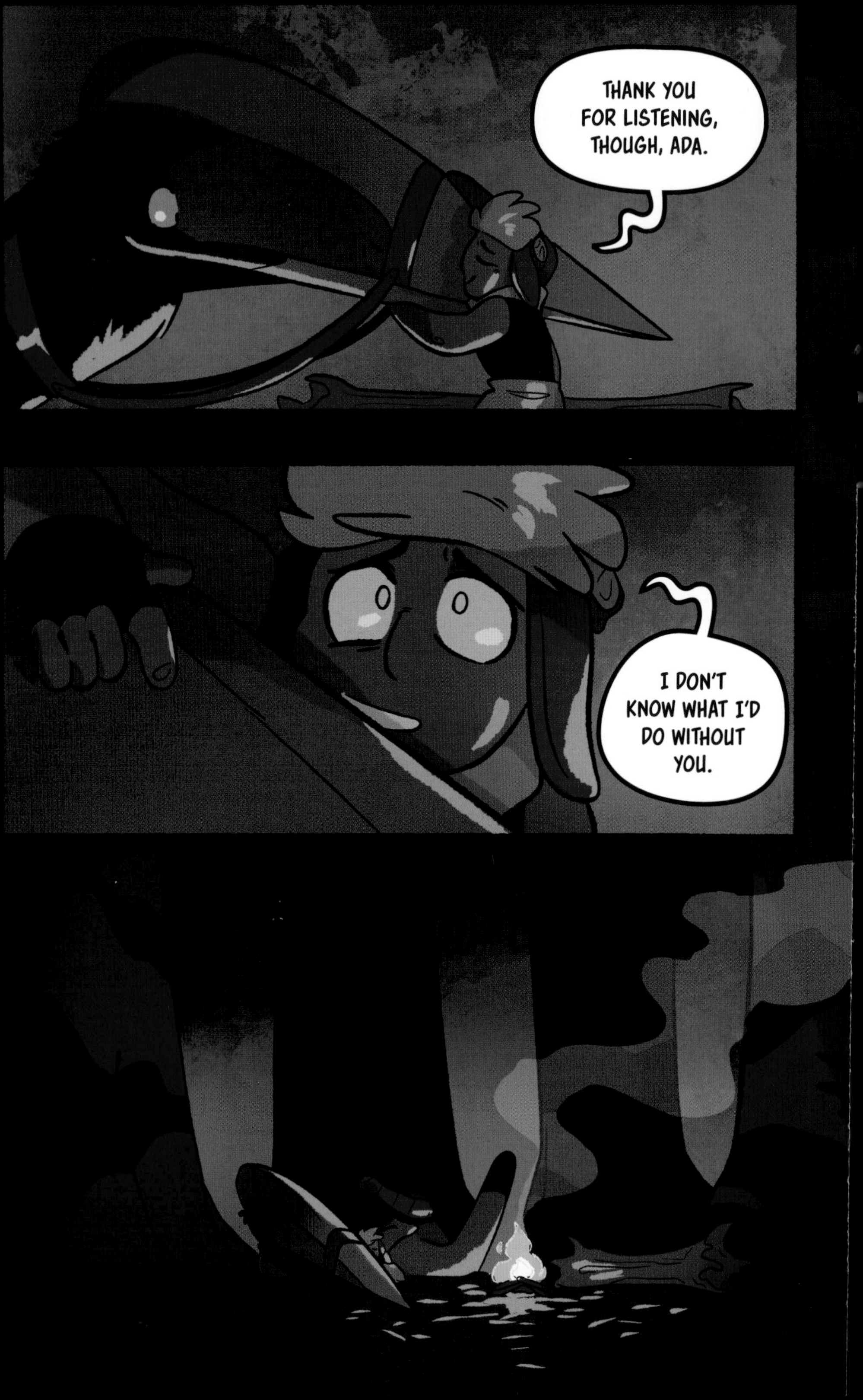
THANK YOU FOR LISTENING, THOUGH, ADA.
I DON'T KNOW WHAT I'D DO WITHOUT YOU.

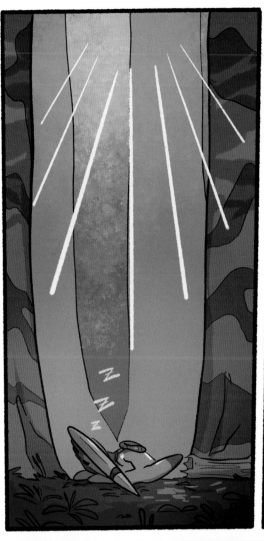

ADA!

ADA, COME LOOK AT THIS!

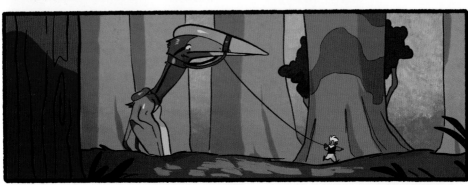

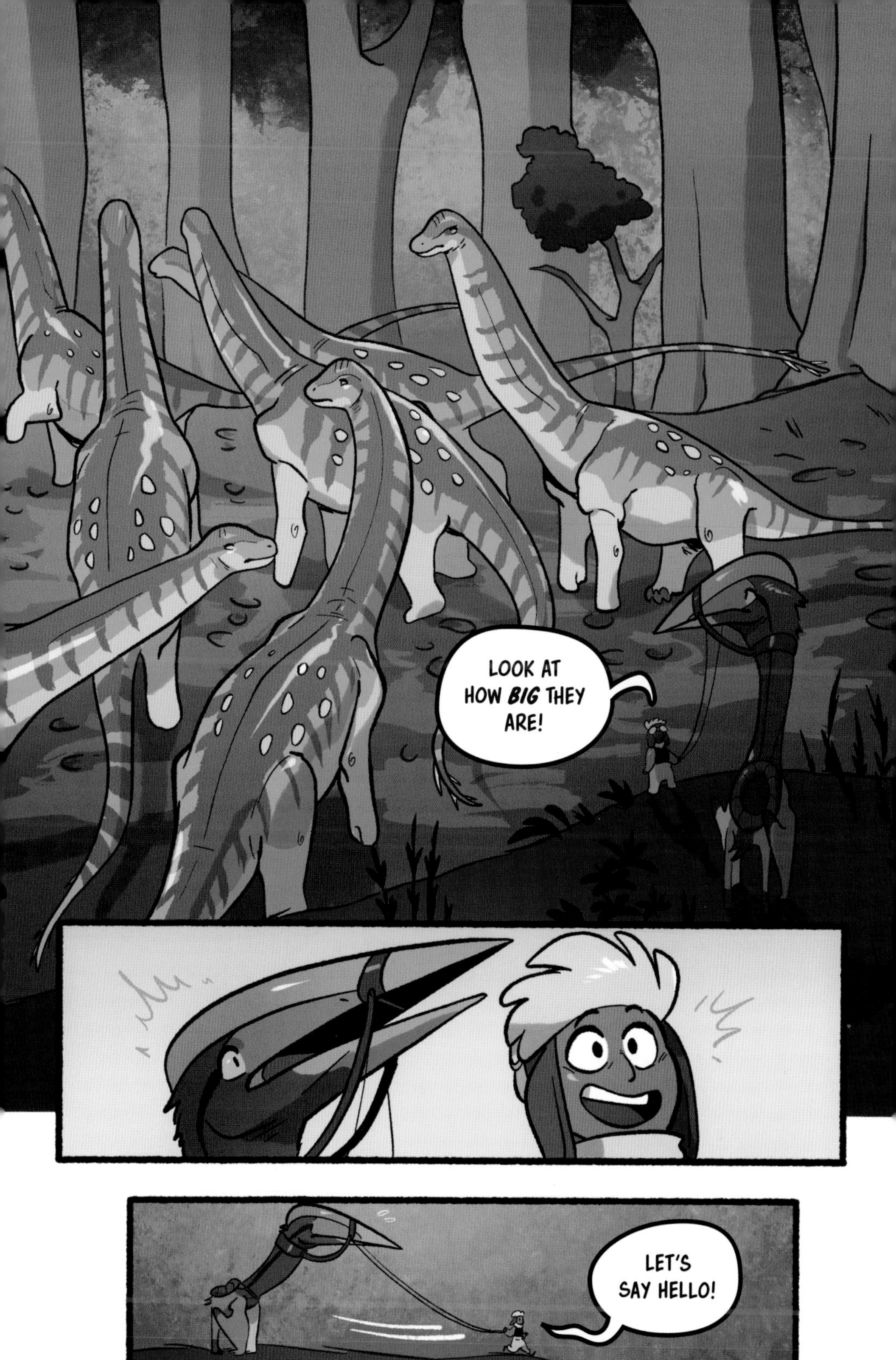
LOOK AT HOW BIG THEY ARE!
LET'S SAY HELLO!

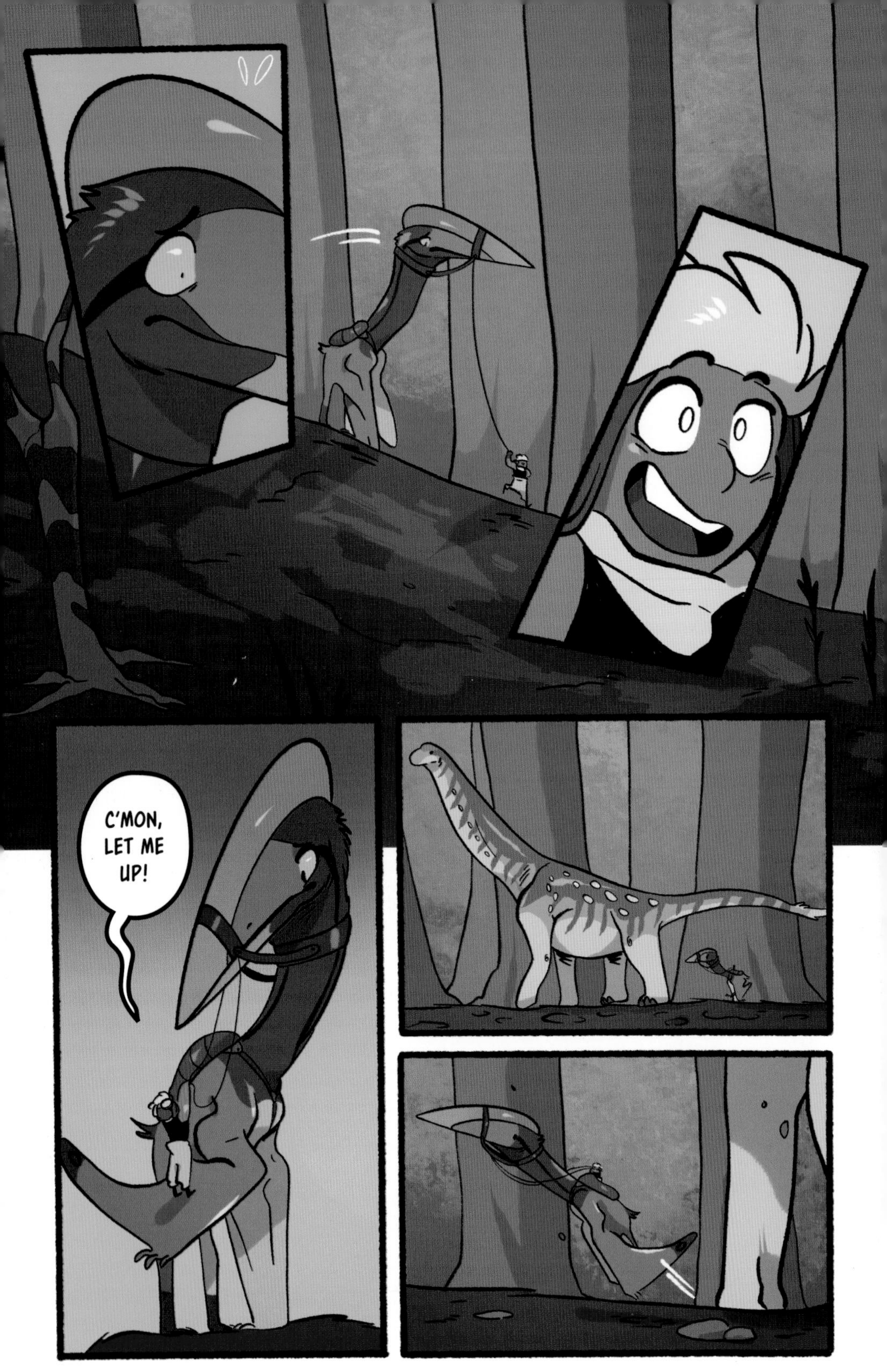
C'MON, LET ME UP!

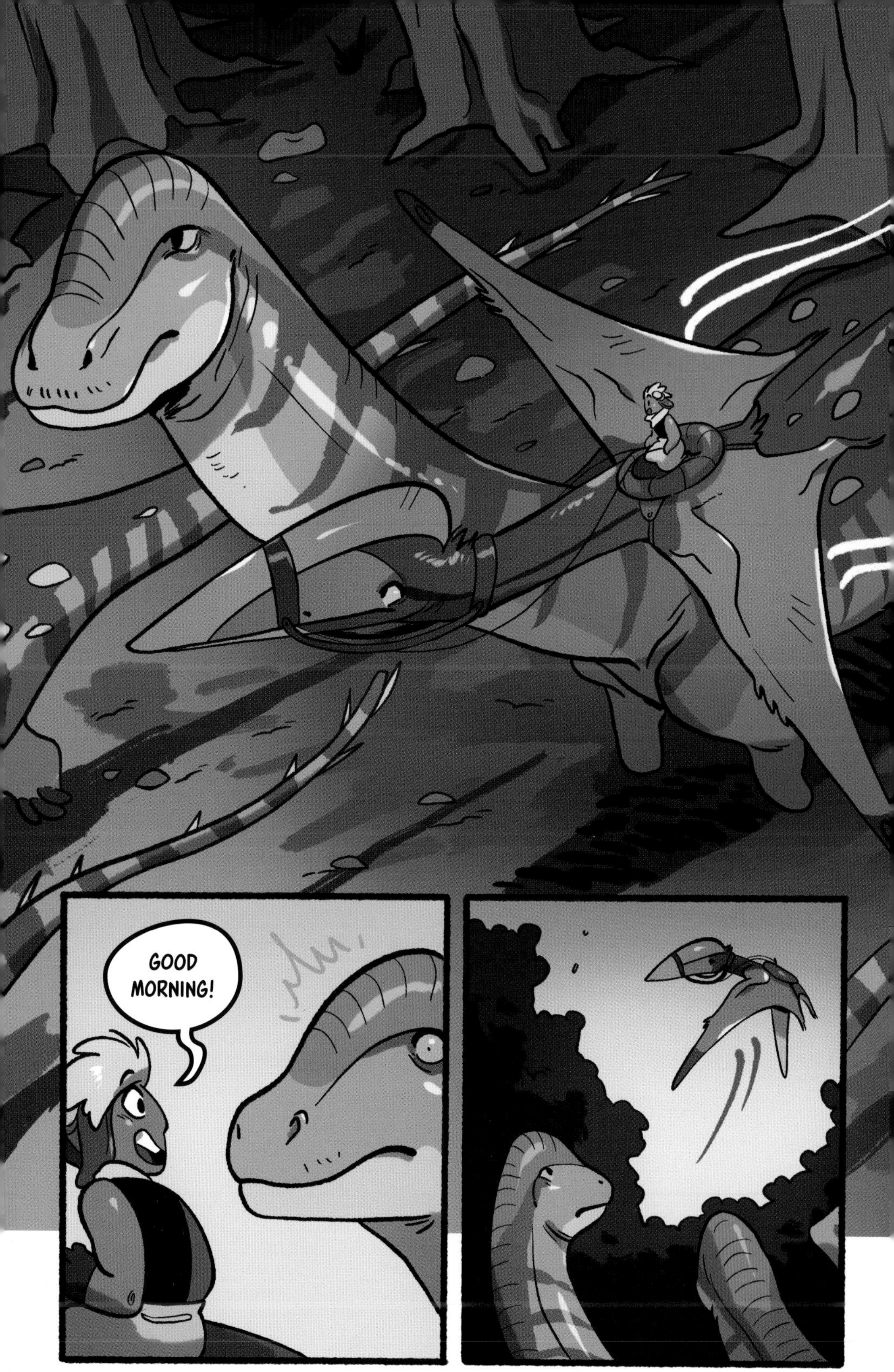
GOOD MORNING!

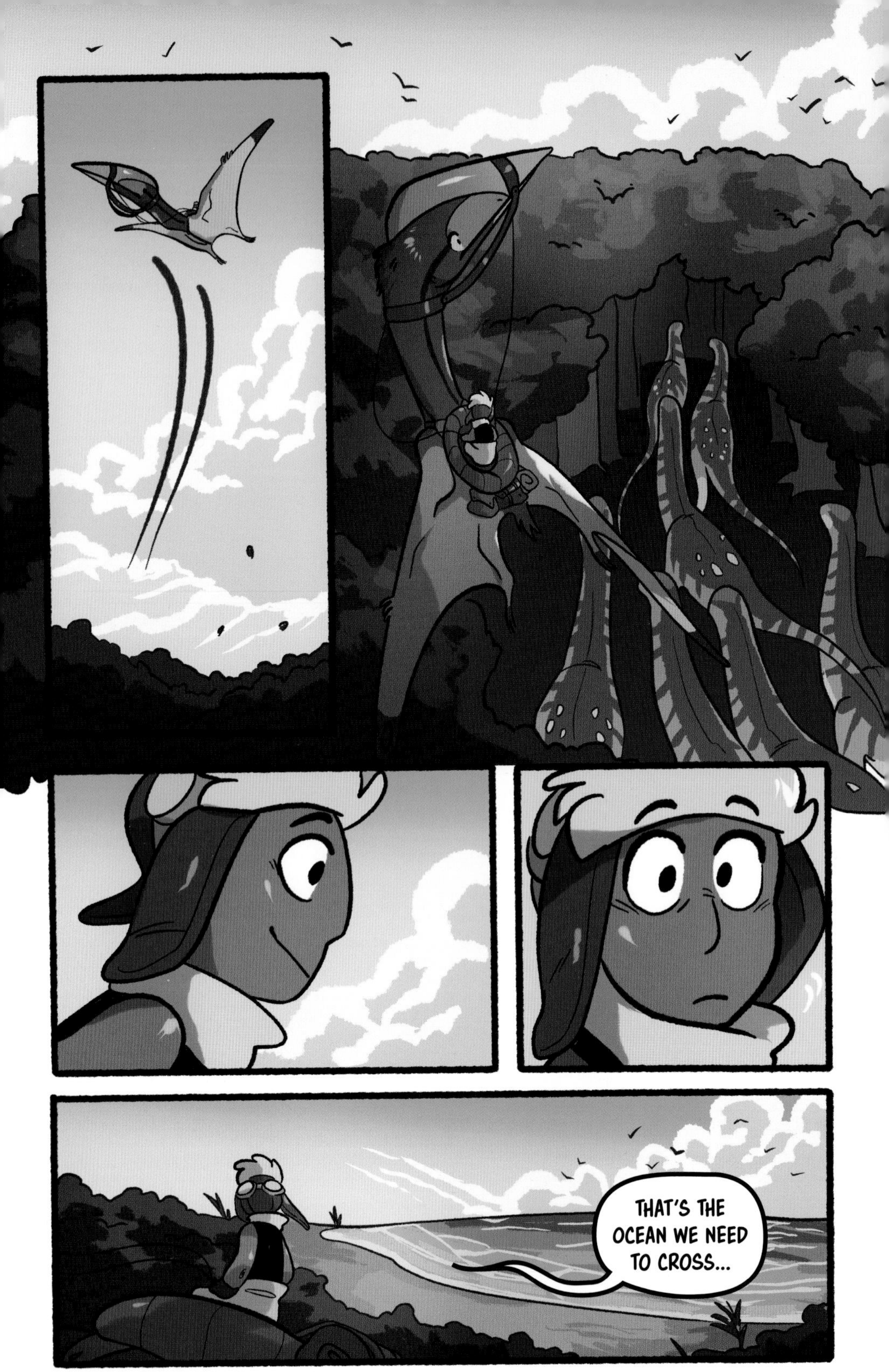
THAT'S THE OCEAN WE NEED TO CROSS...

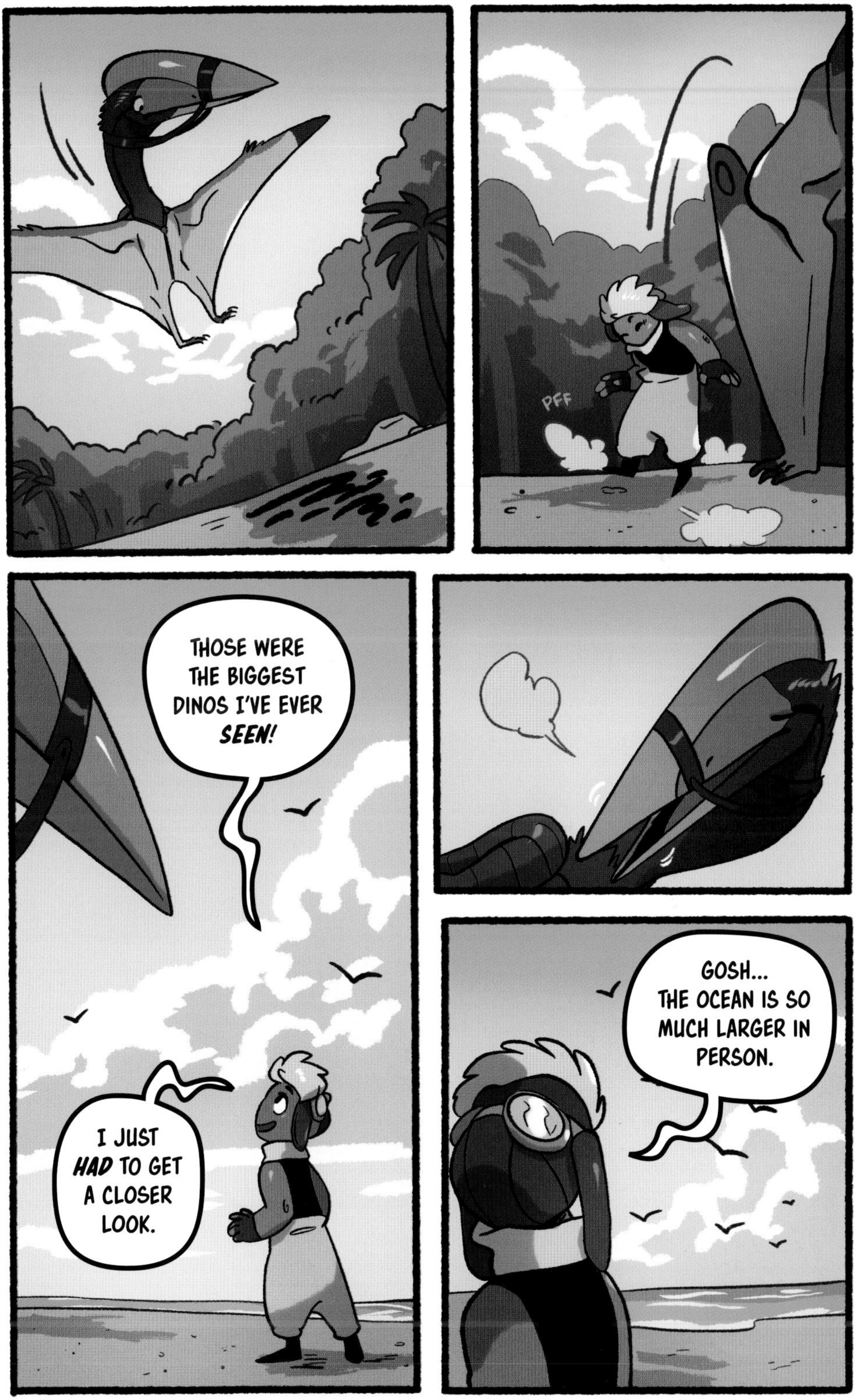
PFF
THOSE WERE THE BIGGEST DINOS I'VE EVER SEEN!
I JUST HAD TO GET A CLOSER LOOK.
GOSH... THE OCEAN IS SO MUCH LARGER IN PERSON.

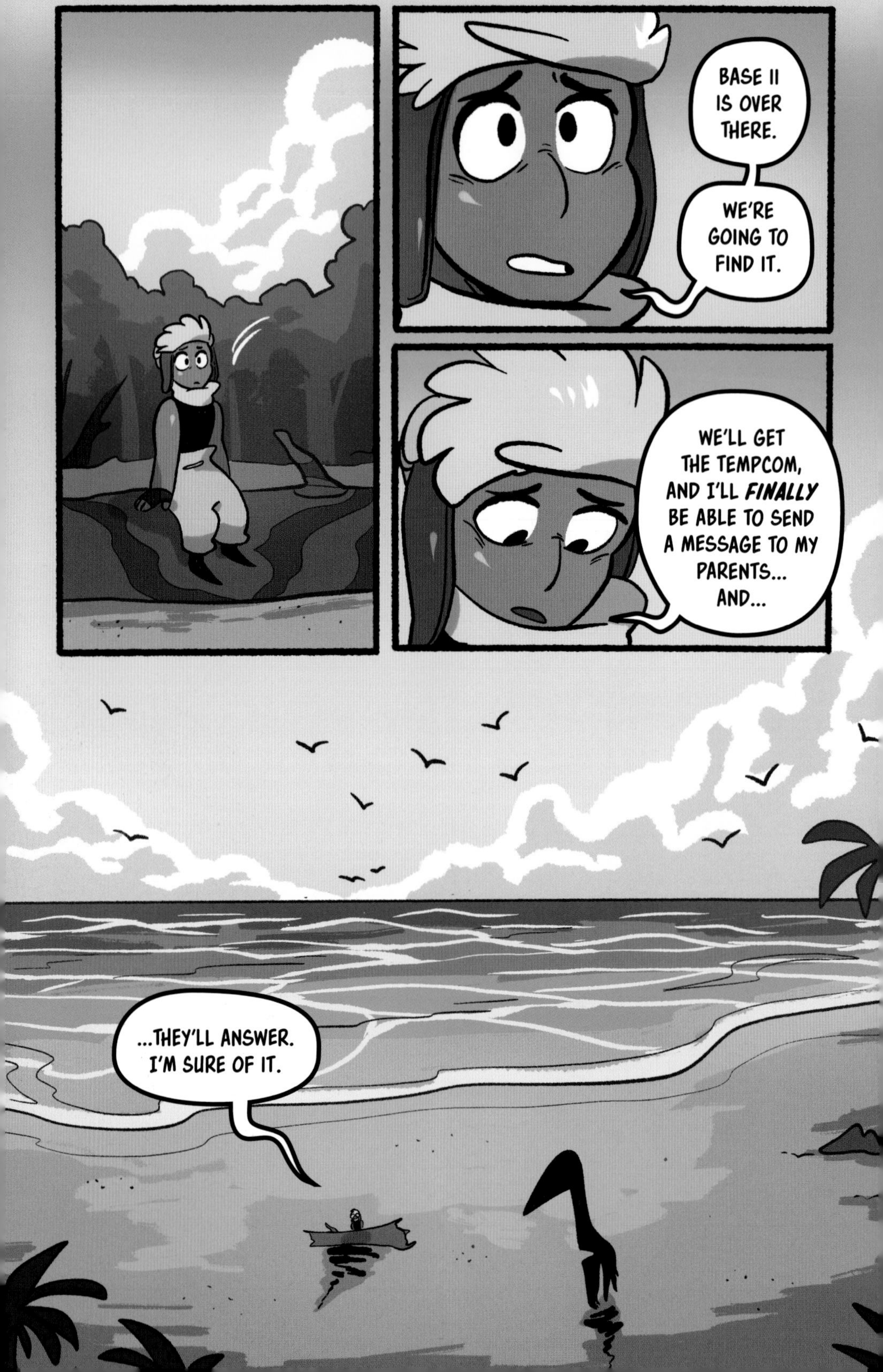
BASE II IS OVER THERE.
WE'RE GOING TO FIND IT.
WE'LL GET THE TEMPCOM, AND I'LL *FINALLY* BE ABLE TO SEND A MESSAGE TO MY PARENTS... AND...
...THEY'LL ANSWER. I'M SURE OF IT.

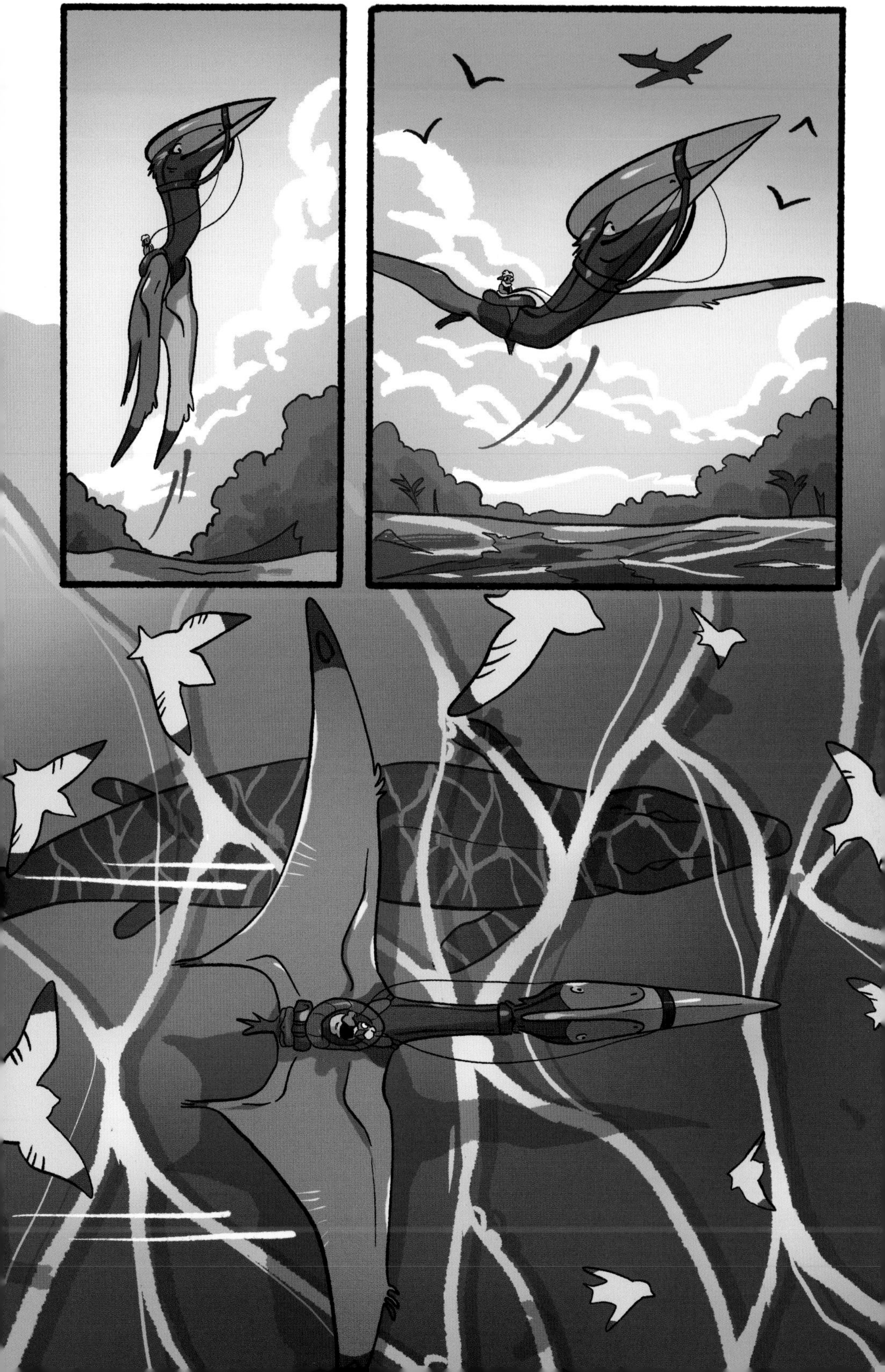

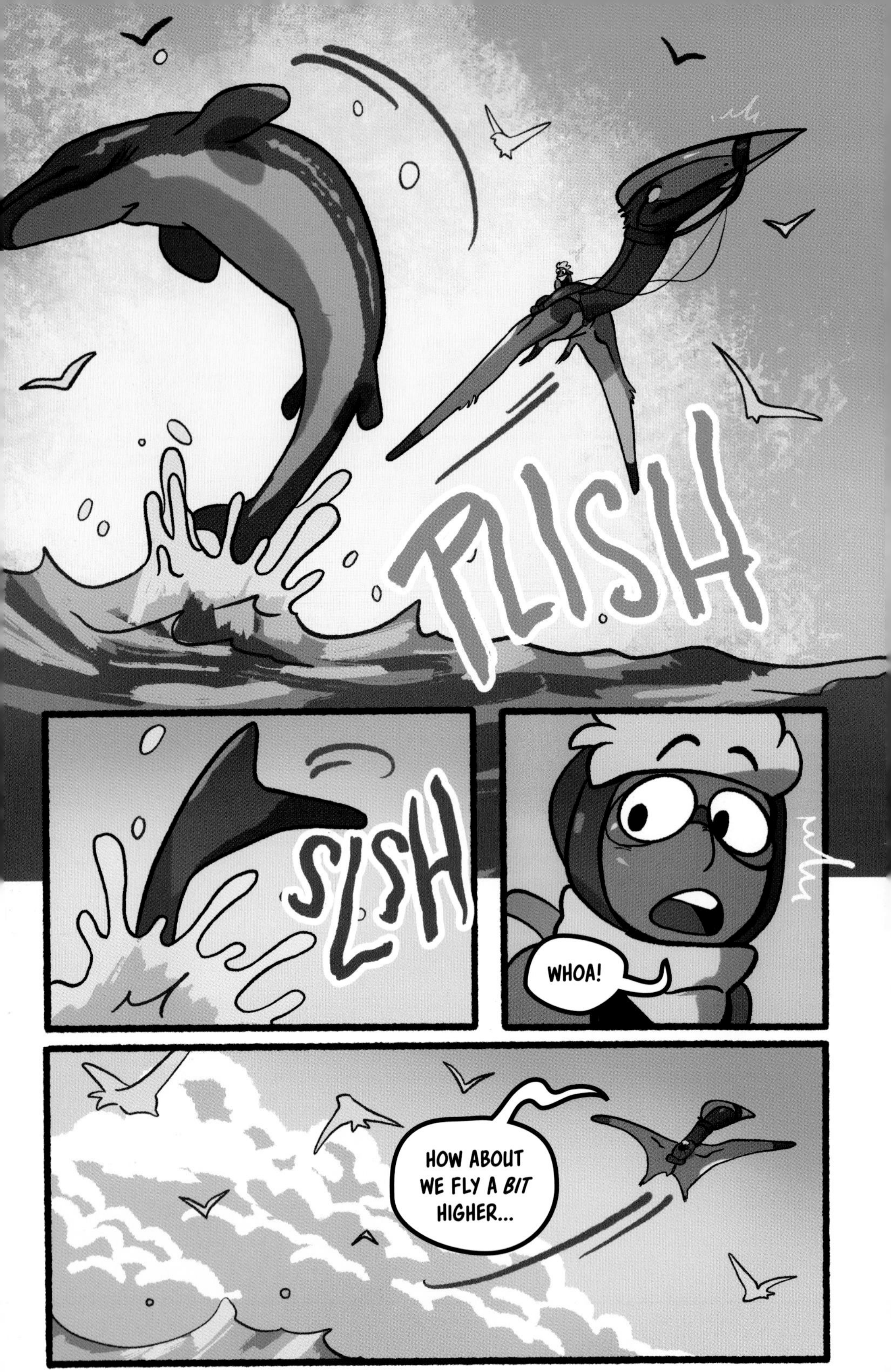
PLISH
SLSH
WHOA!
HOW ABOUT WE FLY A *BIT* HIGHER...

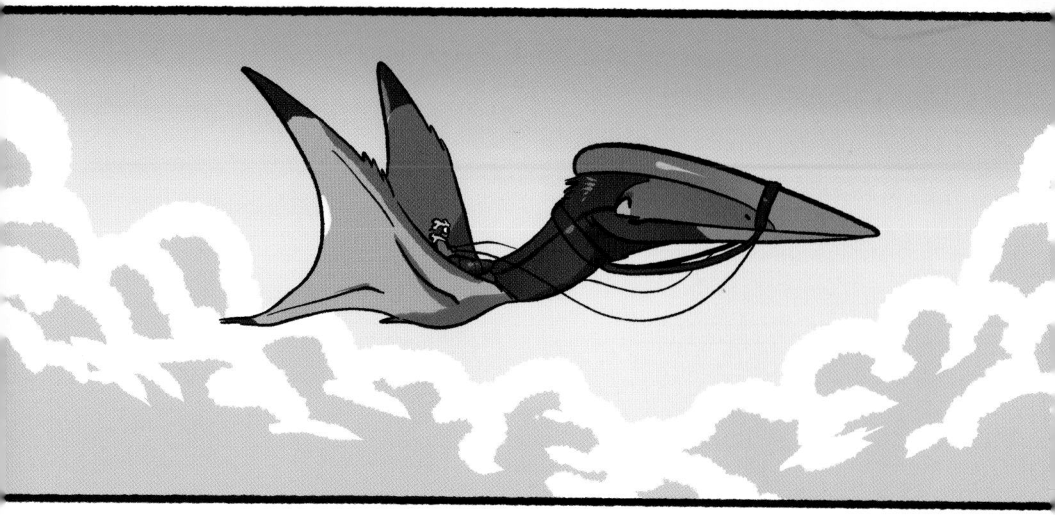

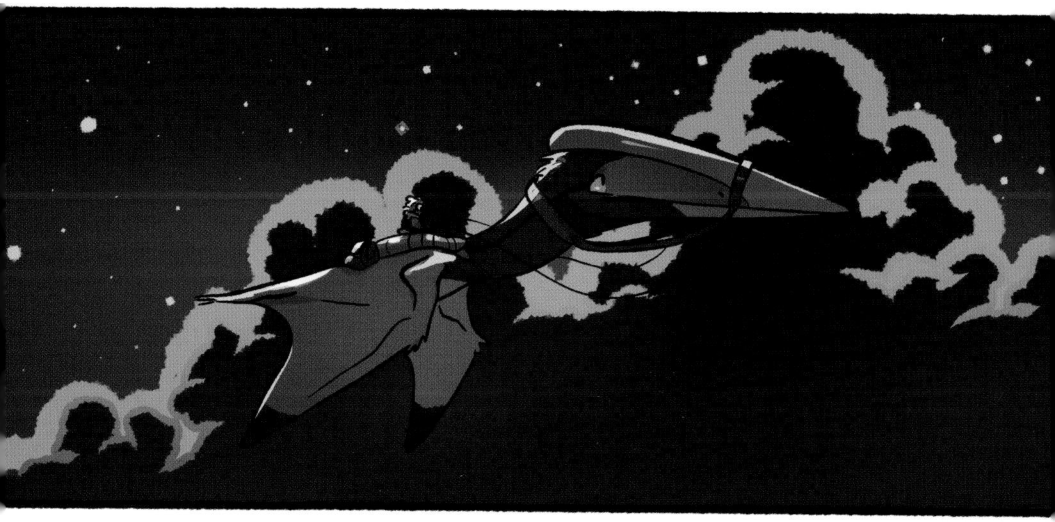

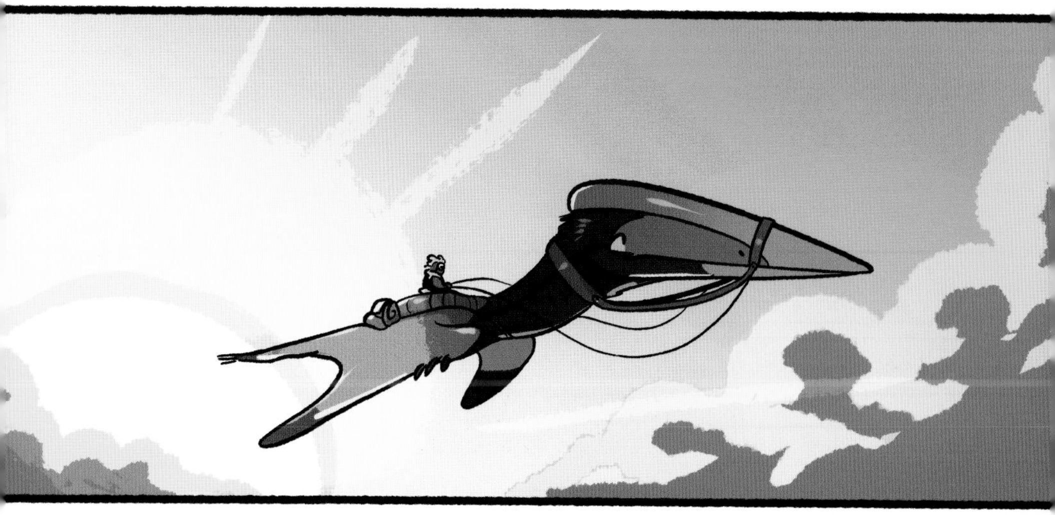

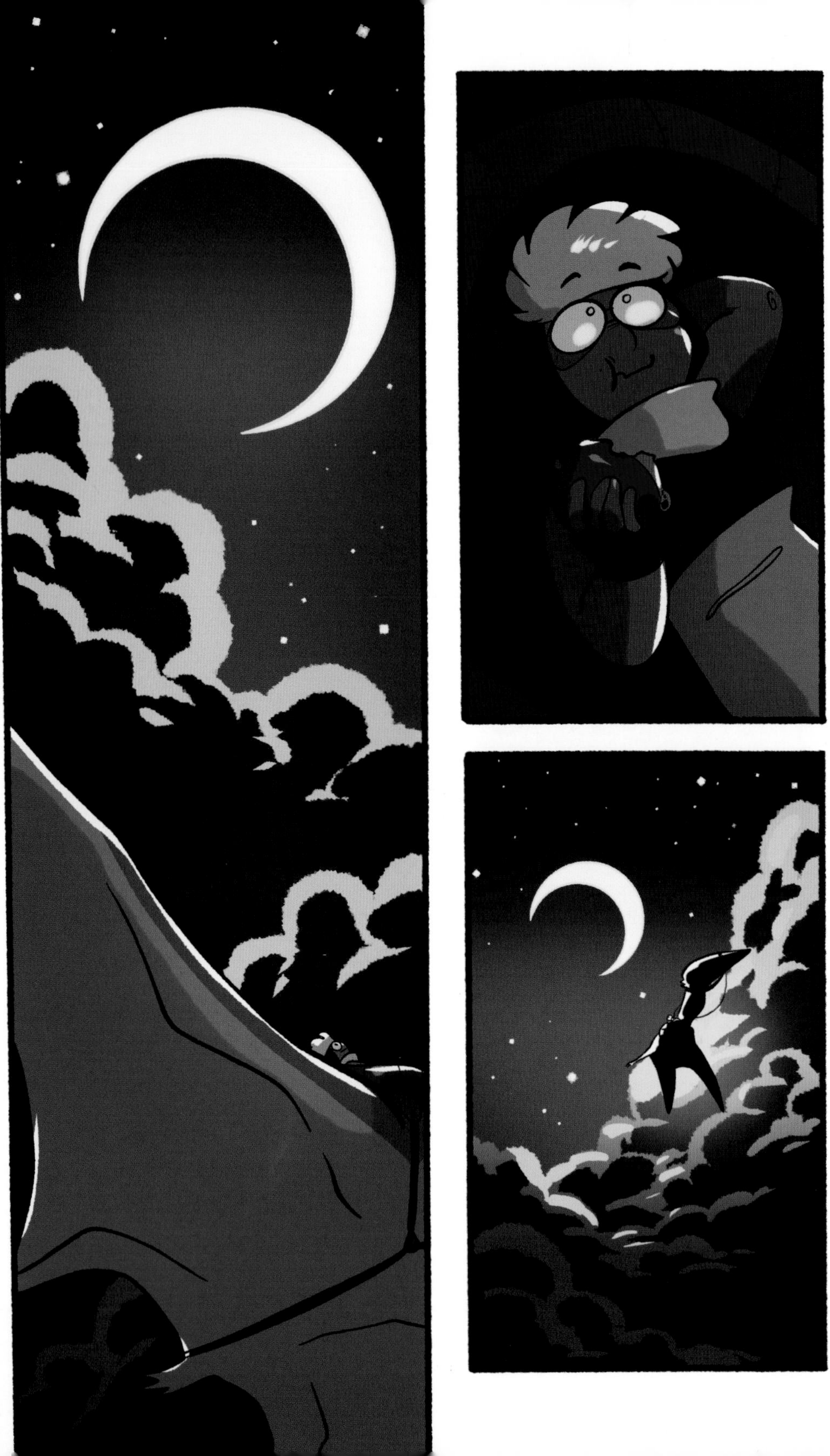

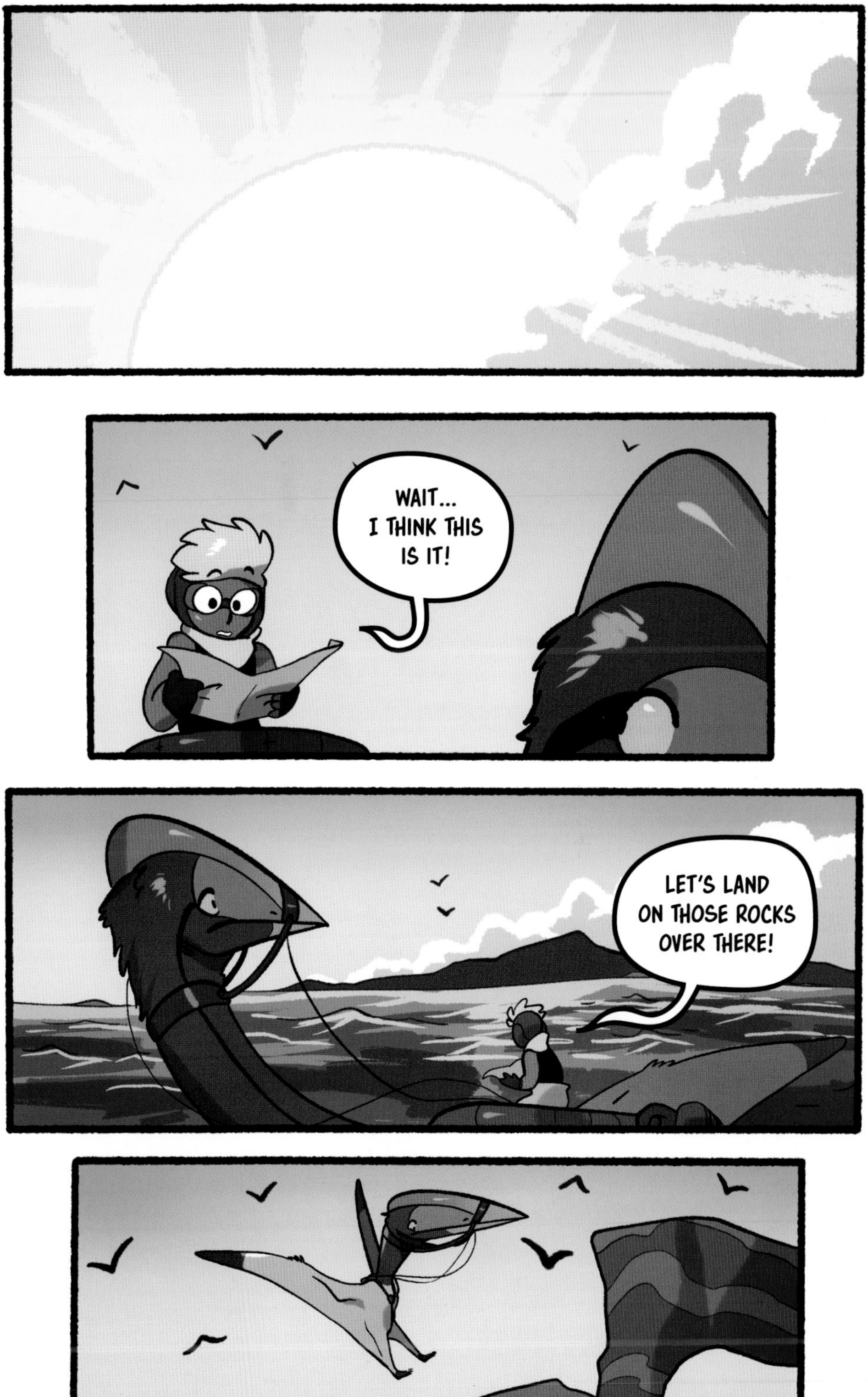
WAIT... I THINK THIS IS IT!
LET'S LAND ON THOSE ROCKS OVER THERE!

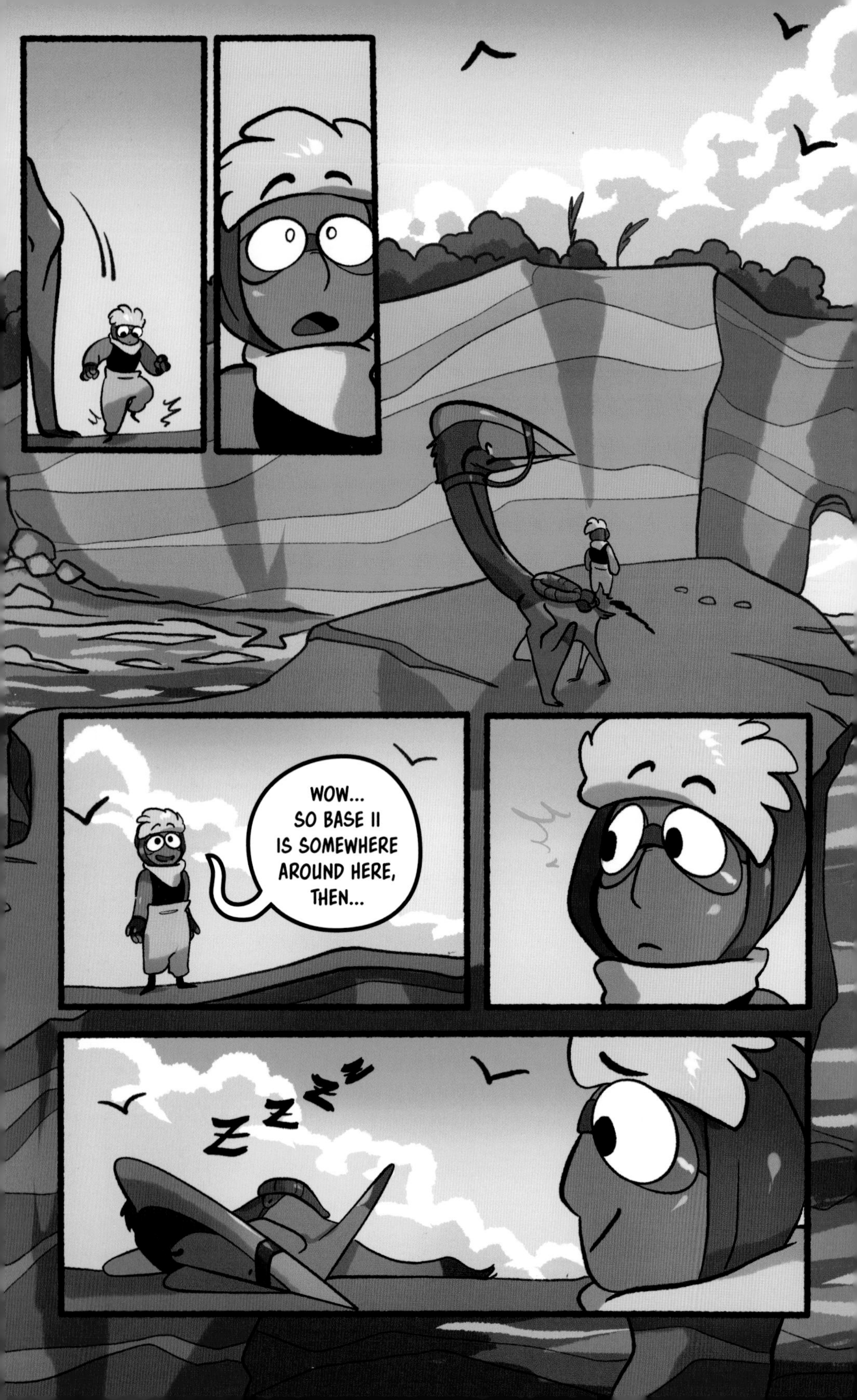
WOW...
SO BASE II
IS SOMEWHERE
AROUND HERE,
THEN...
ZZZZ

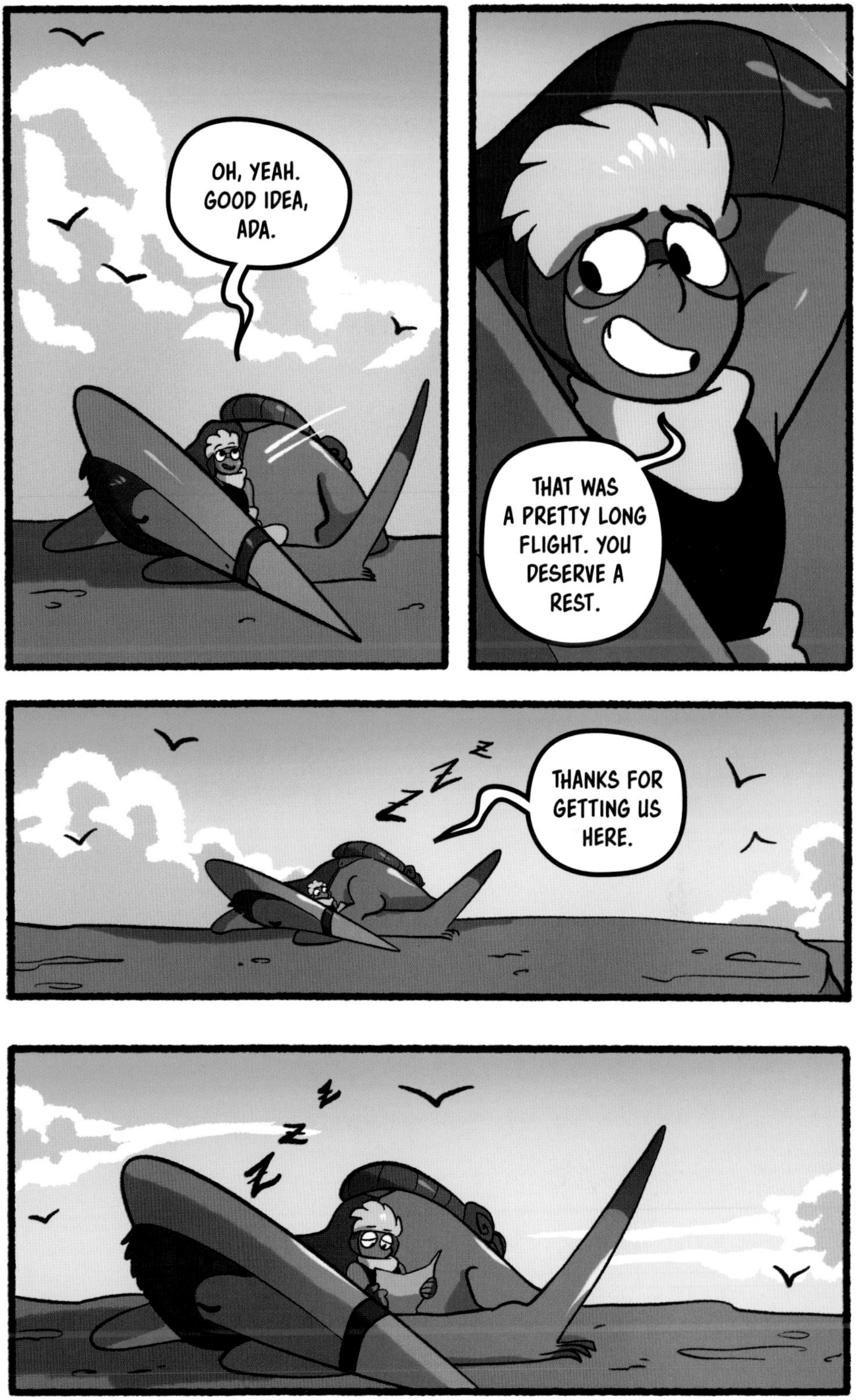
OH, YEAH. GOOD IDEA, ADA.
THAT WAS A PRETTY LONG FLIGHT. YOU DESERVE A REST.
Z Z Z
THANKS FOR GETTING US HERE.
Z Z Z

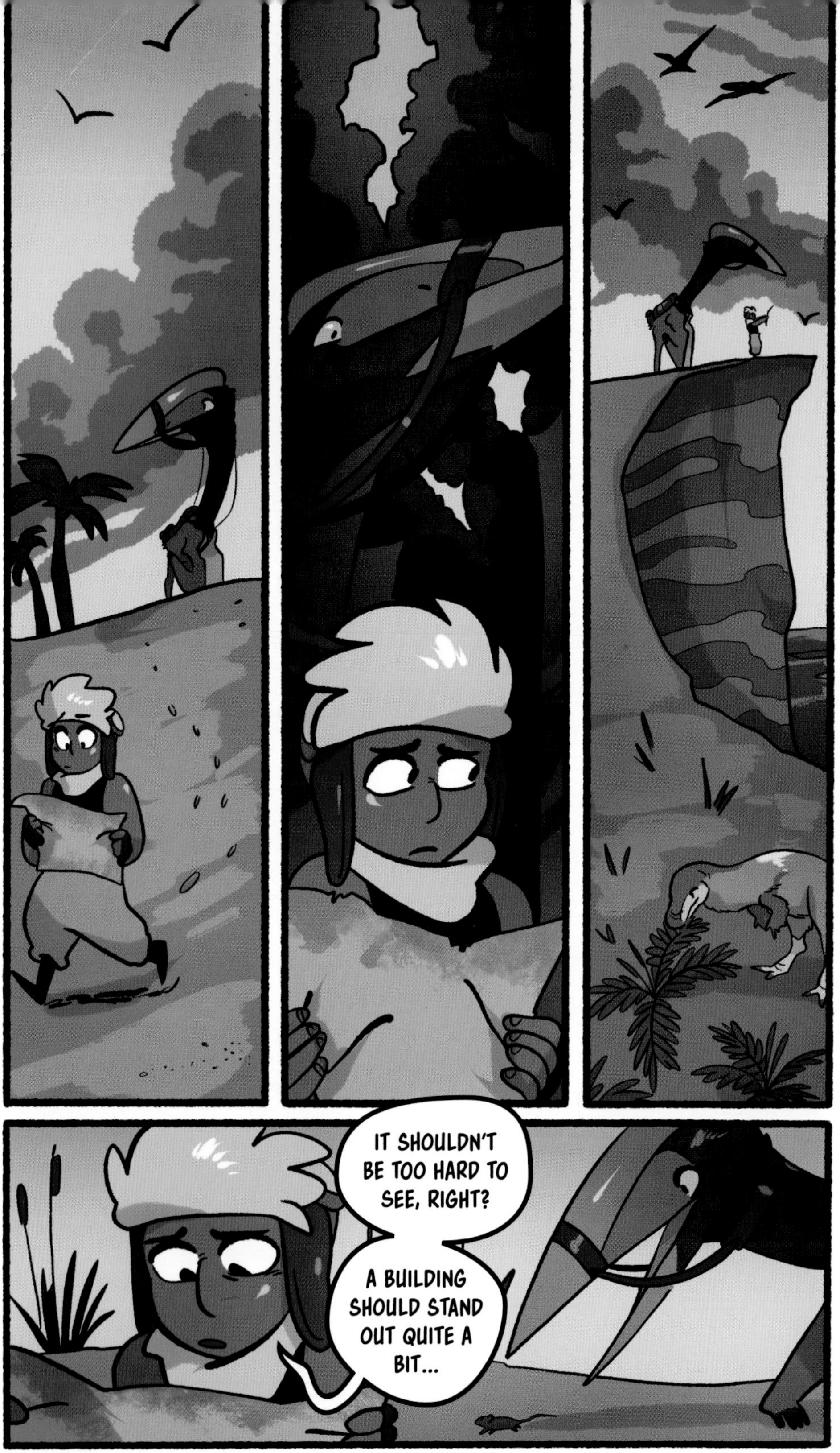
IT SHOULDN'T BE TOO HARD TO SEE, RIGHT?
A BUILDING SHOULD STAND OUT QUITE A BIT...

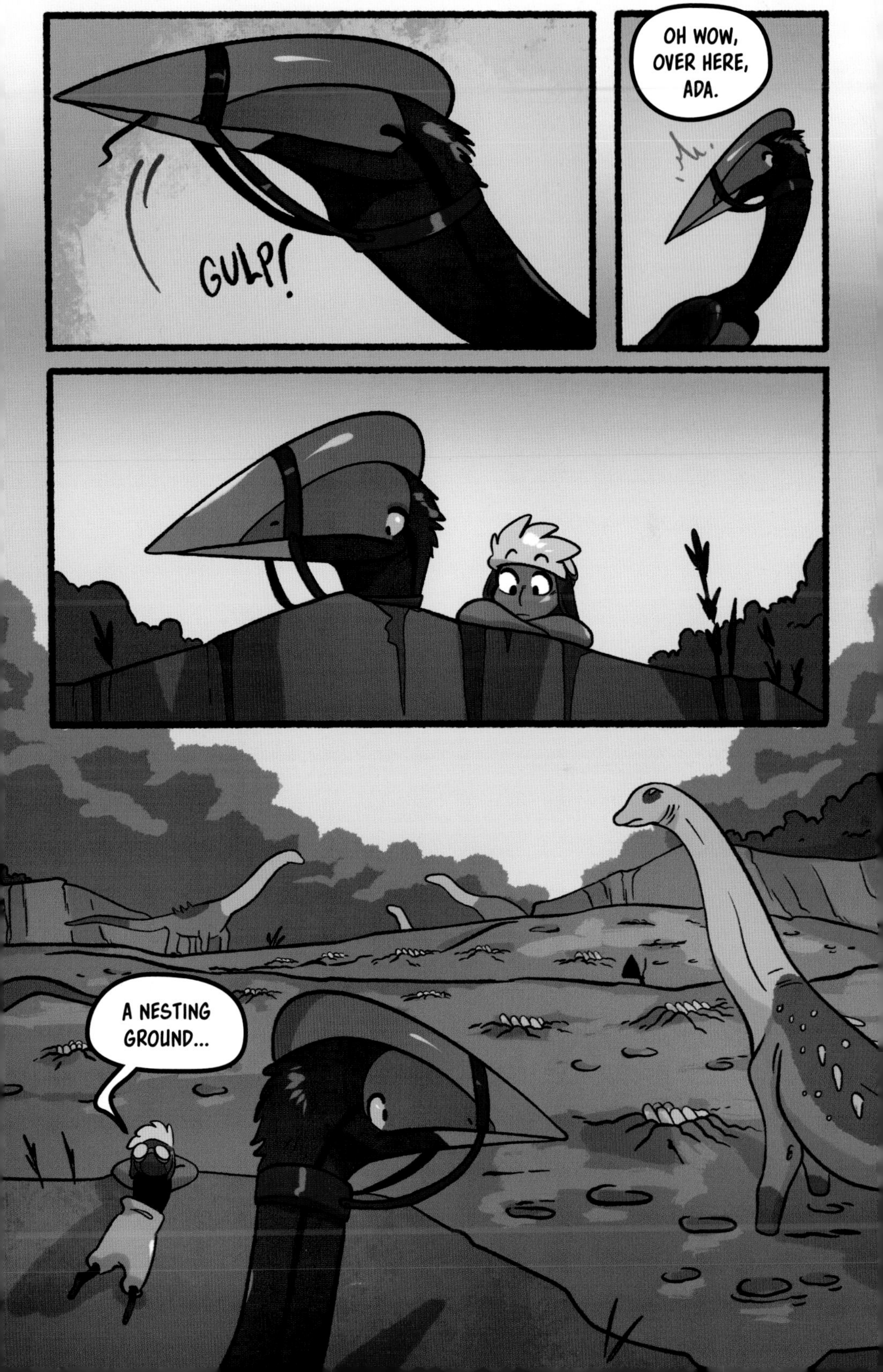
GULP!
OH WOW, OVER HERE, ADA.
A NESTING GROUND...

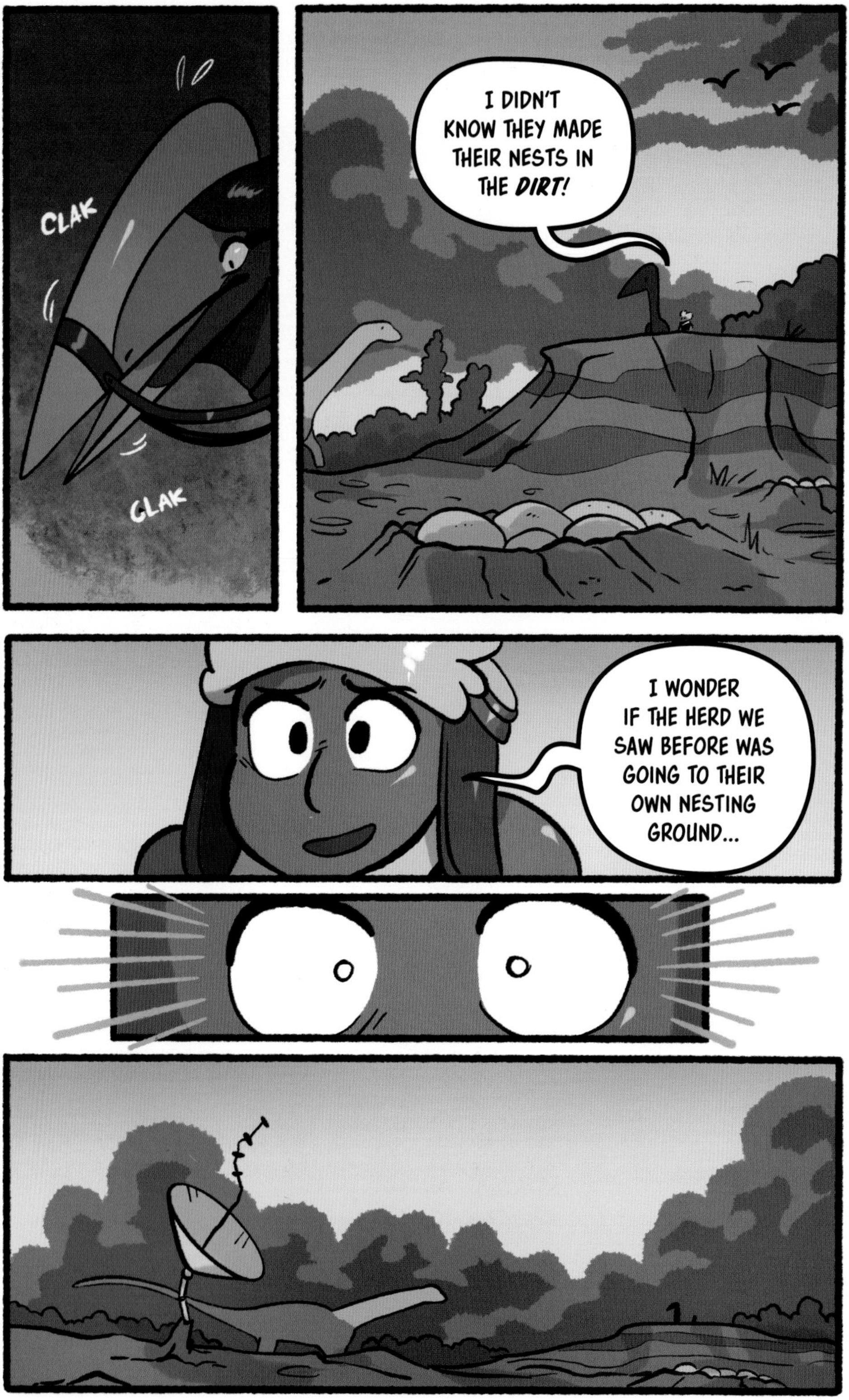
CLAK
CLAK
I DIDN'T KNOW THEY MADE THEIR NESTS IN THE *DIRT!*
I WONDER IF THE HERD WE SAW BEFORE WAS GOING TO THEIR OWN NESTING GROUND...

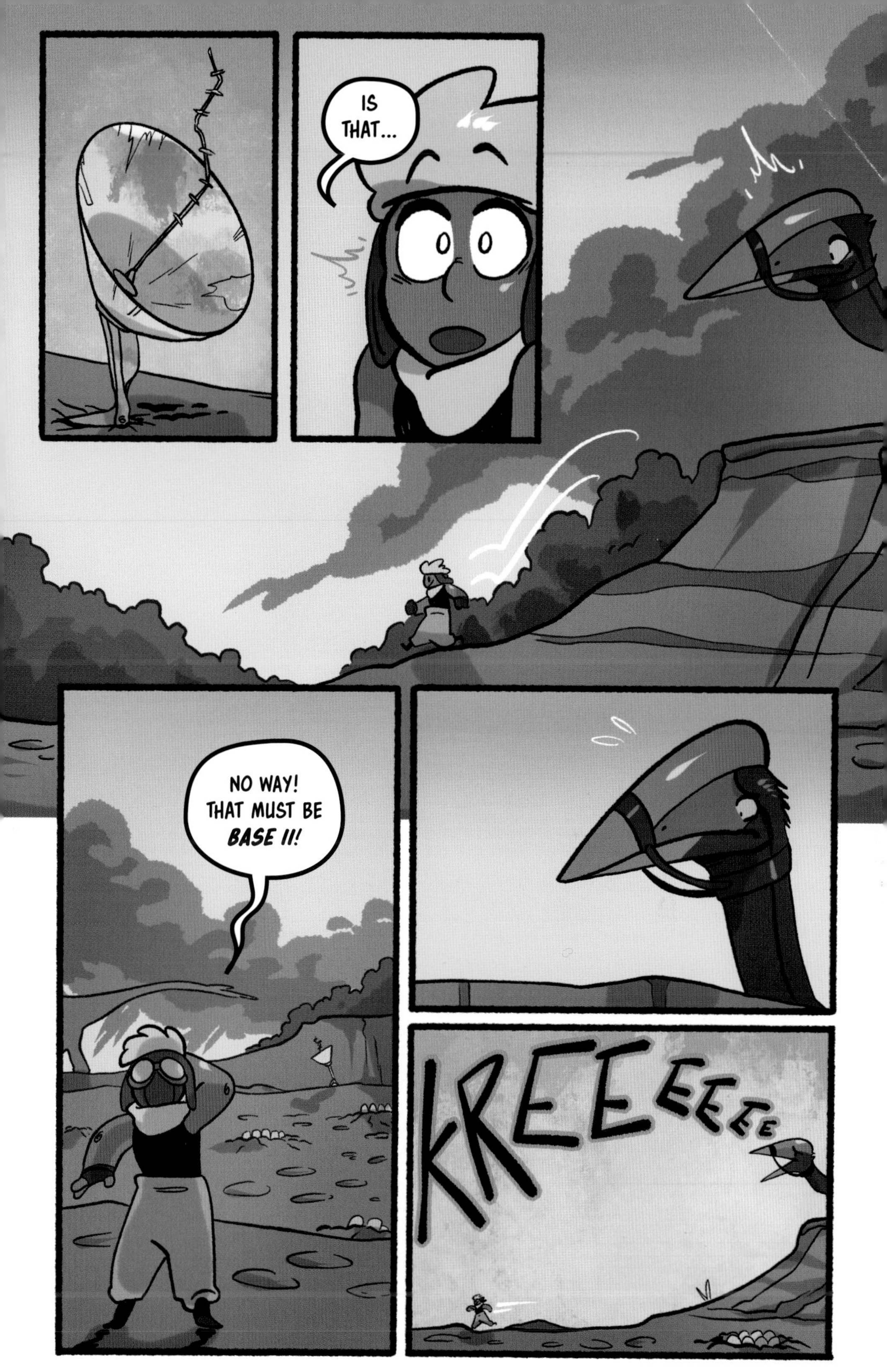
IS THAT...
NO WAY! THAT MUST BE BASE II!
KREEEEEEE

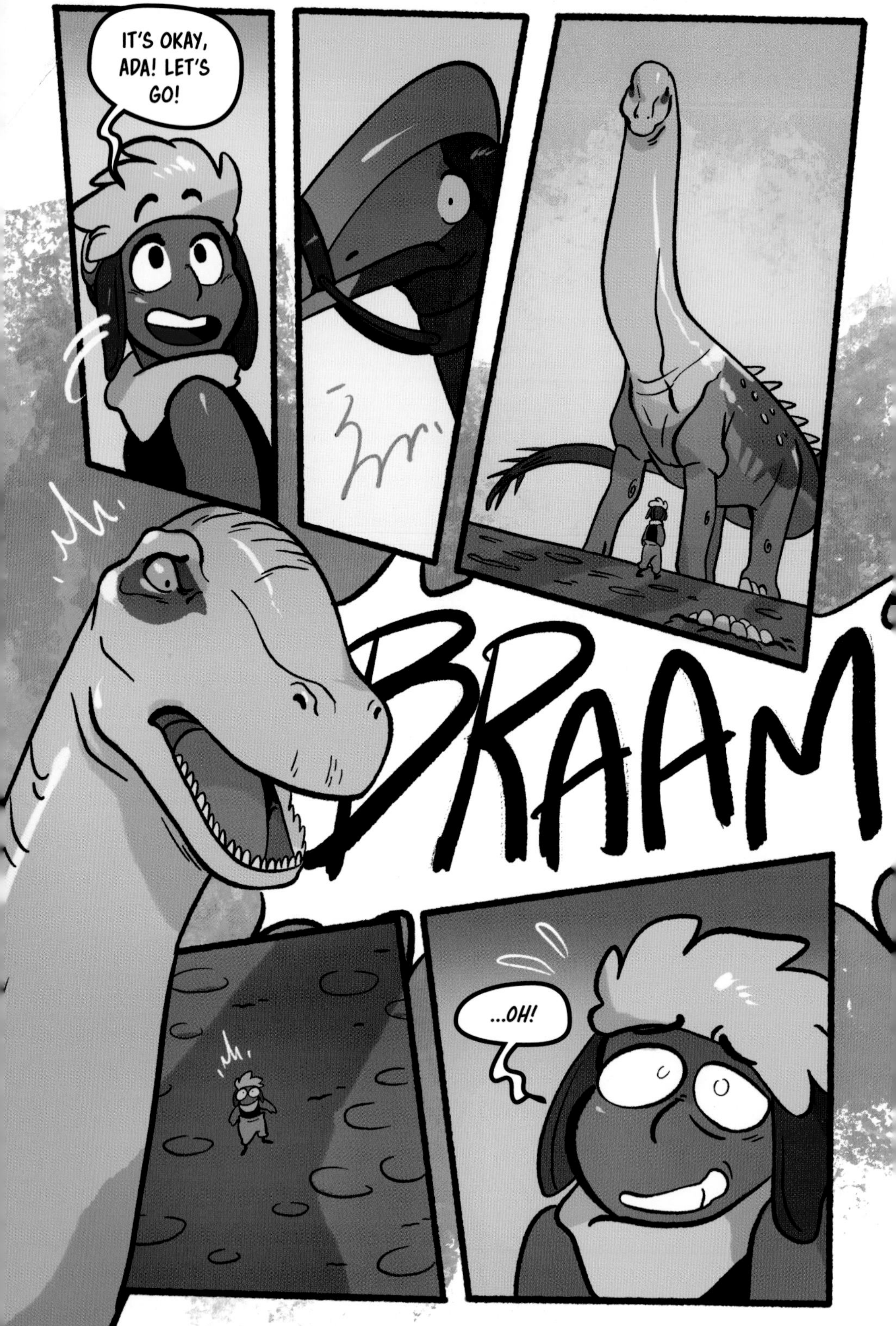
IT'S OKAY, ADA! LET'S GO!
BRAAM
...OH!

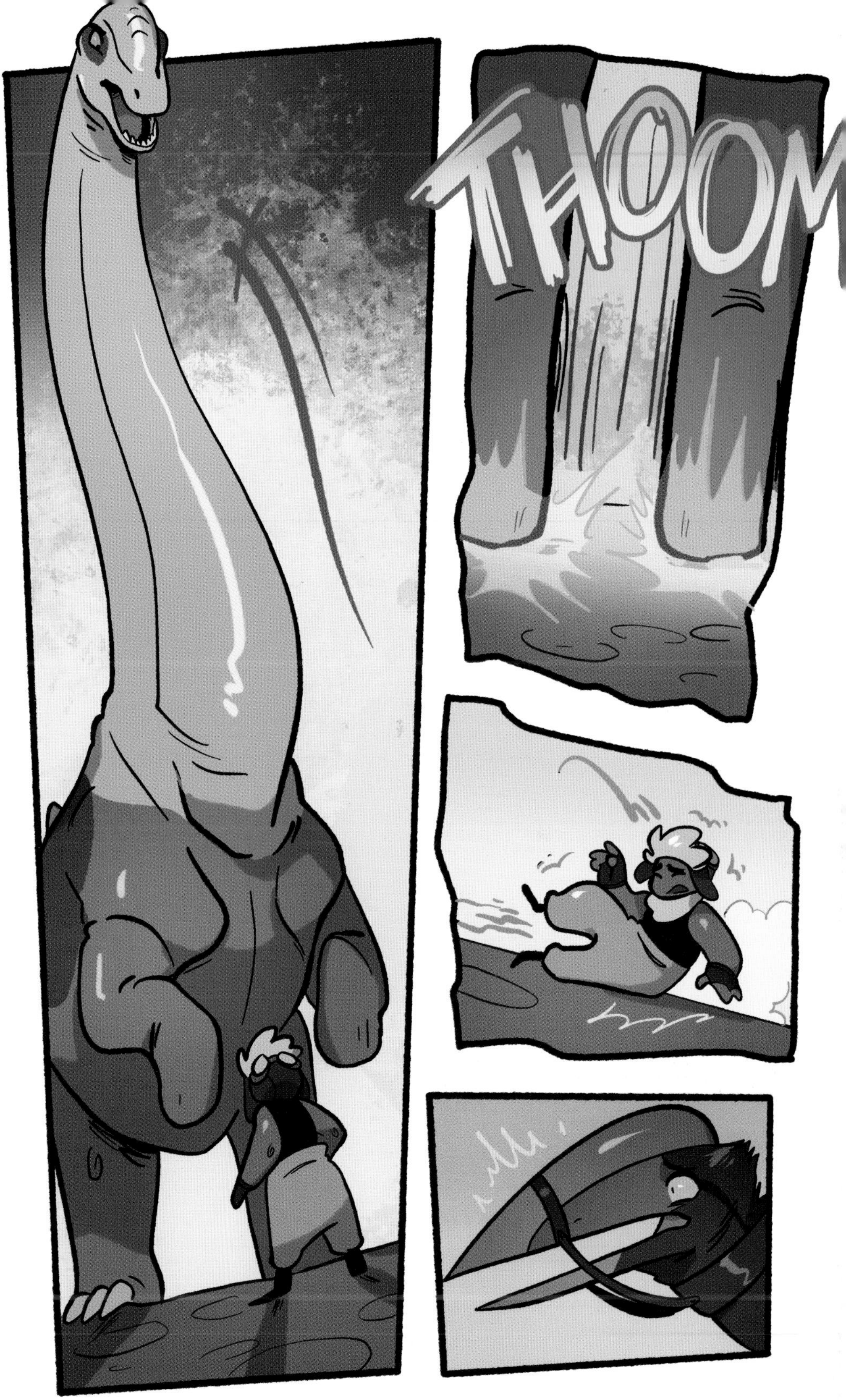
THOOM

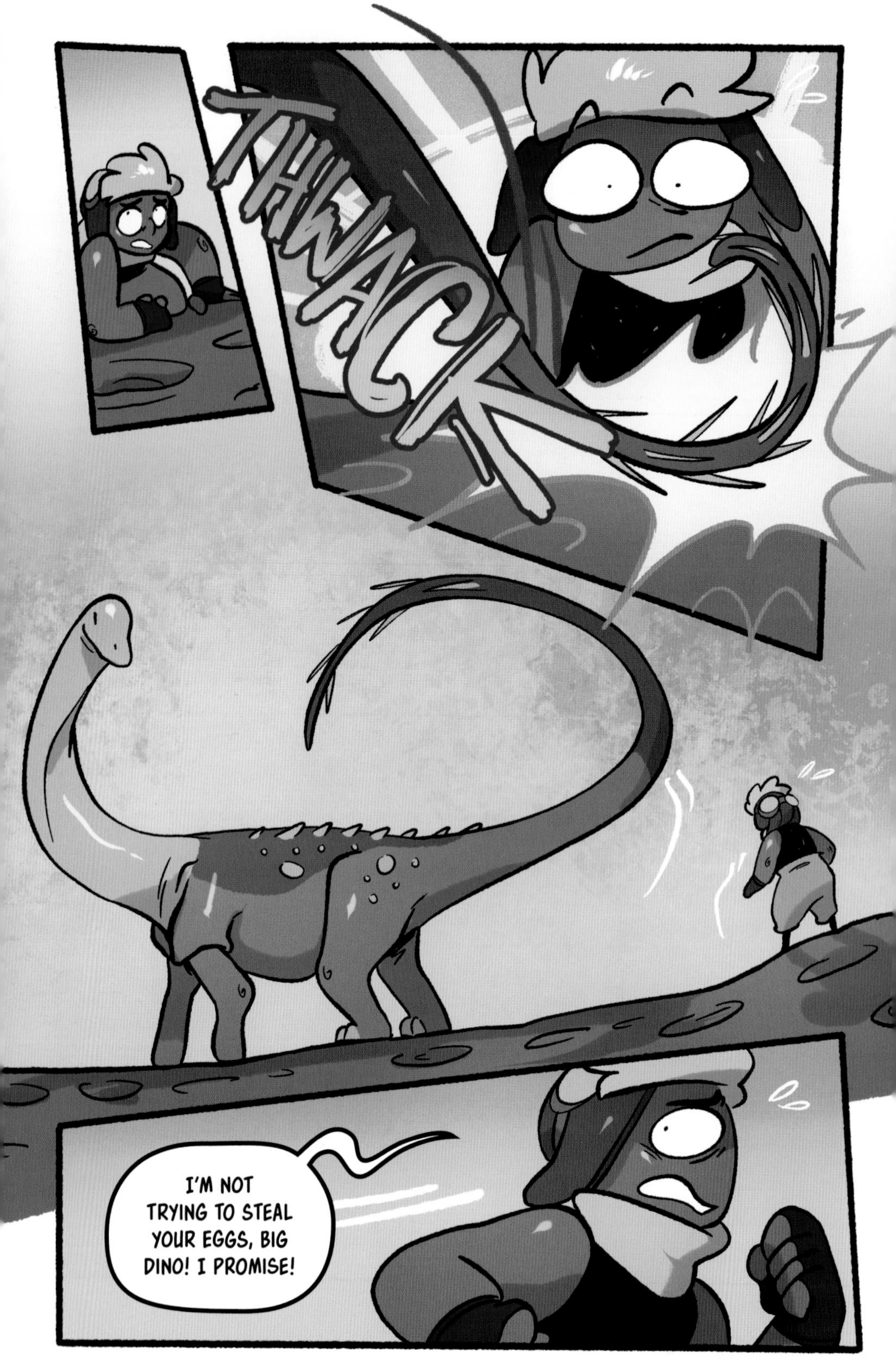
THWACK
I'M NOT TRYING TO STEAL YOUR EGGS, BIG DINO! I PROMISE!

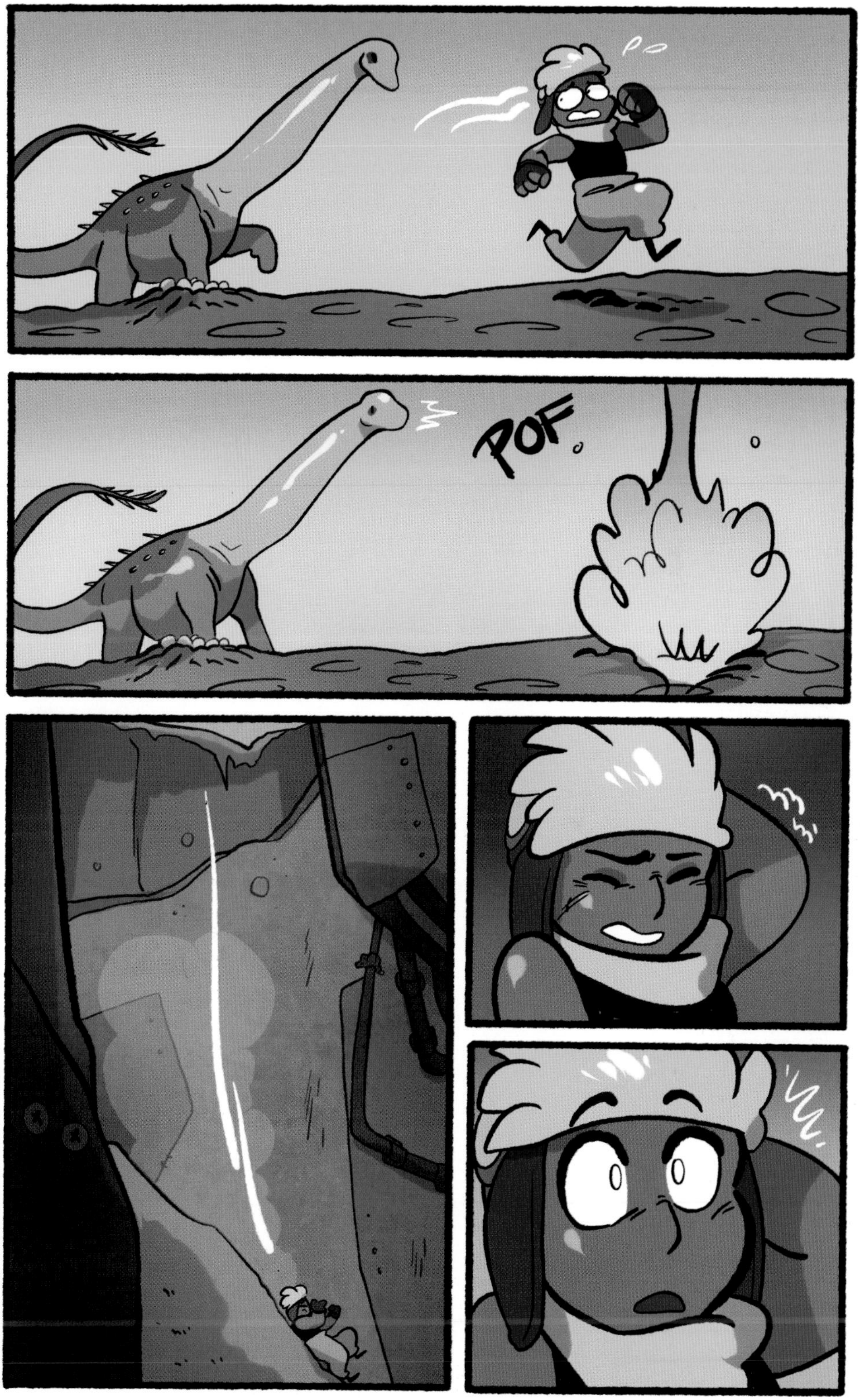
POF

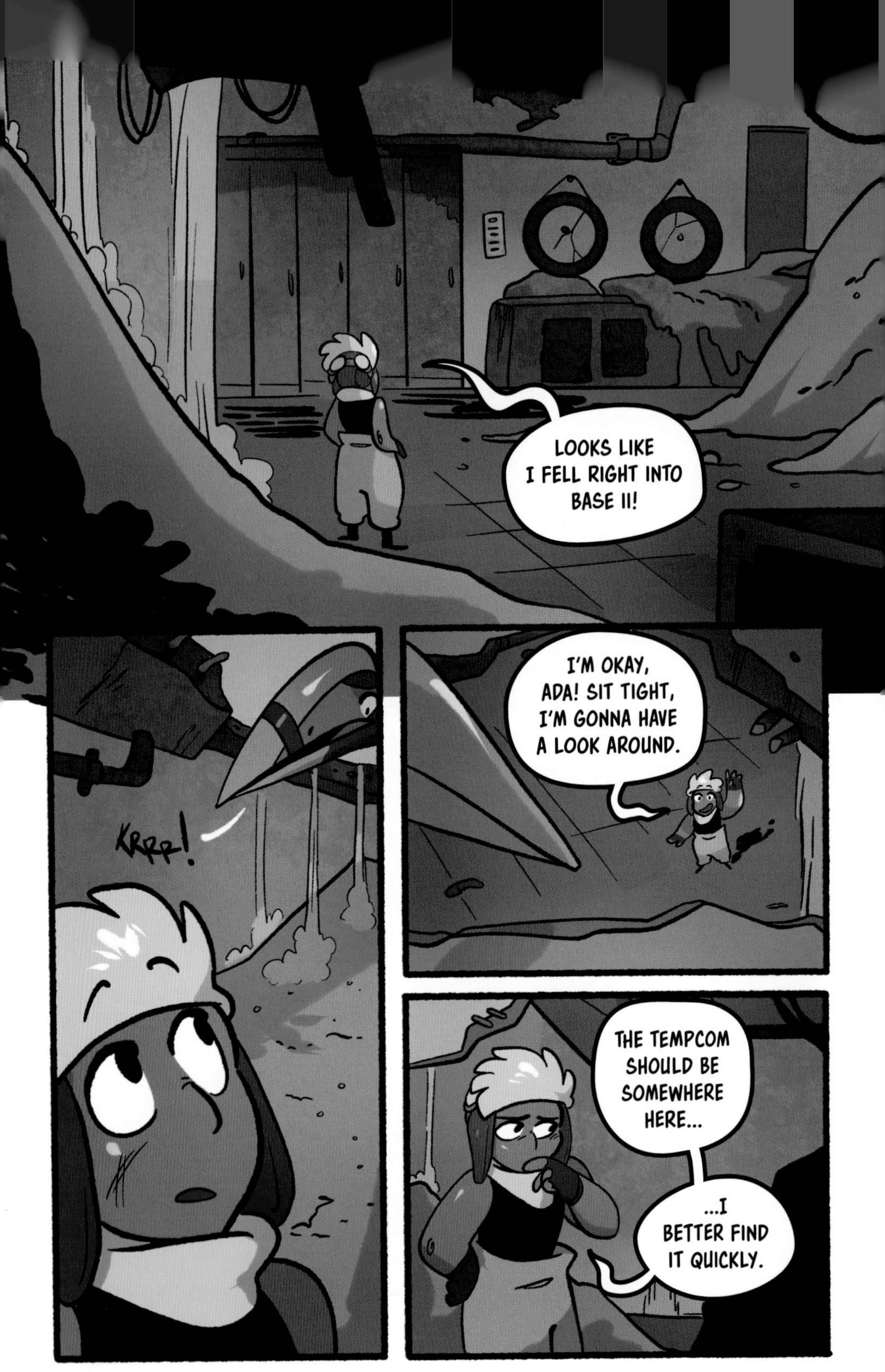
LOOKS LIKE I FELL RIGHT INTO BASE II!
KRRR!
I'M OKAY, ADA! SIT TIGHT, I'M GONNA HAVE A LOOK AROUND.
THE TEMPCOM SHOULD BE SOMEWHERE HERE...
...I BETTER FIND IT QUICKLY.

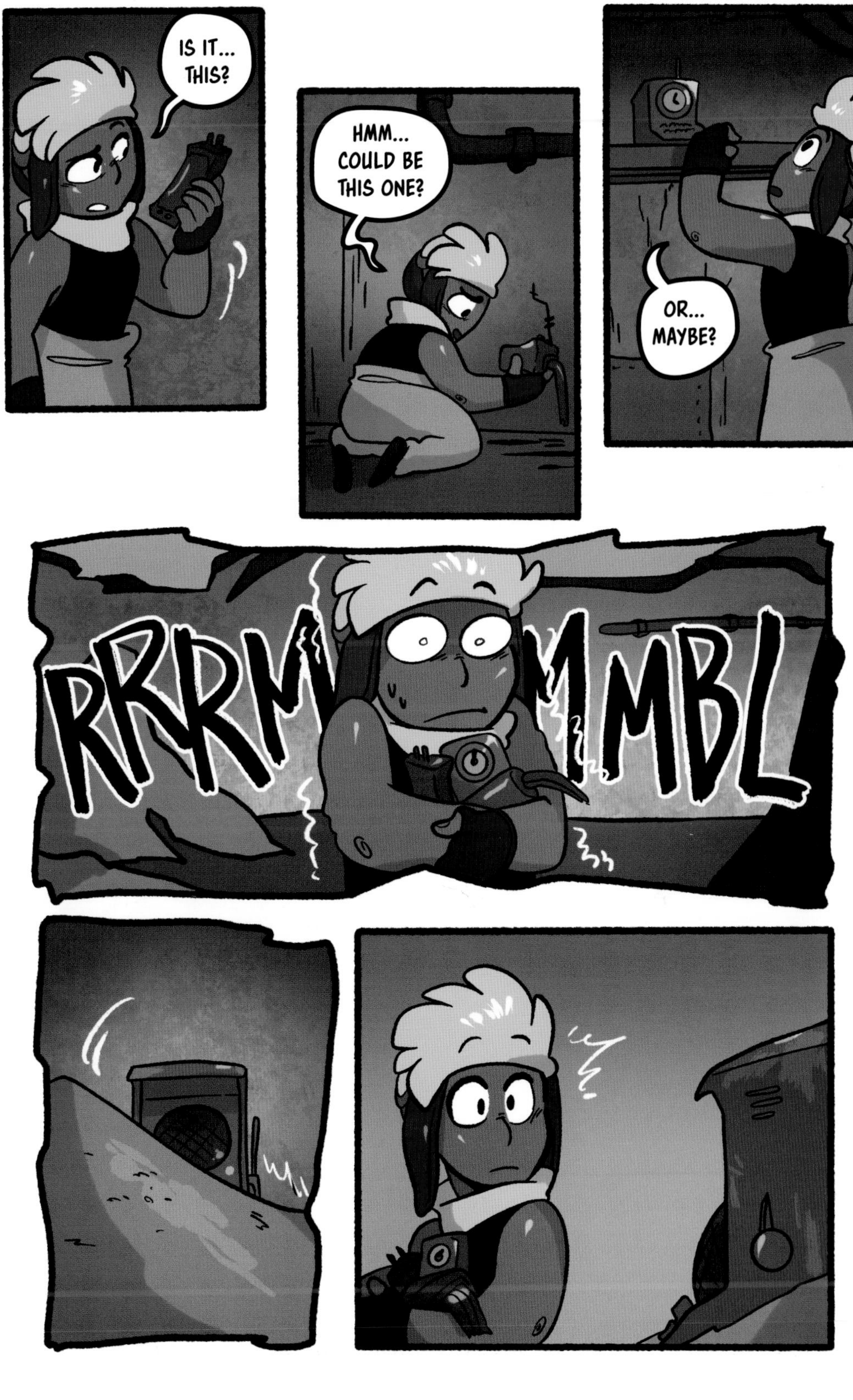
IS IT... THIS?
HMM... COULD BE THIS ONE?
OR... MAYBE?
RRRMMMBL

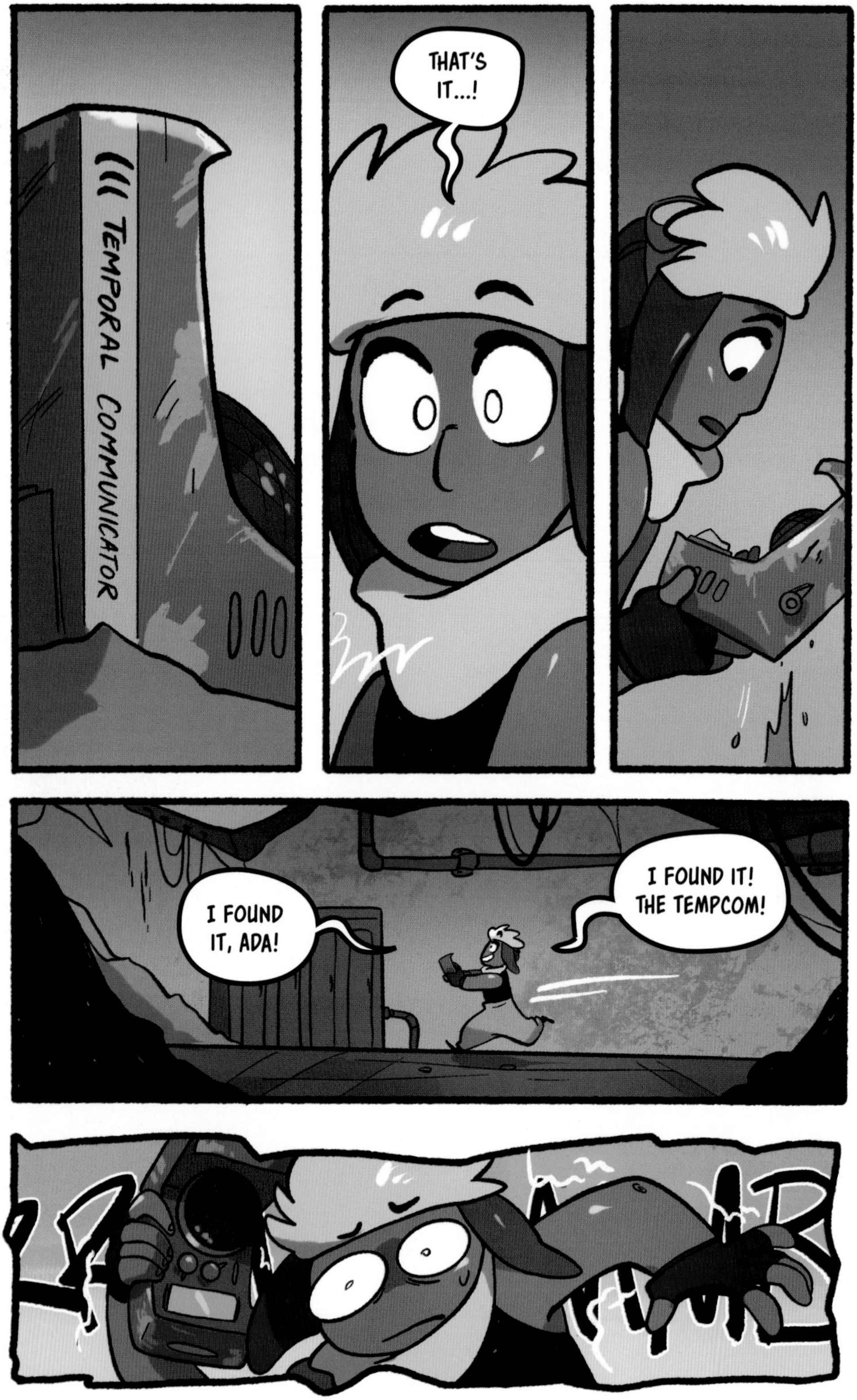
TEMPORAL COMMUNICATOR
THAT'S IT...!
I FOUND IT, ADA!
I FOUND IT! THE TEMPCOM!

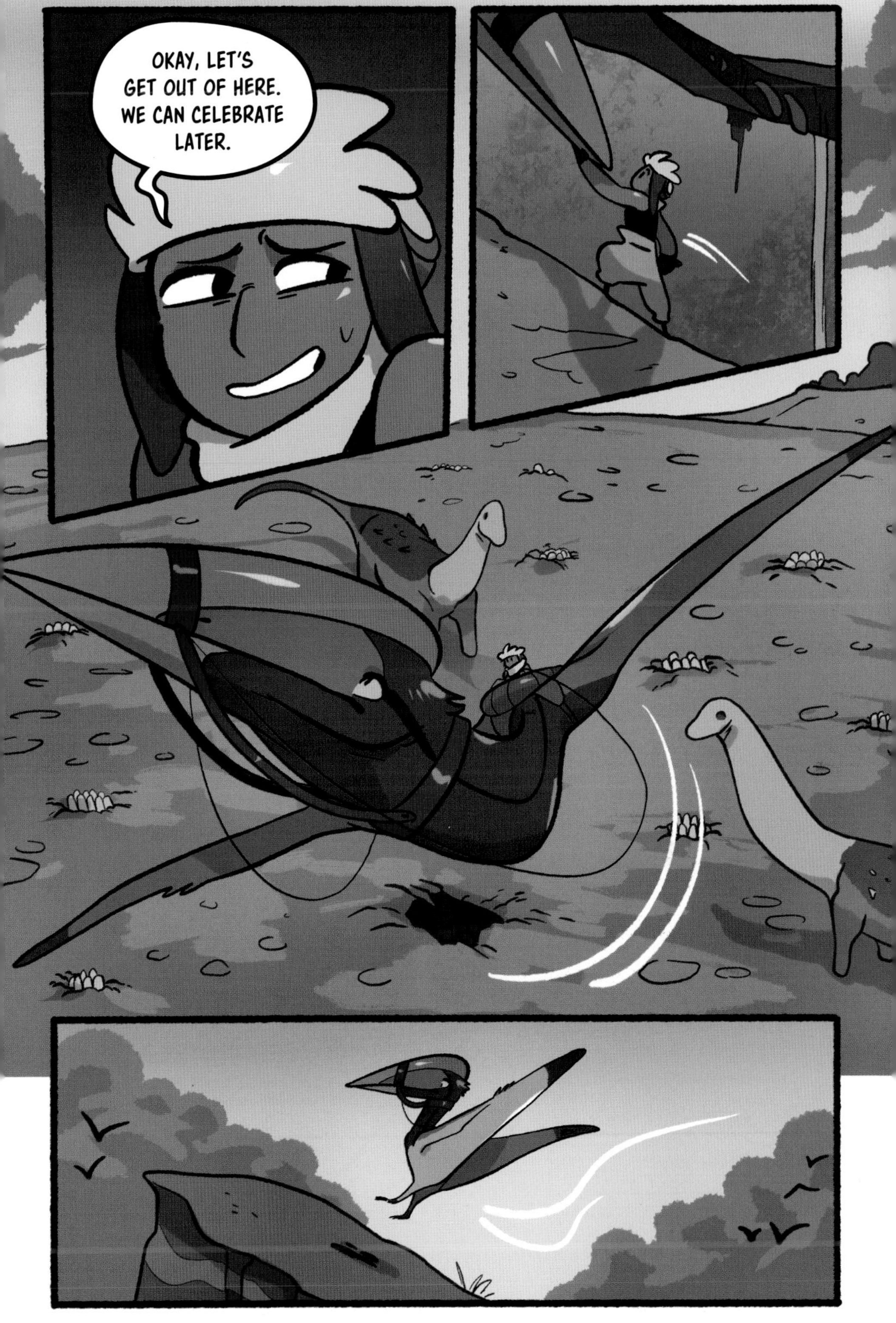
OKAY, LET'S GET OUT OF HERE. WE CAN CELEBRATE LATER.

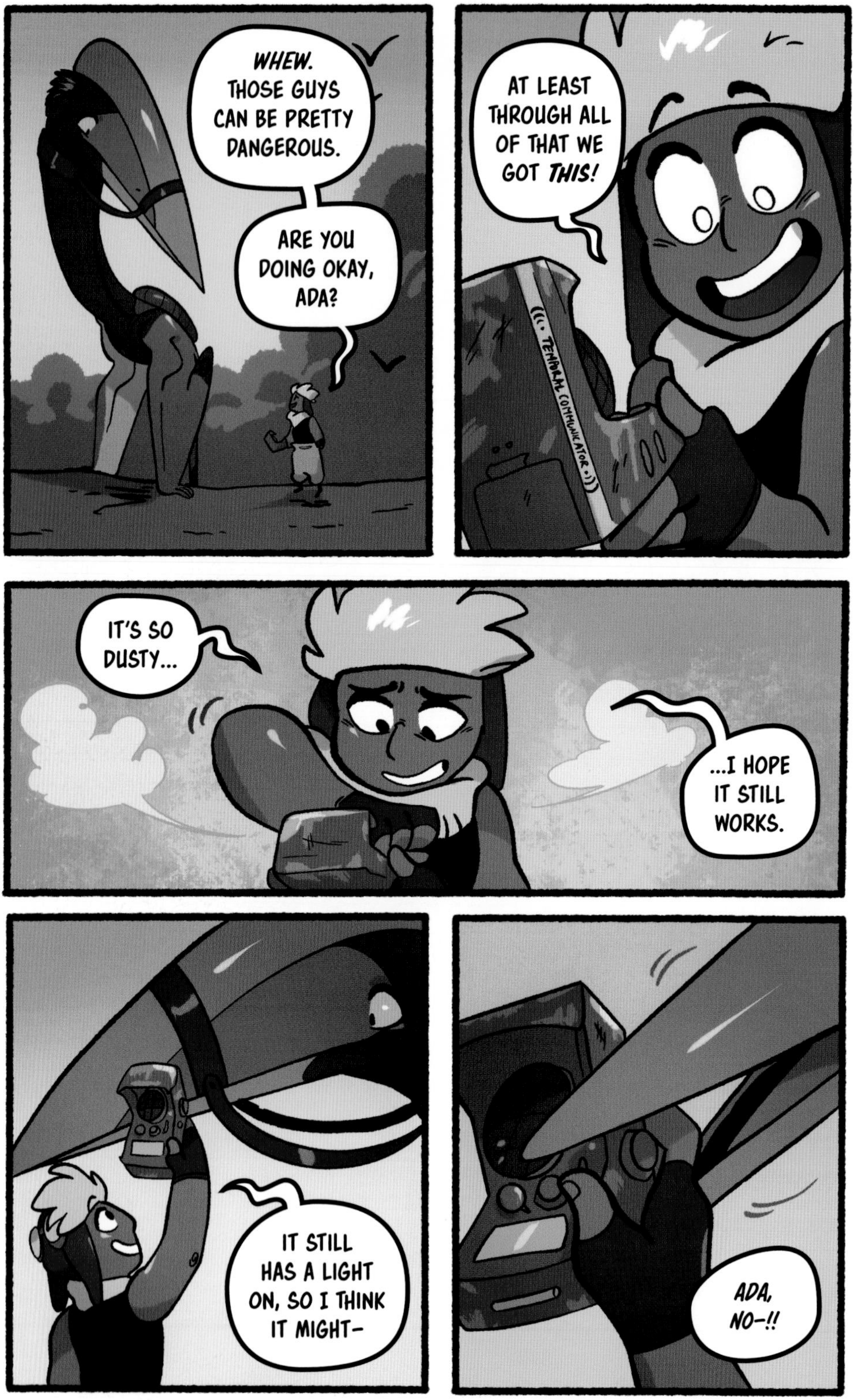
WHEW. THOSE GUYS CAN BE PRETTY DANGEROUS.
ARE YOU DOING OKAY, ADA?
AT LEAST THROUGH ALL OF THAT WE GOT THIS!
TEMPORAL COMMUNICATOR
IT'S SO DUSTY...
...I HOPE IT STILL WORKS.
IT STILL HAS A LIGHT ON, SO I THINK IT MIGHT-
ADA, NO-!!

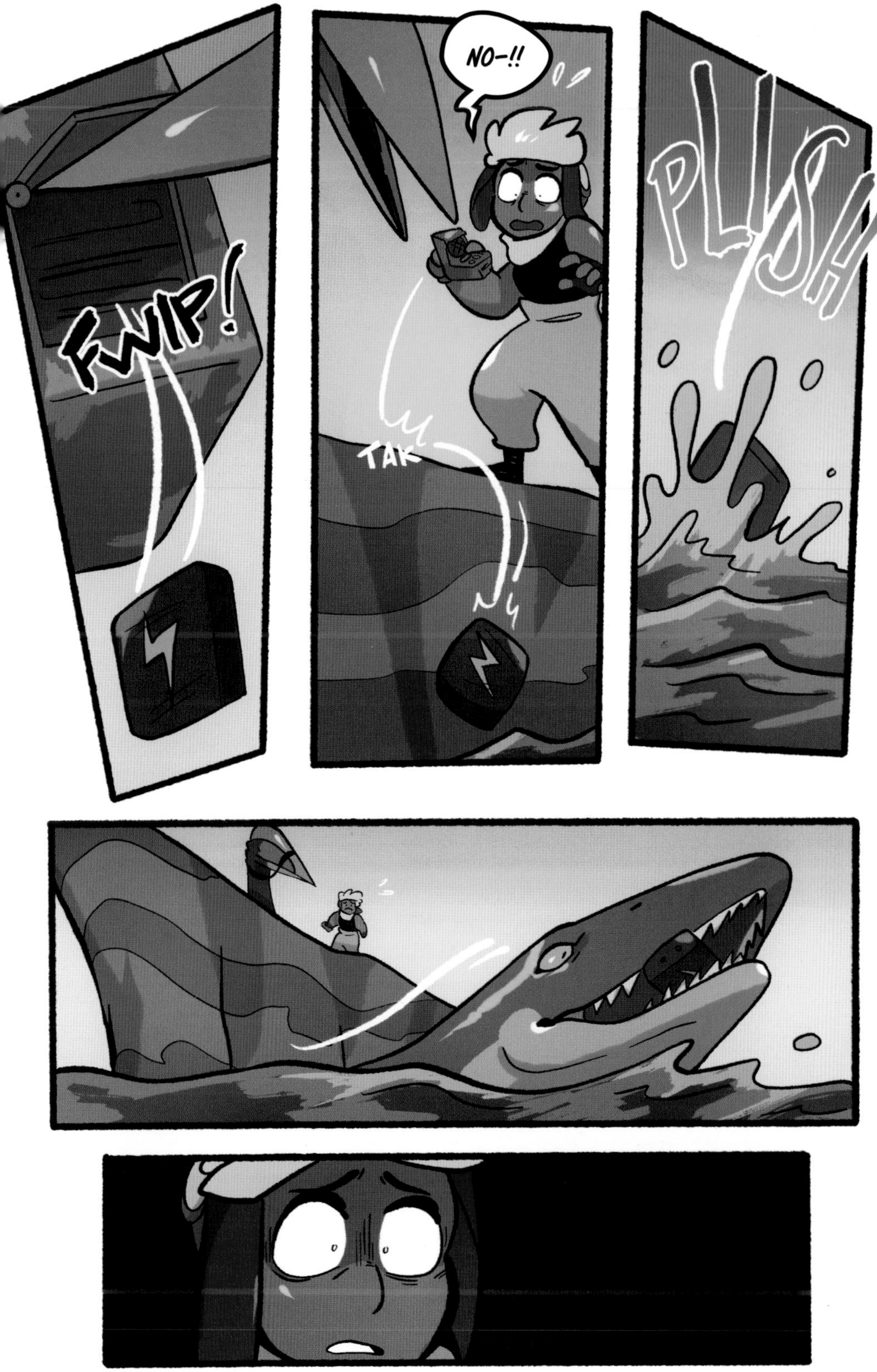
FWIP!
NO-!!
TAK
PLISH

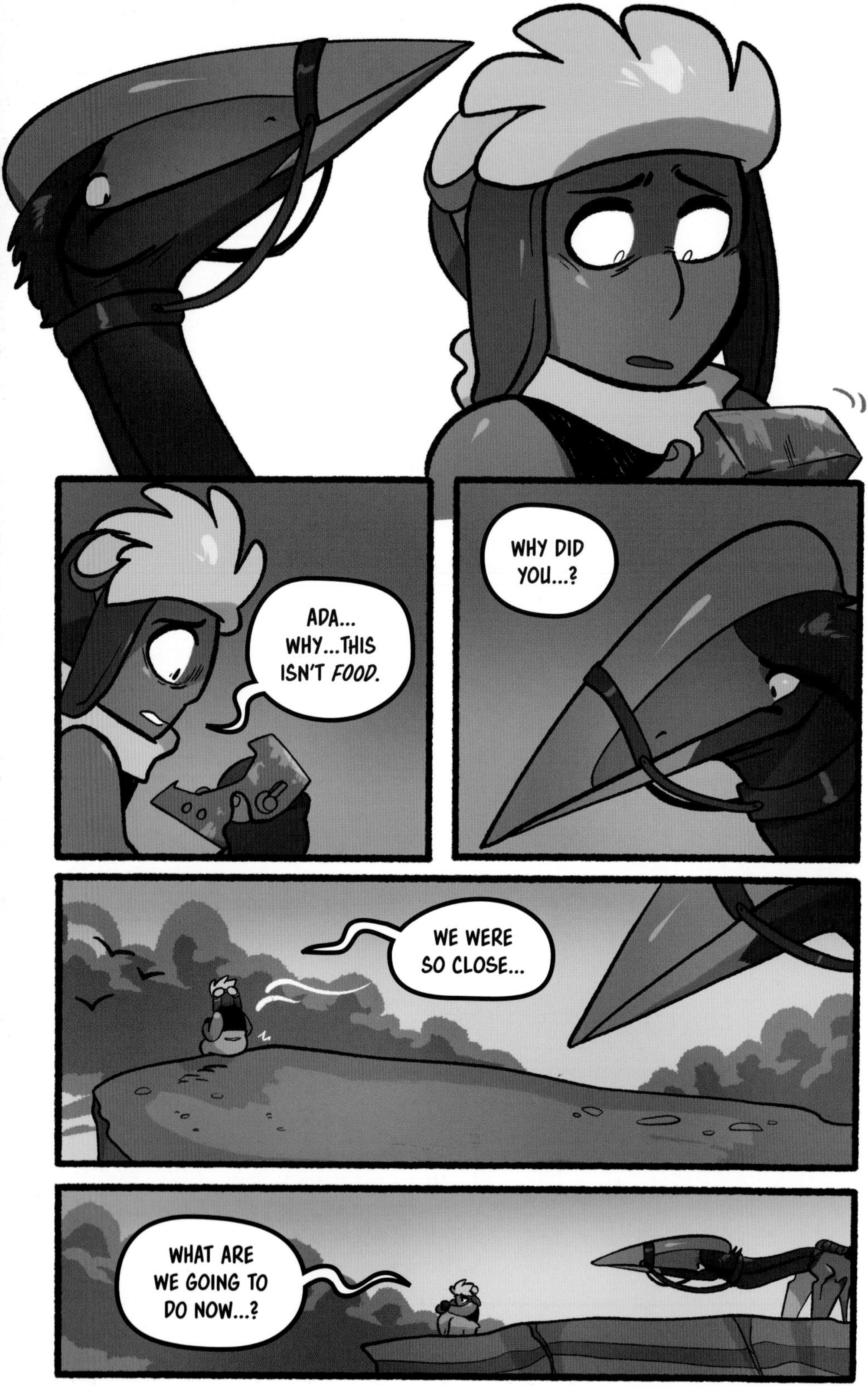
ADA... WHY...THIS ISN'T *FOOD.*
WHY DID YOU...?
WE WERE SO CLOSE...
WHAT ARE WE GOING TO DO NOW...?

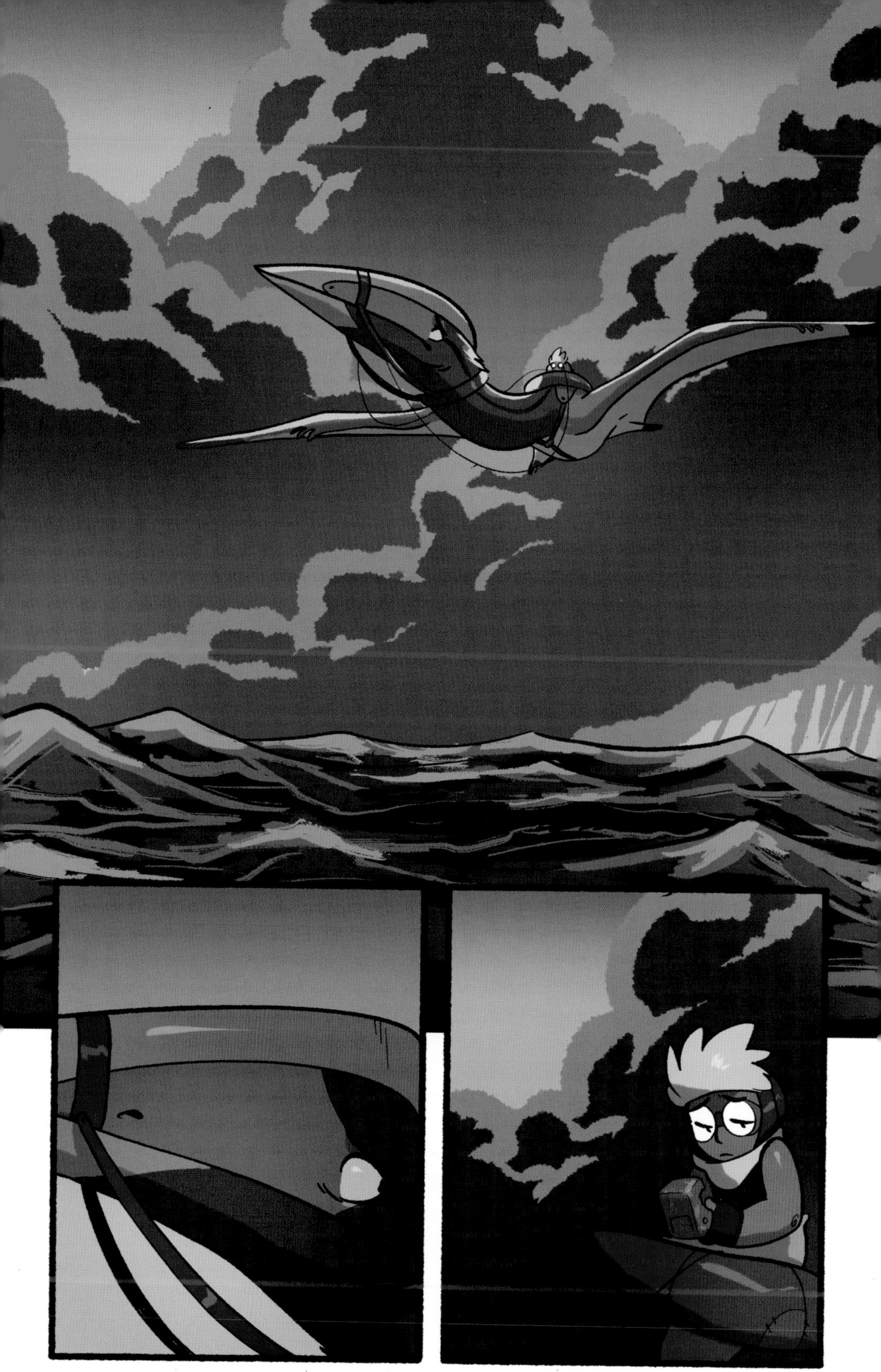

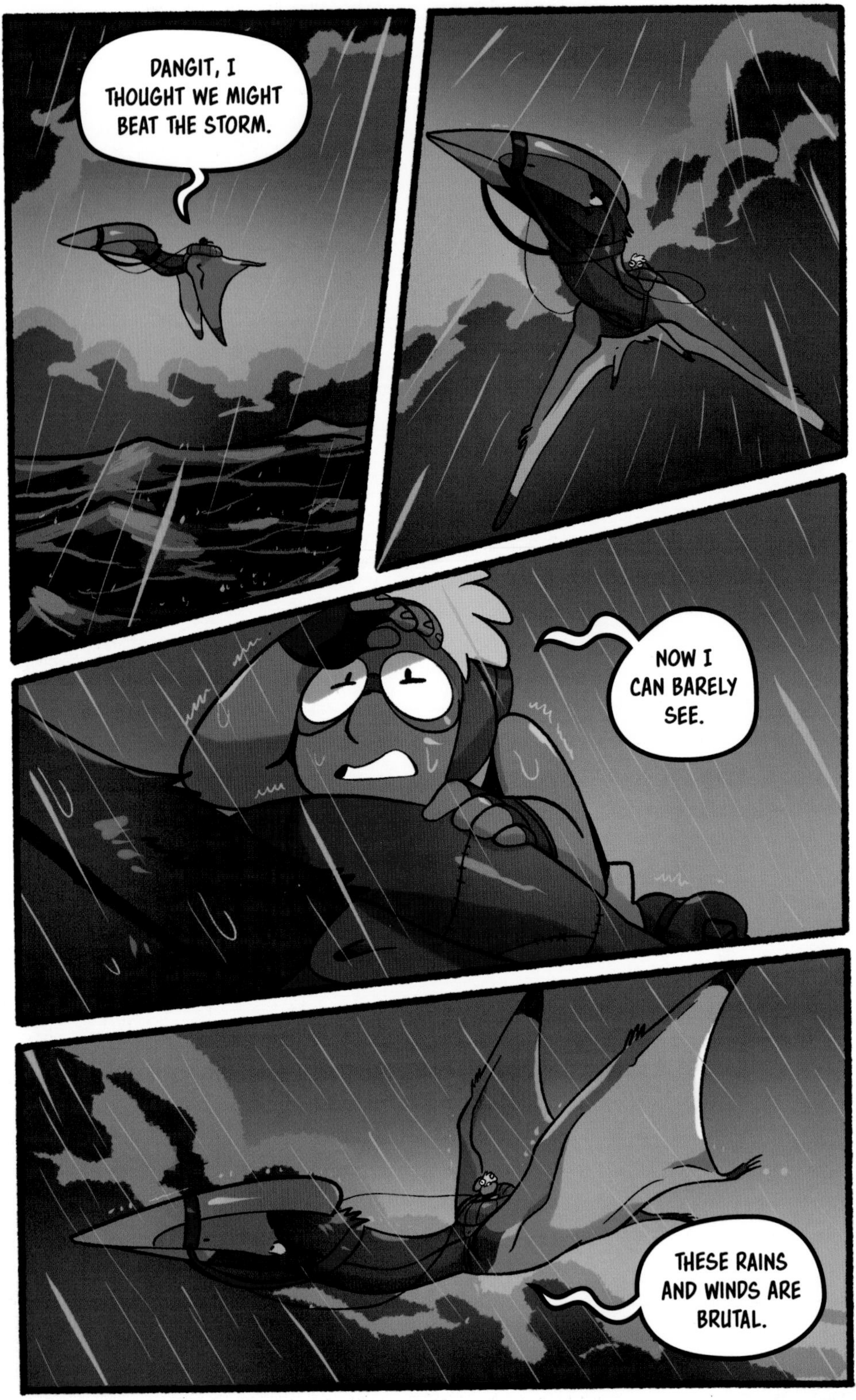
DANGIT, I THOUGHT WE MIGHT BEAT THE STORM.
NOW I CAN BARELY SEE.
THESE RAINS AND WINDS ARE BRUTAL.

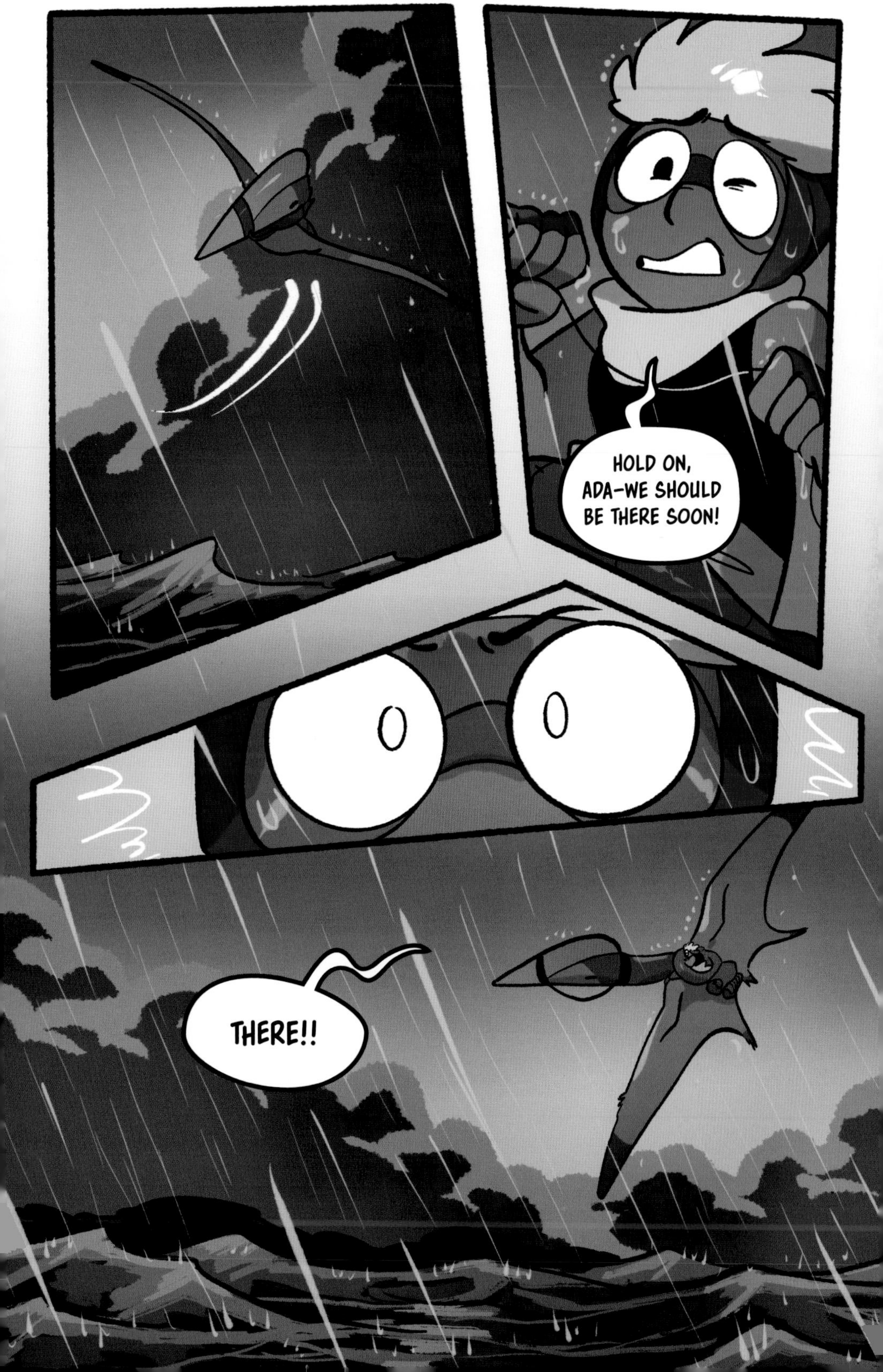
HOLD ON, ADA—WE SHOULD BE THERE SOON!
THERE!!

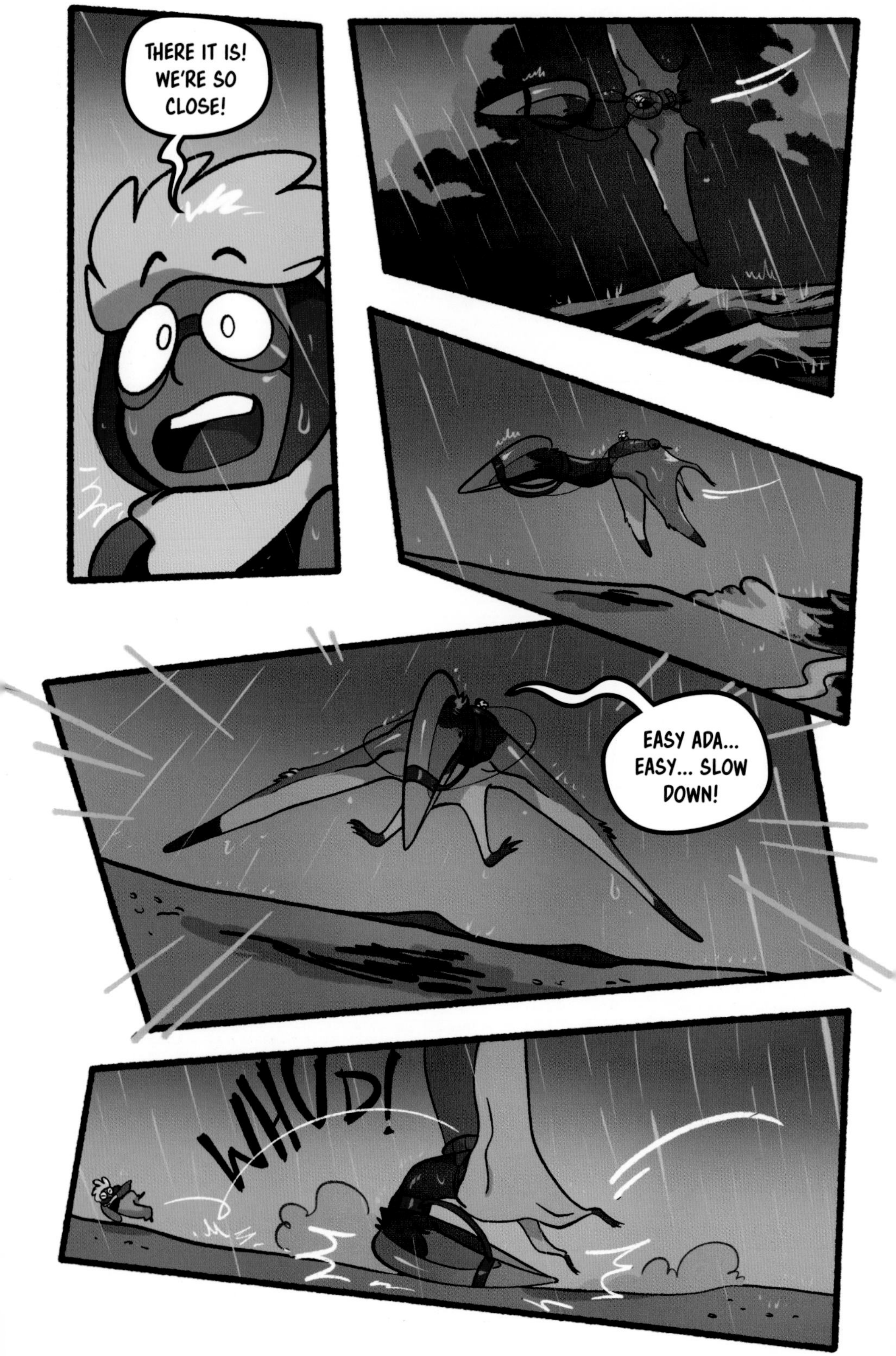
THERE IT IS! WE'RE SO CLOSE!
EASY ADA... EASY... SLOW DOWN!
WHUD!

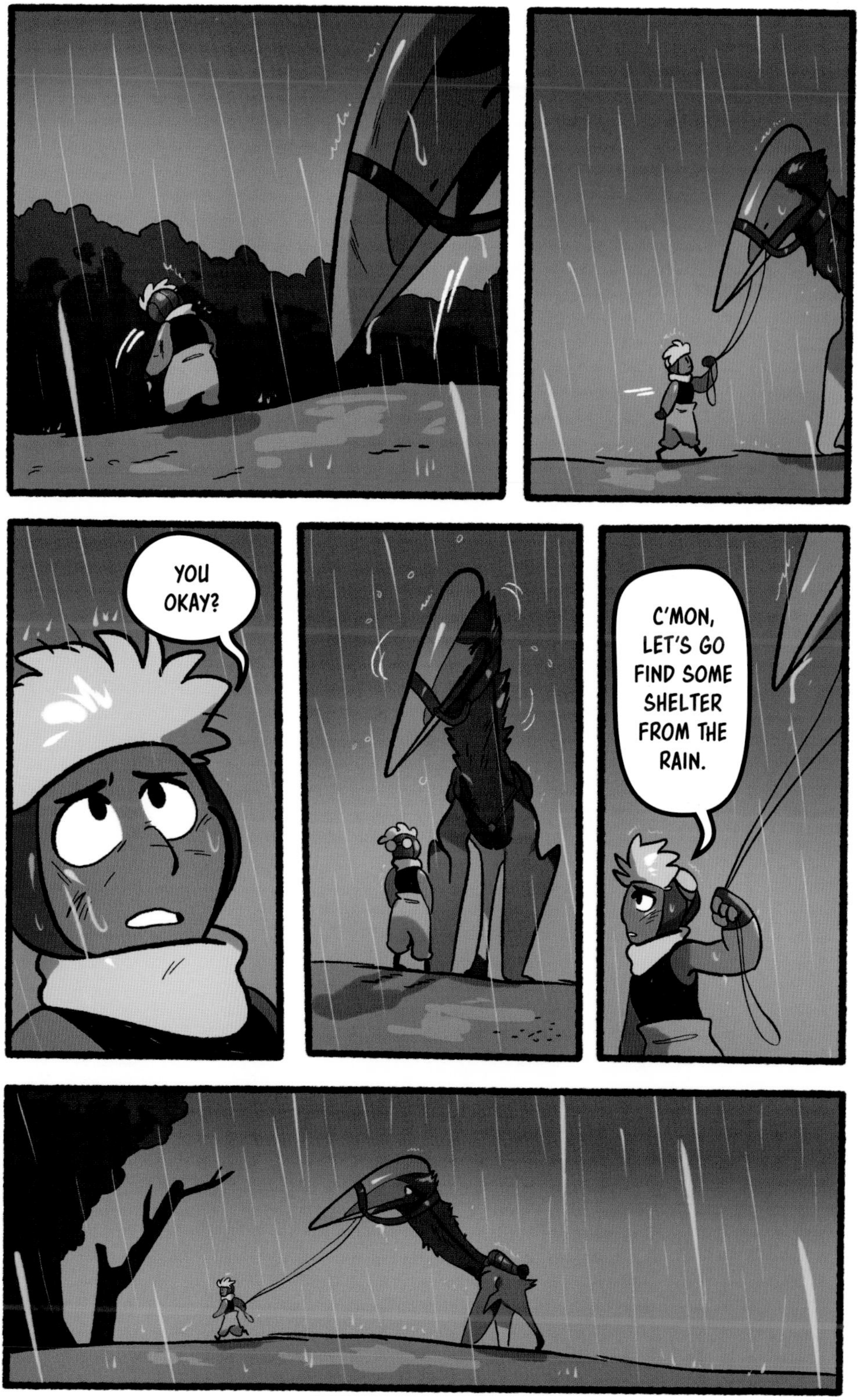
YOU OKAY?
C'MON, LET'S GO FIND SOME SHELTER FROM THE RAIN.

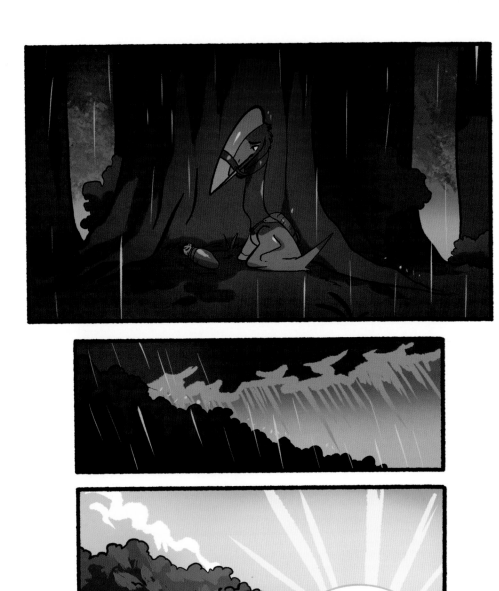

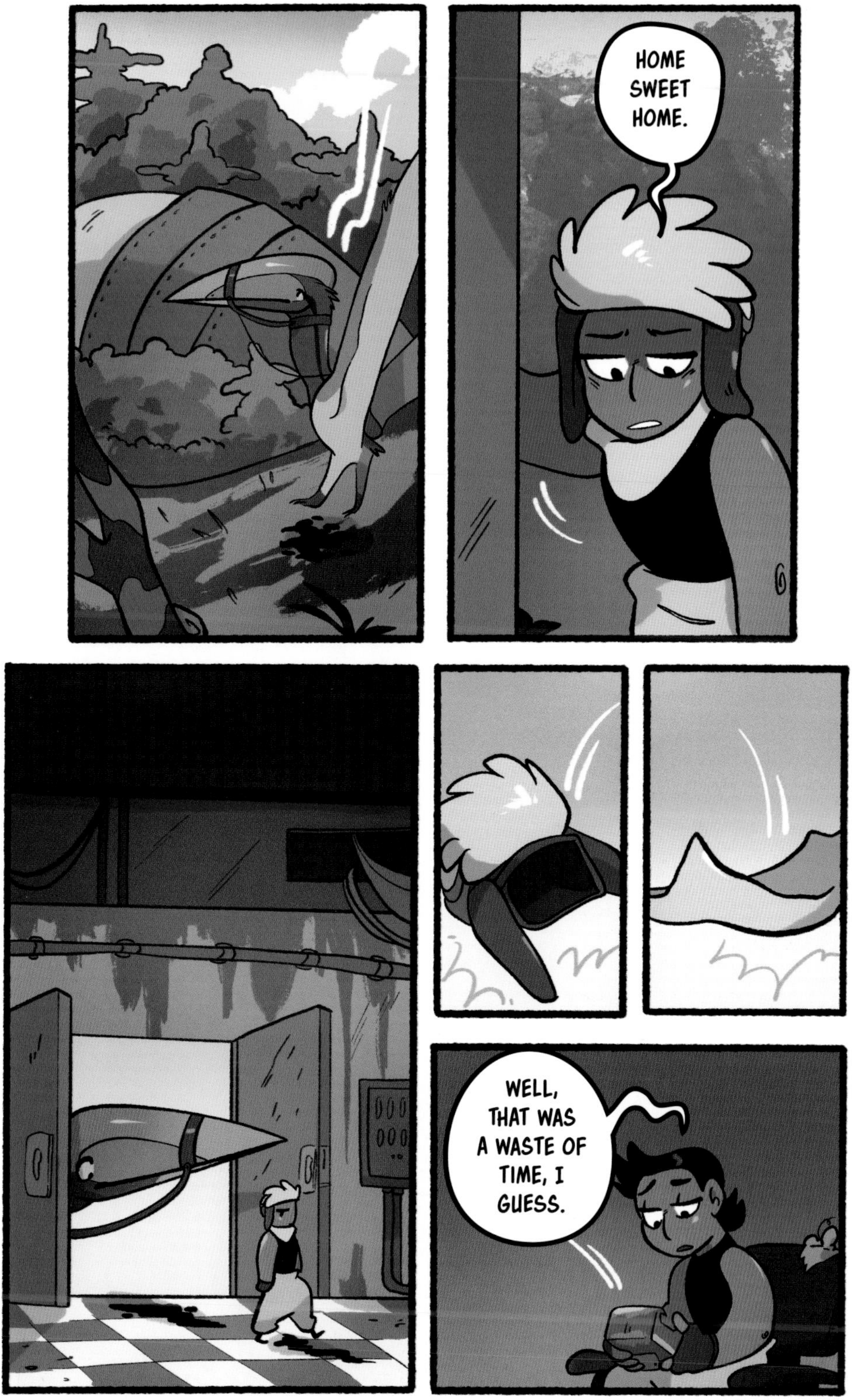
HOME SWEET HOME.
WELL, THAT WAS A WASTE OF TIME, I GUESS.

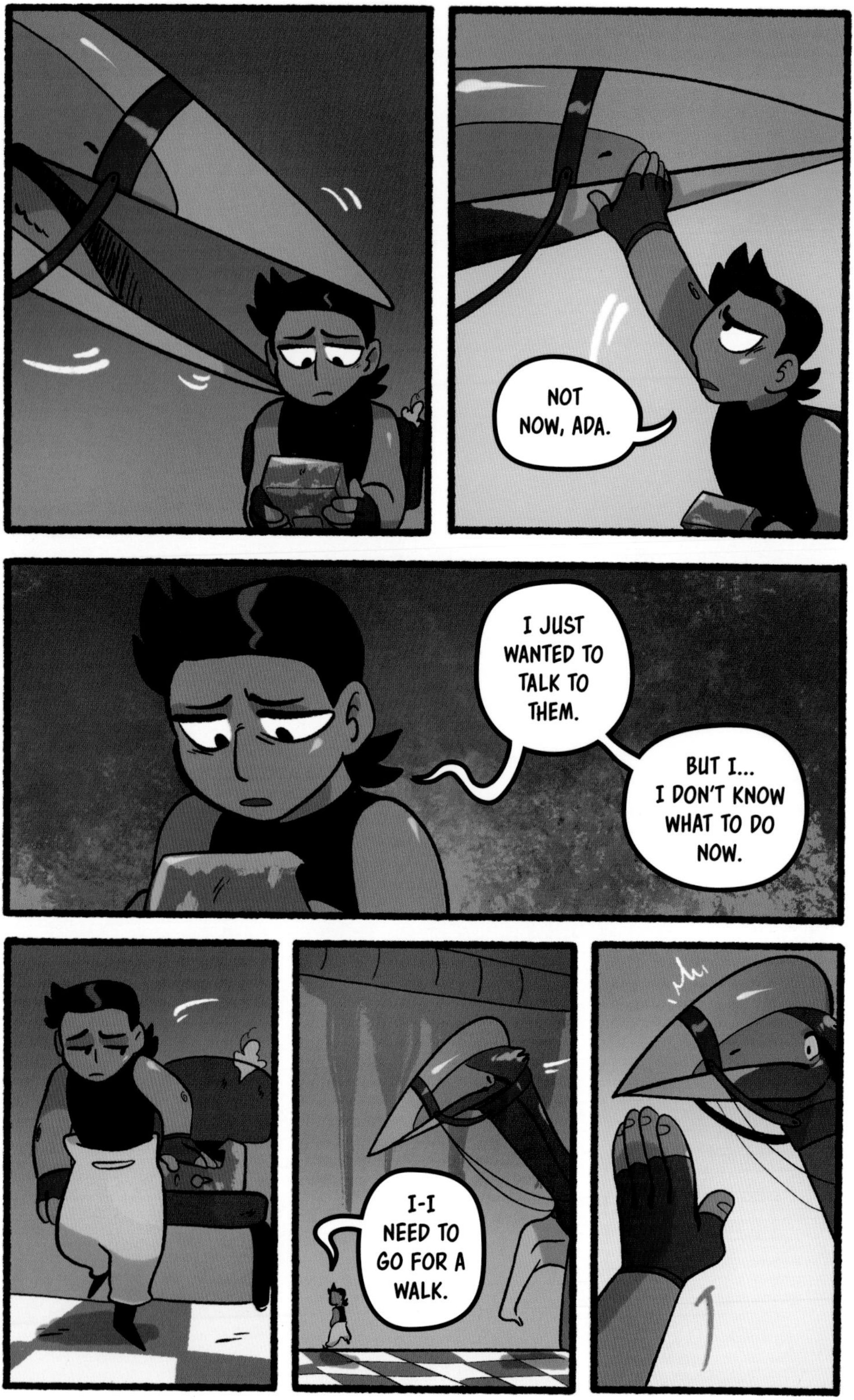
NOT NOW, ADA.
I JUST WANTED TO TALK TO THEM.
BUT I... I DON'T KNOW WHAT TO DO NOW.
I-I NEED TO GO FOR A WALK.

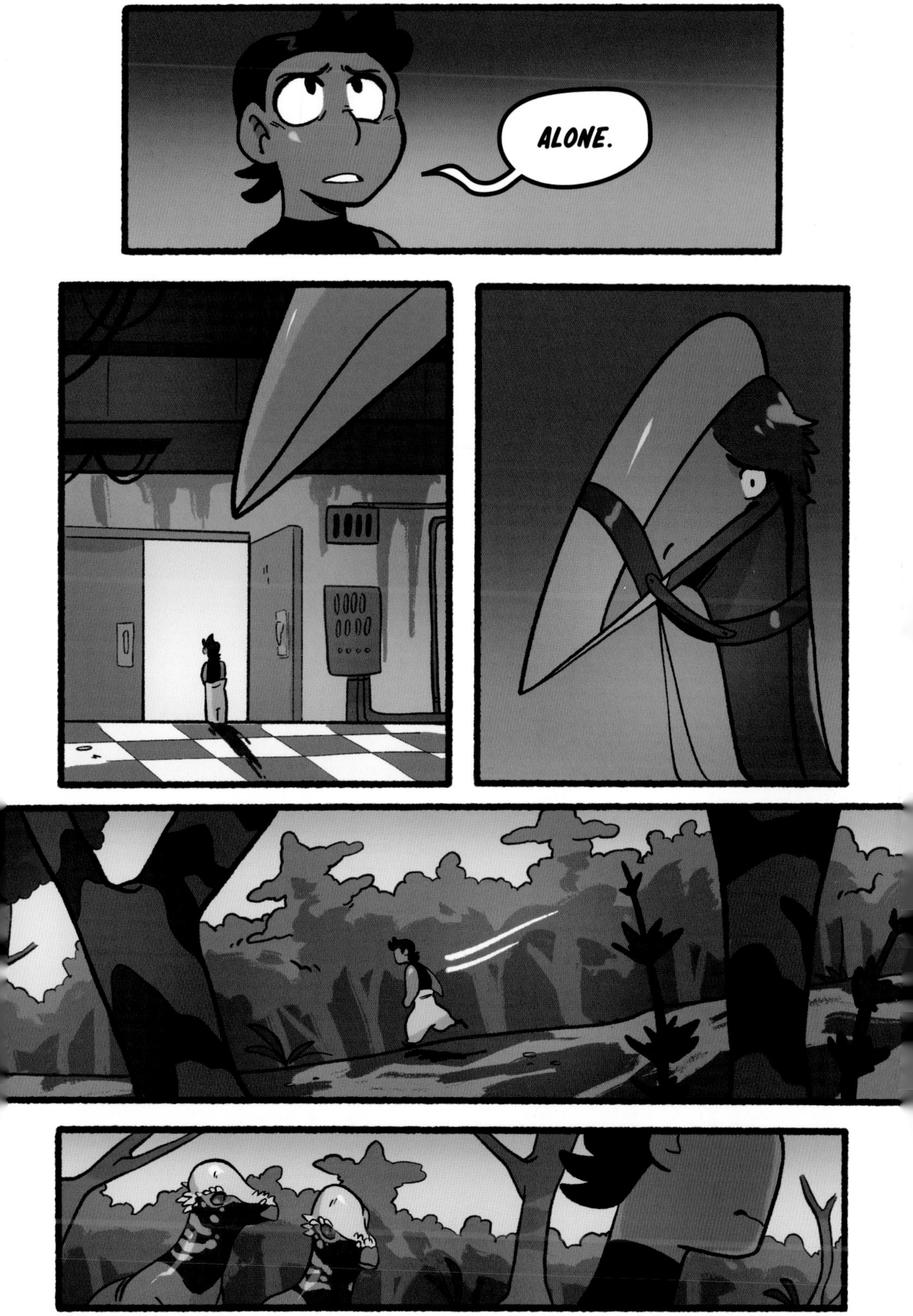
ALONE.

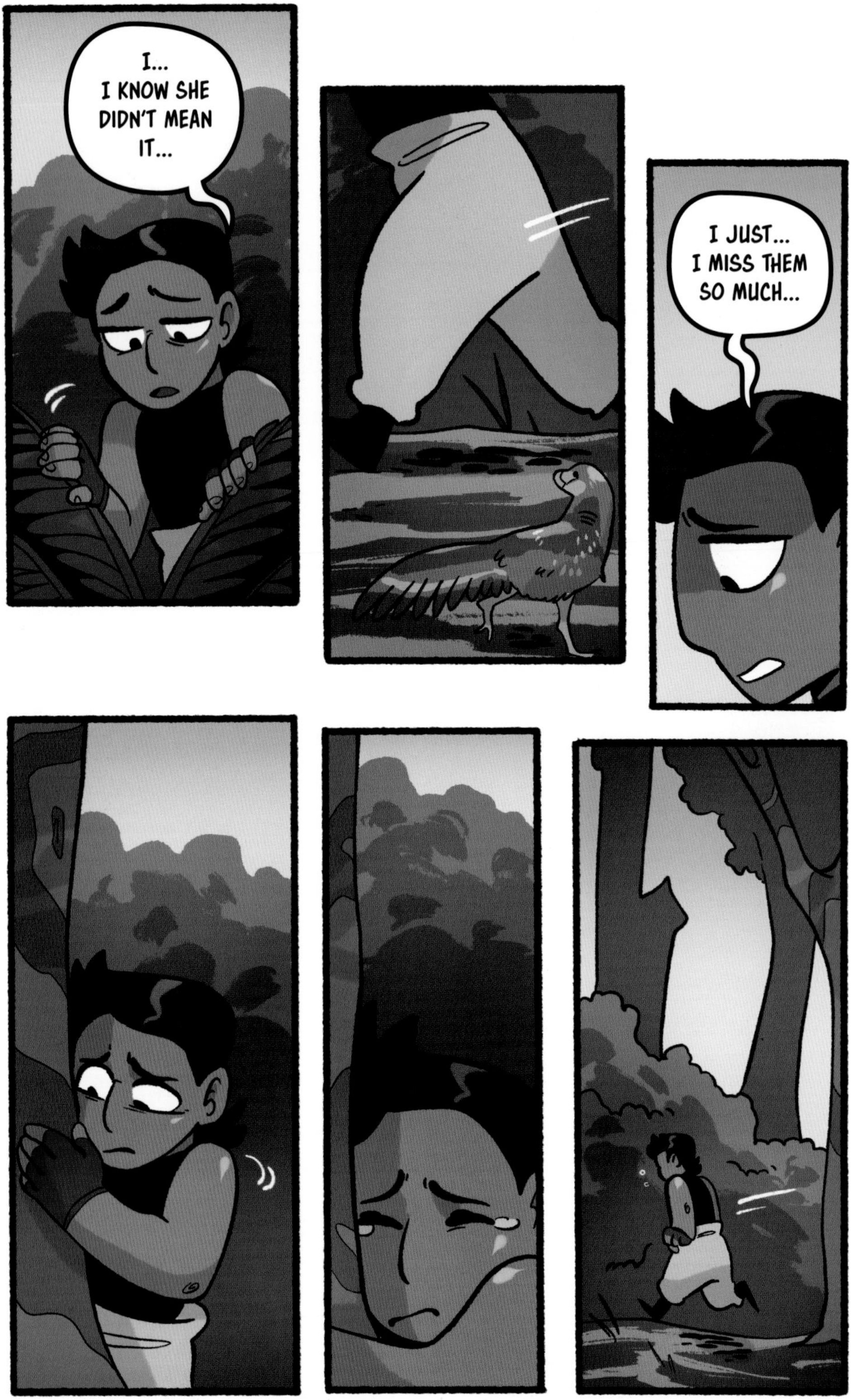
I... I KNOW SHE DIDN'T MEAN IT...
I JUST... I MISS THEM SO MUCH...

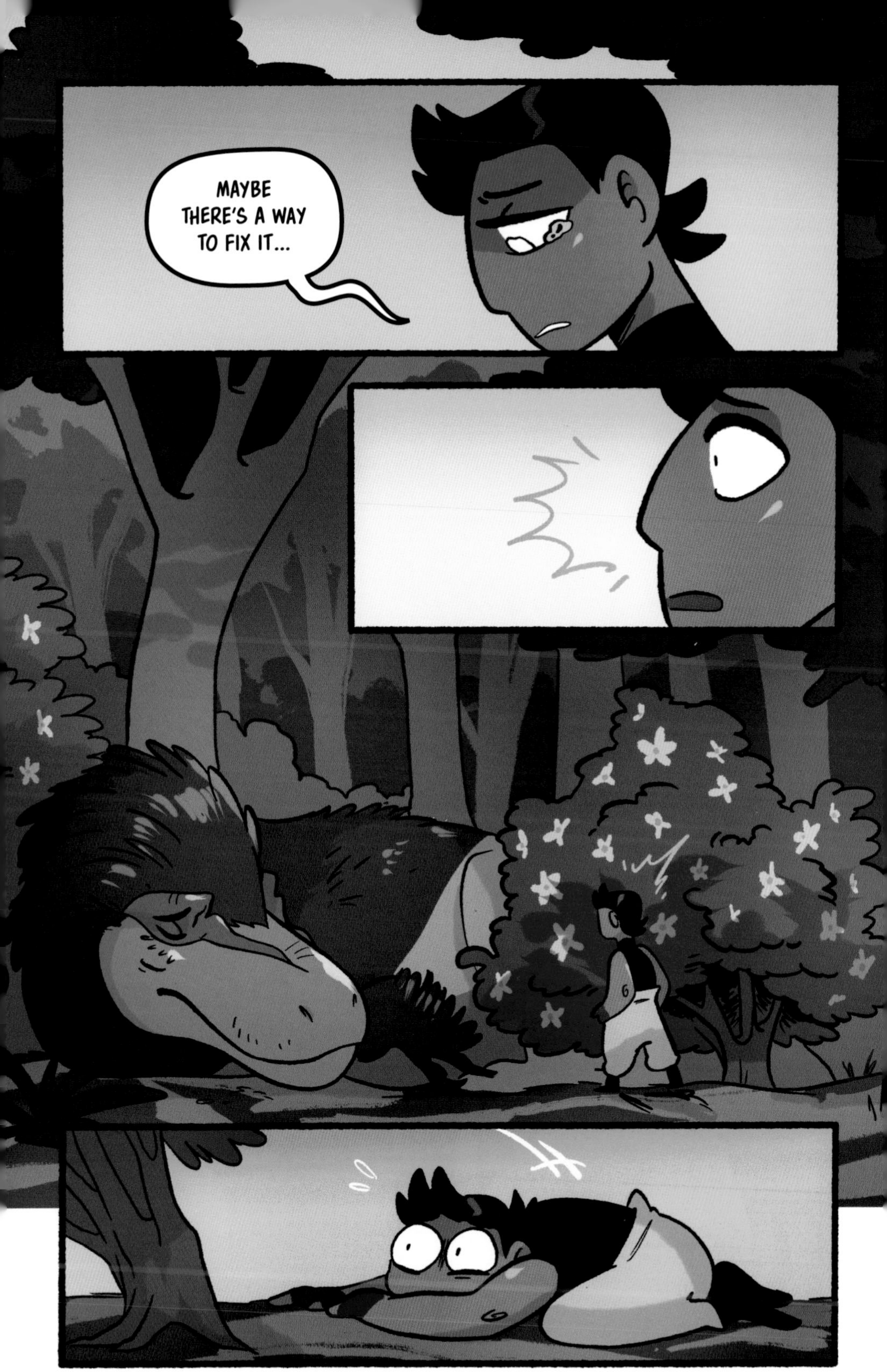
MAYBE THERE'S A WAY TO FIX IT...

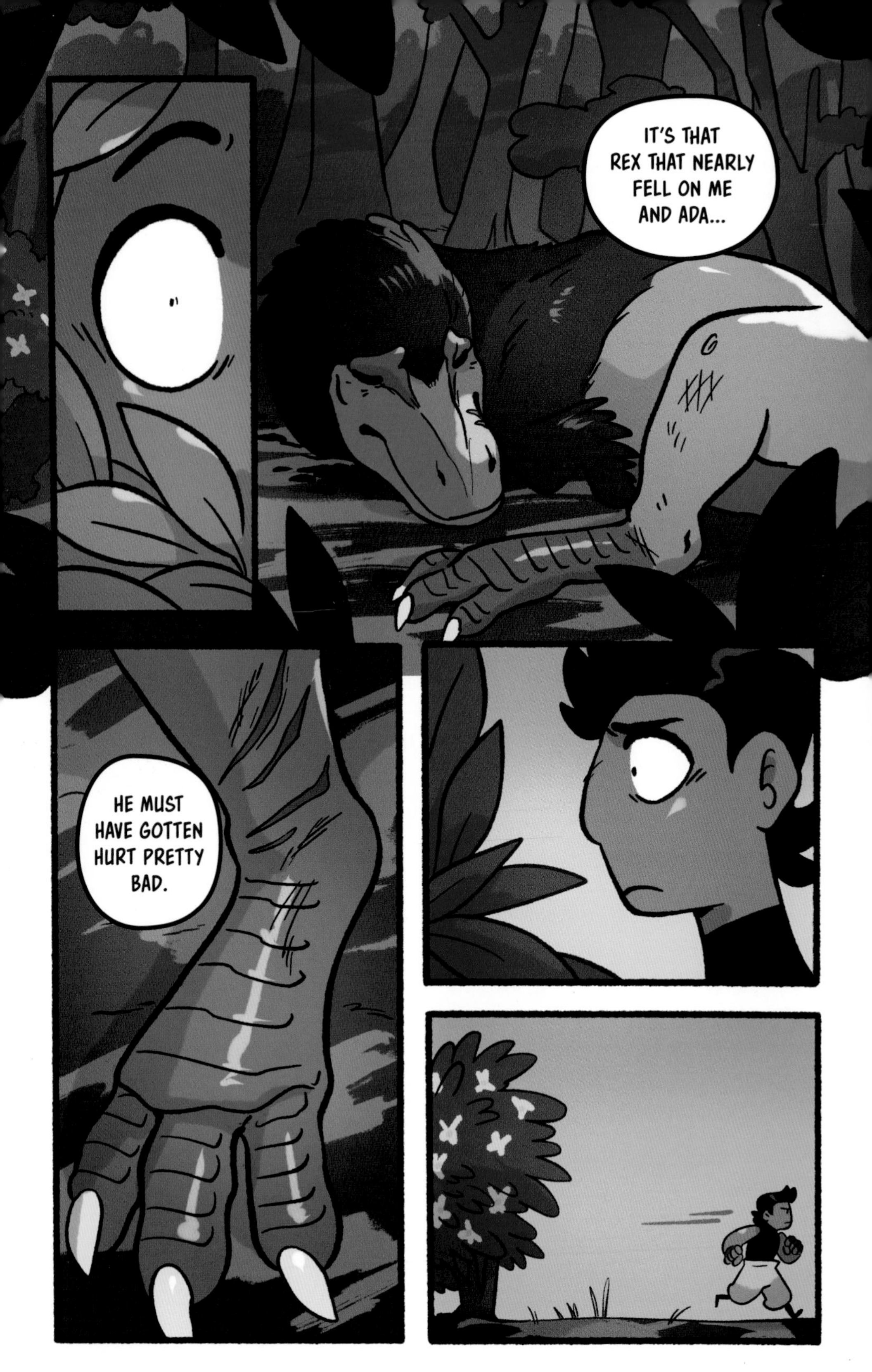
IT'S THAT REX THAT NEARLY FELL ON ME AND ADA...
HE MUST HAVE GOTTEN HURT PRETTY BAD.

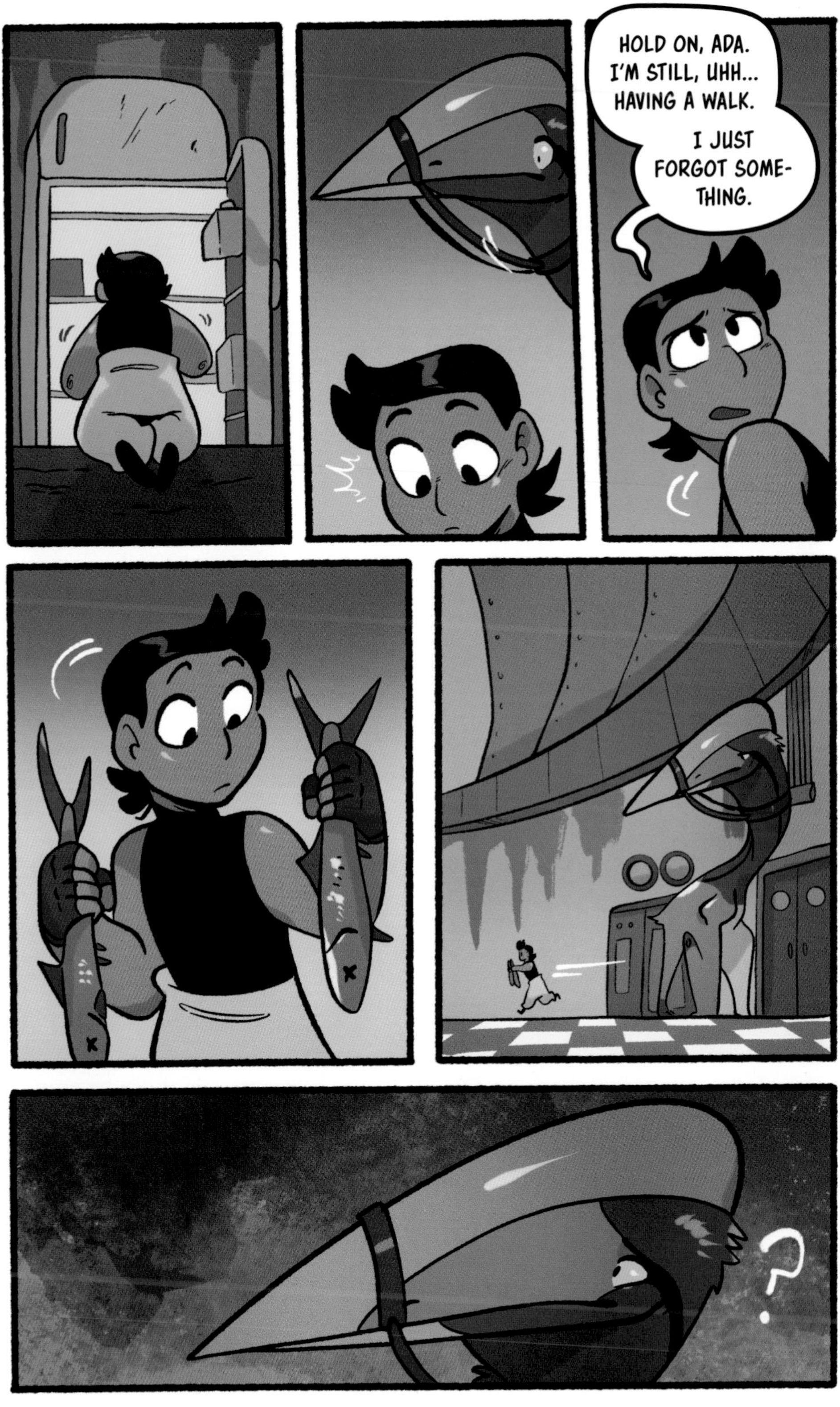
HOLD ON, ADA. I'M STILL, UHH... HAVING A WALK.
I JUST FORGOT SOME-THING.
?

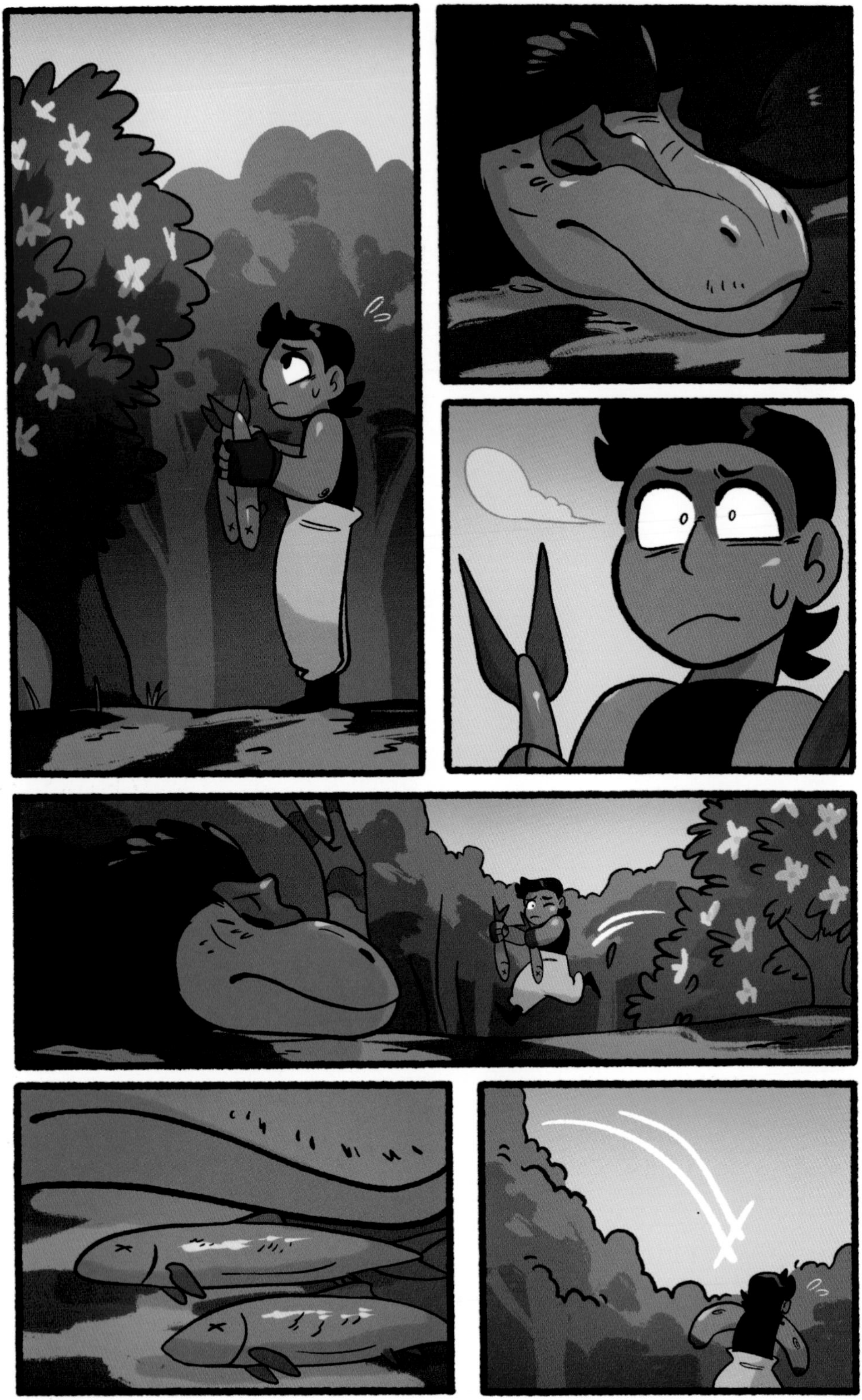

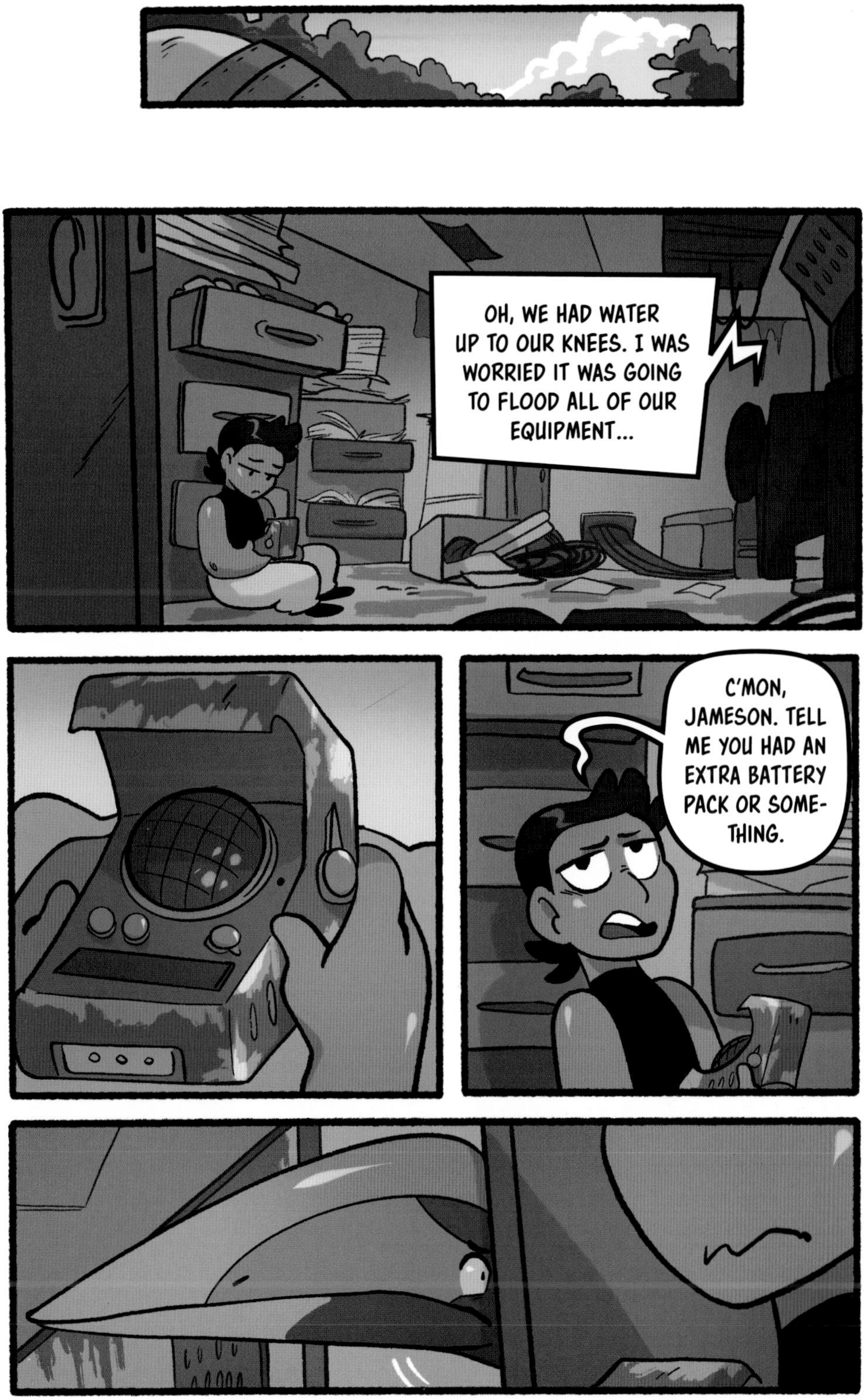
OH, WE HAD WATER UP TO OUR KNEES. I WAS WORRIED IT WAS GOING TO FLOOD ALL OF OUR EQUIPMENT...
C'MON, JAMESON. TELL ME YOU HAD AN EXTRA BATTERY PACK OR SOME-THING.

krr?

HEY, ADA.

NOT NOW, ADA.

I'M TRYING TO GO BACK OVER THE RECORDINGS AND SEE IF JAMESON MENTIONS ANYTHING THAT WILL HELP ME FIX THE TEMPCOM...

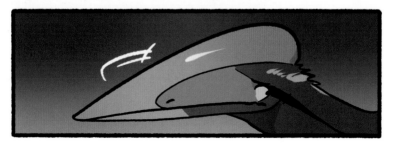

THESE AREN'T FOR YOU, ADA.
STAY HERE, OKAY? I'LL BE BACK.

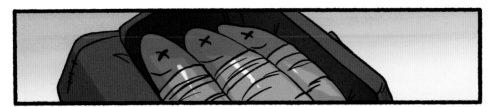

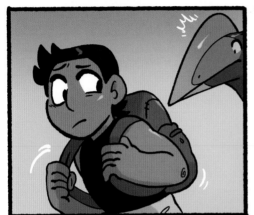

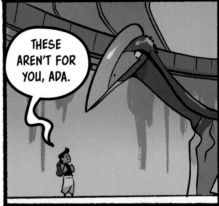

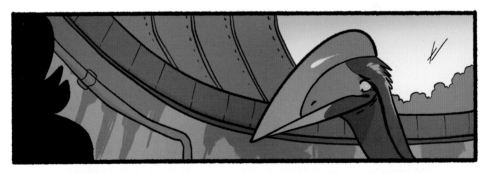

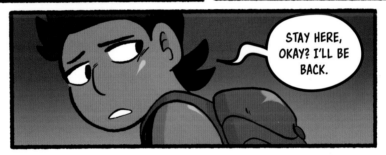

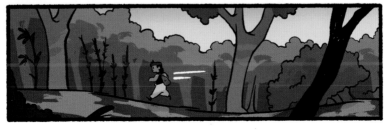

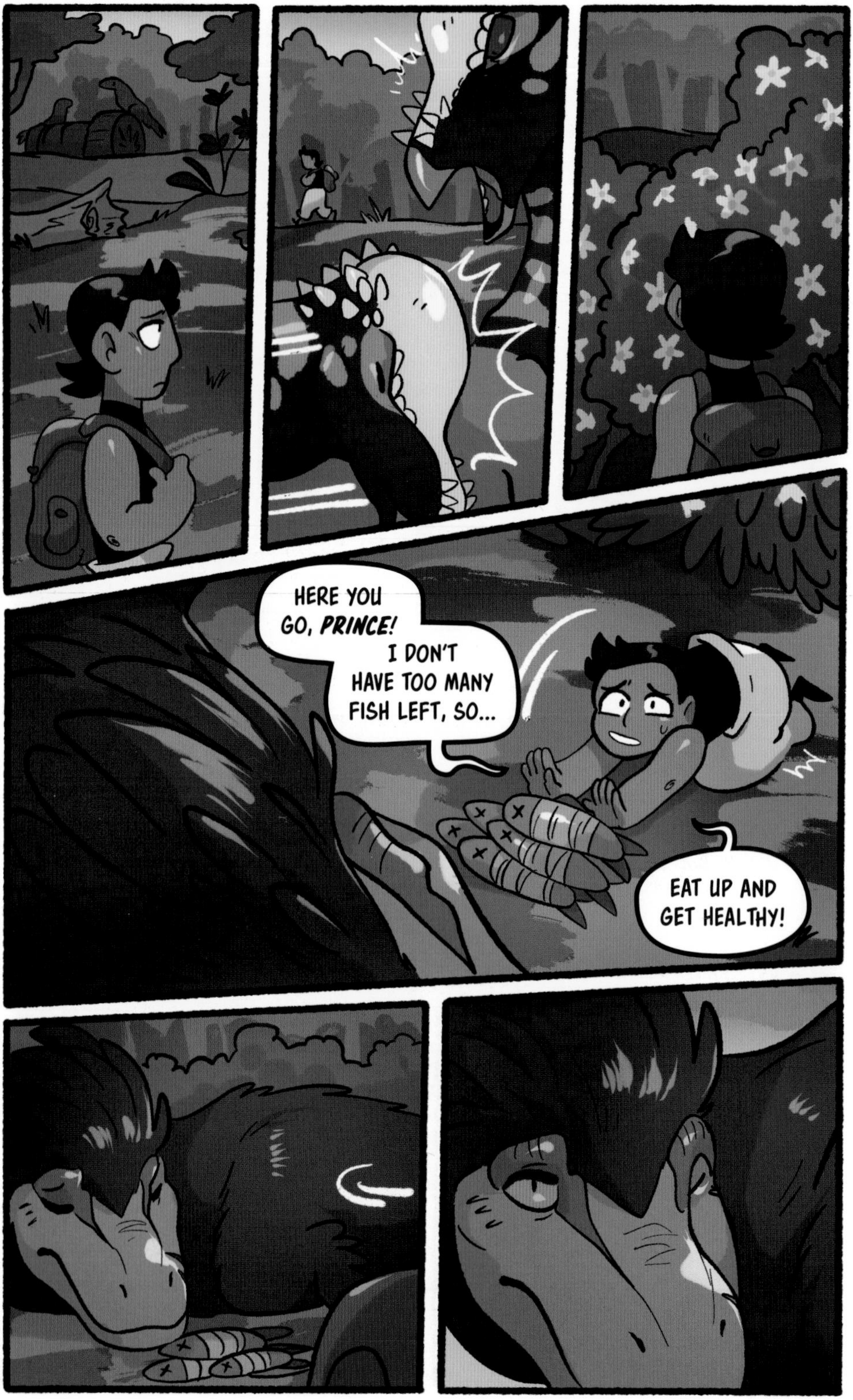
HERE YOU GO, *PRINCE!*
I DON'T HAVE TOO MANY FISH LEFT, SO...
EAT UP AND GET HEALTHY!

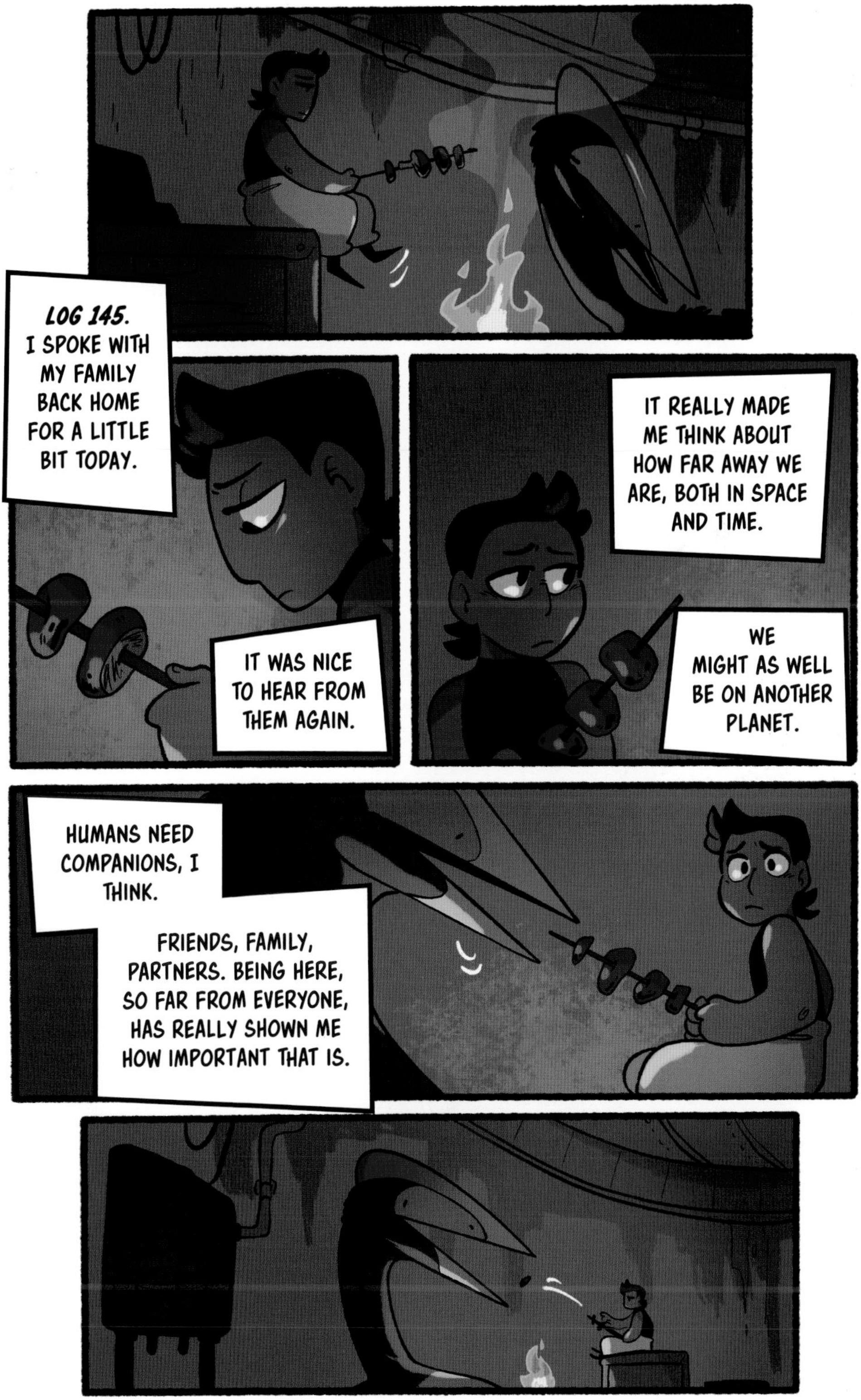
LOG 145.
I SPOKE WITH MY FAMILY BACK HOME FOR A LITTLE BIT TODAY.
IT WAS NICE TO HEAR FROM THEM AGAIN.
IT REALLY MADE ME THINK ABOUT HOW FAR AWAY WE ARE, BOTH IN SPACE AND TIME.
WE MIGHT AS WELL BE ON ANOTHER PLANET.
HUMANS NEED COMPANIONS, I THINK.
FRIENDS, FAMILY, PARTNERS. BEING HERE, SO FAR FROM EVERYONE, HAS REALLY SHOWN ME HOW IMPORTANT THAT IS.

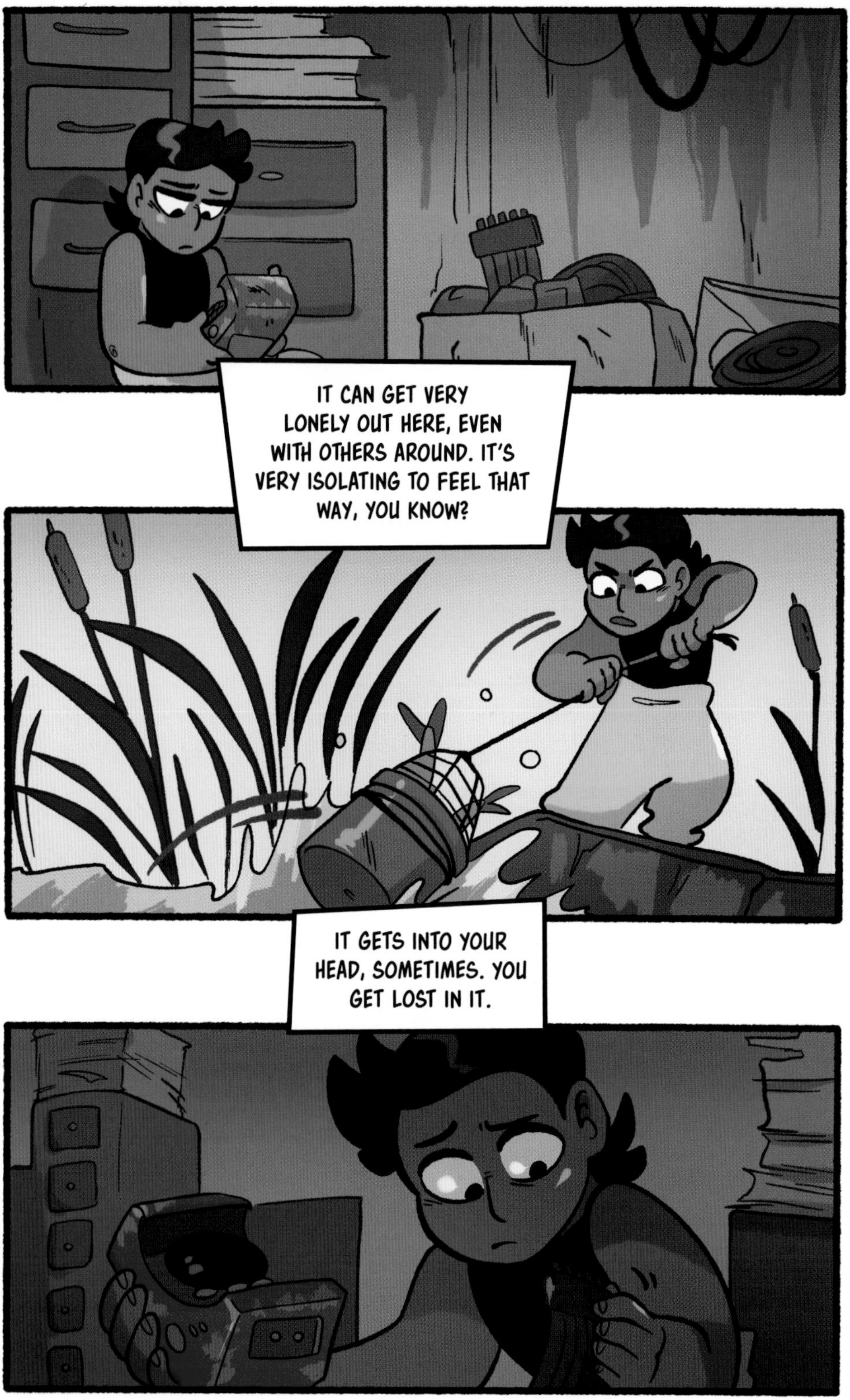
IT CAN GET VERY LONELY OUT HERE, EVEN WITH OTHERS AROUND. IT'S VERY ISOLATING TO FEEL THAT WAY, YOU KNOW?
IT GETS INTO YOUR HEAD, SOMETIMES. YOU GET LOST IN IT.

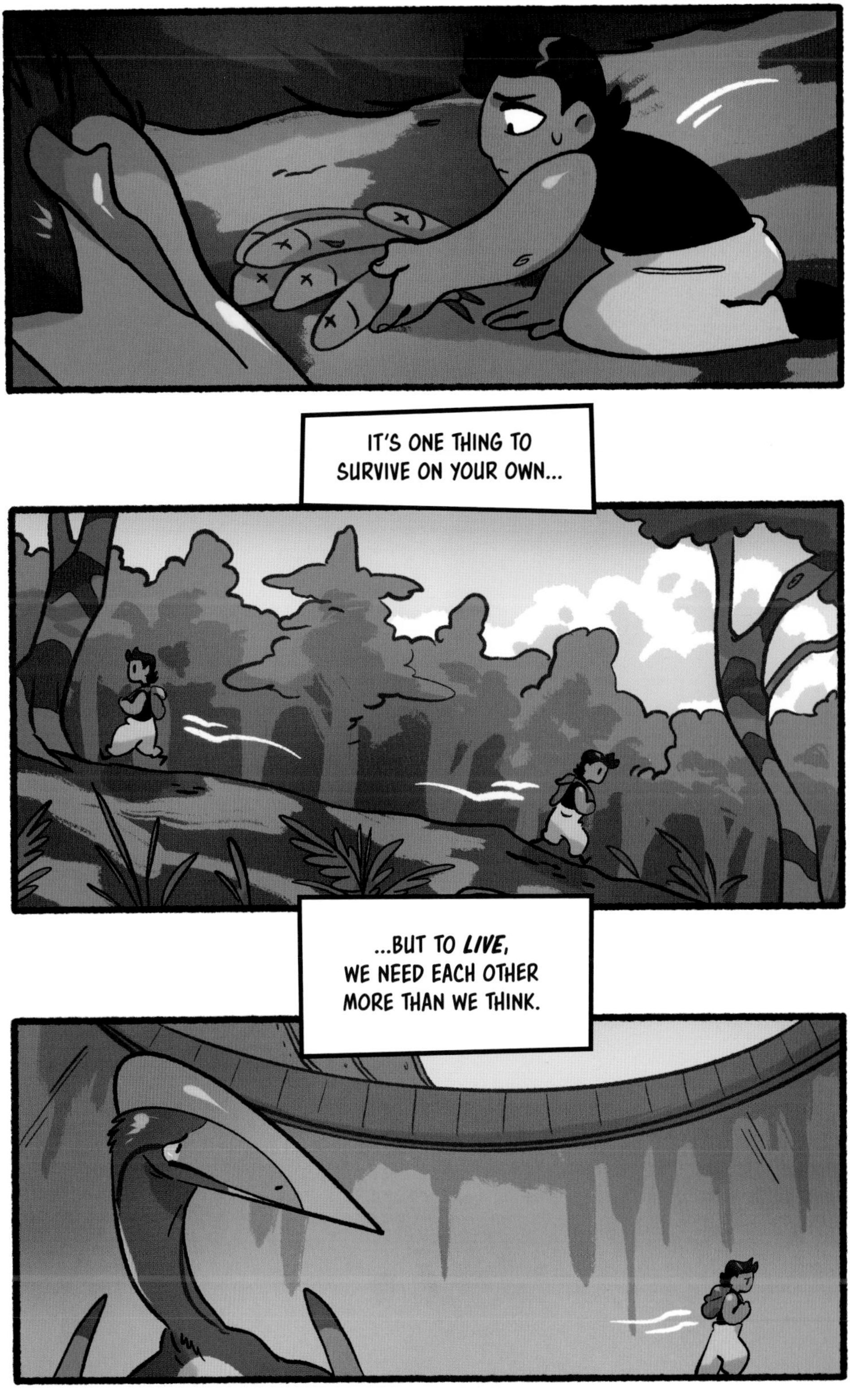
IT'S ONE THING TO SURVIVE ON YOUR OWN...
...BUT TO *LIVE*, WE NEED EACH OTHER MORE THAN WE THINK.

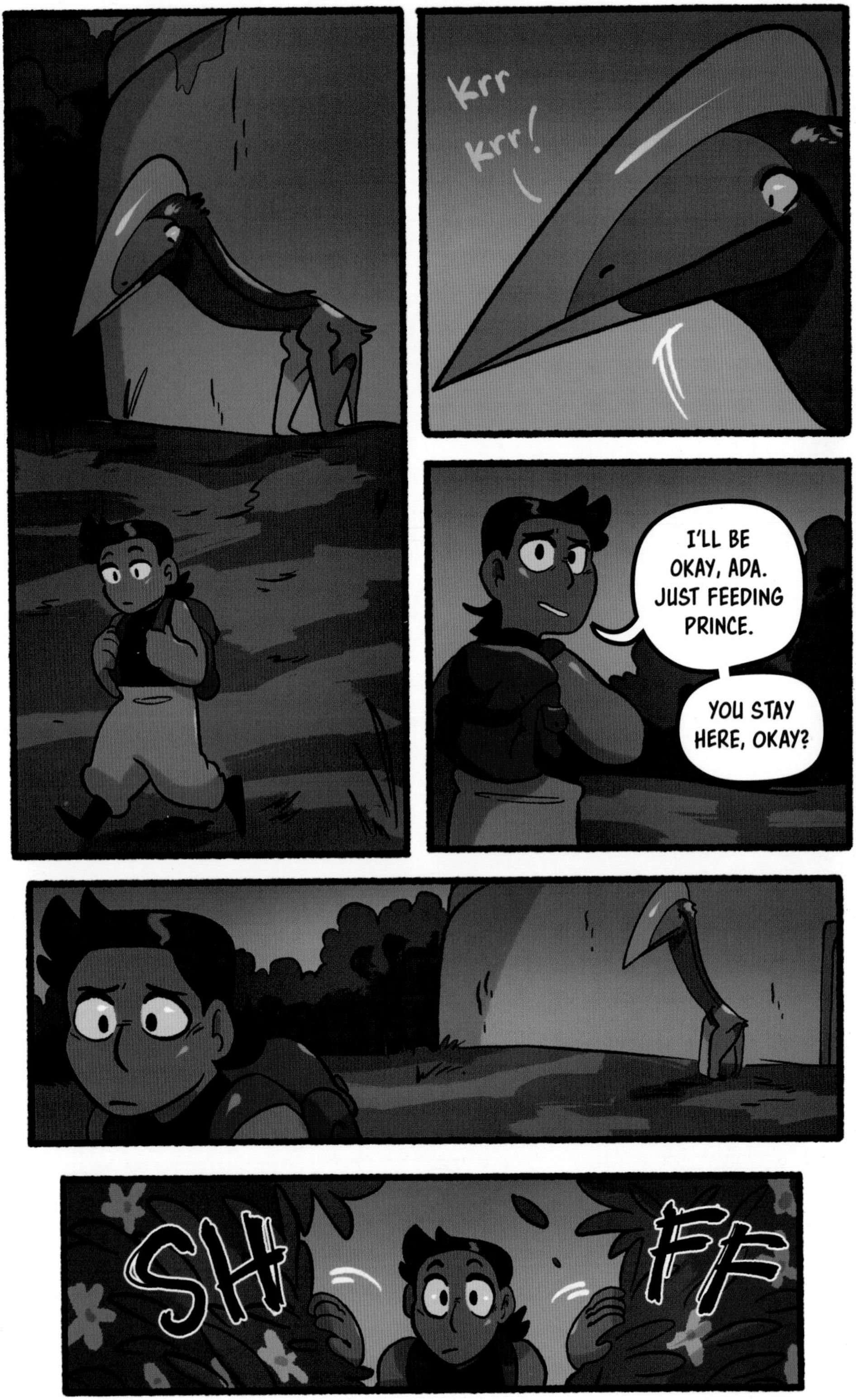

Krr krr!
I'LL BE OKAY, ADA. JUST FEEDING PRINCE.
YOU STAY HERE, OKAY?
SH FF

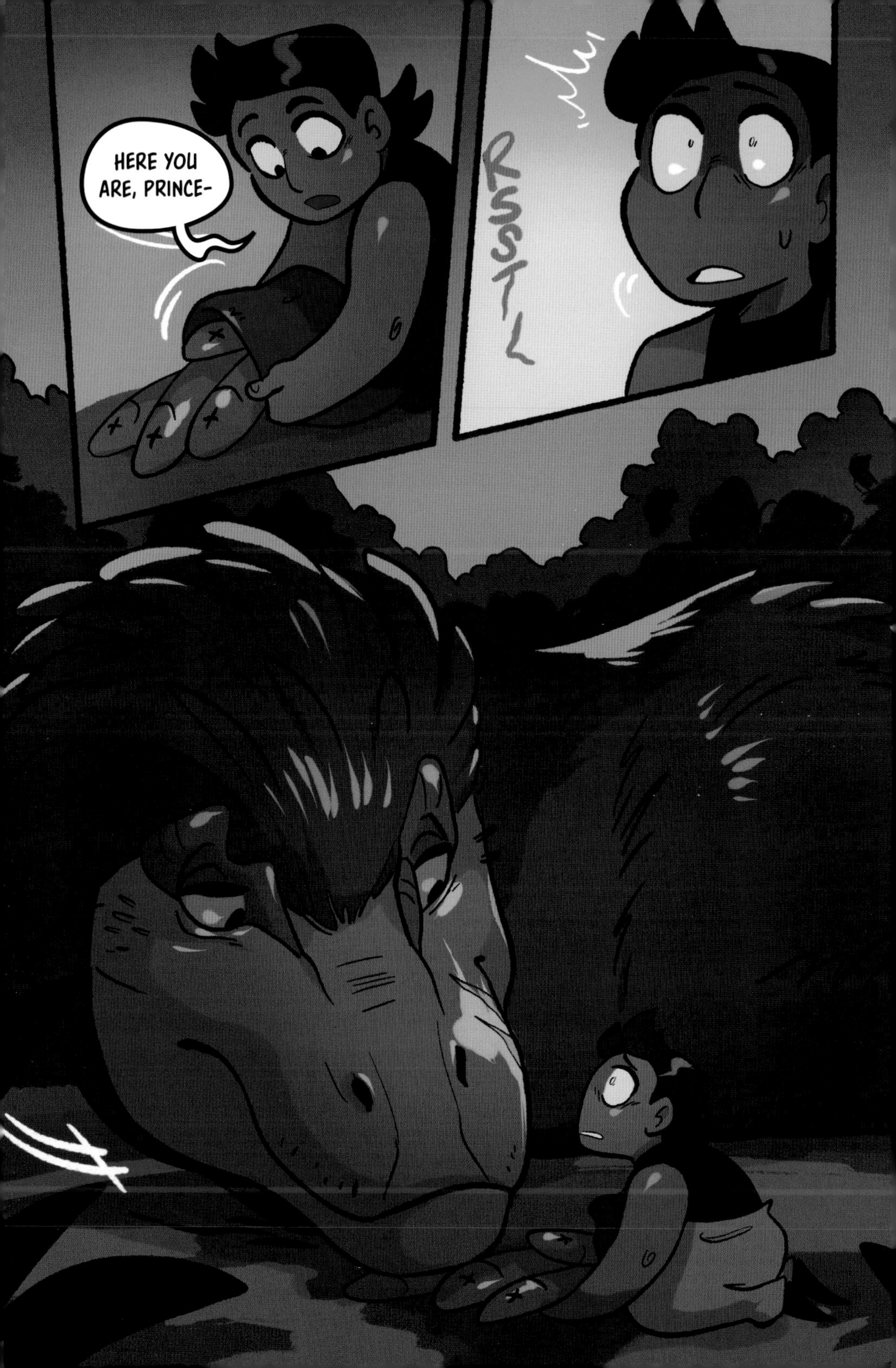
HERE YOU ARE, PRINCE-
RSSTTL

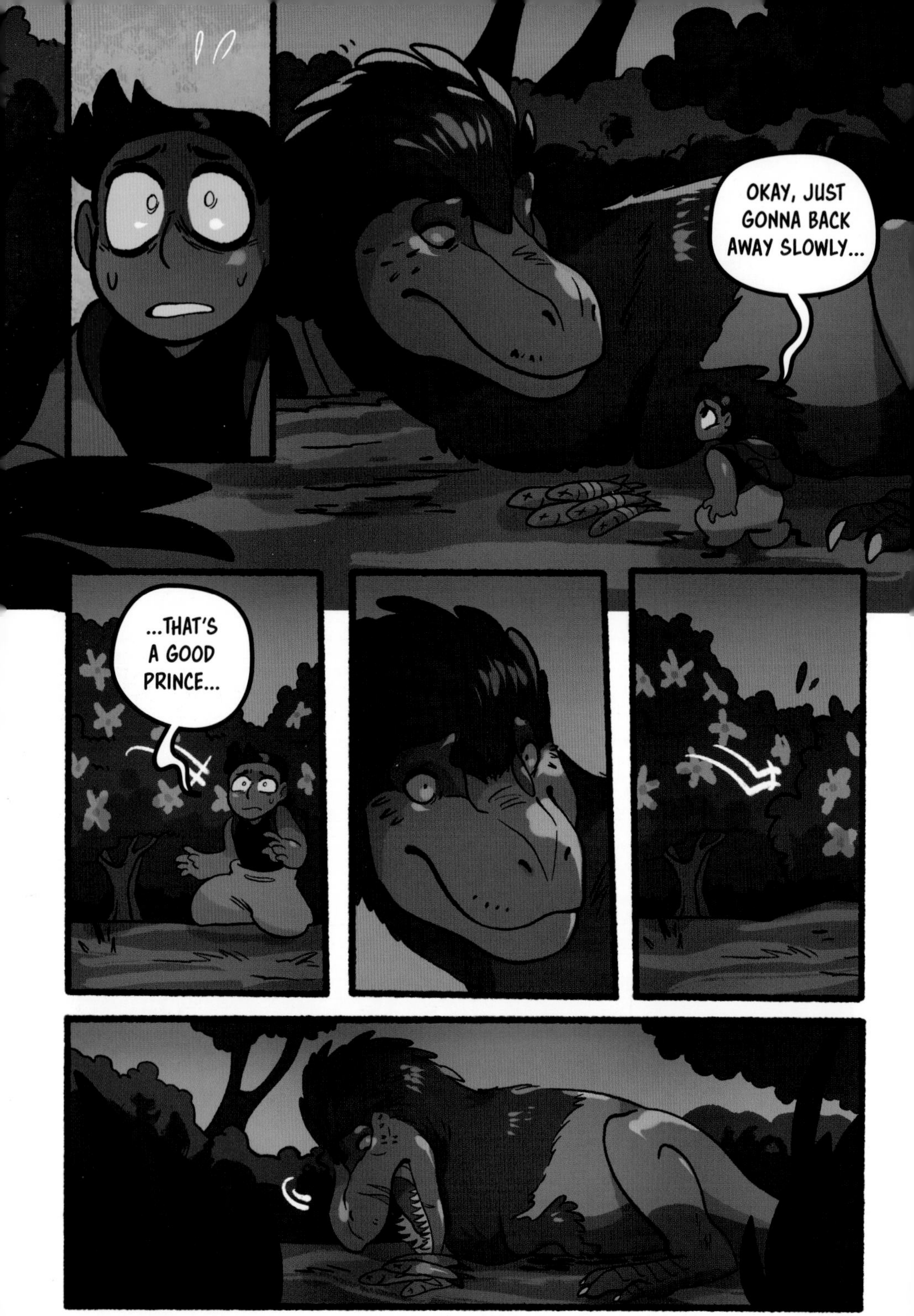
OKAY, JUST GONNA BACK AWAY SLOWLY...
...THAT'S A GOOD PRINCE...

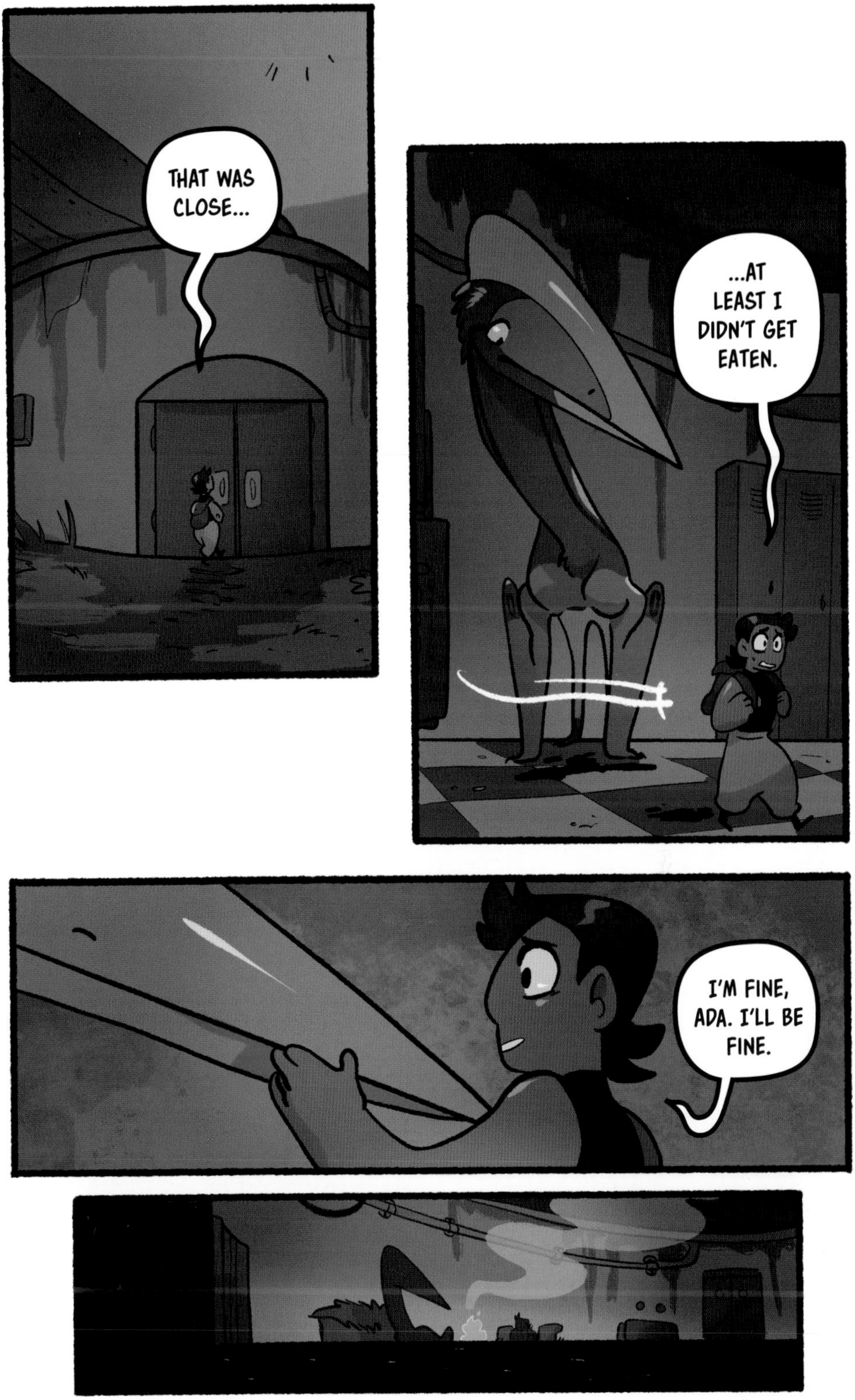
THAT WAS CLOSE...
...AT LEAST I DIDN'T GET EATEN.
I'M FINE, ADA. I'LL BE FINE.

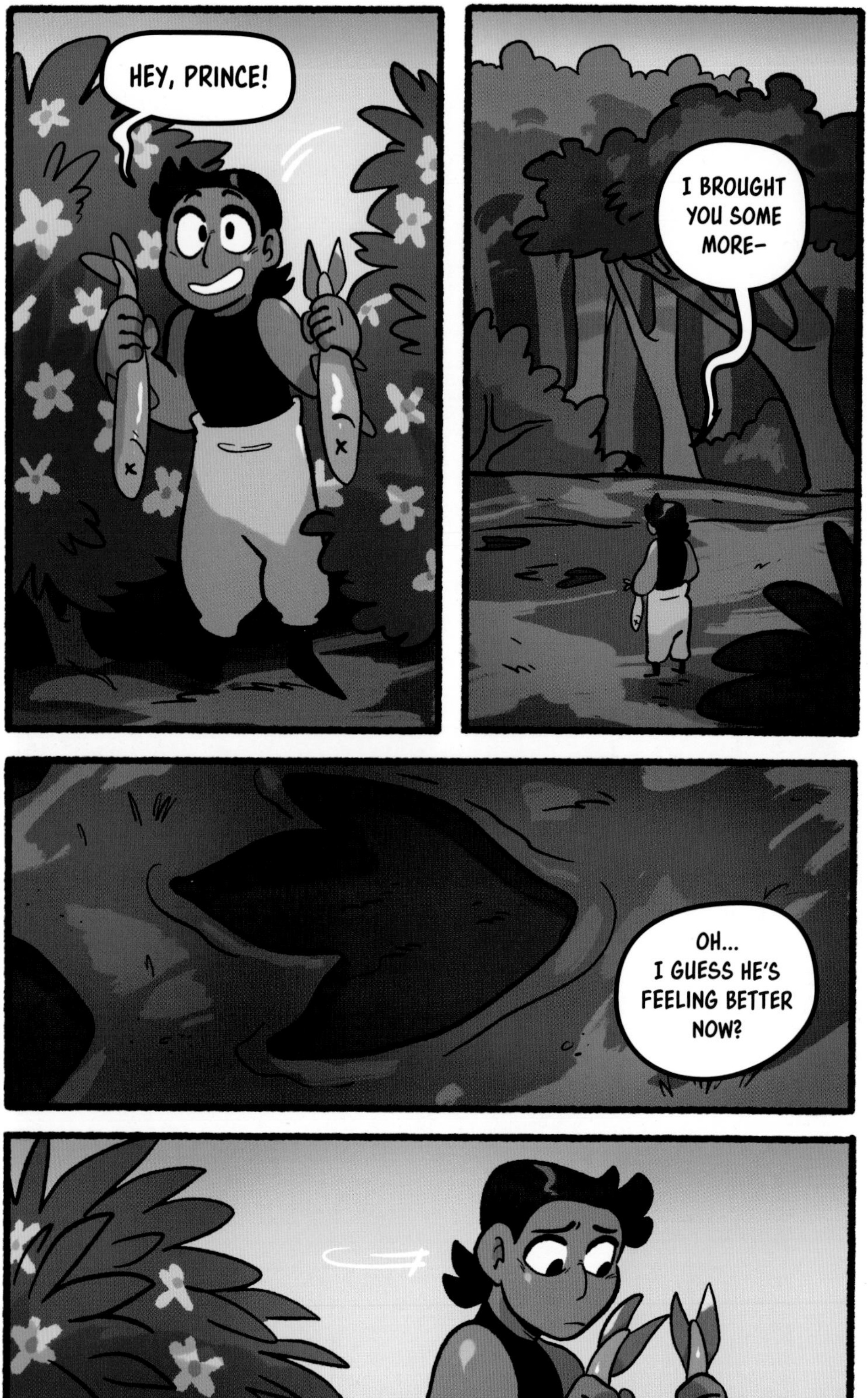
HEY, PRINCE!
I BROUGHT YOU SOME MORE-
OH... I GUESS HE'S FEELING BETTER NOW?

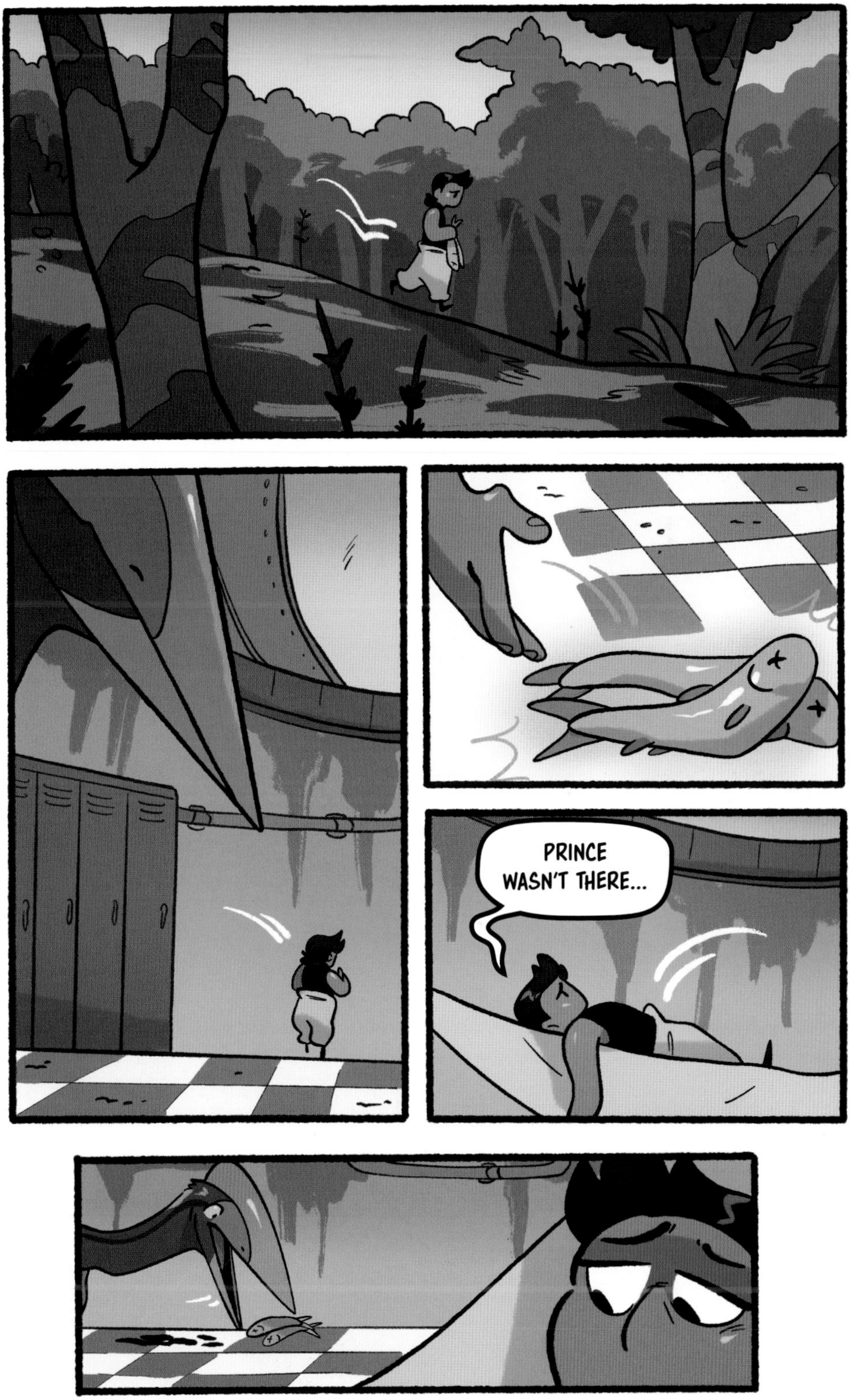
PRINCE
WASN'T THERE...

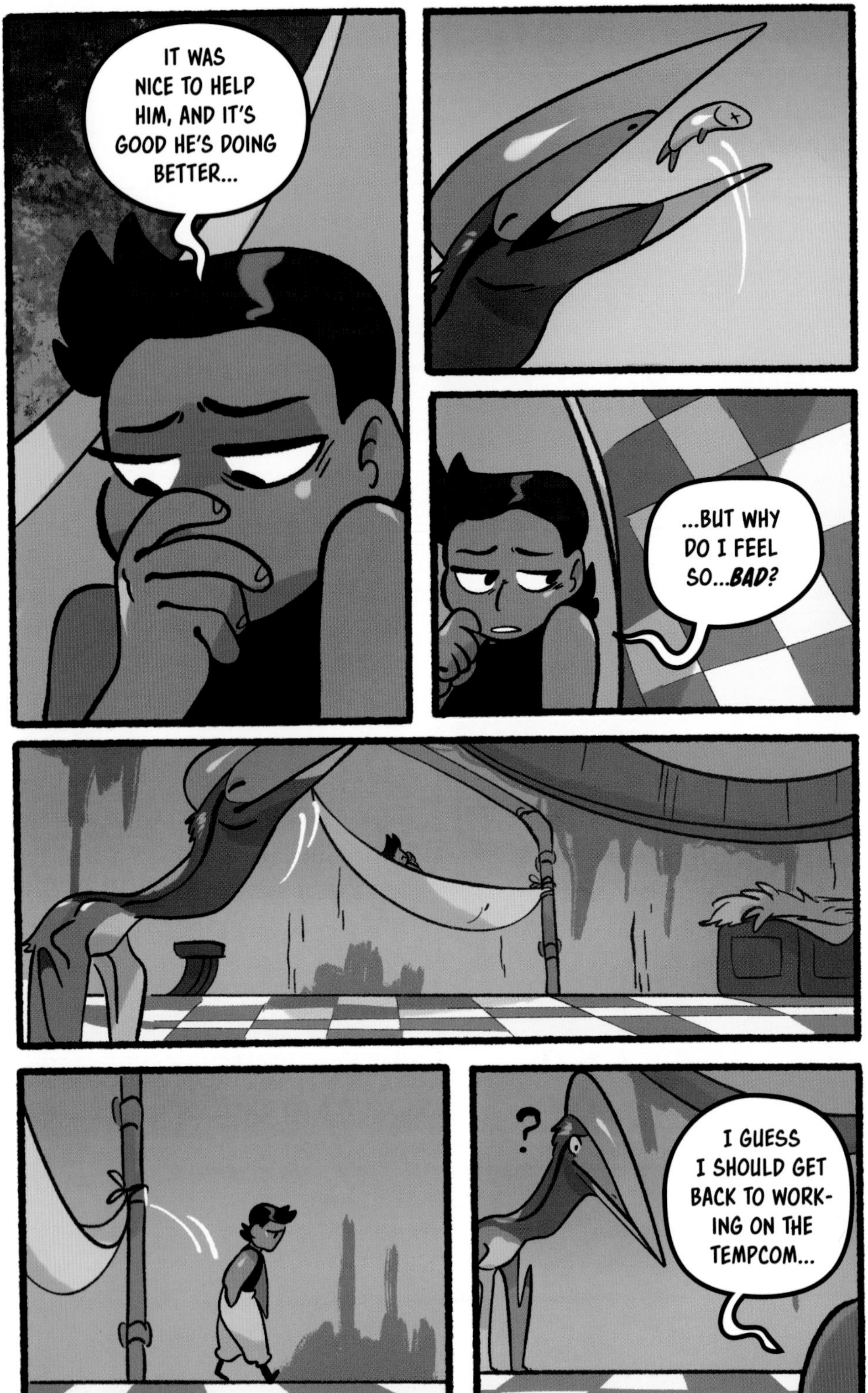
IT WAS NICE TO HELP HIM, AND IT'S GOOD HE'S DOING BETTER...
...BUT WHY DO I FEEL SO...*BAD?*
?
I GUESS I SHOULD GET BACK TO WORK-ING ON THE TEMPCOM...

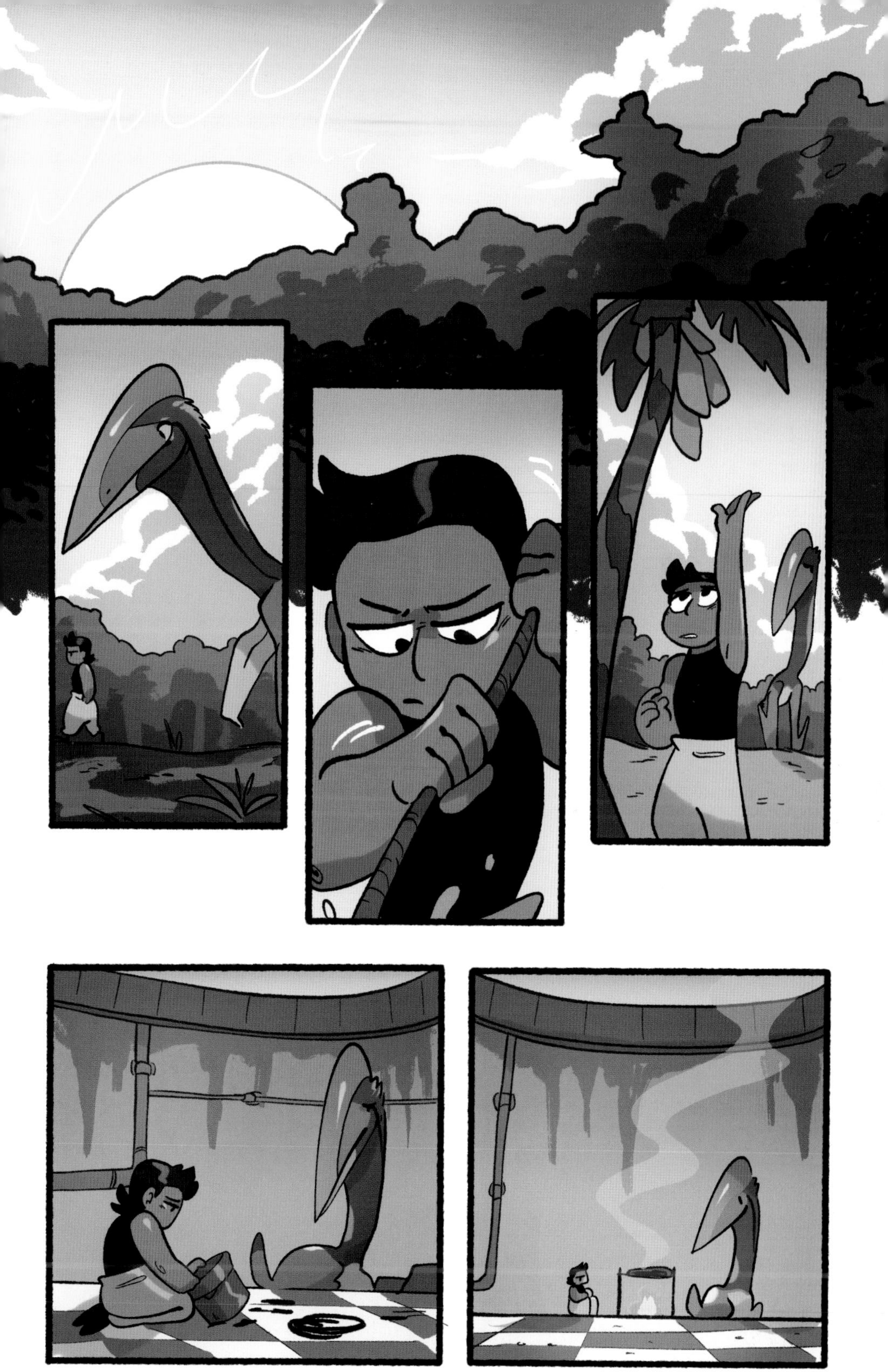

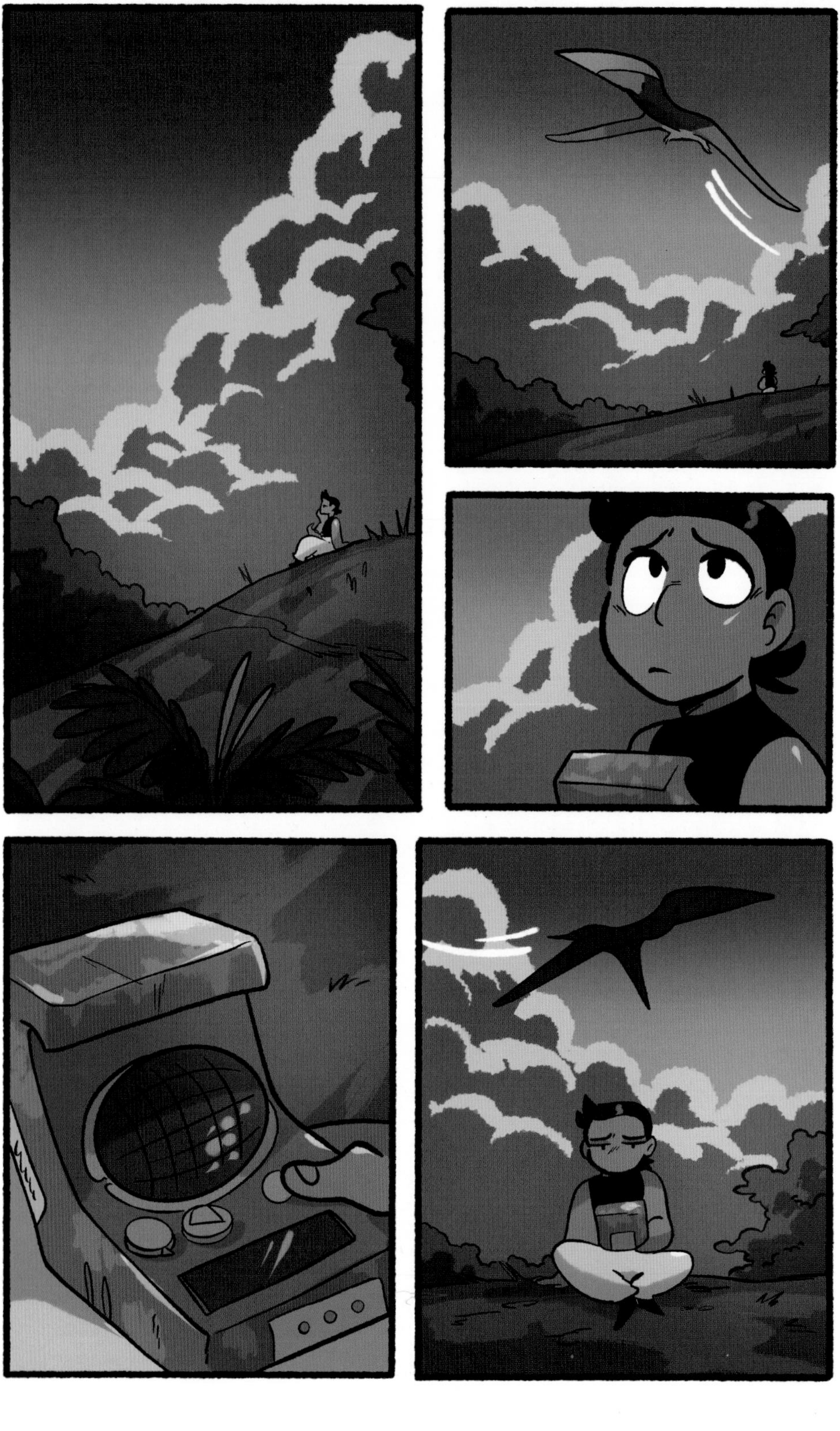

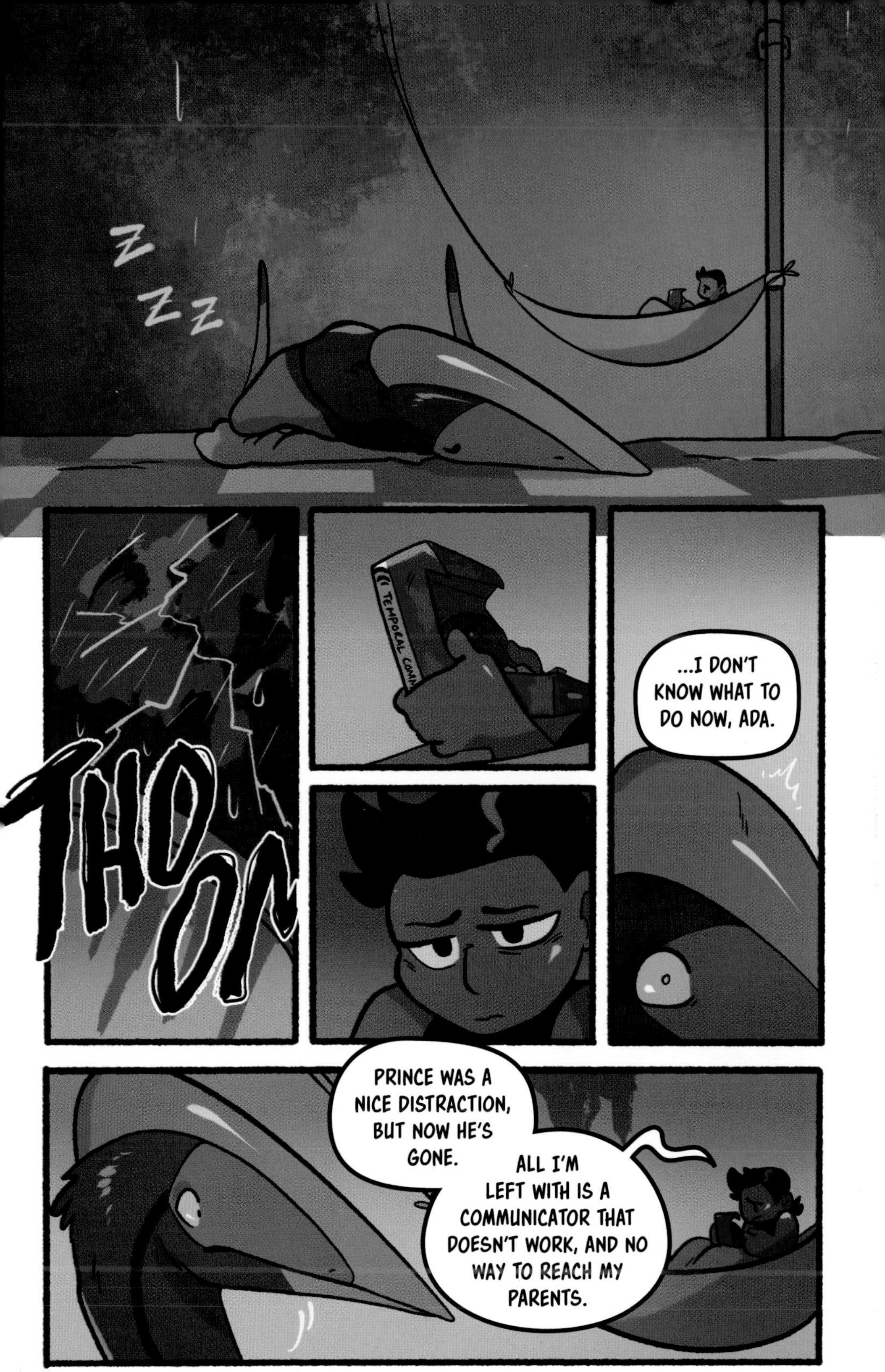
Z Z Z
THOOM
TEMPORAL COMM
...I DON'T KNOW WHAT TO DO NOW, ADA.
PRINCE WAS A NICE DISTRACTION, BUT NOW HE'S GONE.
ALL I'M LEFT WITH IS A COMMUNICATOR THAT DOESN'T WORK, AND NO WAY TO REACH MY PARENTS.

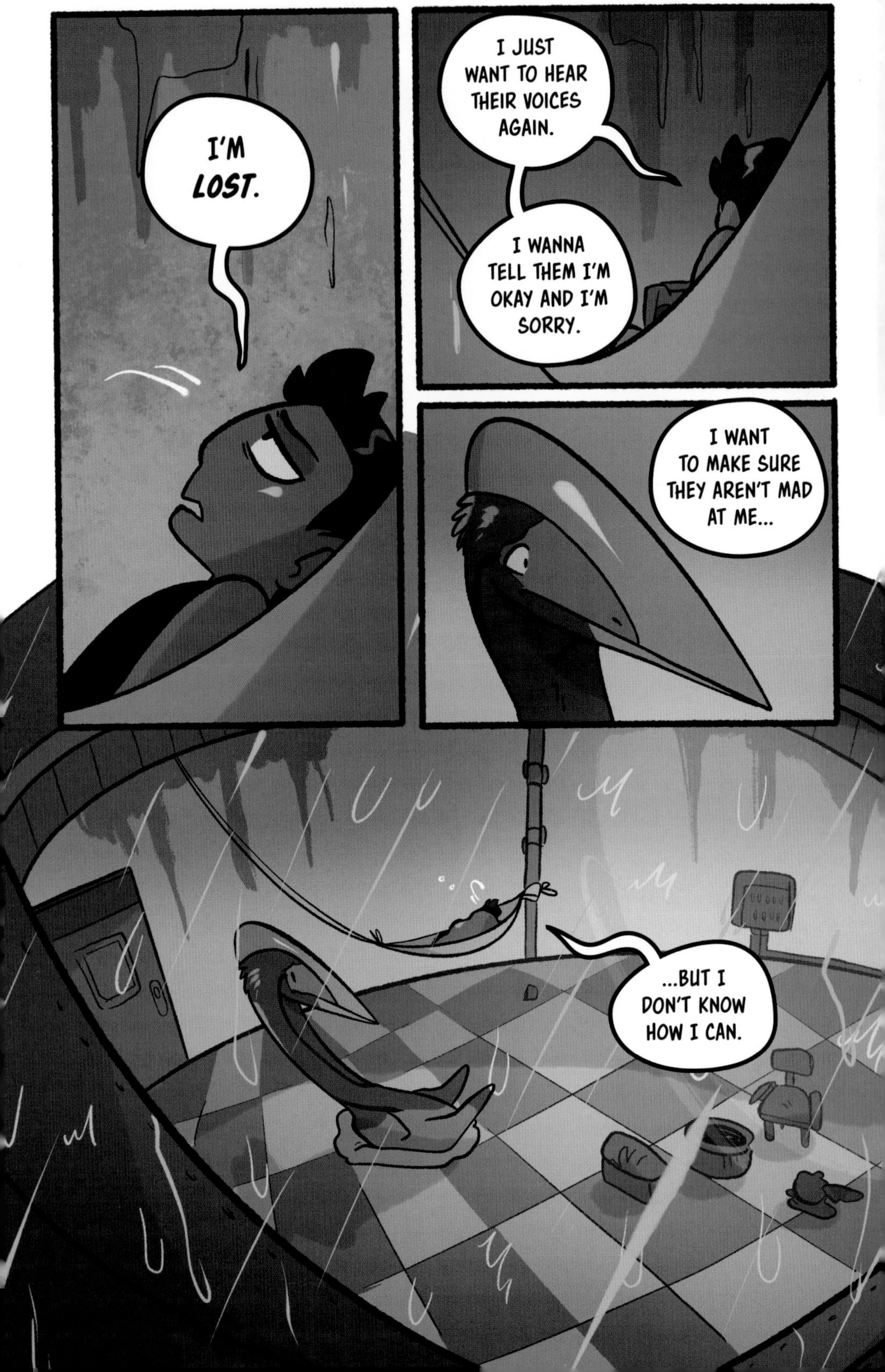
I'M LOST.
I JUST WANT TO HEAR THEIR VOICES AGAIN.
I WANNA TELL THEM I'M OKAY AND I'M SORRY.
I WANT TO MAKE SURE THEY AREN'T MAD AT ME...
...BUT I DON'T KNOW HOW I CAN.

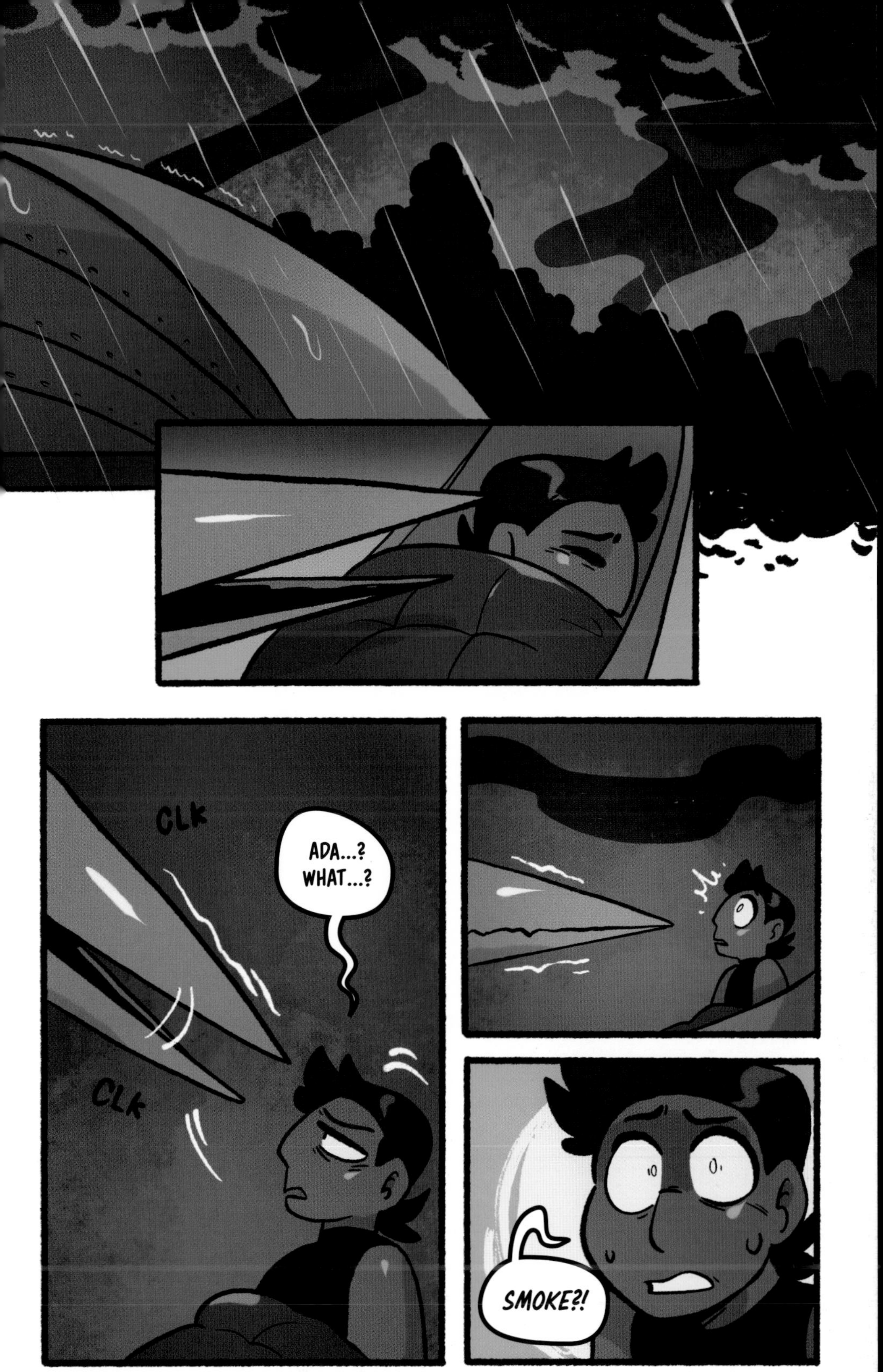
CLK
ADA...? WHAT...?
CLK
SMOKE?!

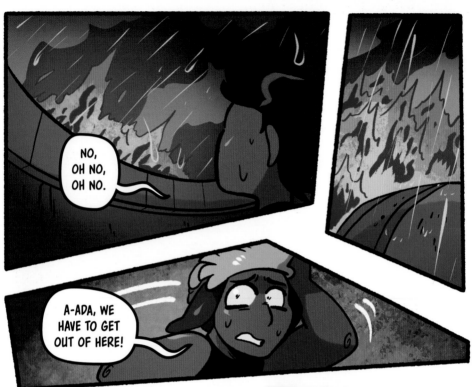

NO,
OH NO,
OH NO.

A-ADA, WE
HAVE TO GET
OUT OF HERE!

IT'S OKAY,
IT'S OKAY!

C'MON!

THAT'S IT,
H-HOLD STILL...

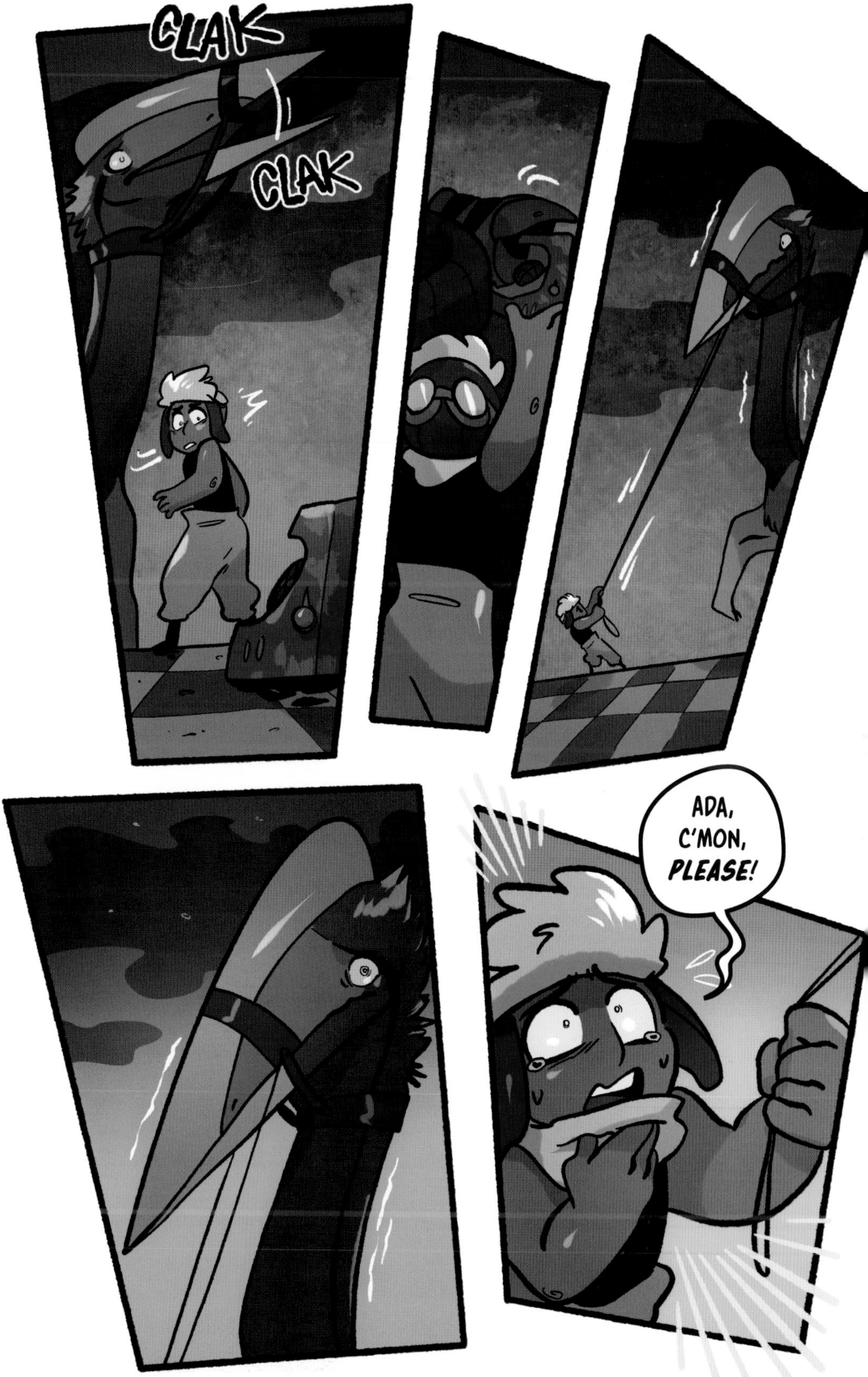
CLAK
CLAK
ADA, C'MON, PLEASE!

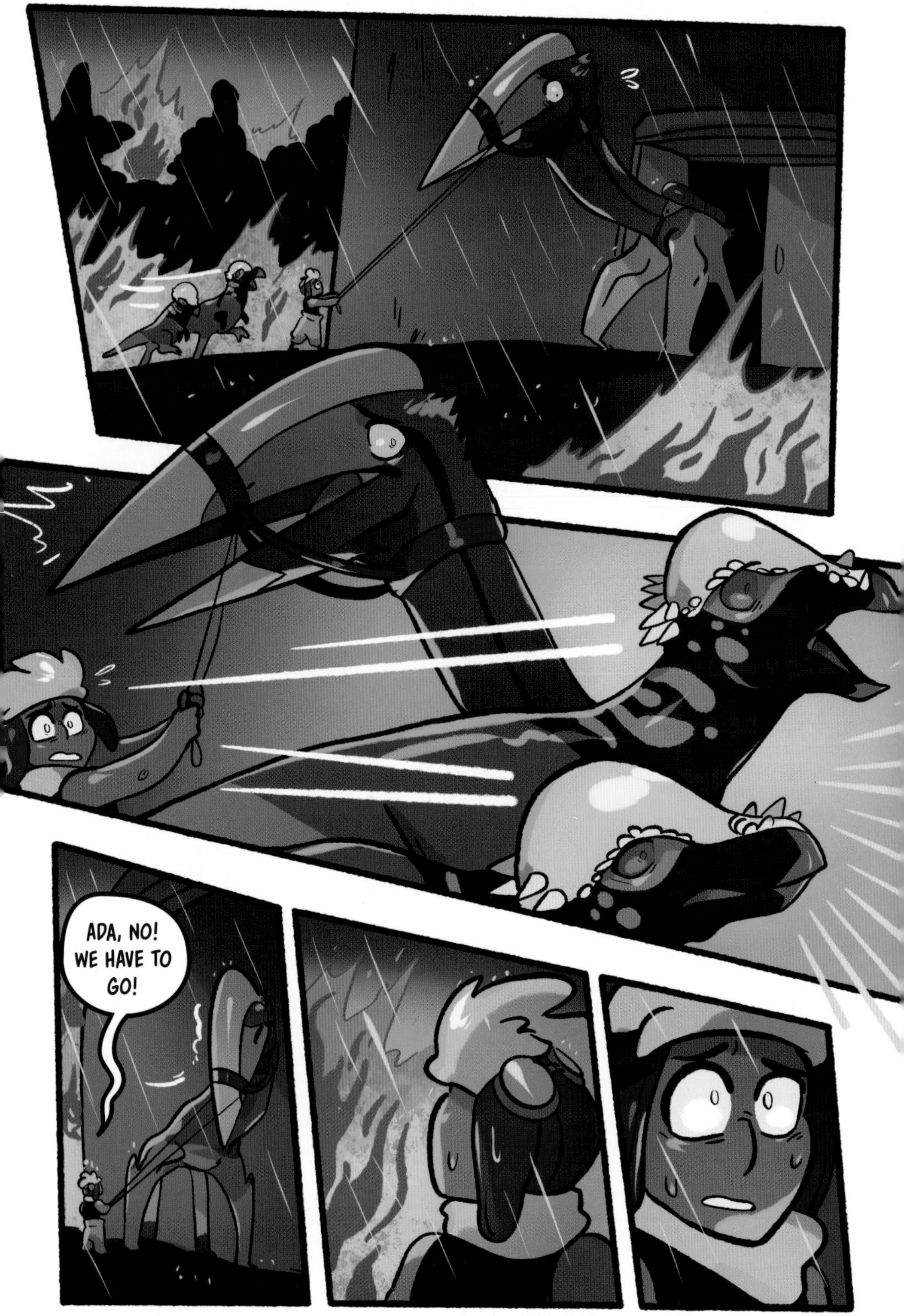
ADA, NO! WE HAVE TO GO!

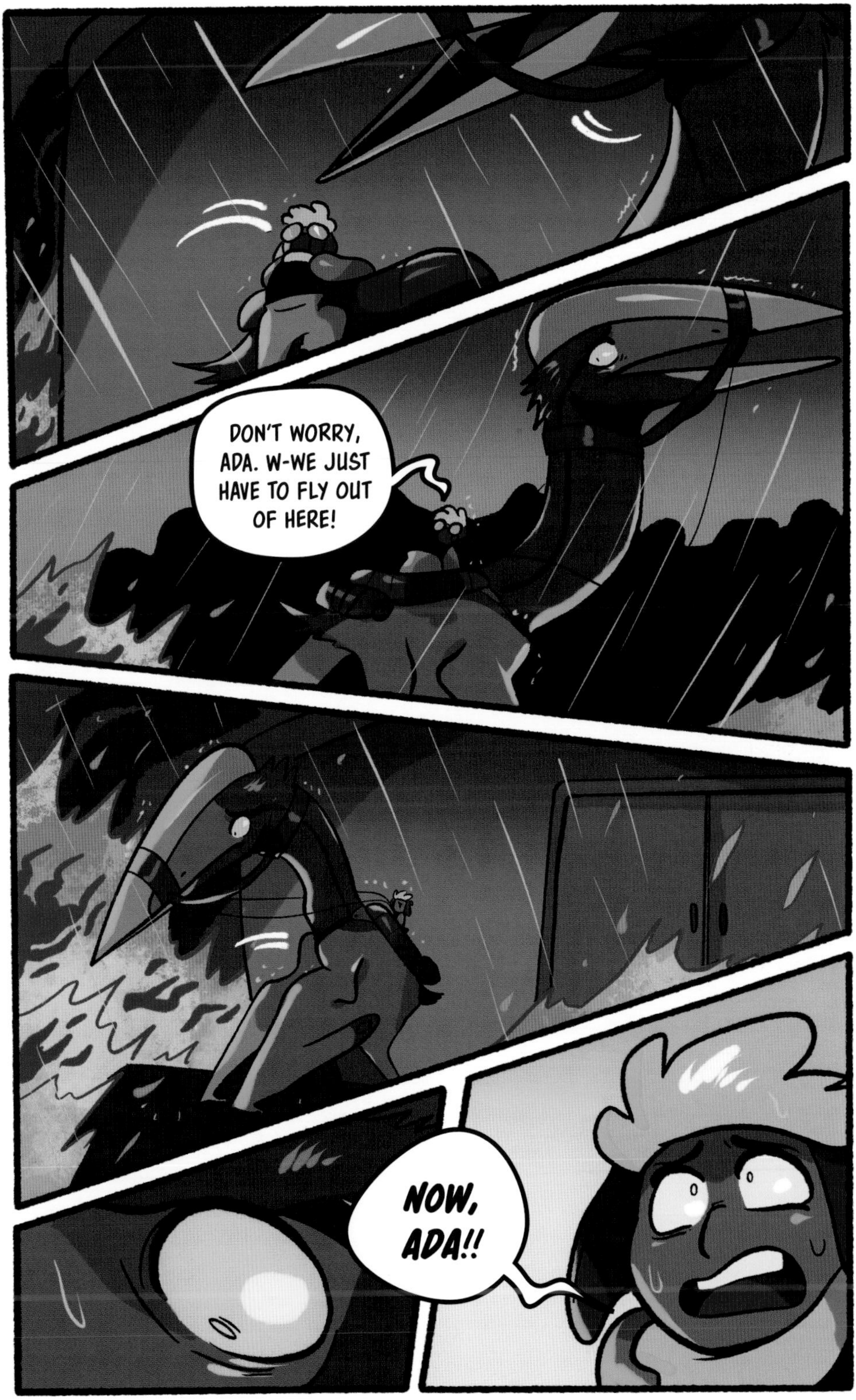
DON'T WORRY, ADA. W-WE JUST HAVE TO FLY OUT OF HERE!
NOW, ADA!!

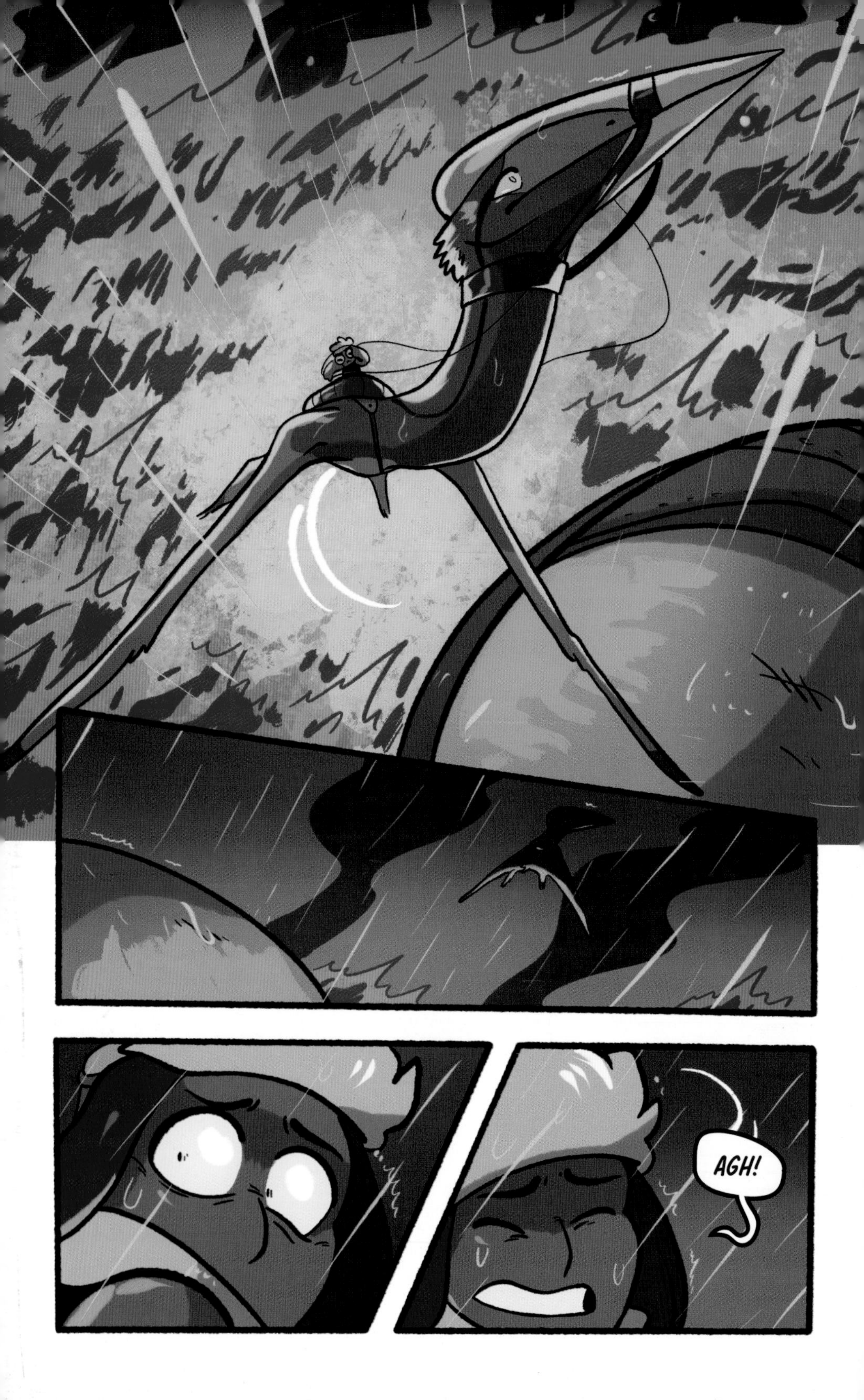
AGH!

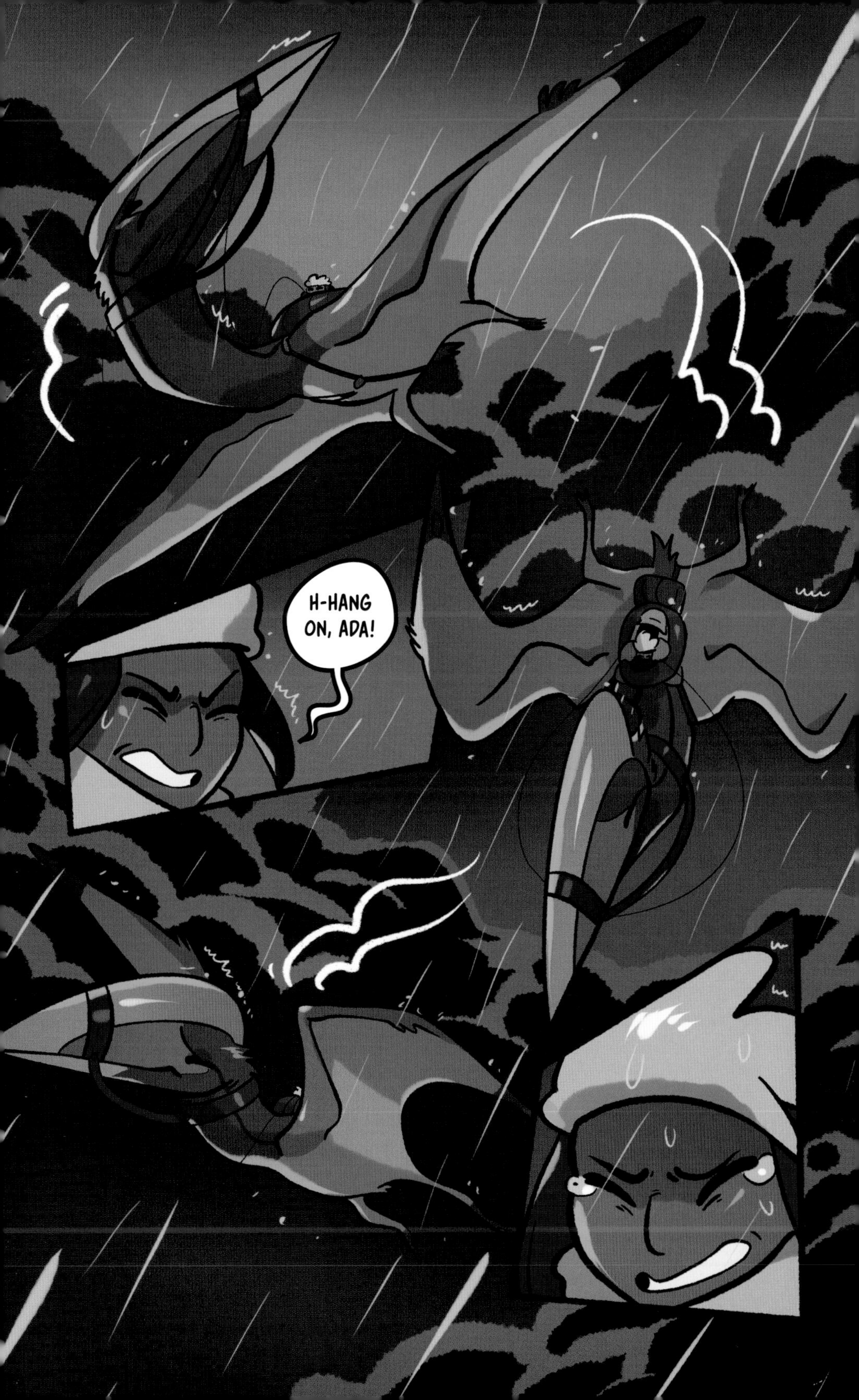
H-HANG ON, ADA!

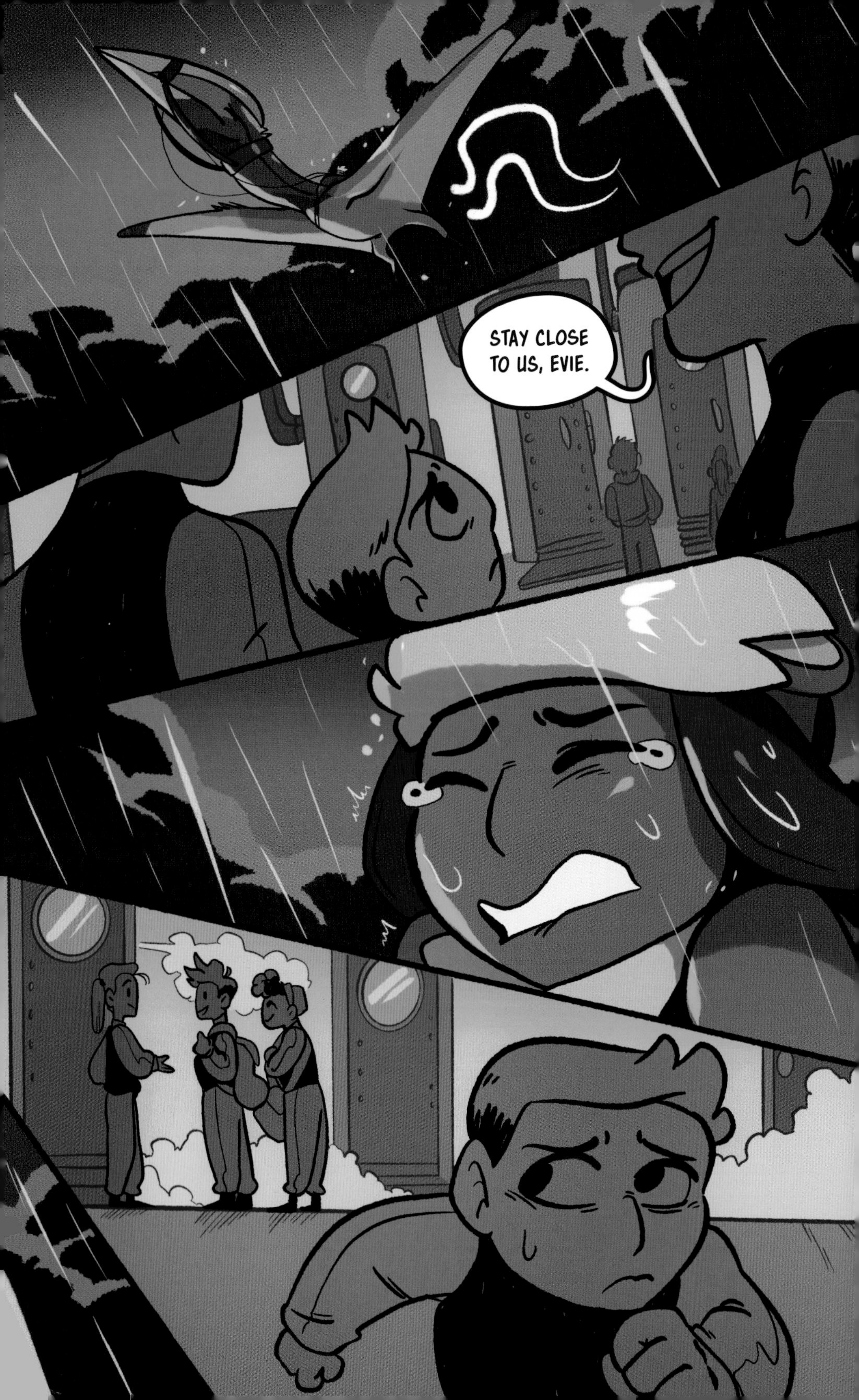
STAY CLOSE TO US, EVIE.

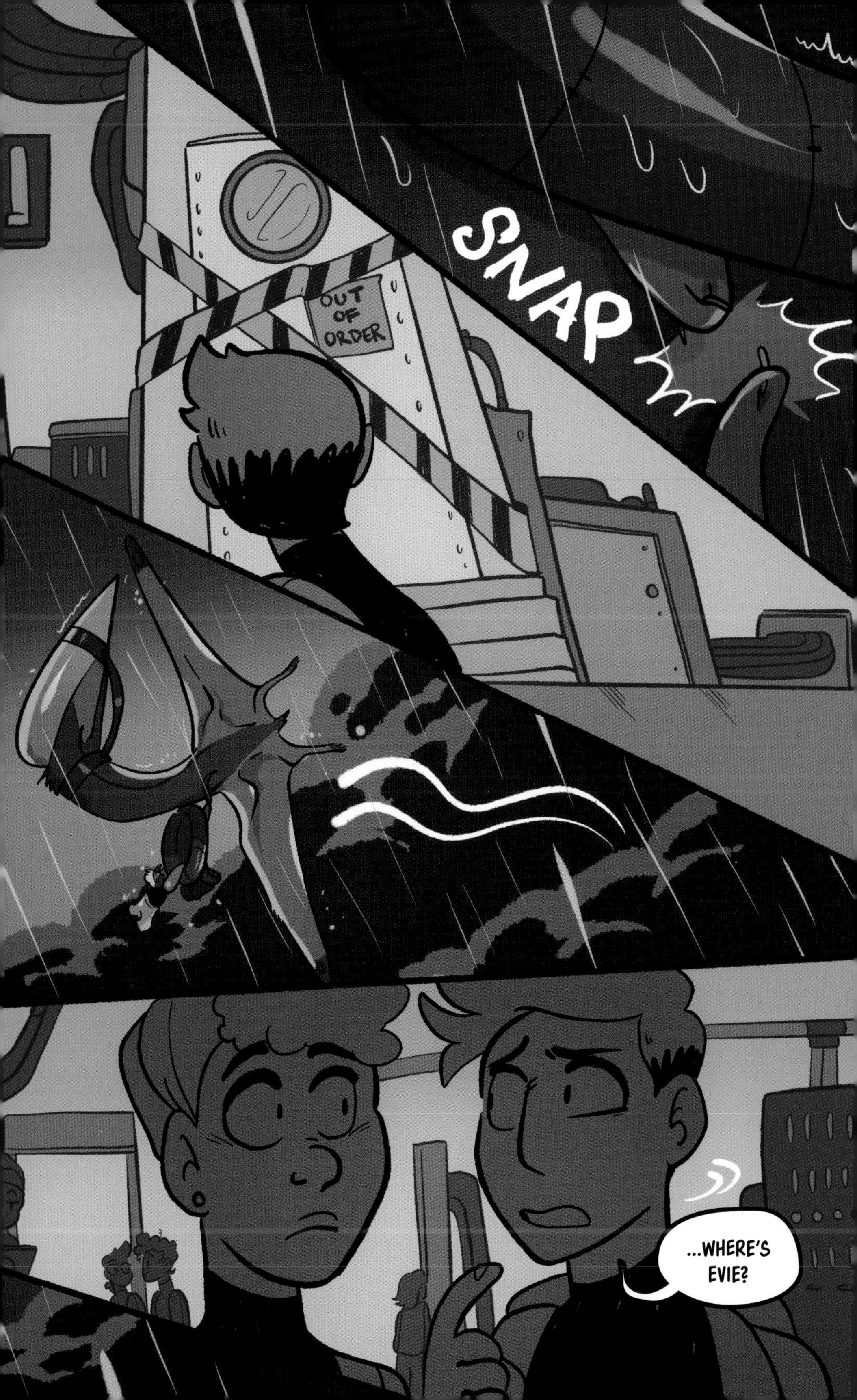
SNAP
OUT OF ORDER
...WHERE'S EVIE?

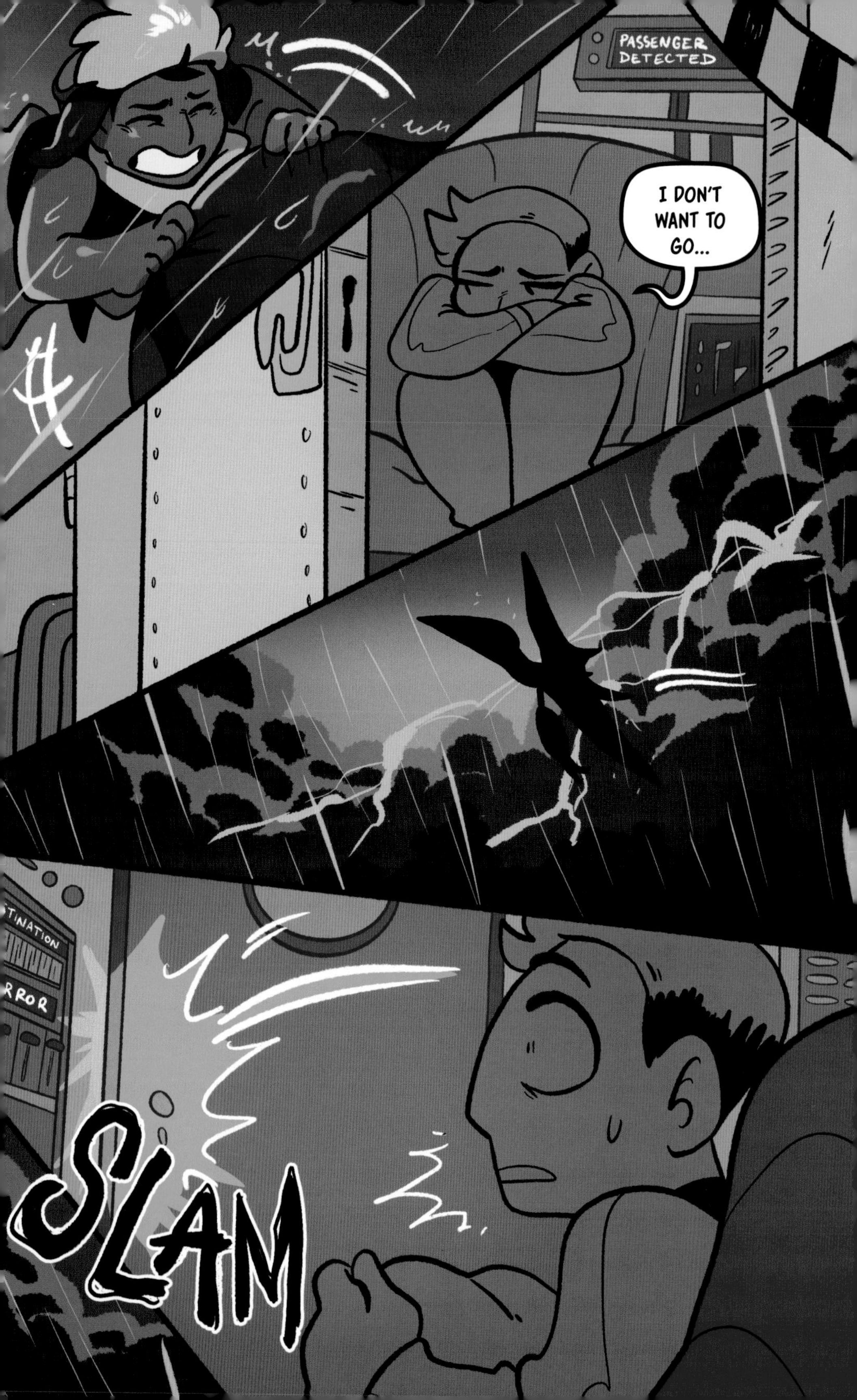
PASSENGER DETECTED
I DON'T WANT TO GO...
SLAM

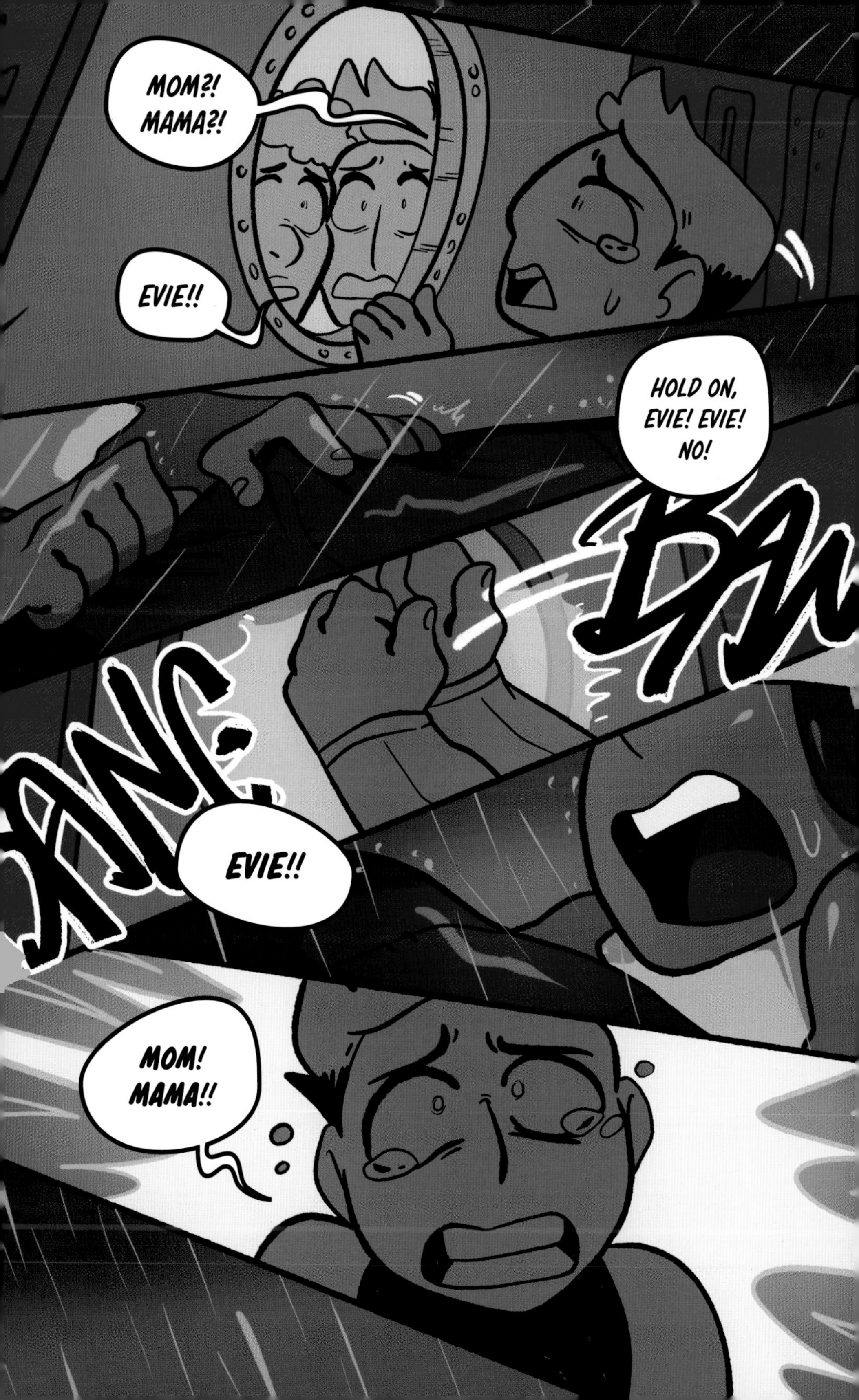
MOM?! MAMA?!
EVIE!!
HOLD ON, EVIE! EVIE! NO!
BANG!
EVIE!!
MOM! MAMA!!

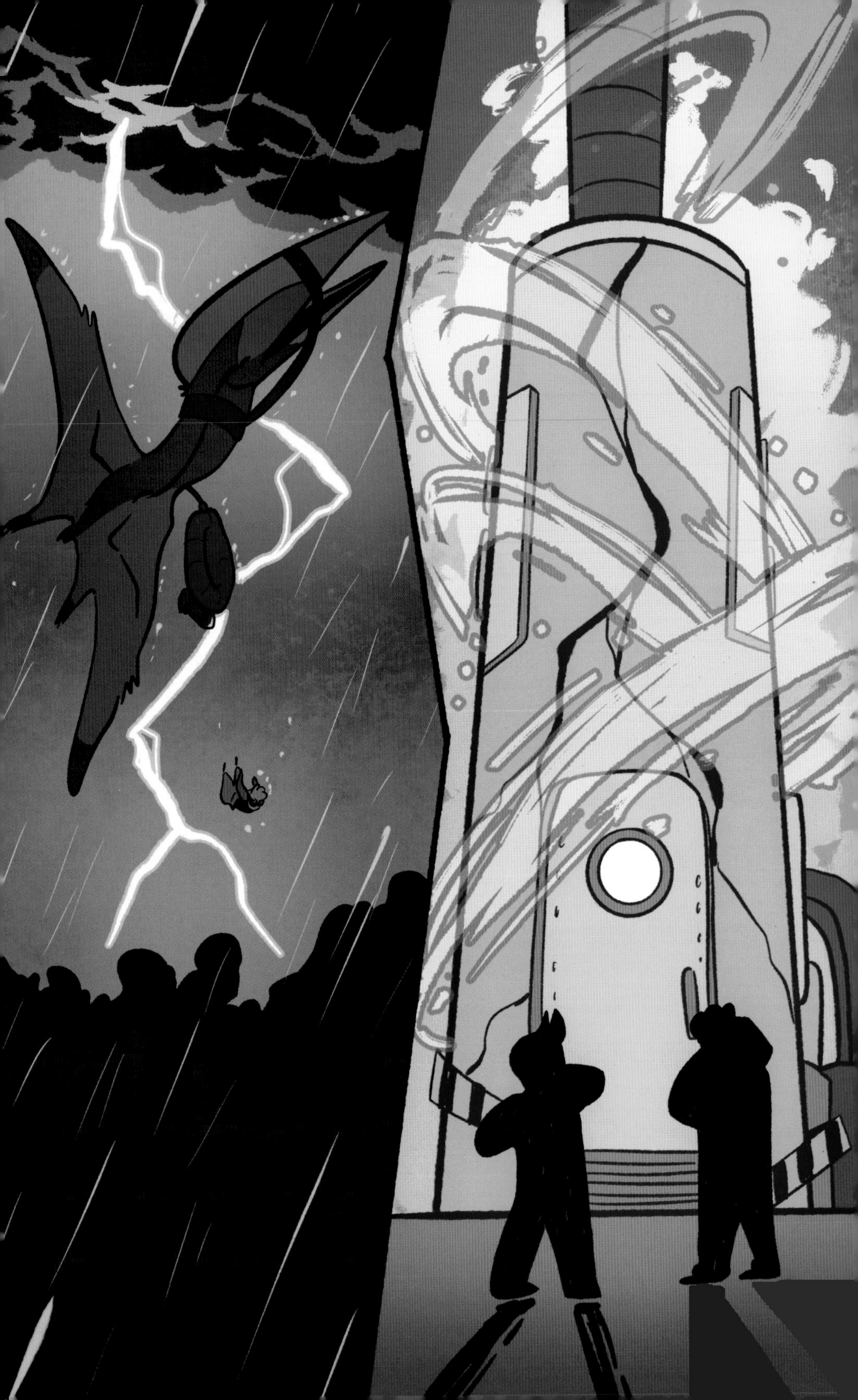

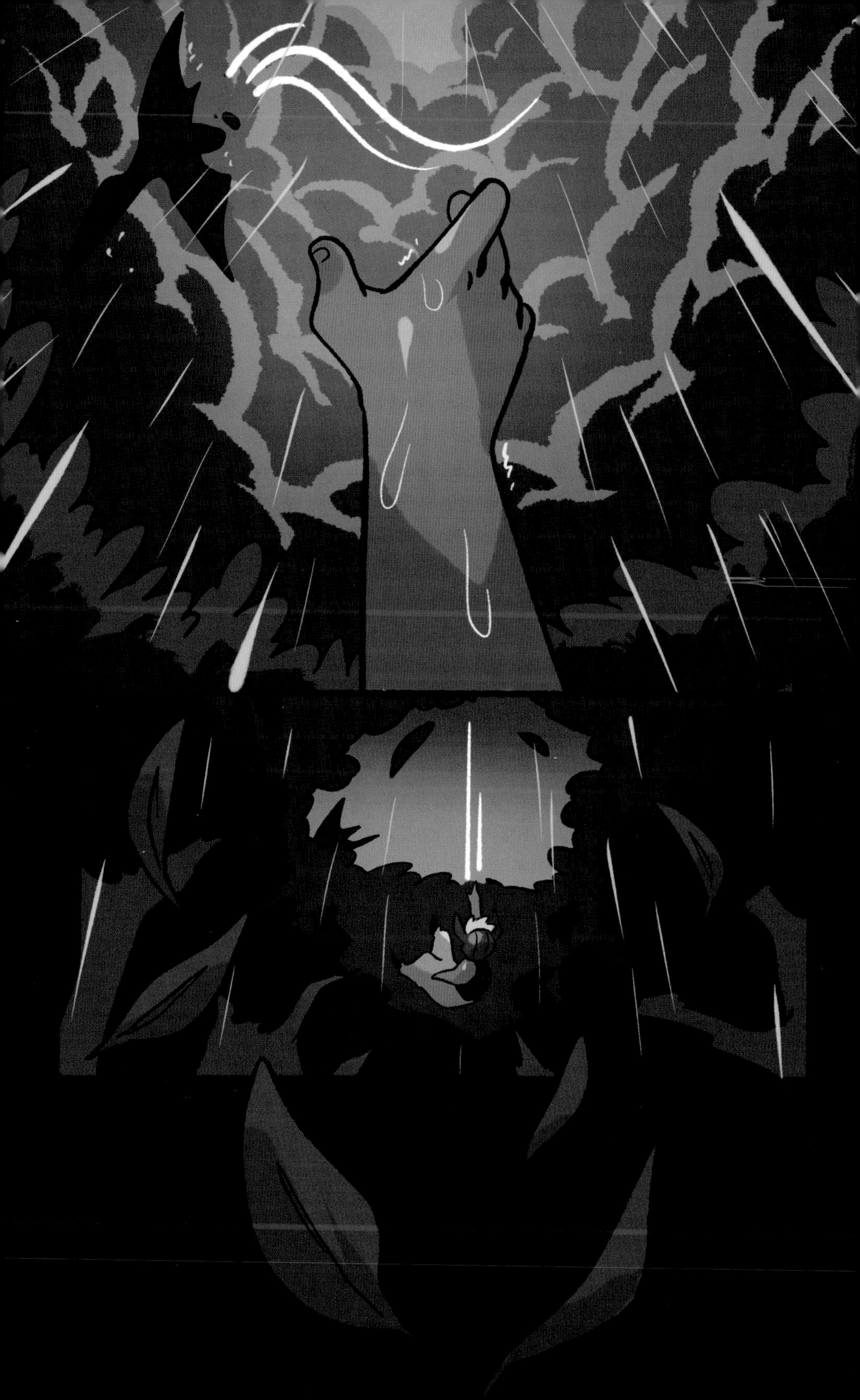

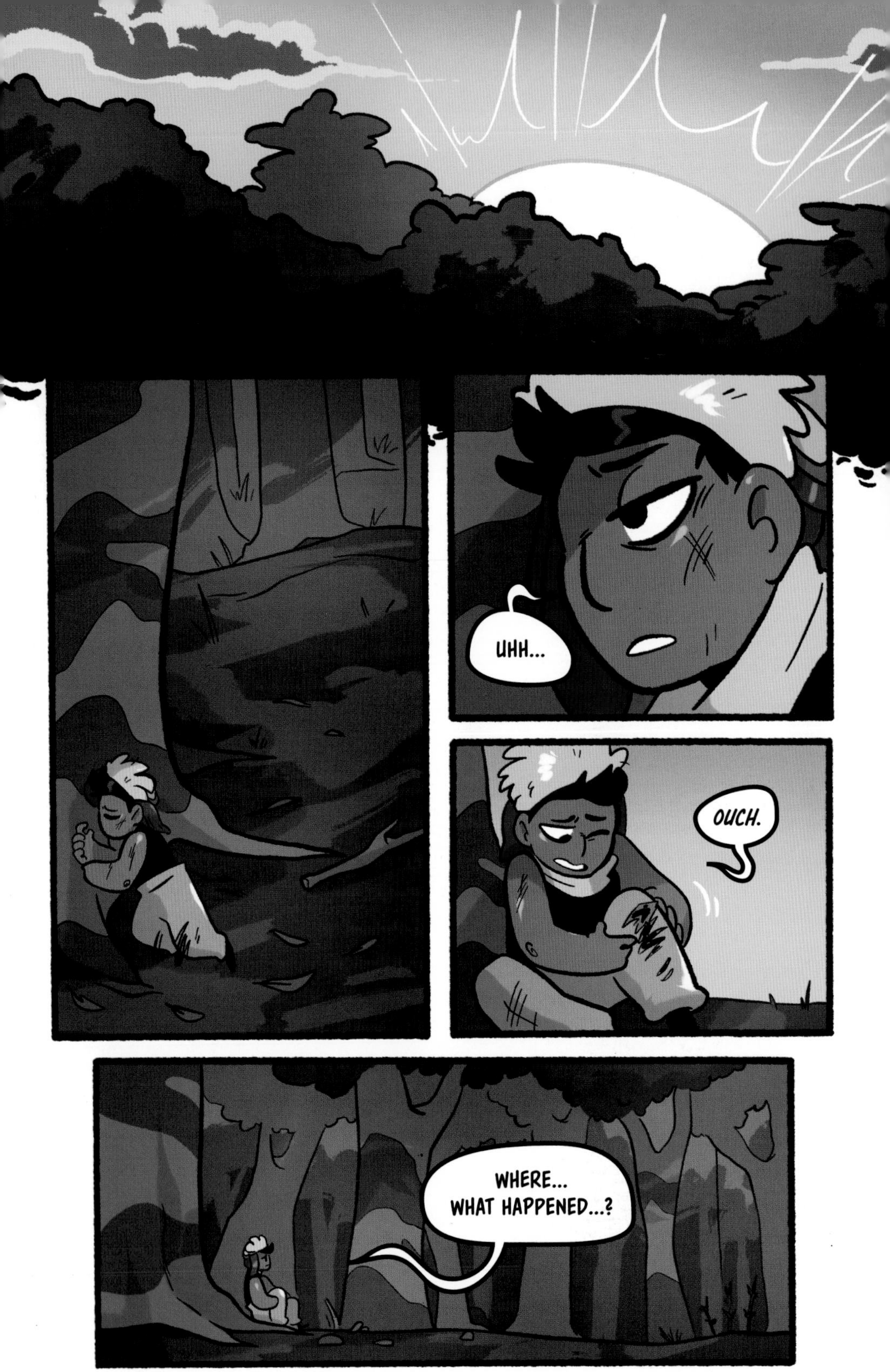
UHH...
OUCH.
WHERE...
WHAT HAPPENED...?

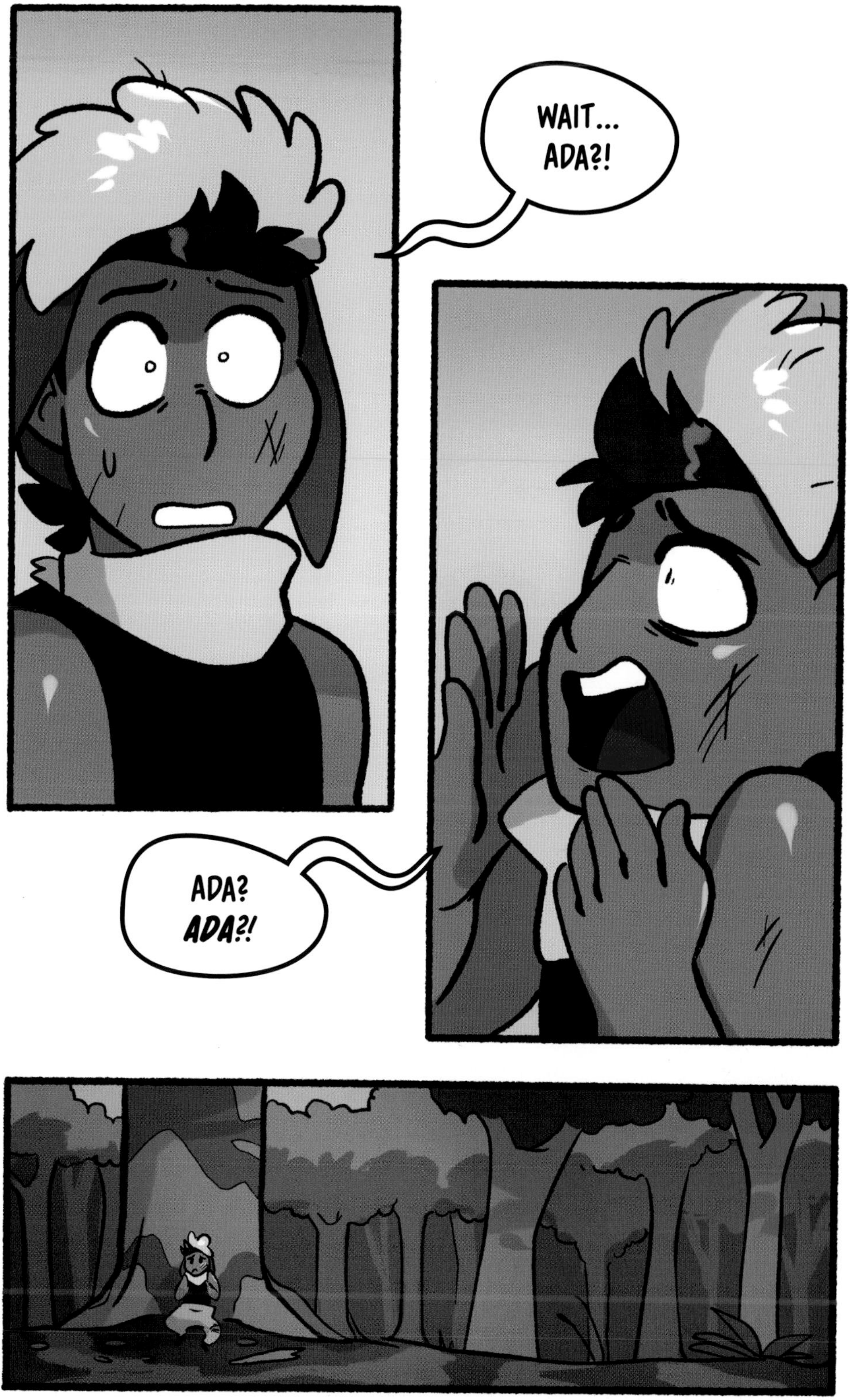
WAIT... ADA?!
ADA? ADA?!

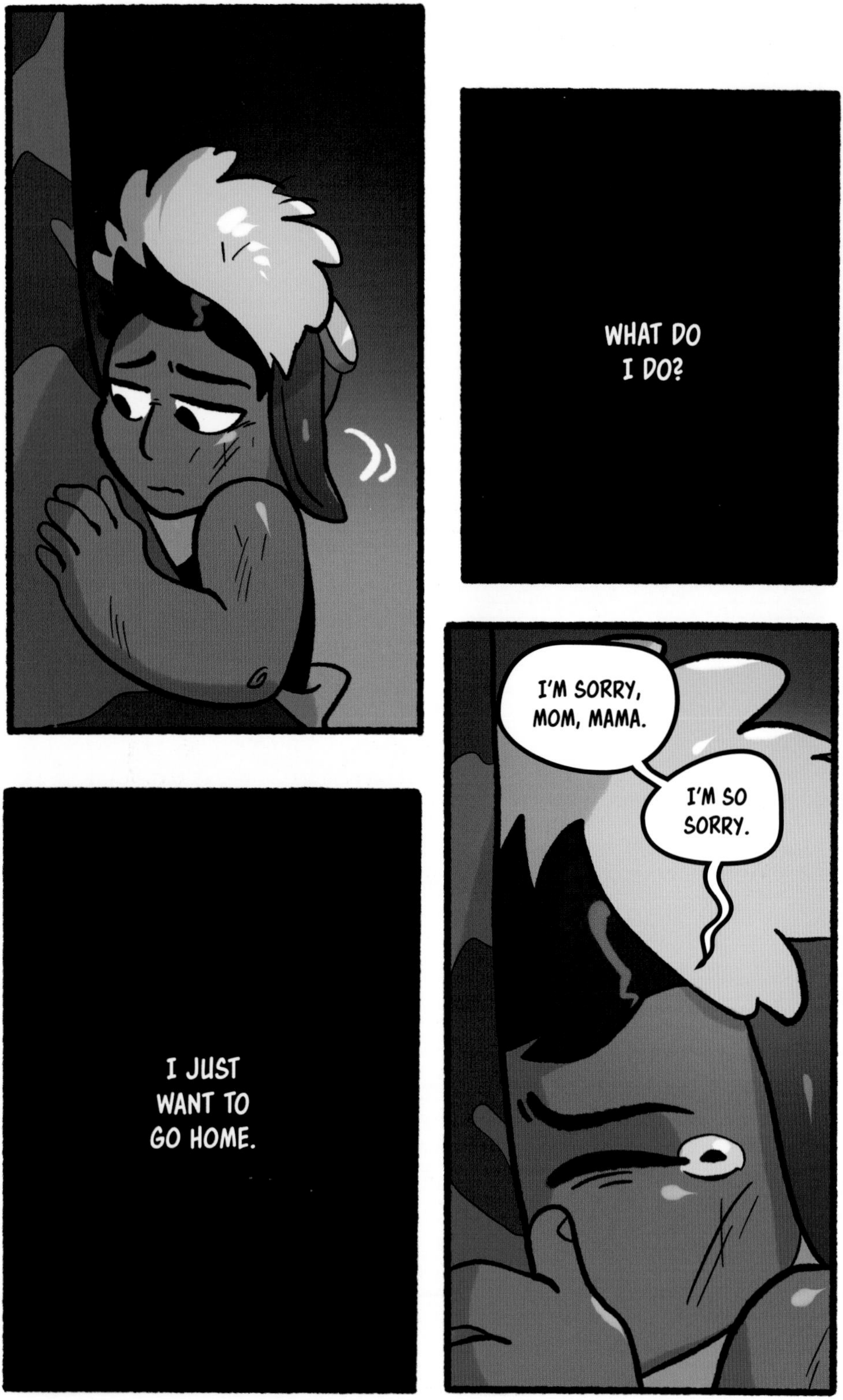
WHAT DO I DO?
I'M SORRY, MOM, MAMA.
I'M SO SORRY.
I JUST WANT TO GO HOME.

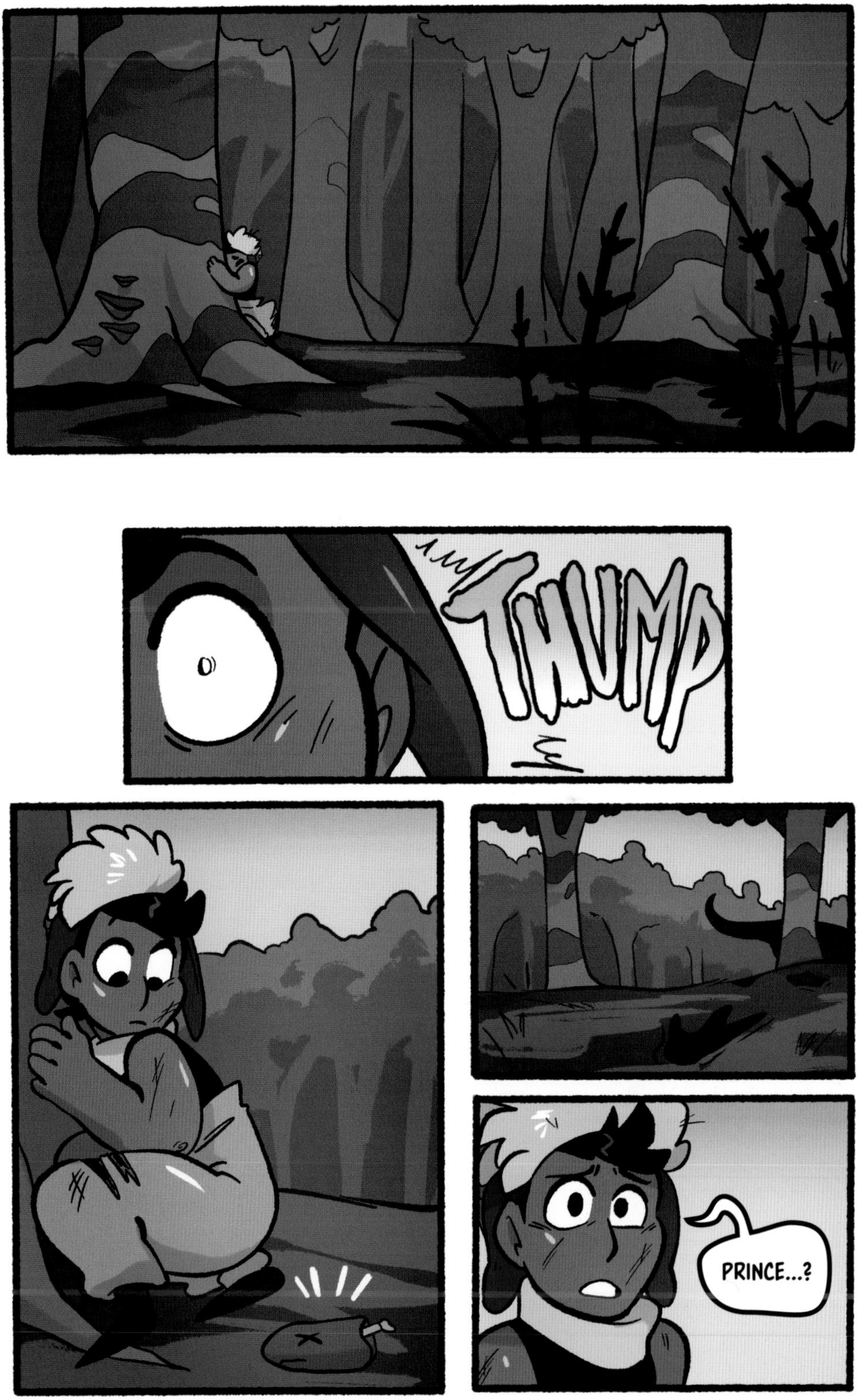
THUMP
PRINCE...?

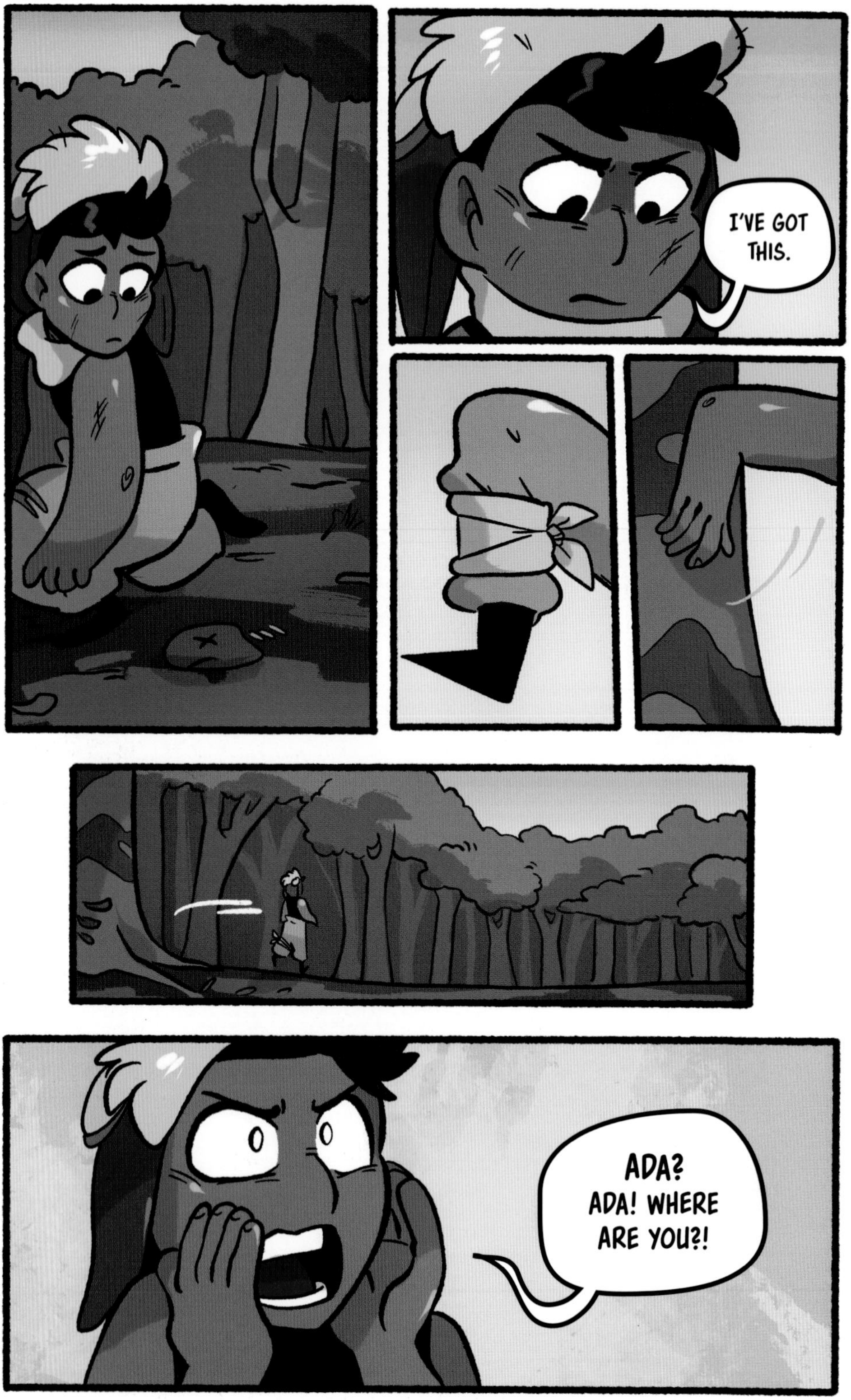
I'VE GOT THIS.
ADA? ADA! WHERE ARE YOU?!

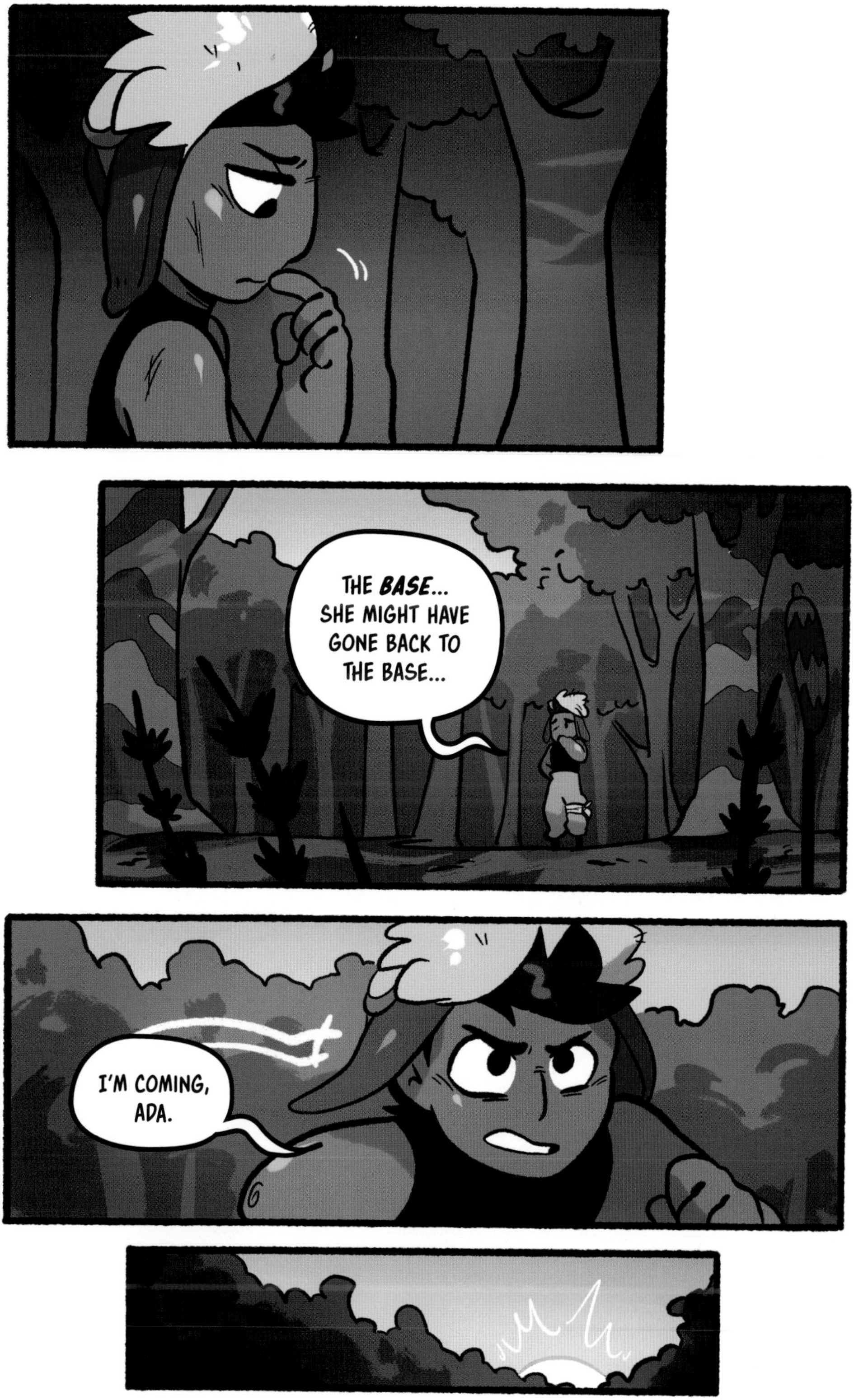
THE *BASE*... SHE MIGHT HAVE GONE BACK TO THE BASE...
I'M COMING, ADA.

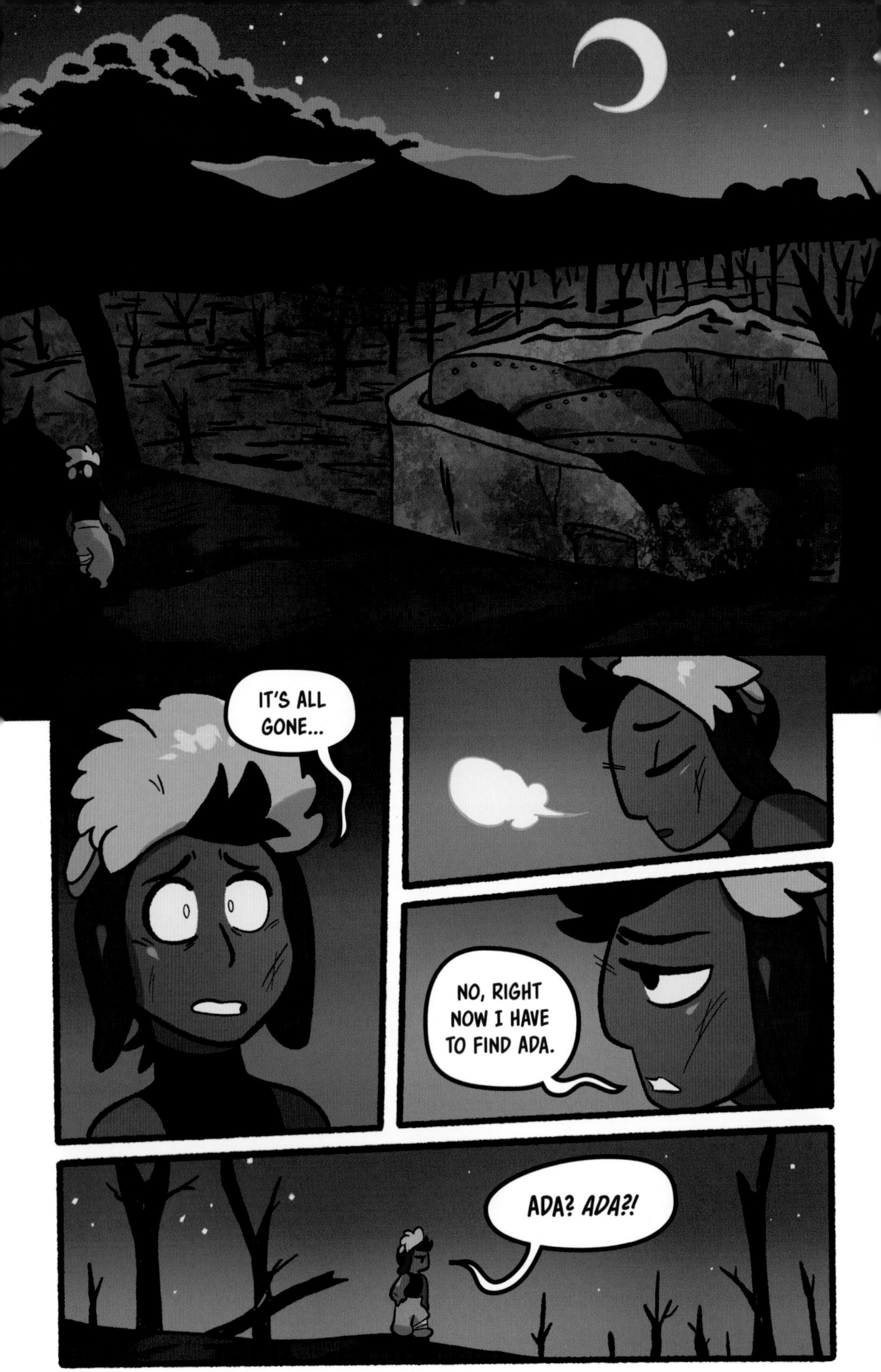
IT'S ALL GONE...
NO, RIGHT NOW I HAVE TO FIND ADA.
ADA? ADA?!

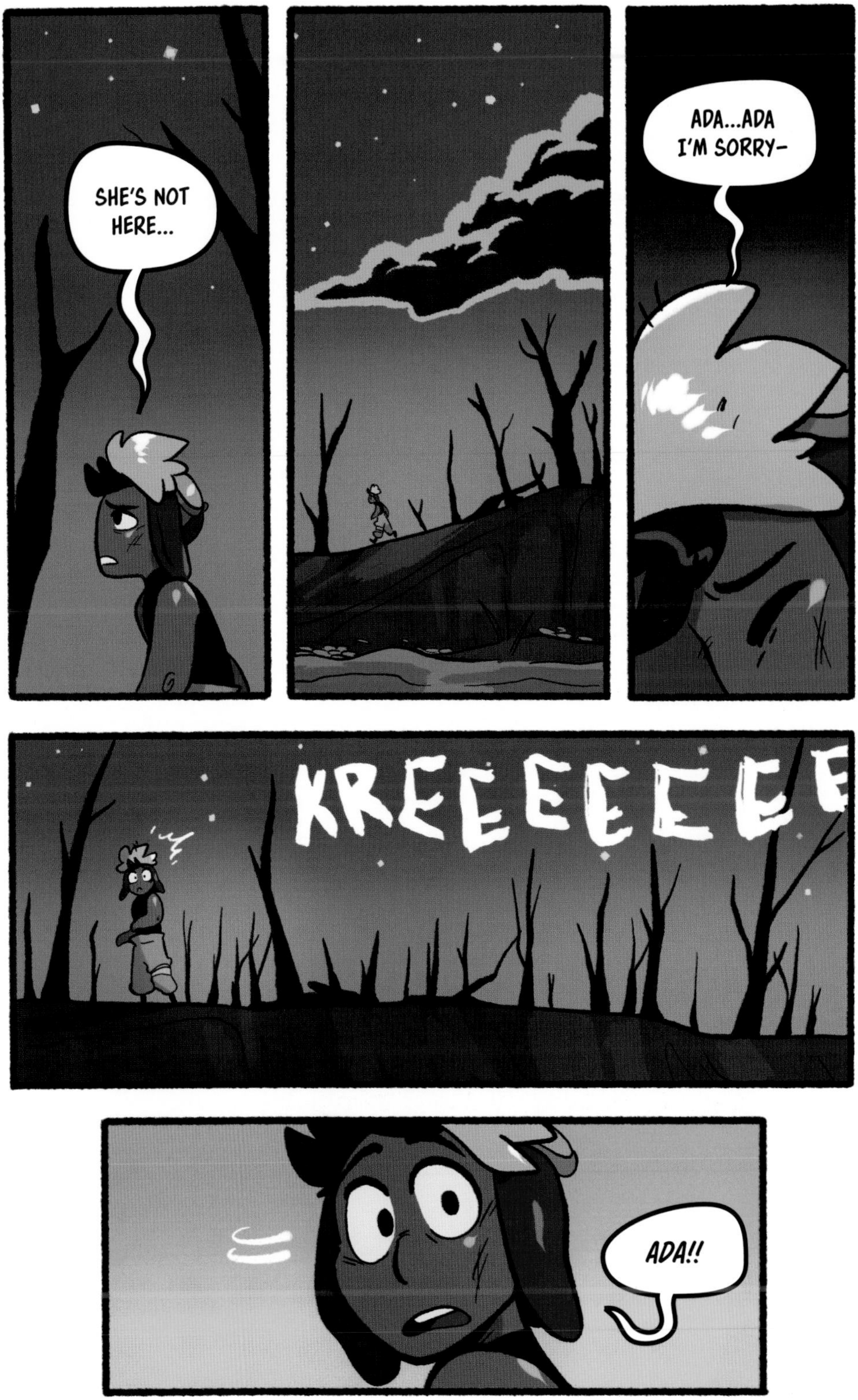
SHE'S NOT HERE...
ADA...ADA I'M SORRY-
KREEEEEEE
ADA!!

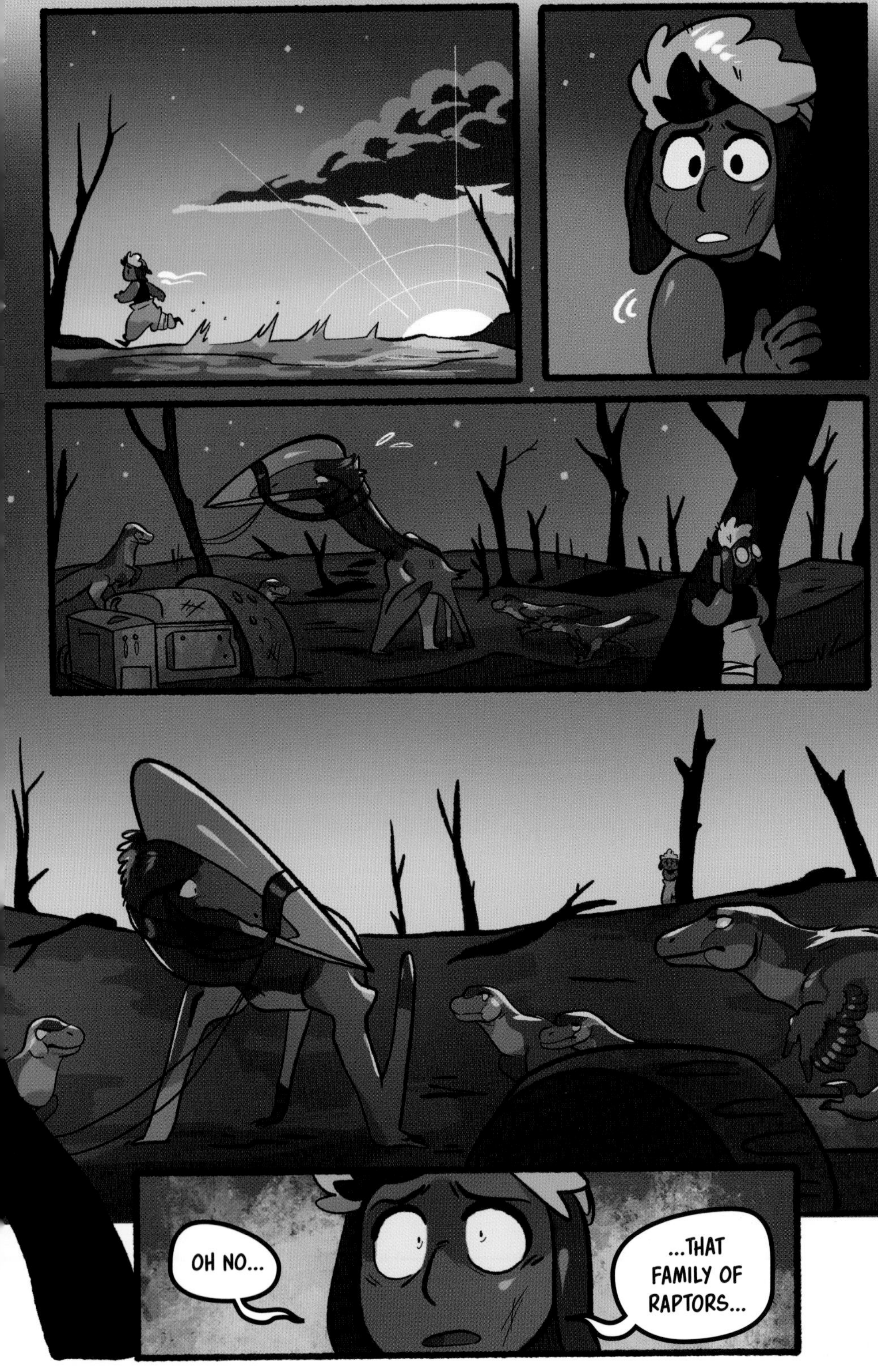
OH NO...
...THAT FAMILY OF RAPTORS...

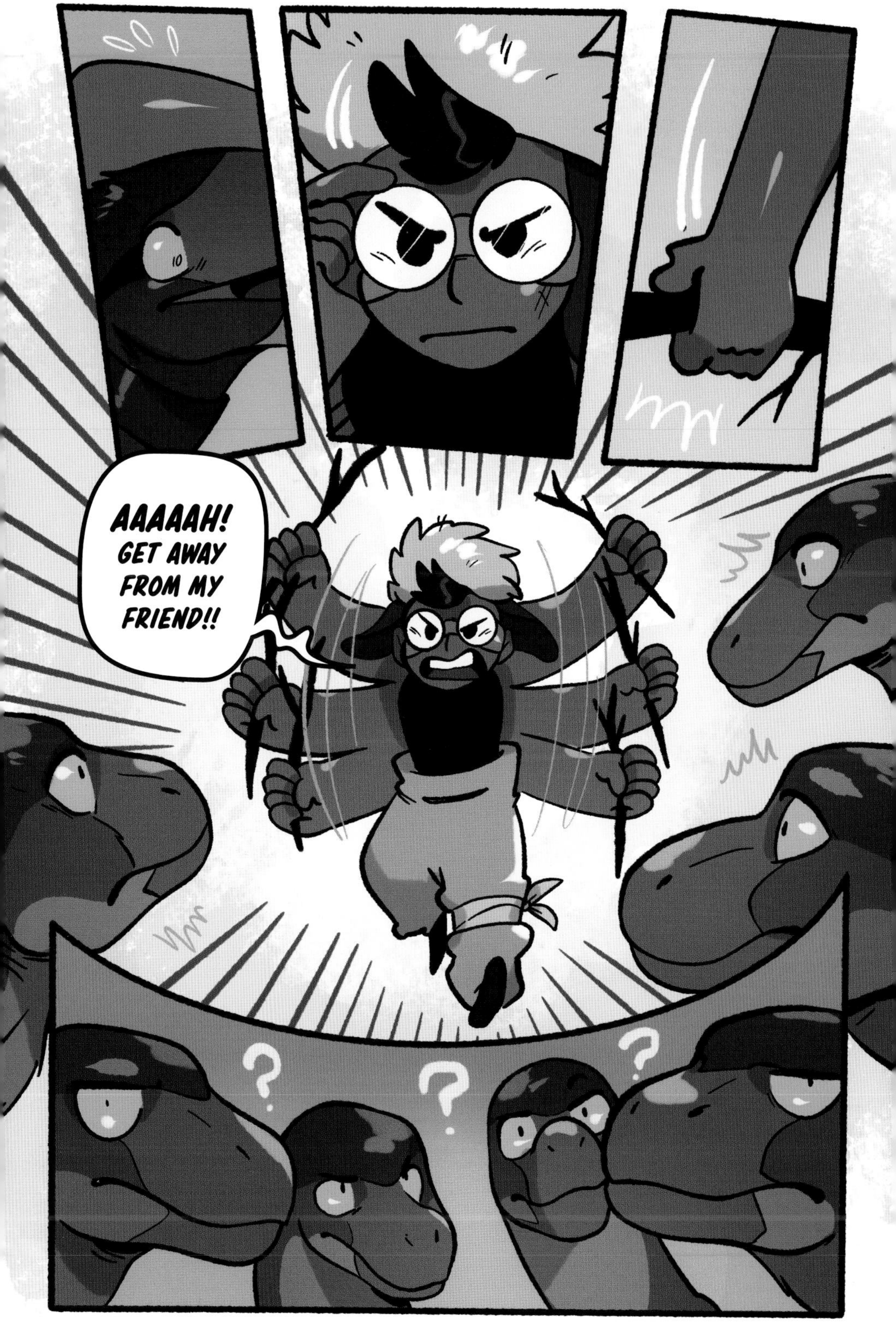
AAAAAH! GET AWAY FROM MY FRIEND!!

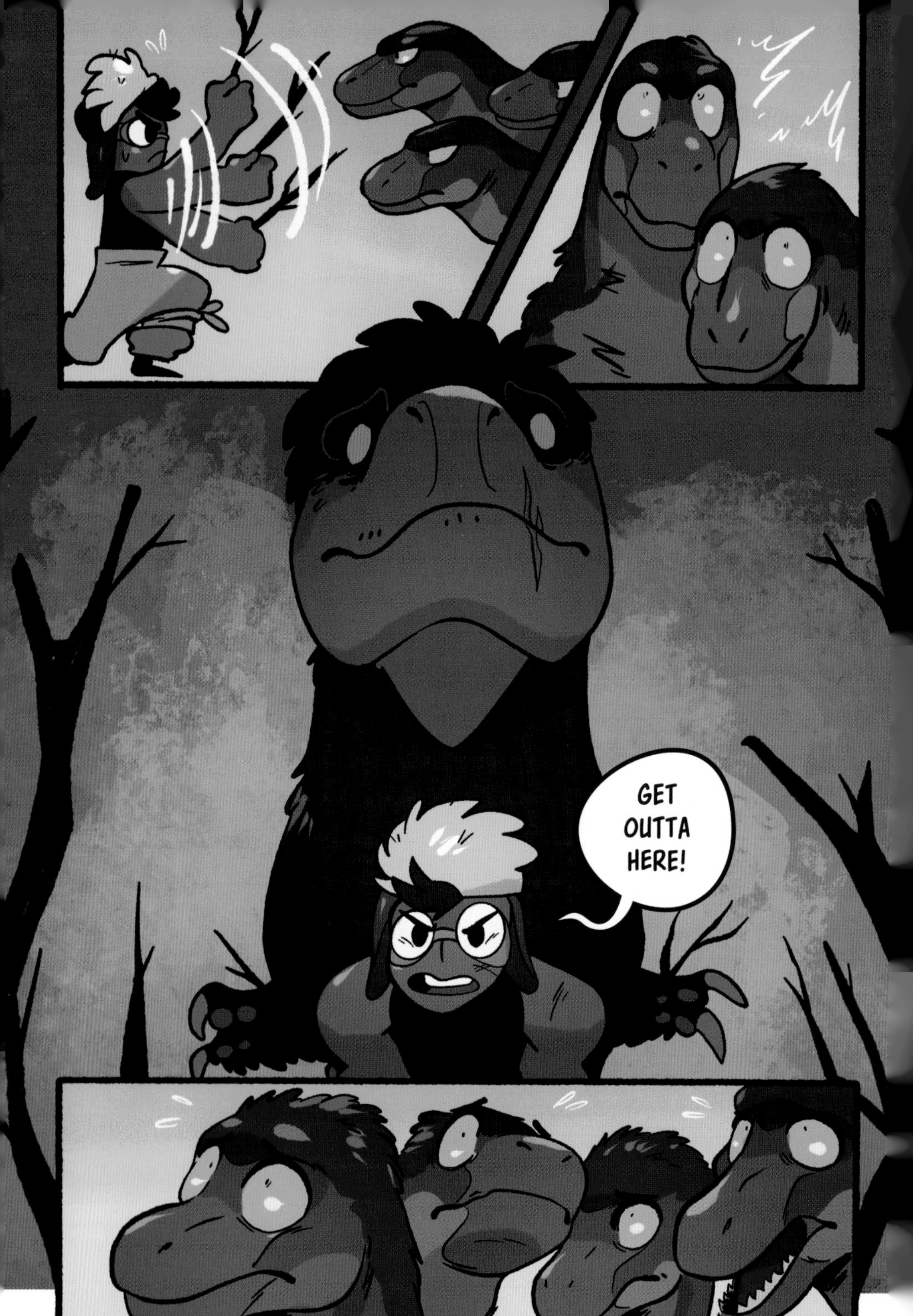
GET OUTTA HERE!

YEAH, YOU BETTER RUN!

SNRT

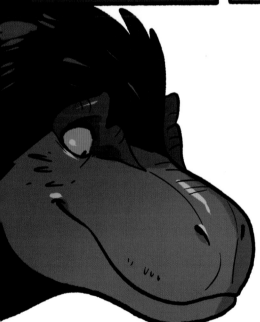

THANK YOU...

PRINCE!

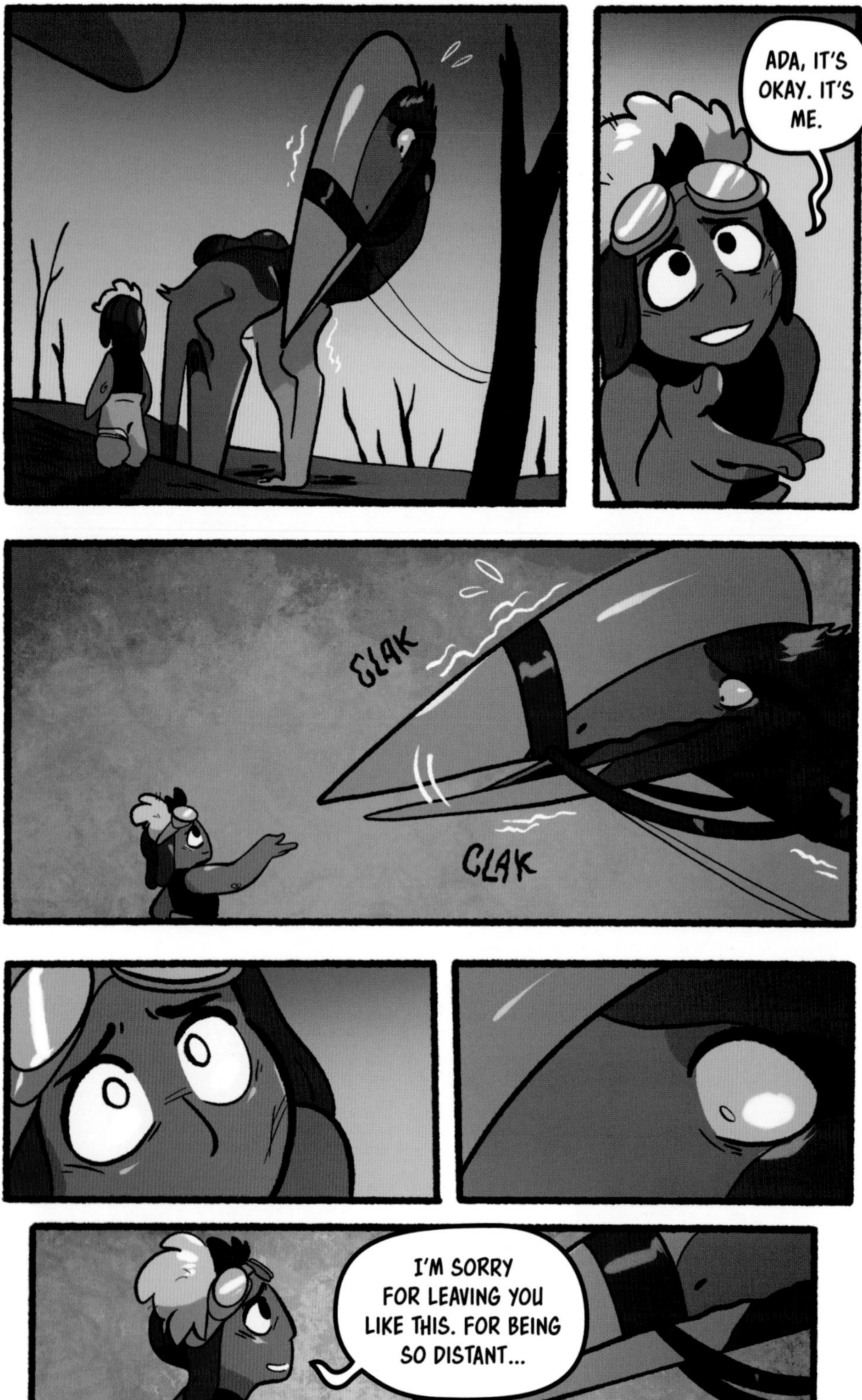
ADA, IT'S OKAY. IT'S ME.
CLAK
CLAK
I'M SORRY FOR LEAVING YOU LIKE THIS. FOR BEING SO DISTANT...

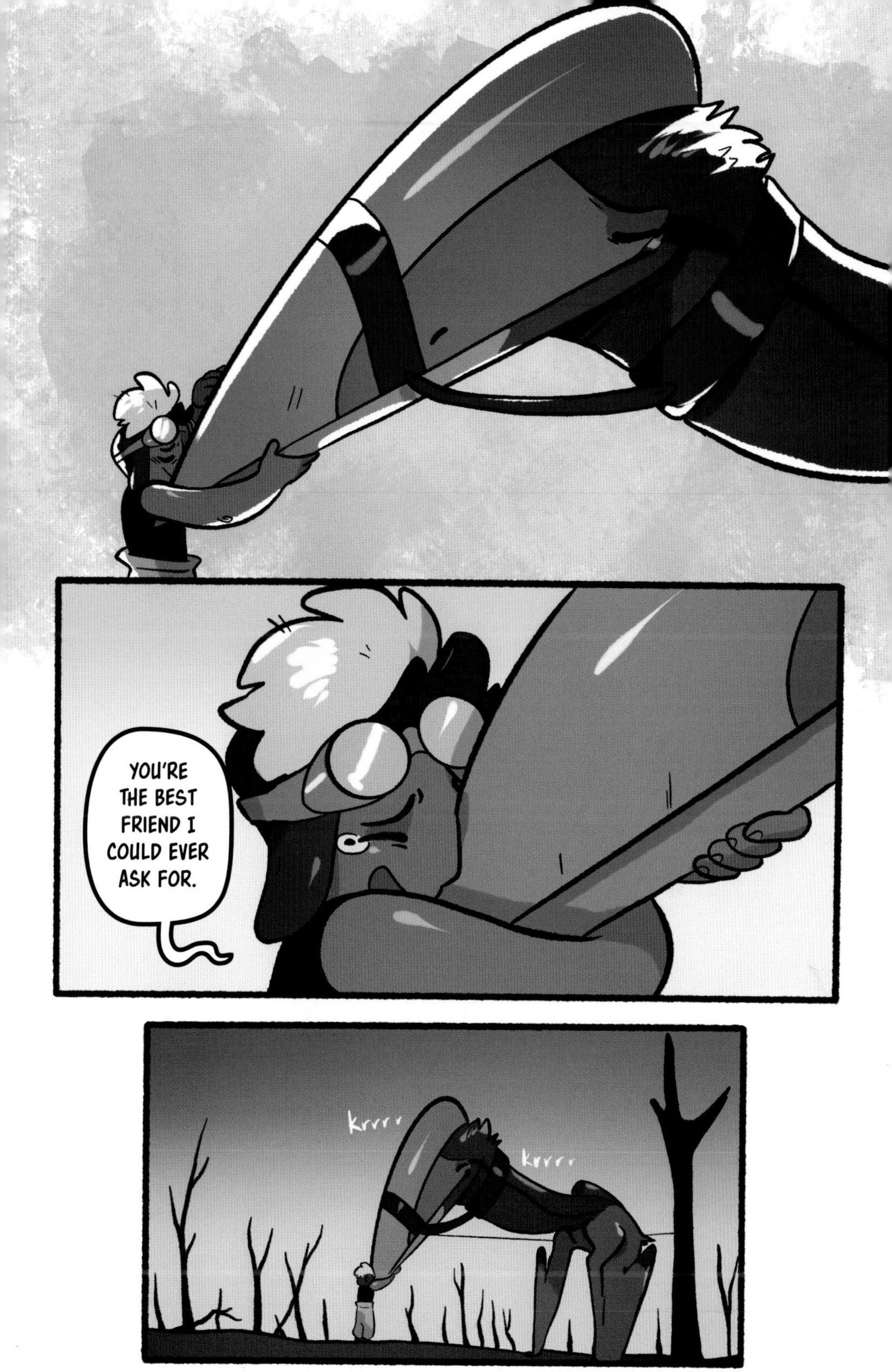
YOU'RE THE BEST FRIEND I COULD EVER ASK FOR.
krrr
krrr

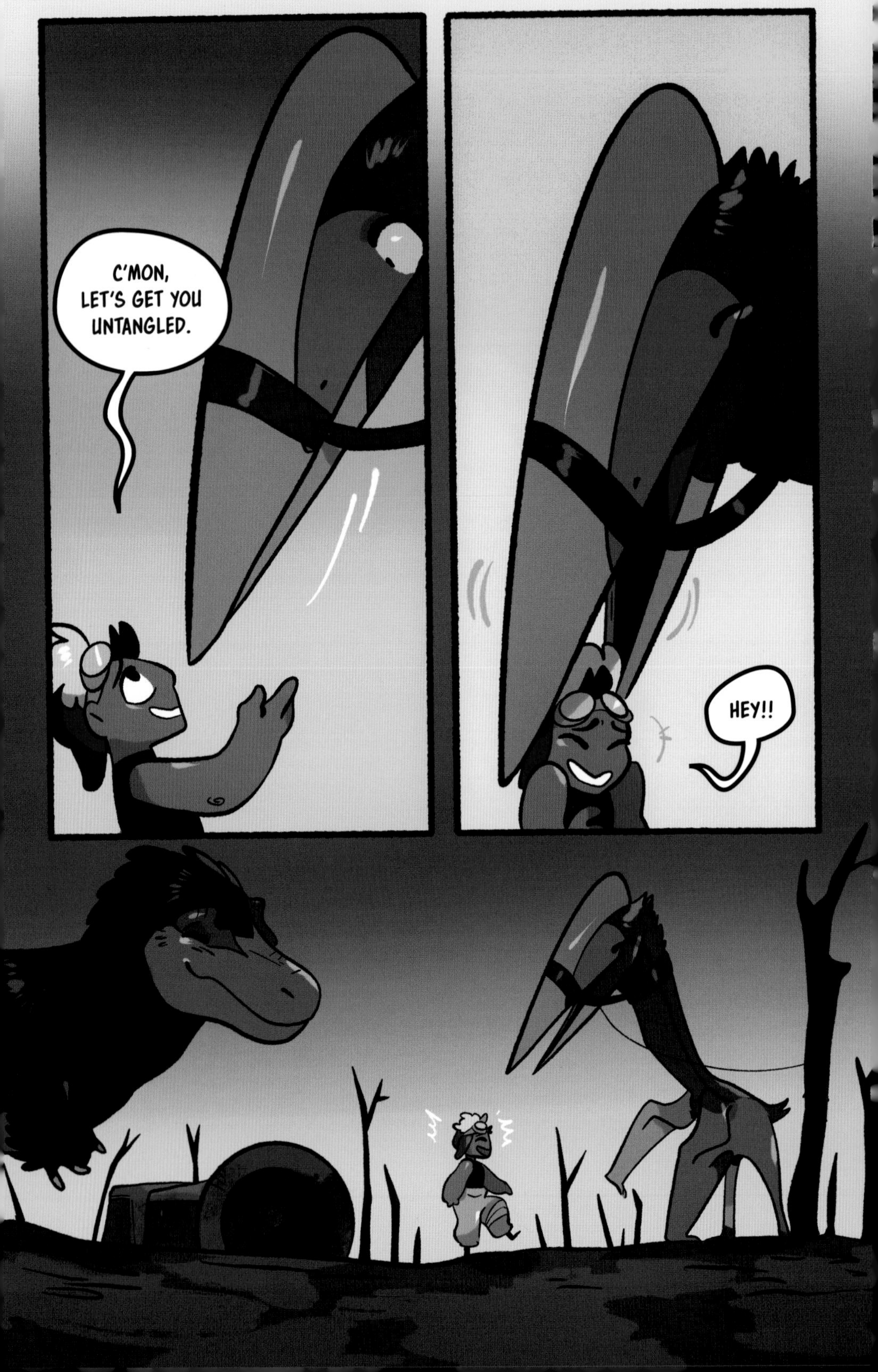
C'MON,
LET'S GET YOU
UNTANGLED.
HEY!!

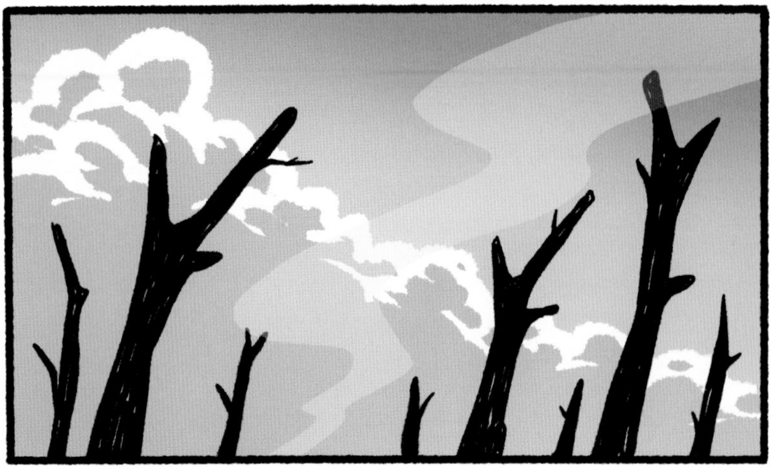

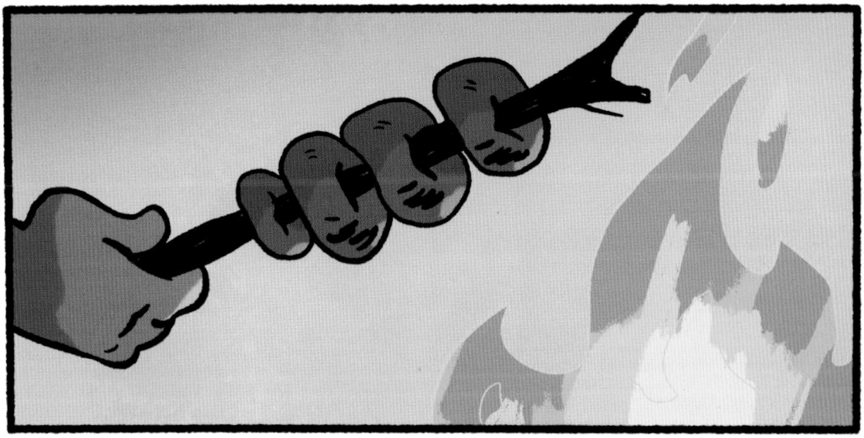

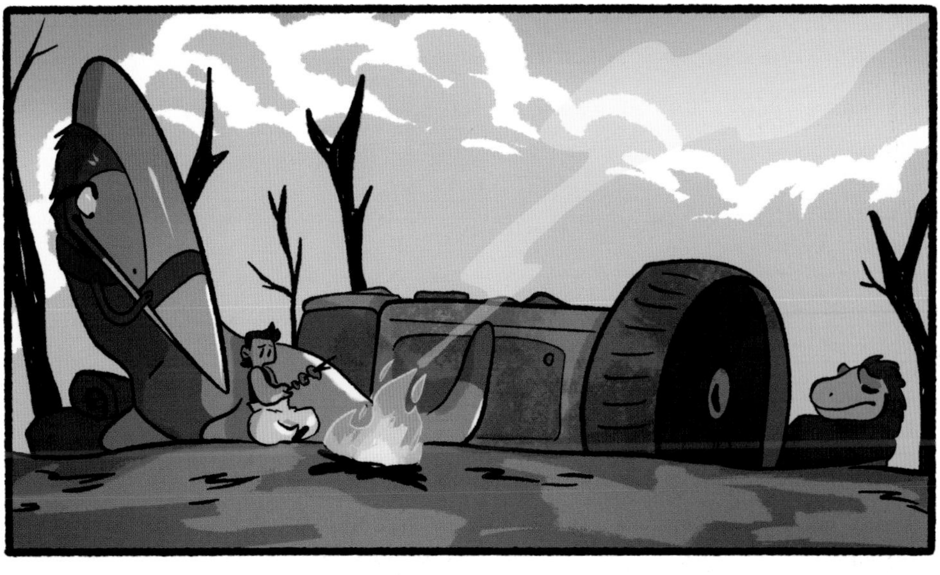

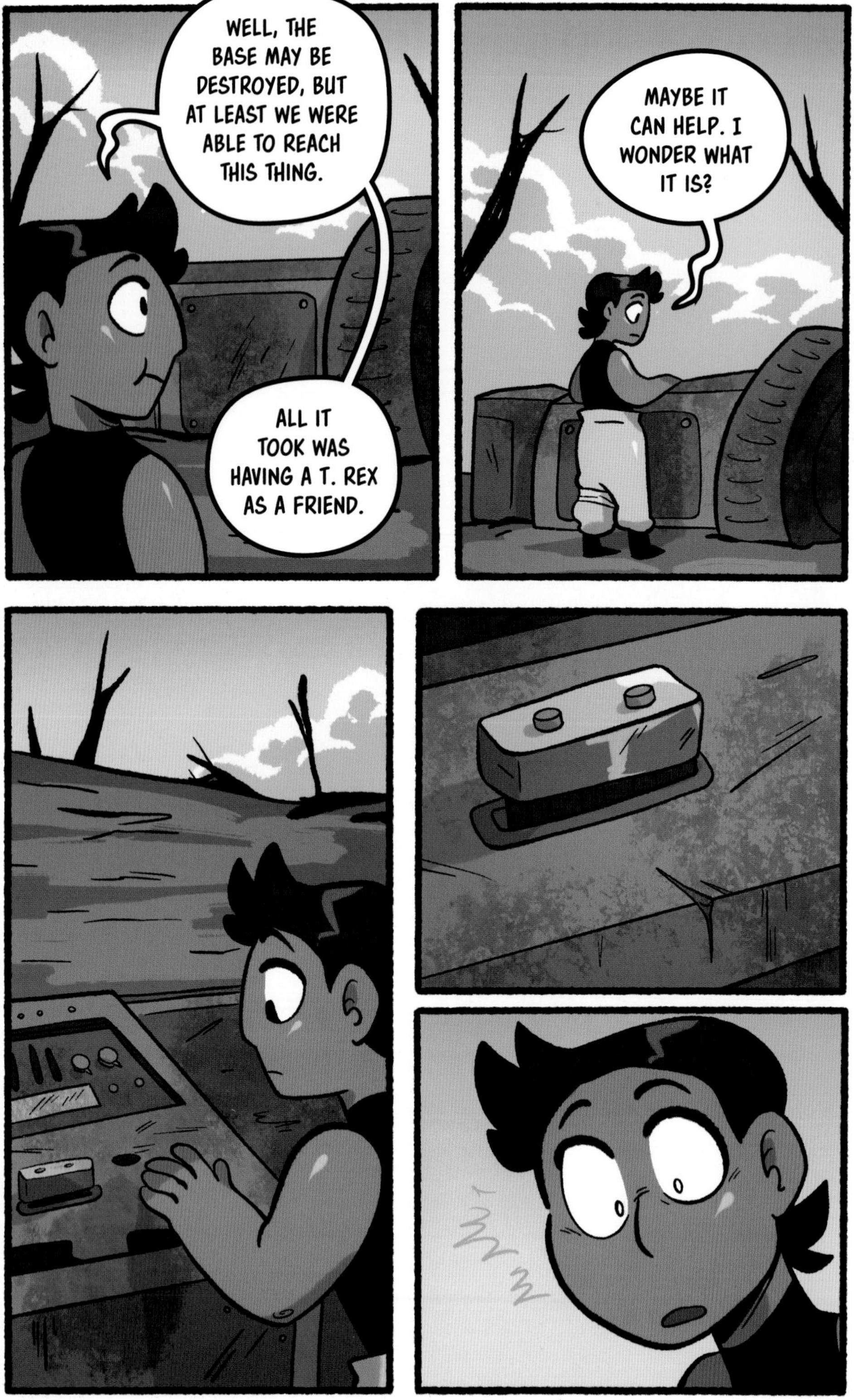
WELL, THE BASE MAY BE DESTROYED, BUT AT LEAST WE WERE ABLE TO REACH THIS THING.
ALL IT TOOK WAS HAVING A T. REX AS A FRIEND.
MAYBE IT CAN HELP. I WONDER WHAT IT IS?

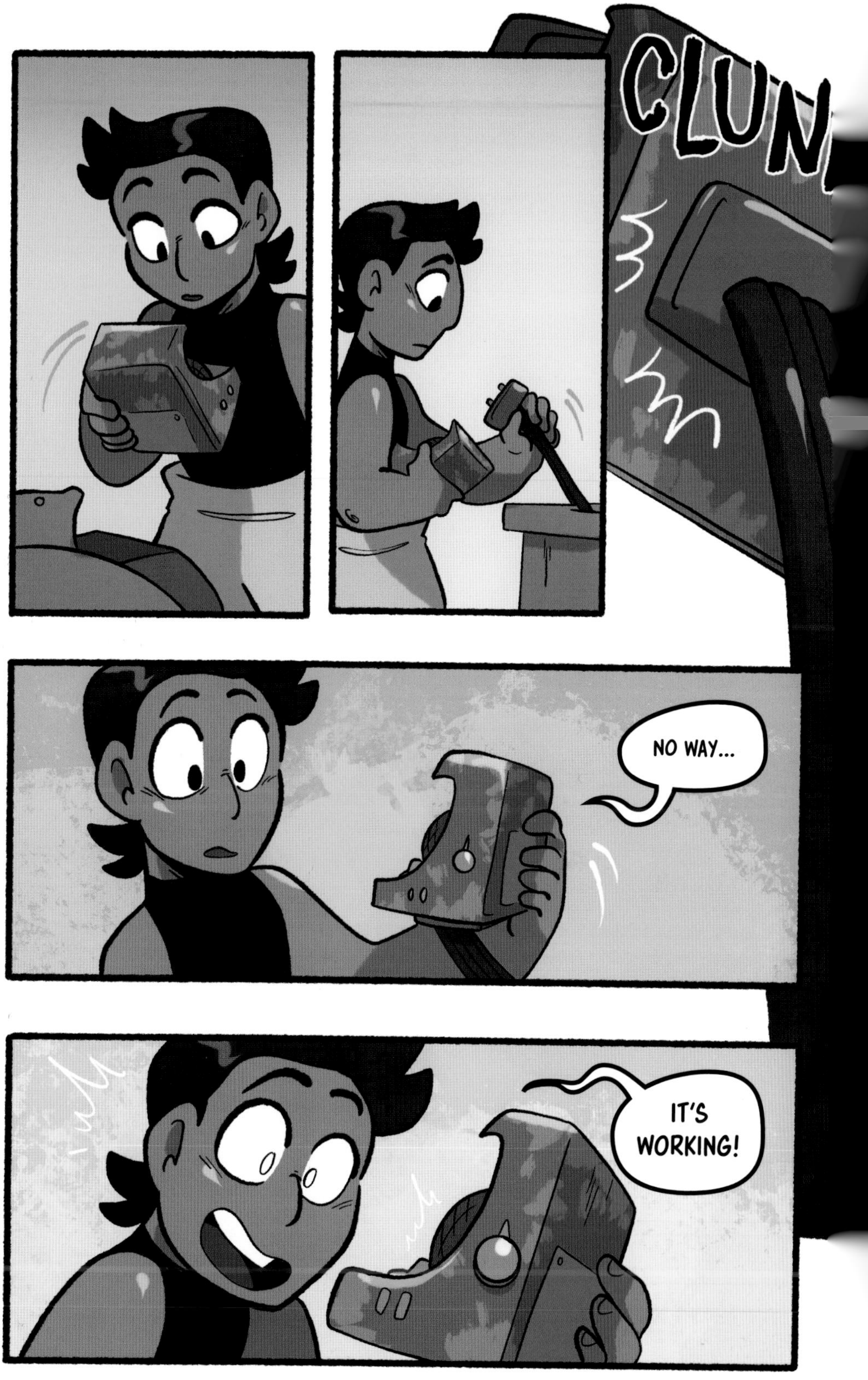
CLUN
NO WAY...
IT'S WORKING!

ADA...THIS IS IT! THIS WILL CHARGE UP THE TEMPCOM!

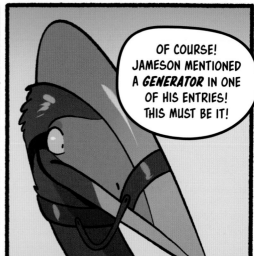

OF COURSE! JAMESON MENTIONED A *GENERATOR* IN ONE OF HIS ENTRIES! THIS MUST BE IT!

ADA!!

I...

...I CAN CONTACT MY PARENTS NOW.

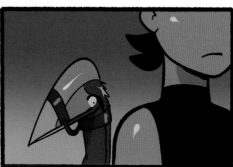

krr

krrr

YEAH. LET'S DO IT.

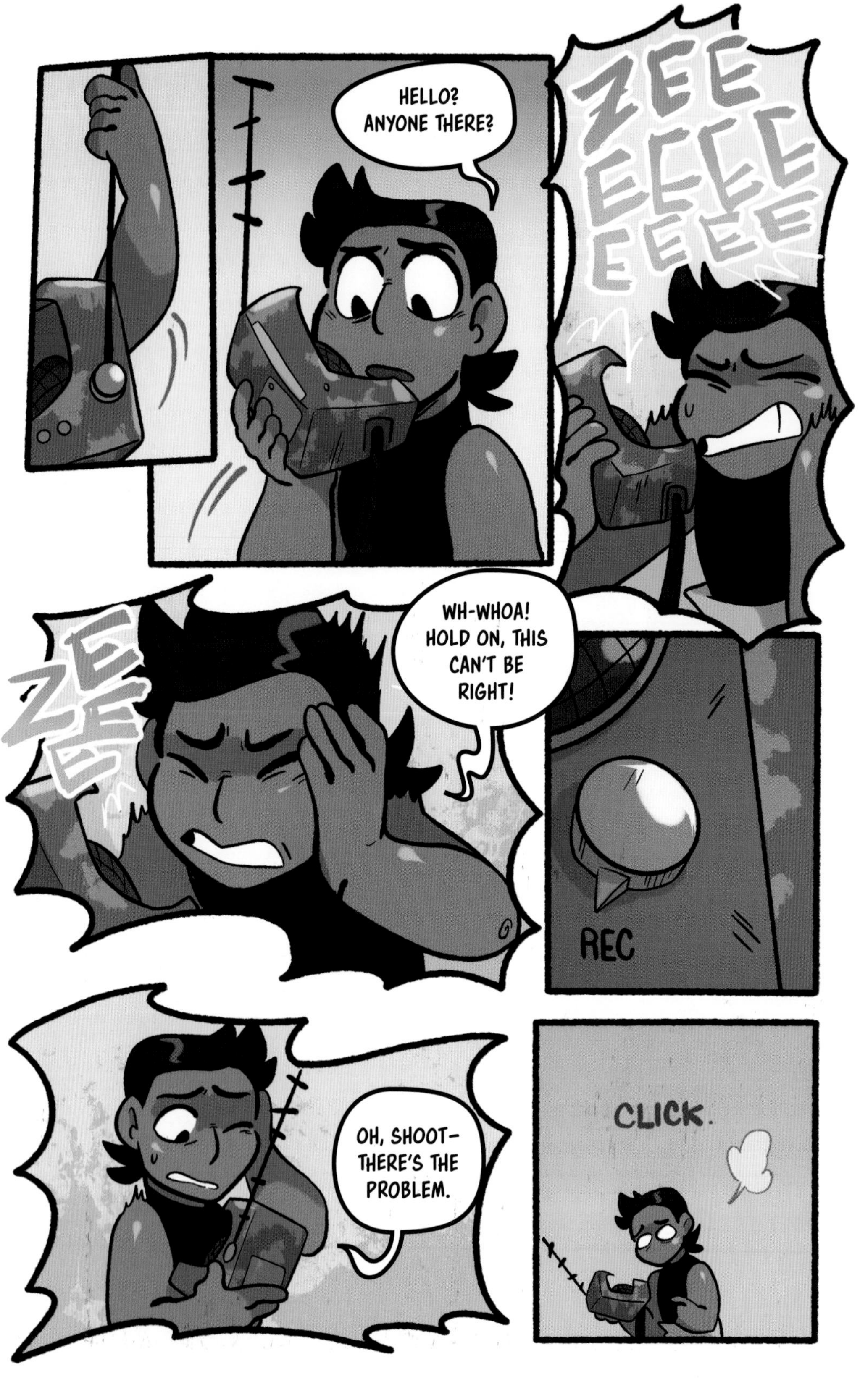
HELLO? ANYONE THERE?
ZEEEEEEEEEEEE
ZEEE
WH-WHOA! HOLD ON, THIS CAN'T BE RIGHT!
REC
OH, SHOOT- THERE'S THE PROBLEM.
CLICK.

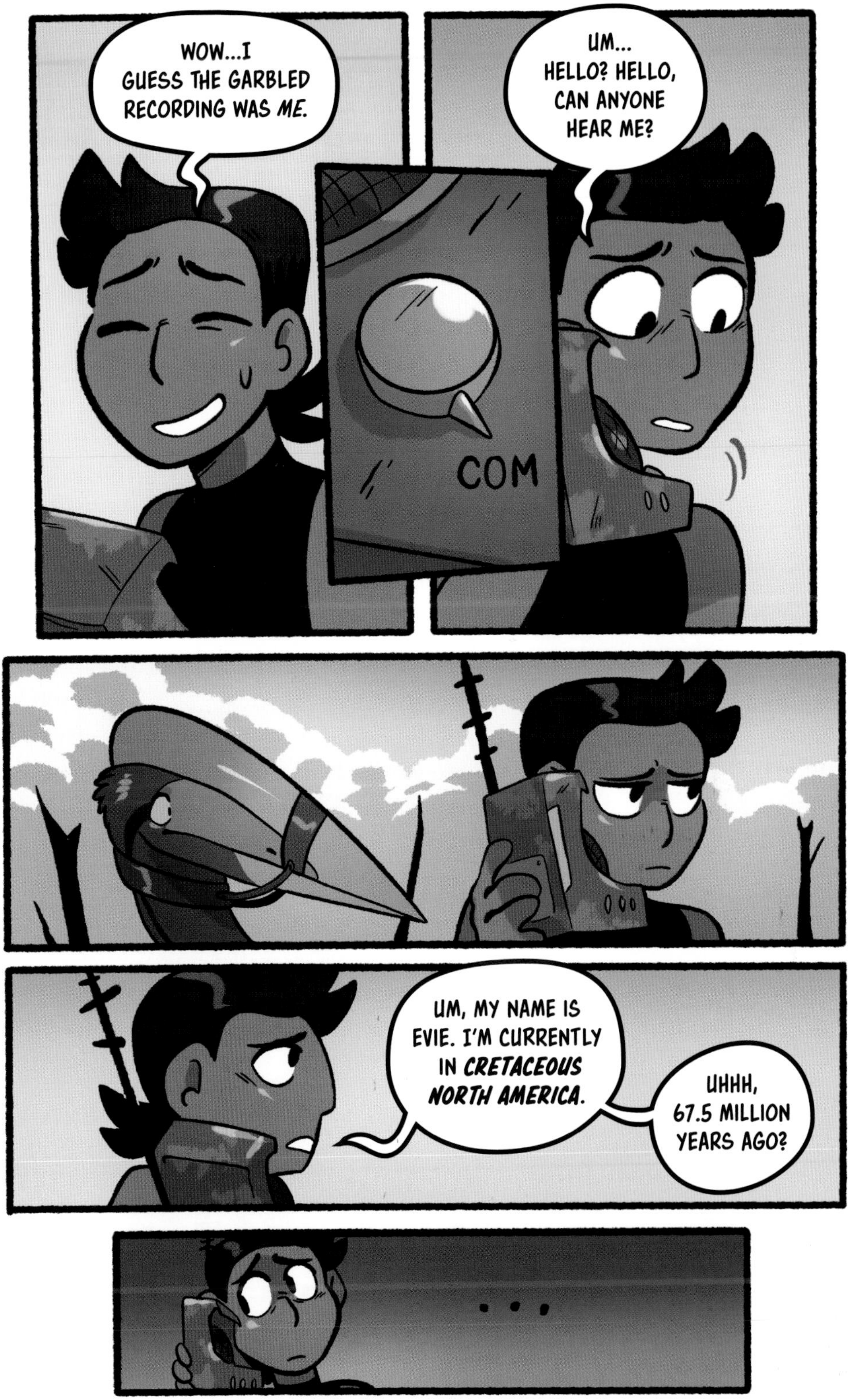
WOW...I GUESS THE GARBLED RECORDING WAS *ME.*
UM... HELLO? HELLO, CAN ANYONE HEAR ME?
COM
UM, MY NAME IS EVIE. I'M CURRENTLY IN ***CRETACEOUS NORTH AMERICA.***
UHHH, 67.5 MILLION YEARS AGO?
. . .

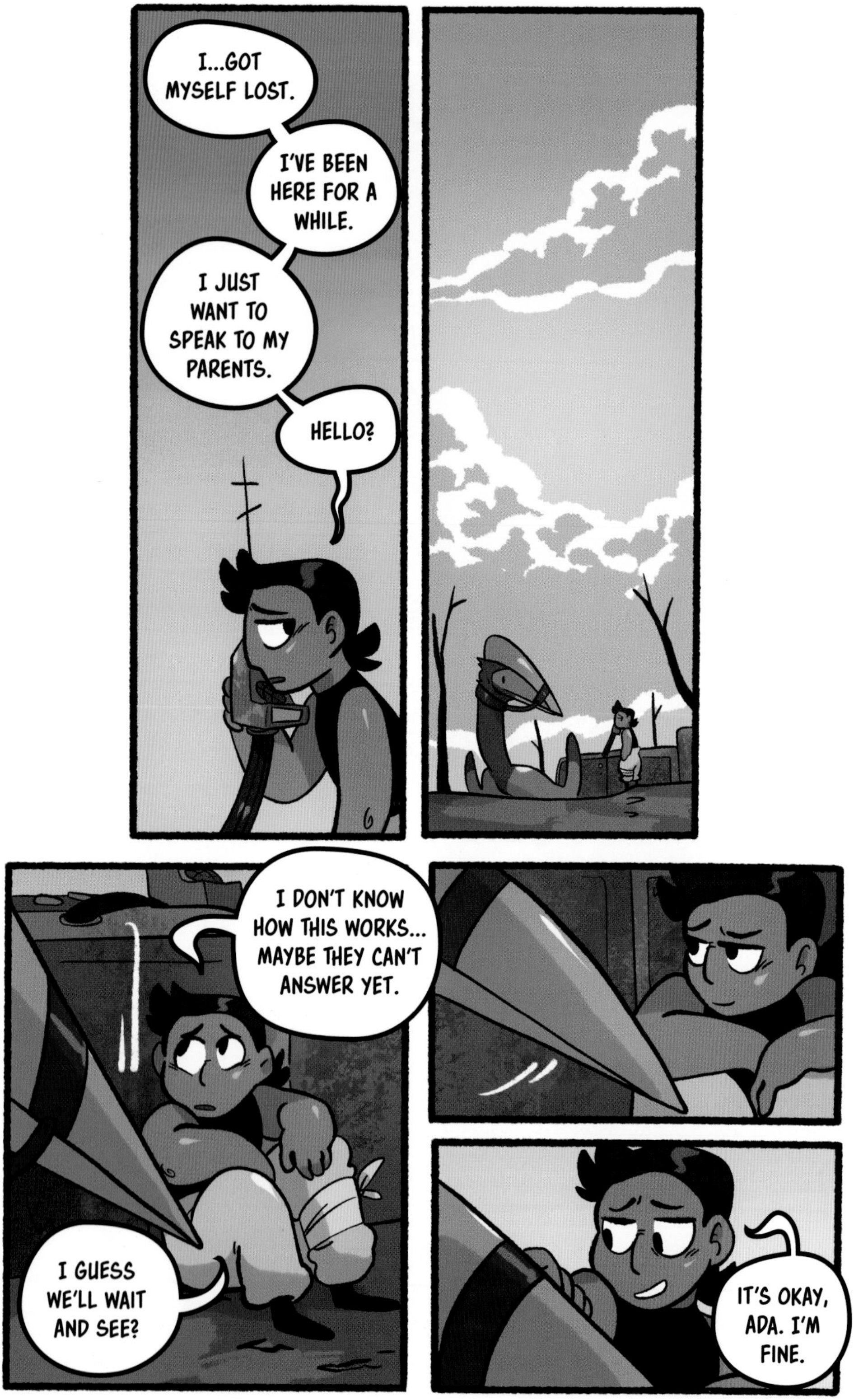
I...GOT MYSELF LOST.
I'VE BEEN HERE FOR A WHILE.
I JUST WANT TO SPEAK TO MY PARENTS.
HELLO?
I DON'T KNOW HOW THIS WORKS... MAYBE THEY CAN'T ANSWER YET.
I GUESS WE'LL WAIT AND SEE?
IT'S OKAY, ADA. I'M FINE.

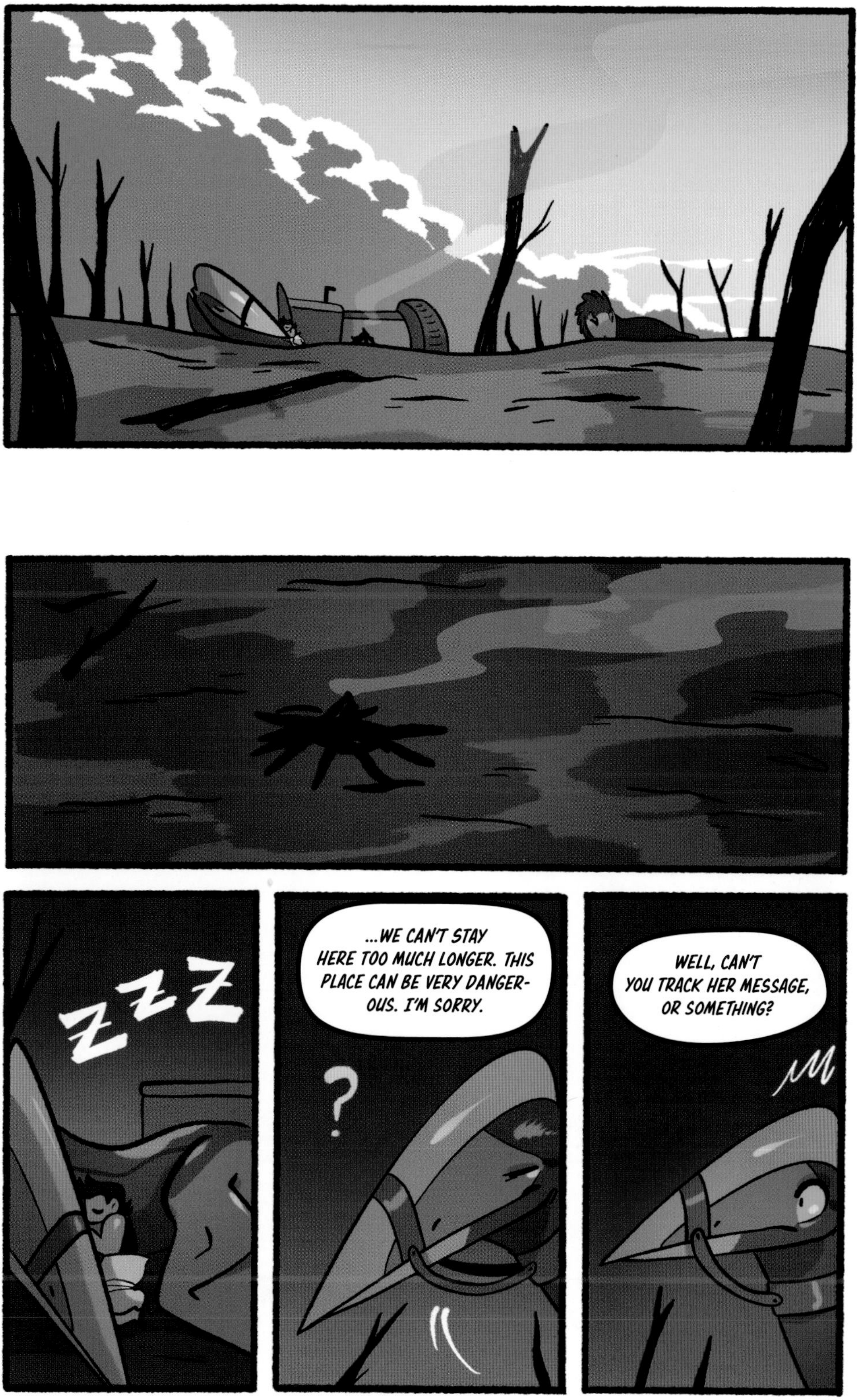
ZZZ
...WE CAN'T STAY HERE TOO MUCH LONGER. THIS PLACE CAN BE VERY DANGER-OUS. I'M SORRY.
?
WELL, CAN'T YOU TRACK HER MESSAGE, OR SOMETHING?

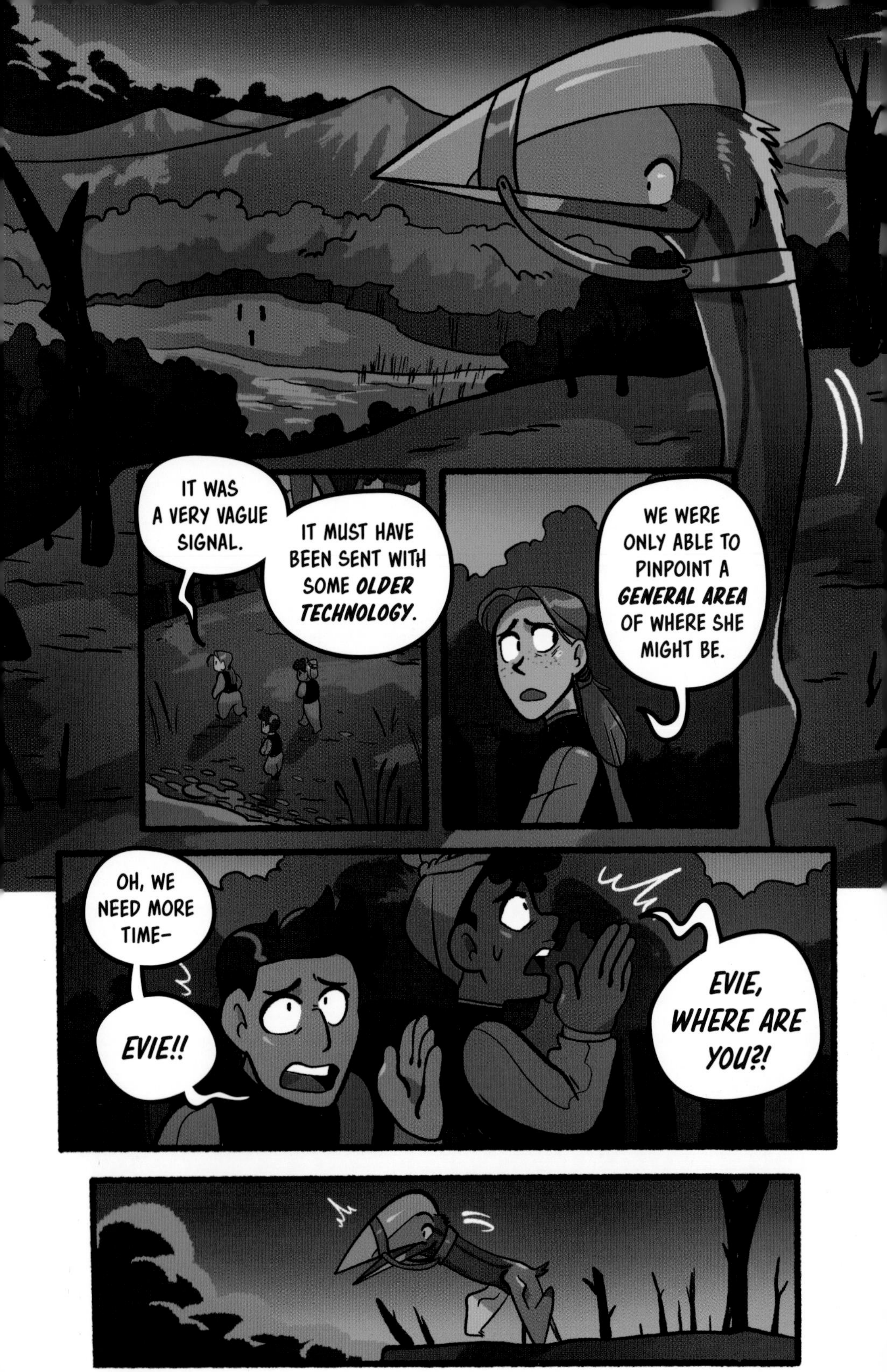
IT WAS A VERY VAGUE SIGNAL.
IT MUST HAVE BEEN SENT WITH SOME *OLDER TECHNOLOGY*.
WE WERE ONLY ABLE TO PINPOINT A *GENERAL AREA* OF WHERE SHE MIGHT BE.
OH, WE NEED MORE TIME-
EVIE!!
EVIE, WHERE ARE YOU?!

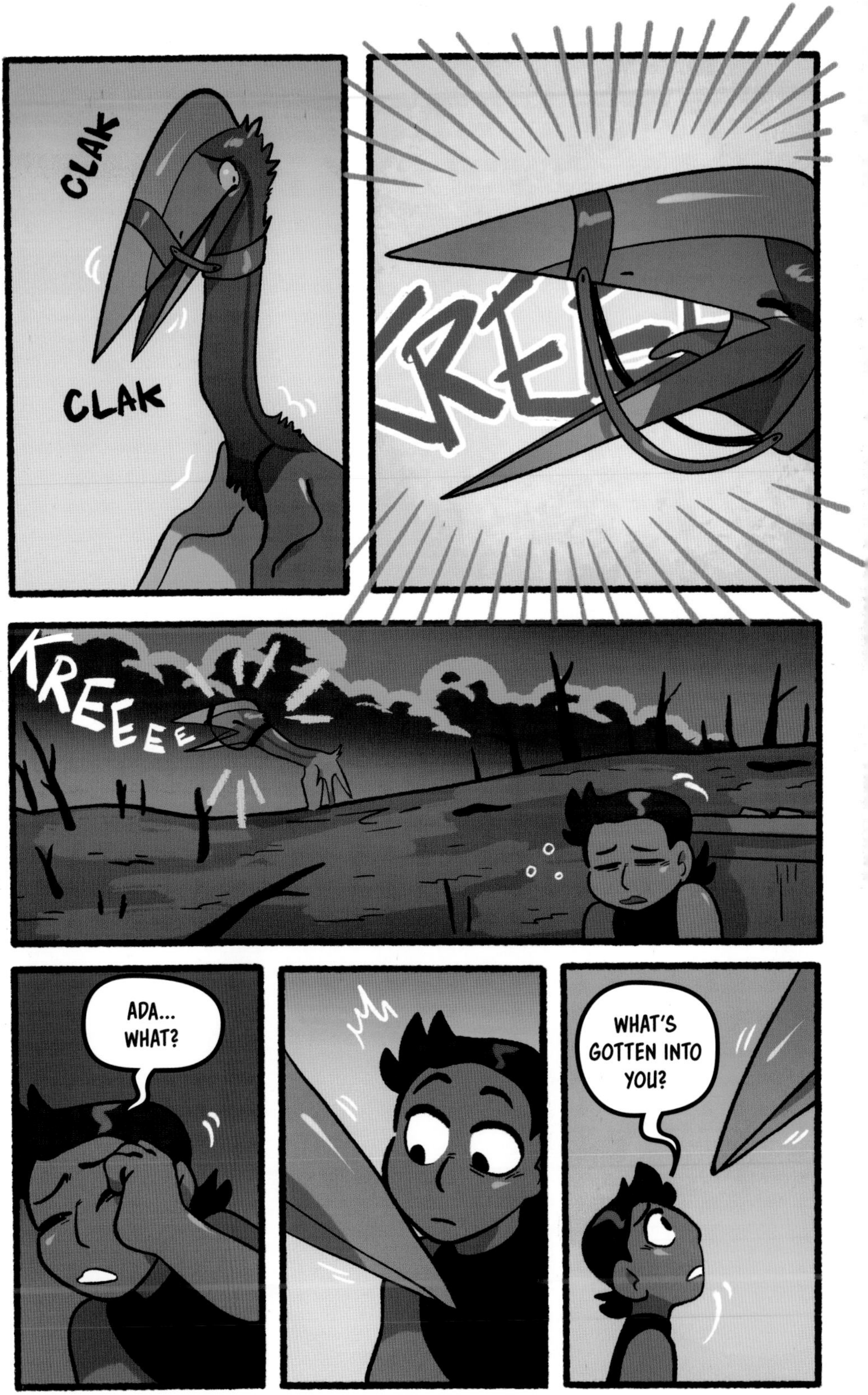
CLAK
CLAK
KREE
KREEEEE
ADA... WHAT?
WHAT'S GOTTEN INTO YOU?

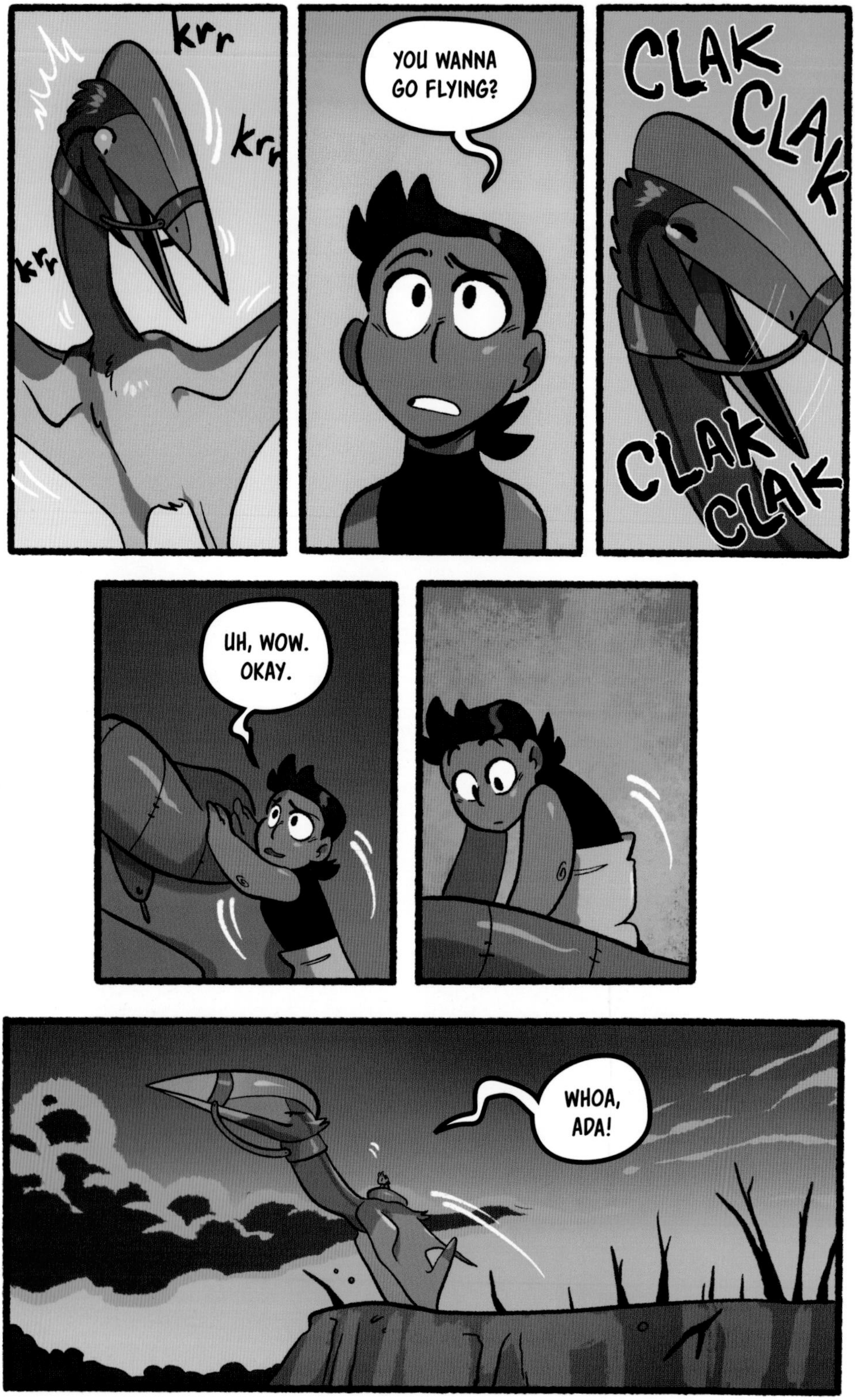
krr
krr
krr
YOU WANNA GO FLYING?
CLAK CLAK
CLAK CLAK
UH, WOW. OKAY.
WHOA, ADA!

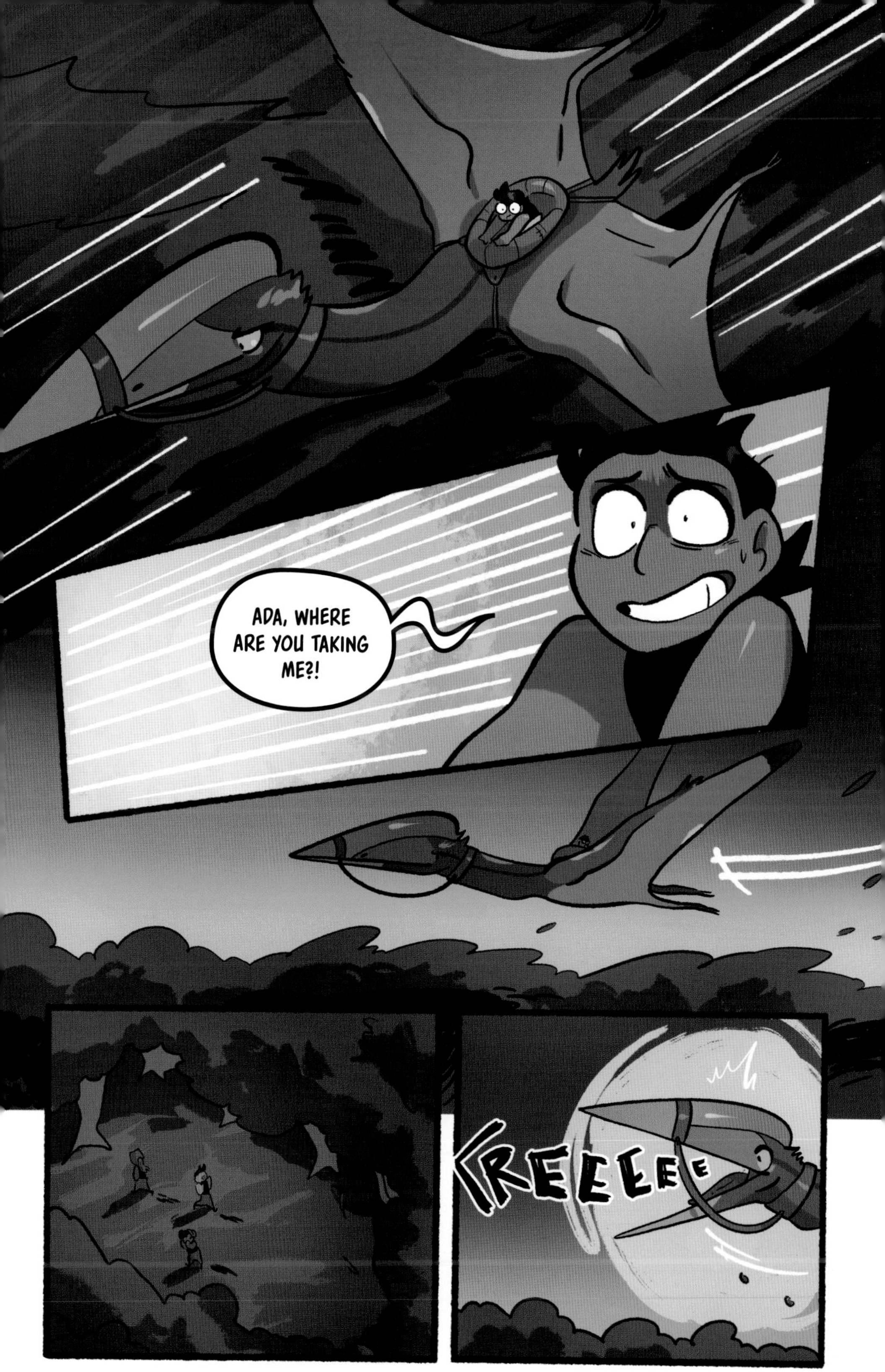
ADA, WHERE ARE YOU TAKING ME?!
KREEEEE

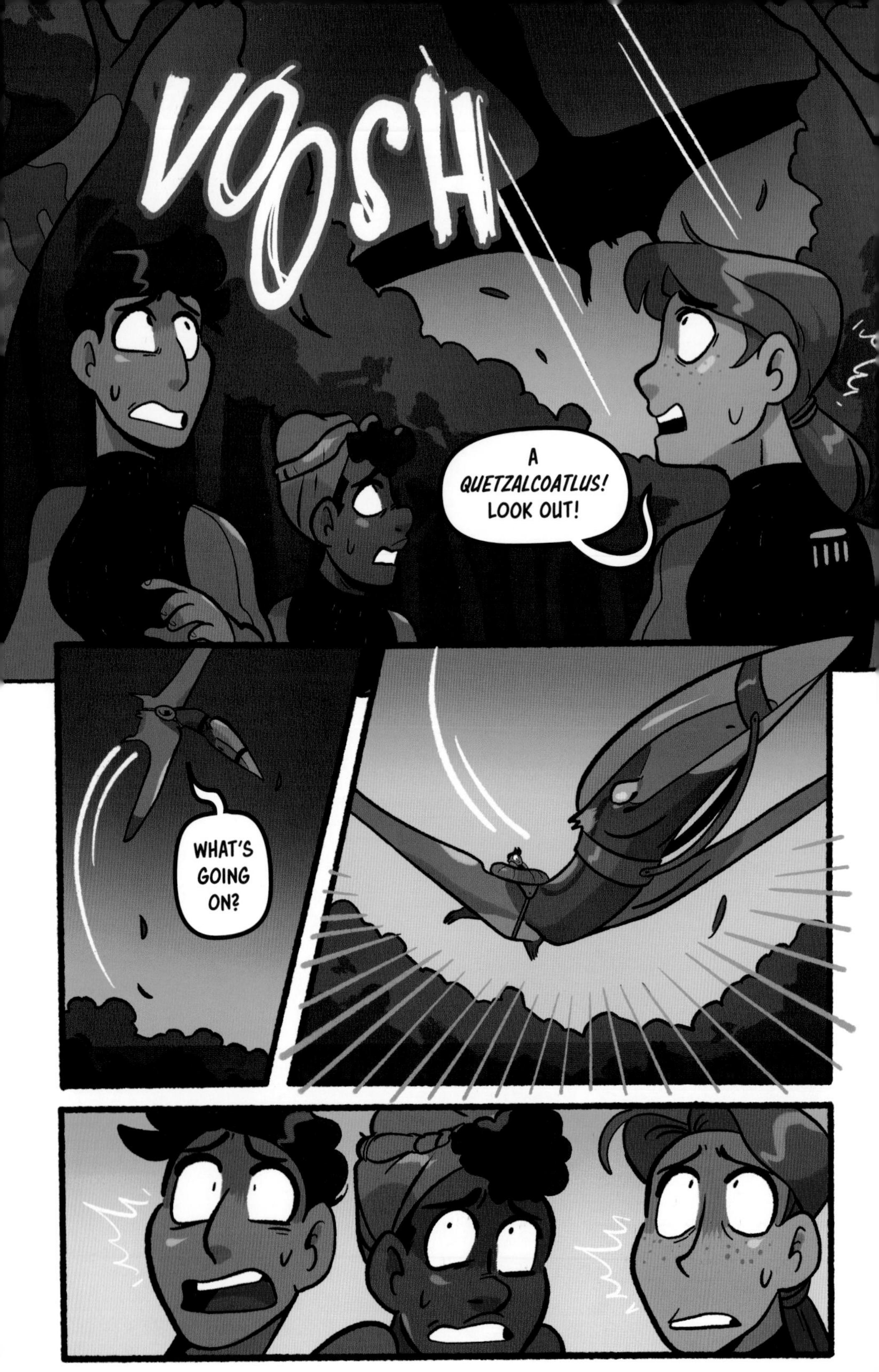
VOOSH
A QUETZALCOATLUS! LOOK OUT!
WHAT'S GOING ON?

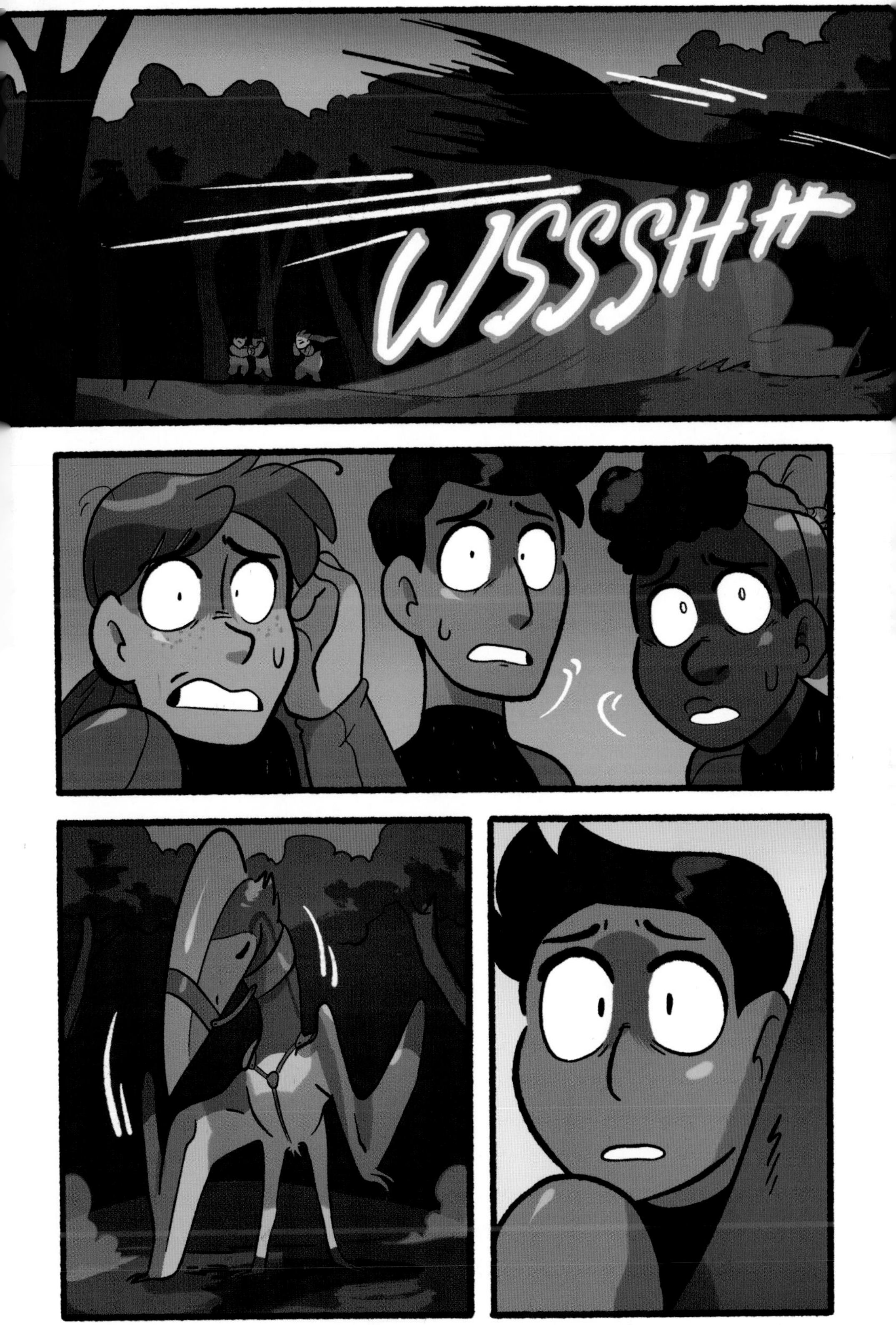
WSSSH!!

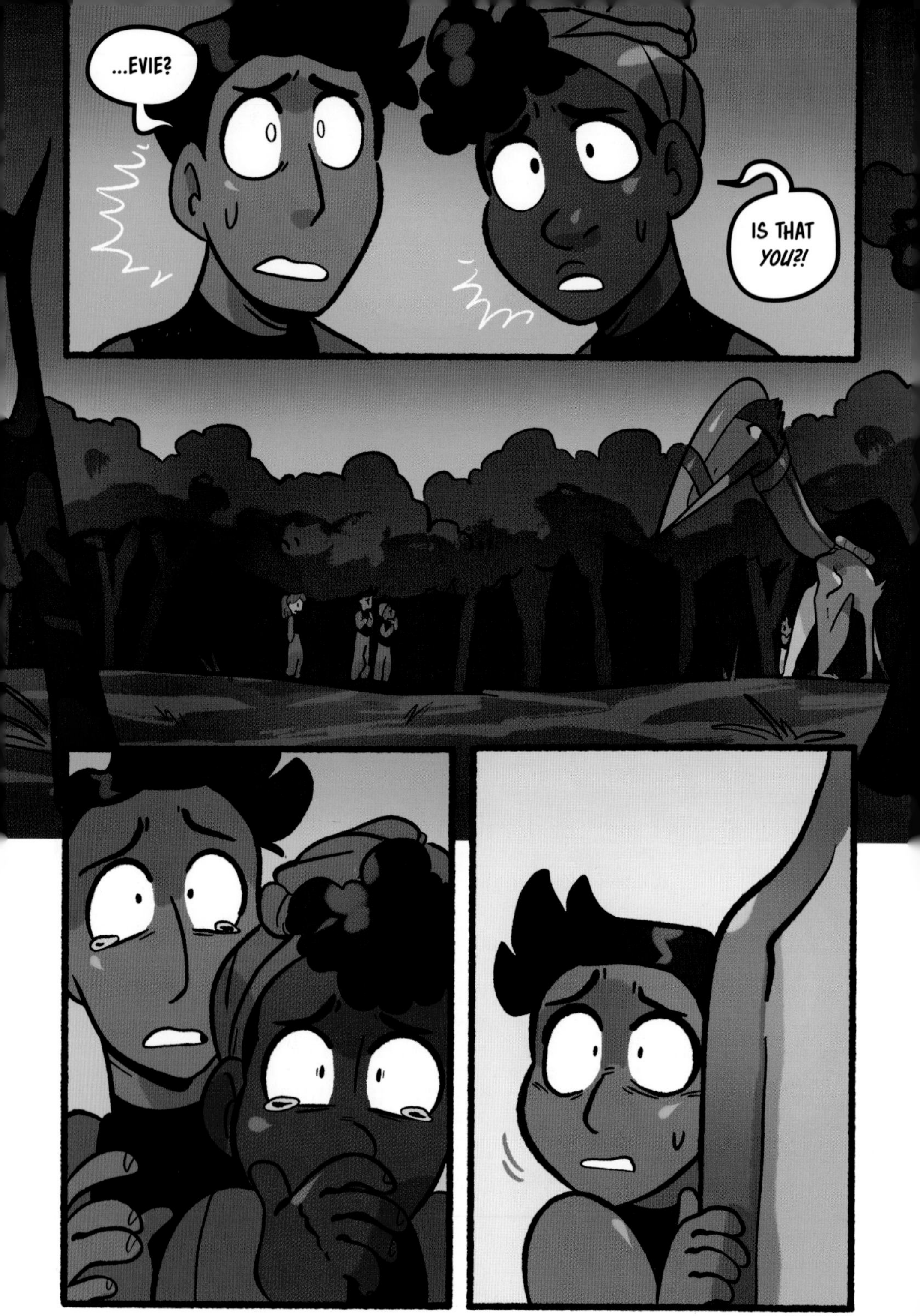
...EVIE?
IS THAT YOU?!

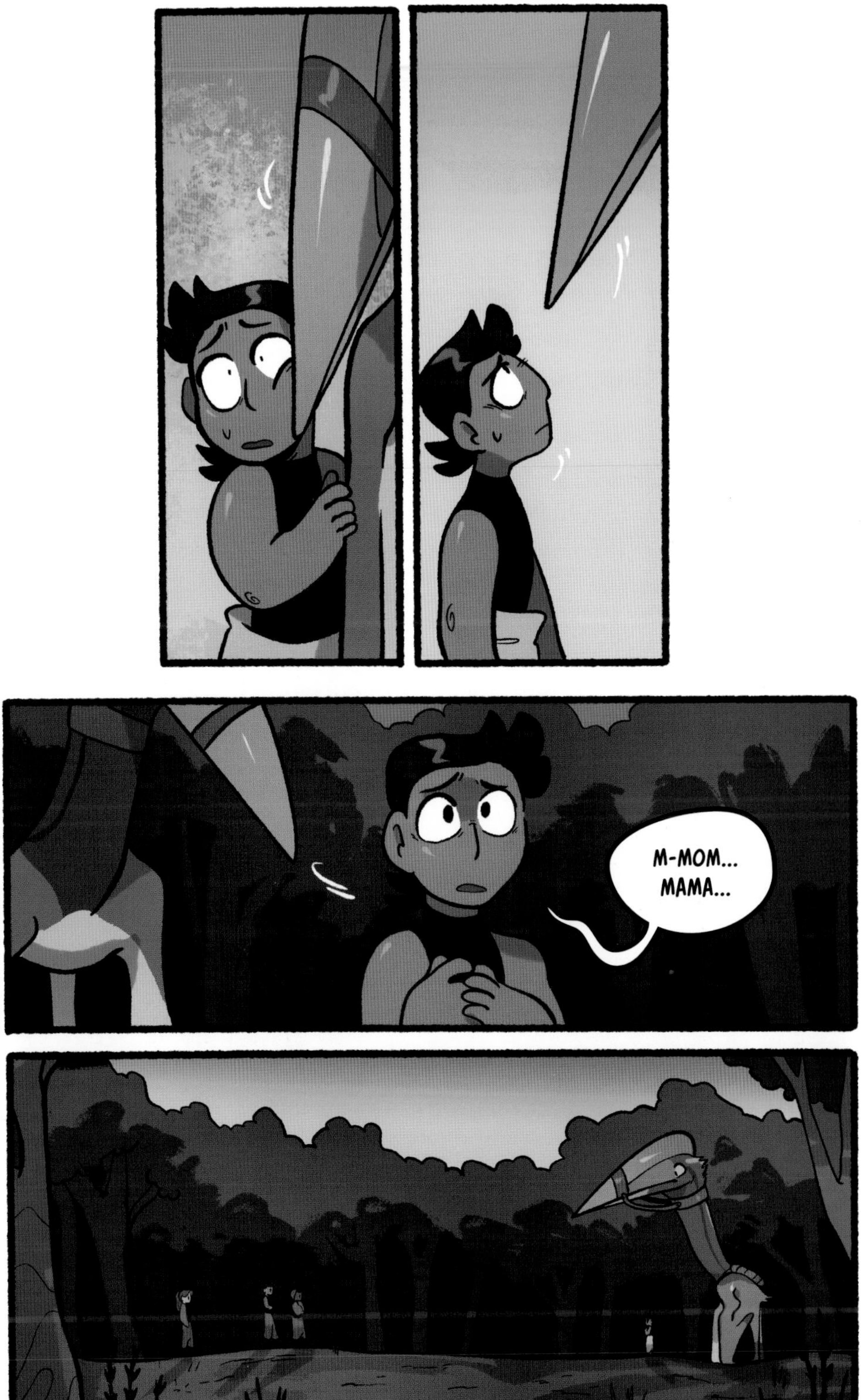
M-MOM...
MAMA...

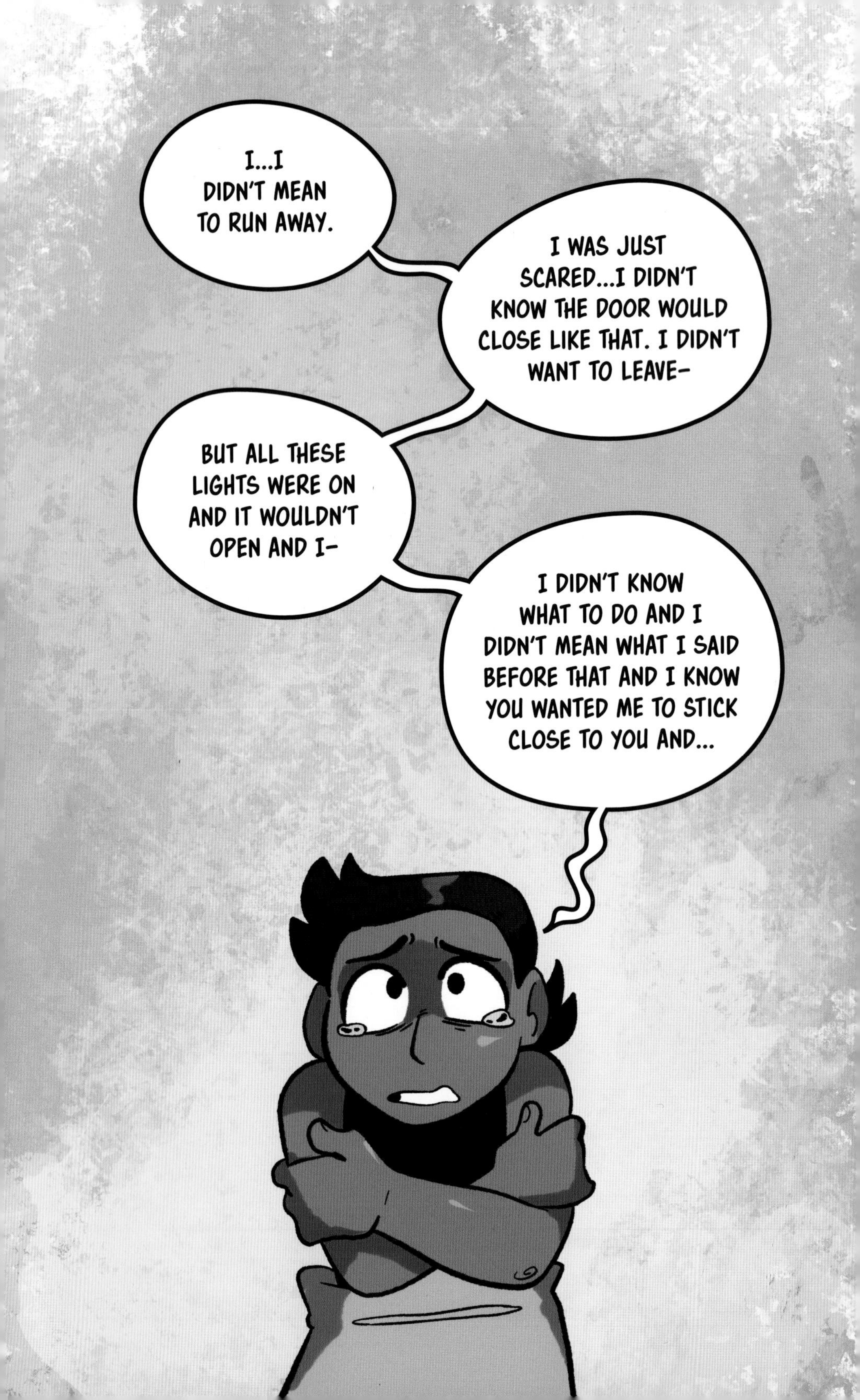
I...I DIDN'T MEAN TO RUN AWAY.
I WAS JUST SCARED...I DIDN'T KNOW THE DOOR WOULD CLOSE LIKE THAT. I DIDN'T WANT TO LEAVE–
BUT ALL THESE LIGHTS WERE ON AND IT WOULDN'T OPEN AND I–
I DIDN'T KNOW WHAT TO DO AND I DIDN'T MEAN WHAT I SAID BEFORE THAT AND I KNOW YOU WANTED ME TO STICK CLOSE TO YOU AND...

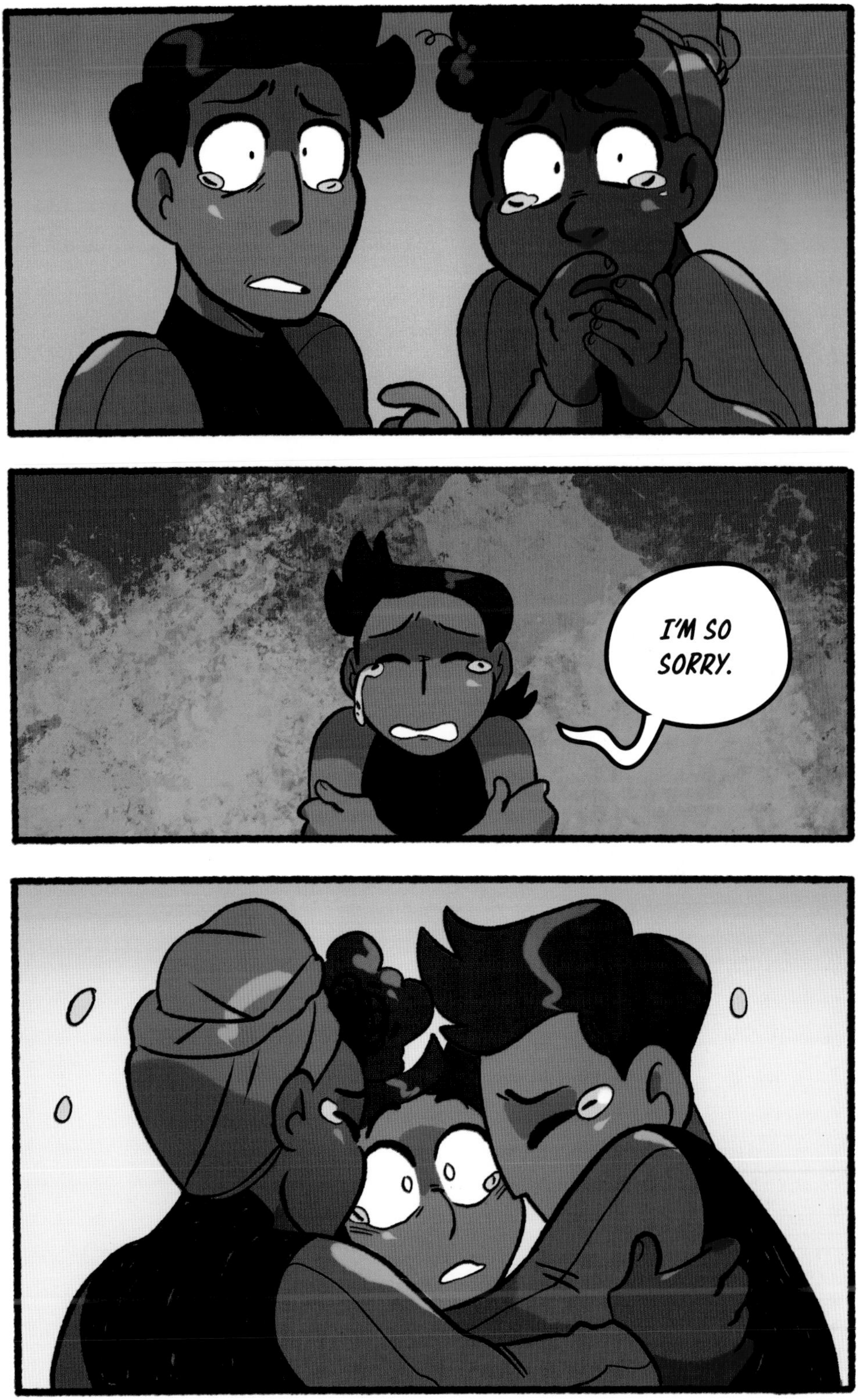
I'M SO SORRY.

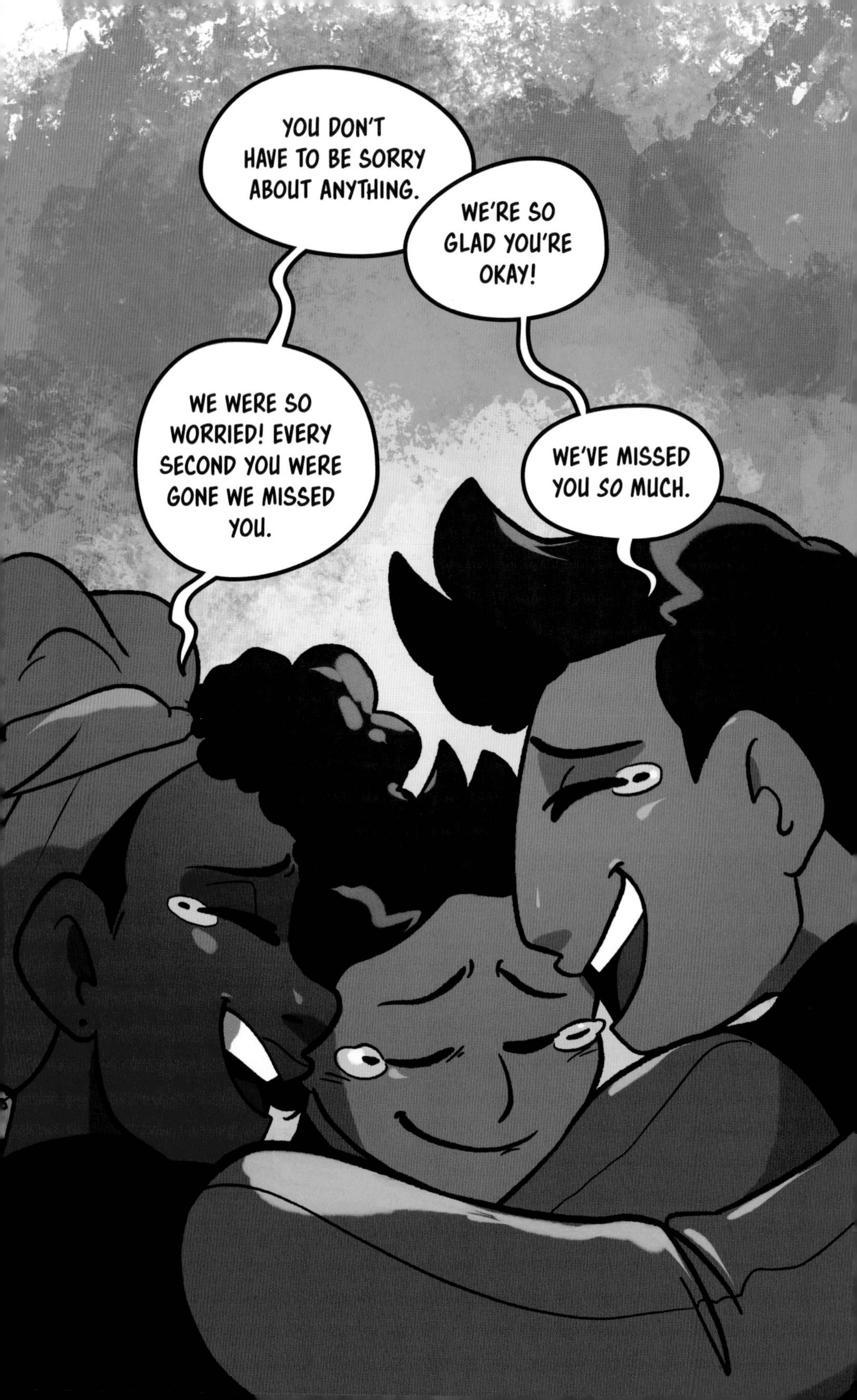
YOU DON'T HAVE TO BE SORRY ABOUT ANYTHING.
WE'RE SO GLAD YOU'RE OKAY!
WE WERE SO WORRIED! EVERY SECOND YOU WERE GONE WE MISSED YOU.
WE'VE MISSED YOU SO MUCH.

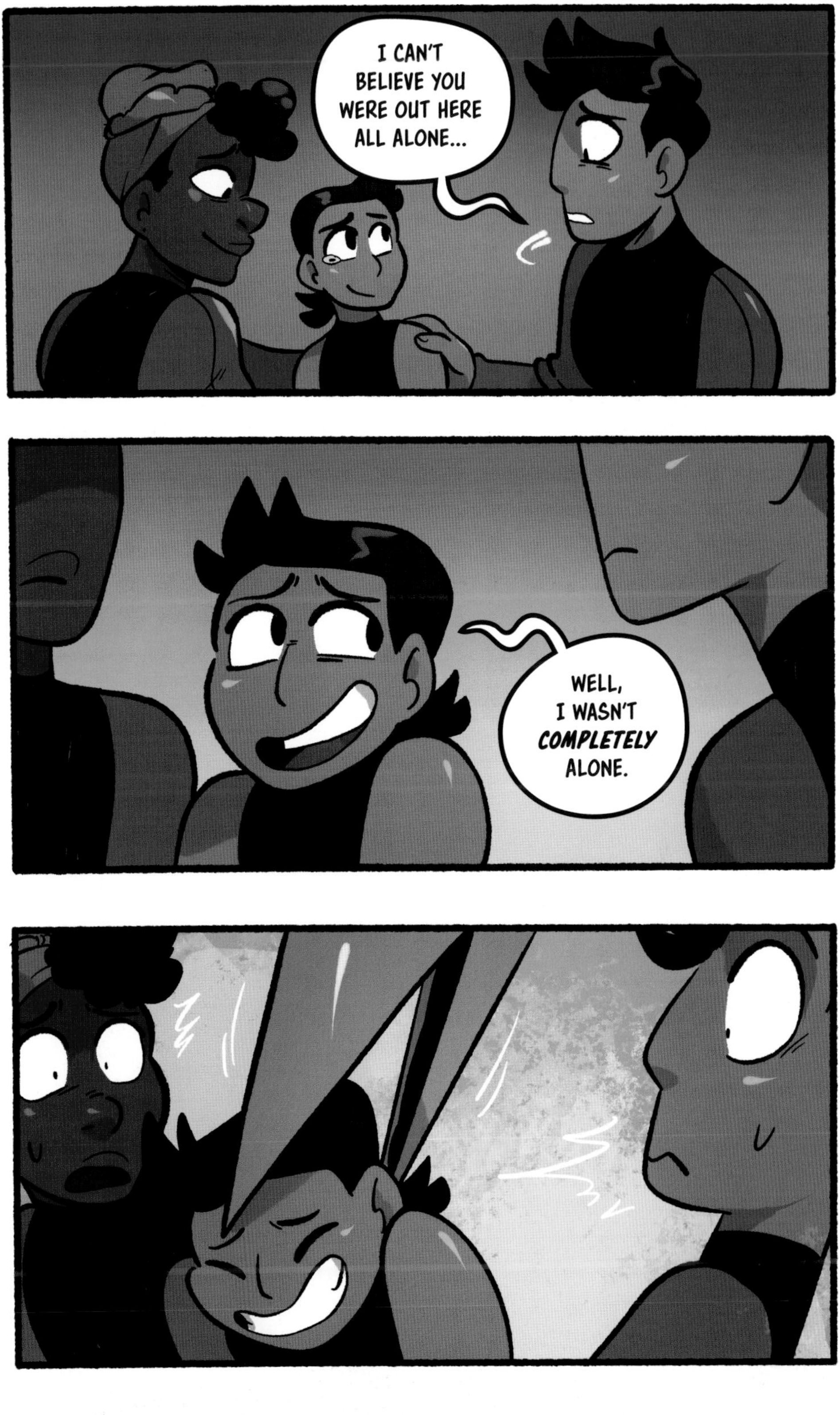
I CAN'T BELIEVE YOU WERE OUT HERE ALL ALONE...
WELL, I WASN'T *COMPLETELY* ALONE.

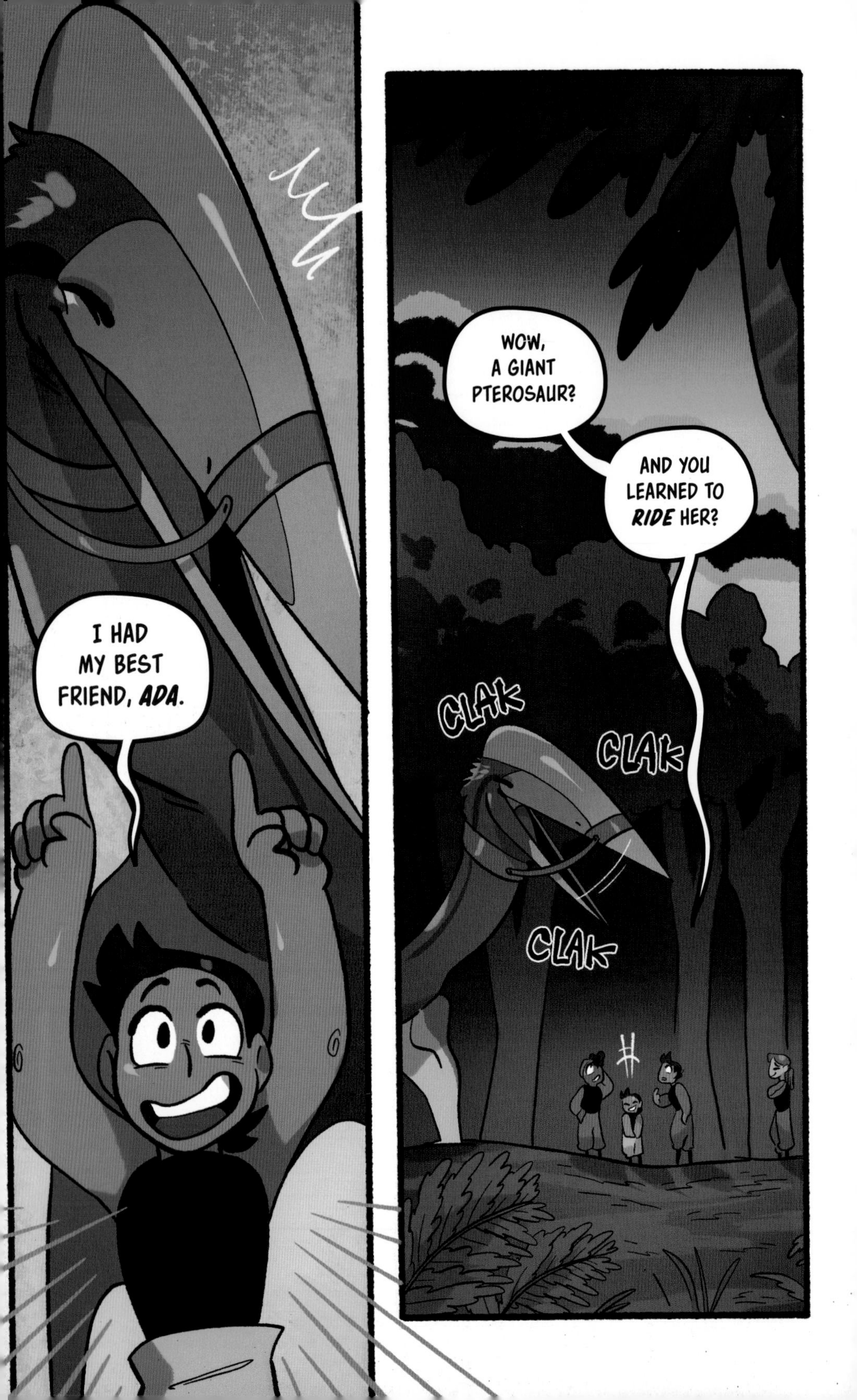
I HAD MY BEST FRIEND, ADA.
WOW, A GIANT PTEROSAUR?
AND YOU LEARNED TO RIDE HER?
CLAK
CLAK
CLAK

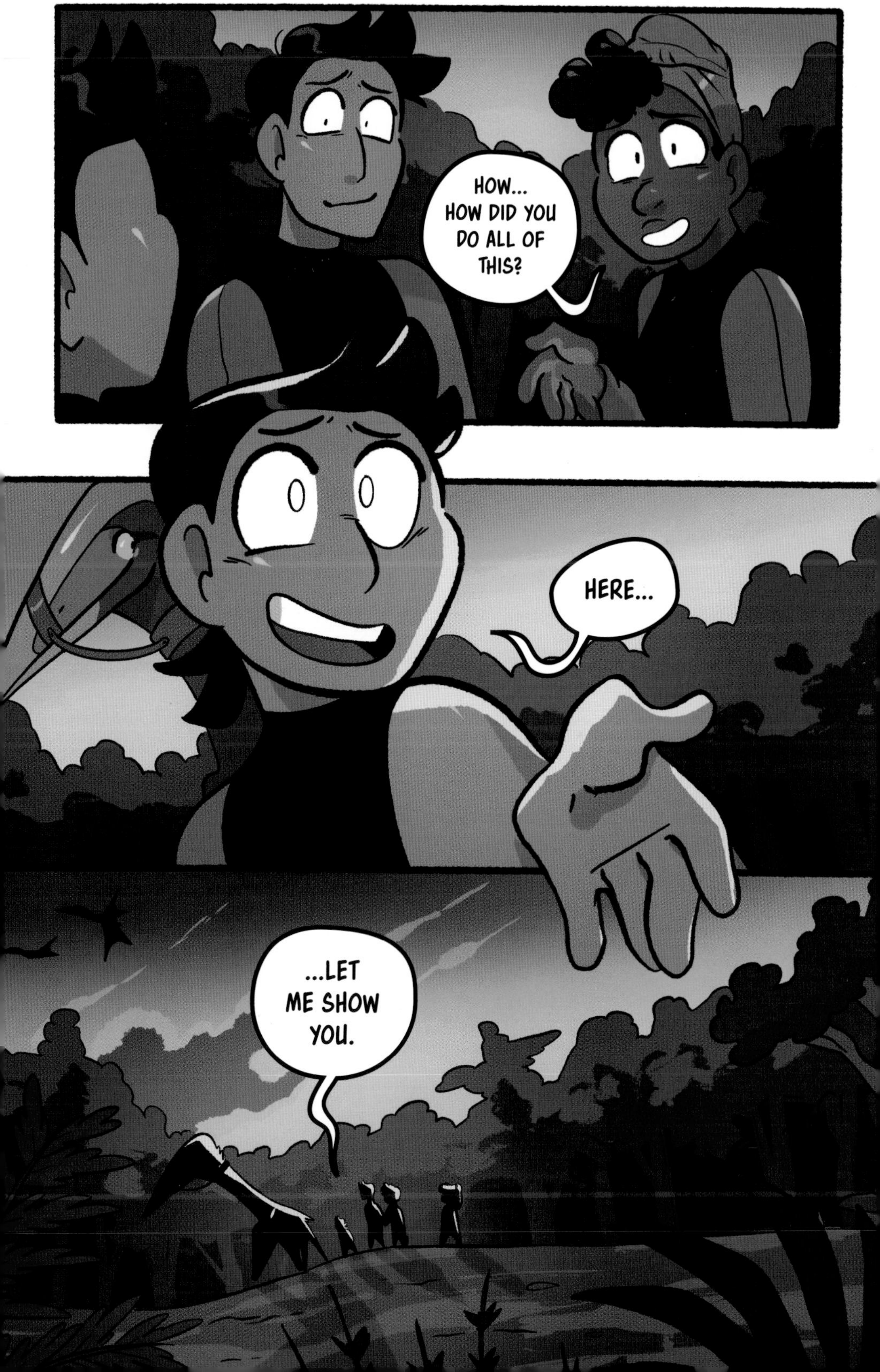
HOW...
HOW DID YOU
DO ALL OF
THIS?
HERE...
...LET
ME SHOW
YOU.

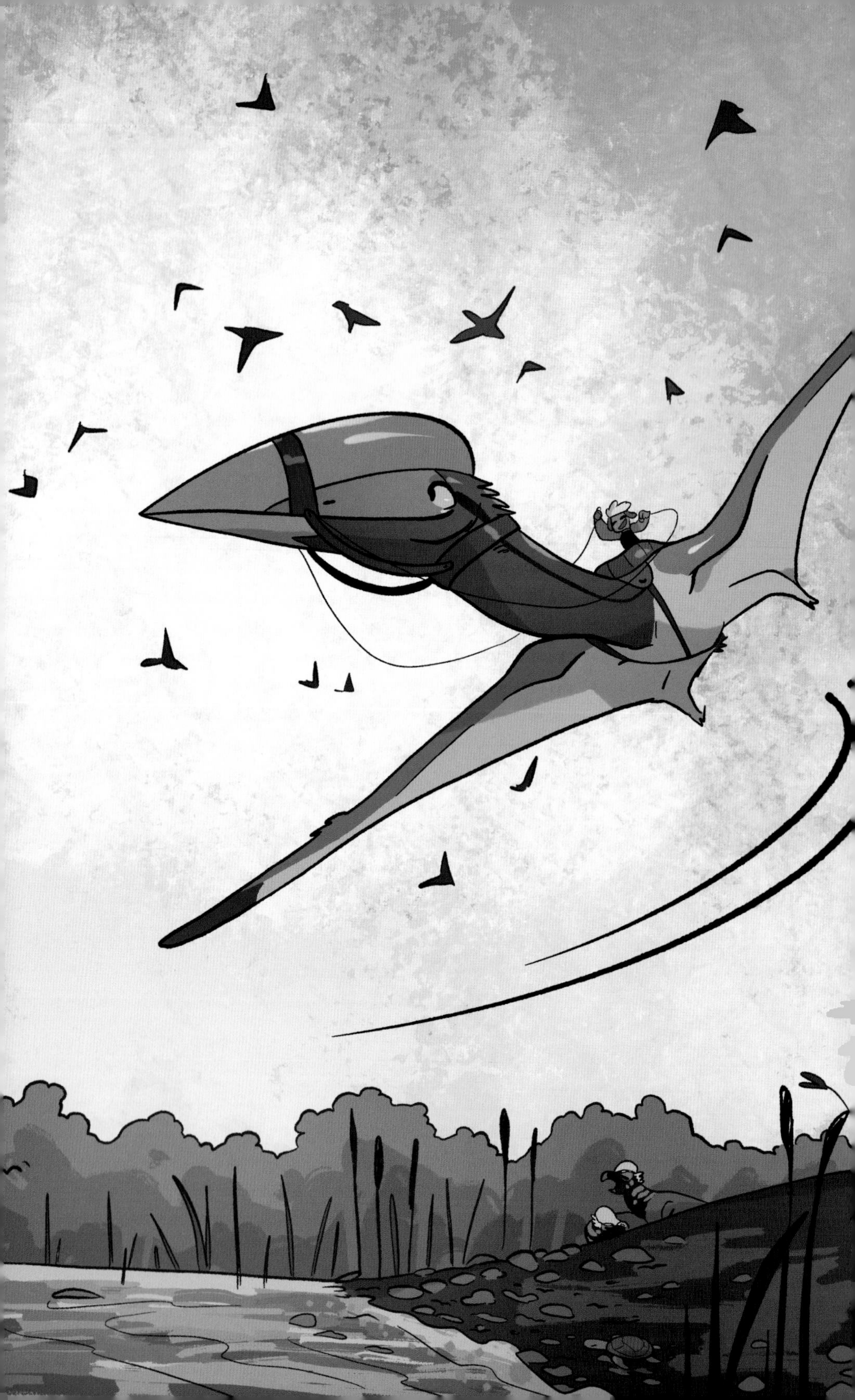

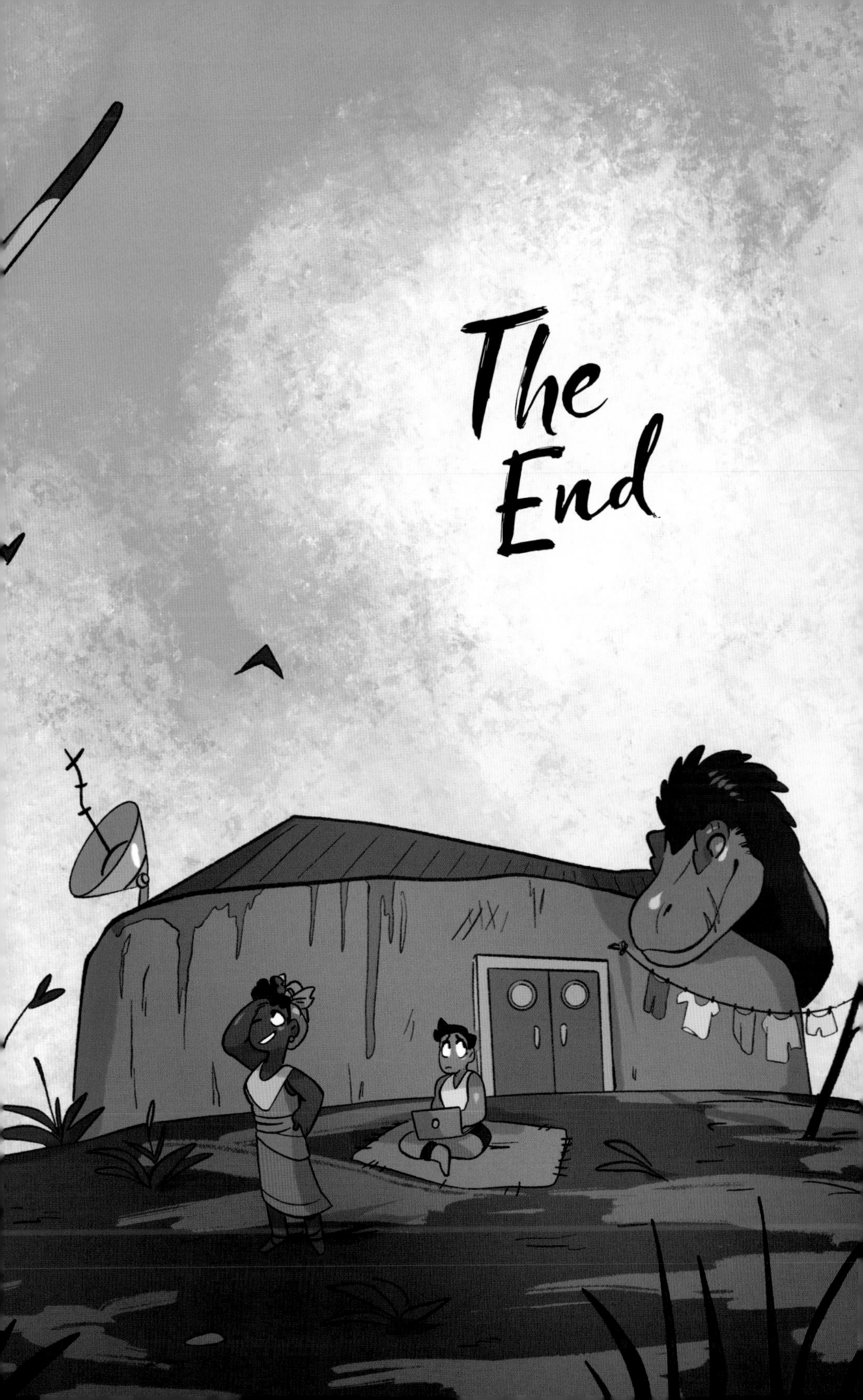
The End

HERE'S A CLOSER LOOK AT SOME OF THE INCREDIBLE ANIMALS EVIE ENCOUNTERS ON HER ADVENTURES!

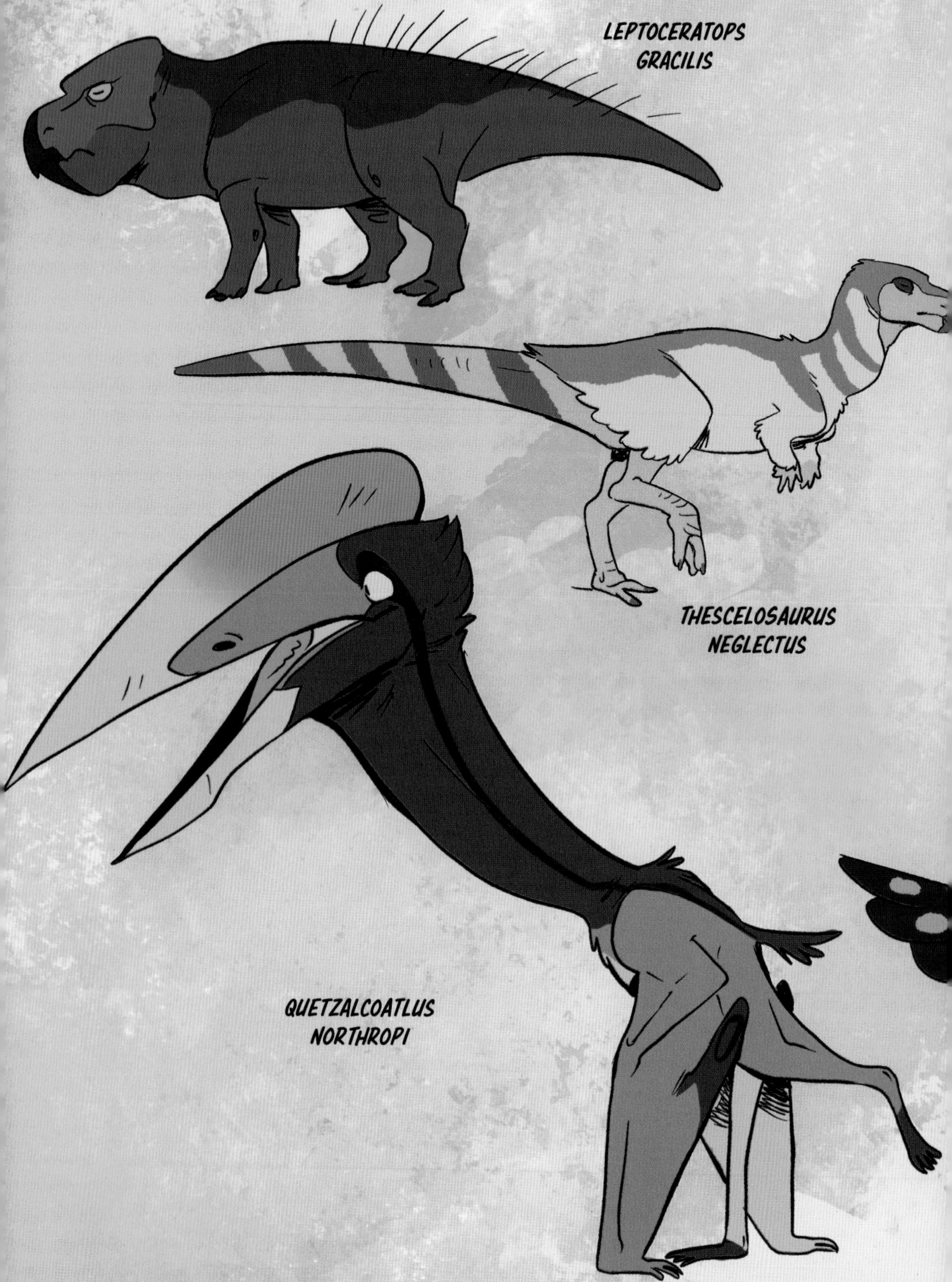
LEPTOCERATOPS GRACILIS
THESCELOSAURUS NEGLECTUS
QUETZALCOATLUS NORTHROPI

Believe it or not, her friend Ada isn't technically a dinosaur. Although often called so, pterosaurs are in fact NOT dinosaurs, but are closely related. And the *Quetzalcoatlus* was one of the largest flying animals to ever exist!

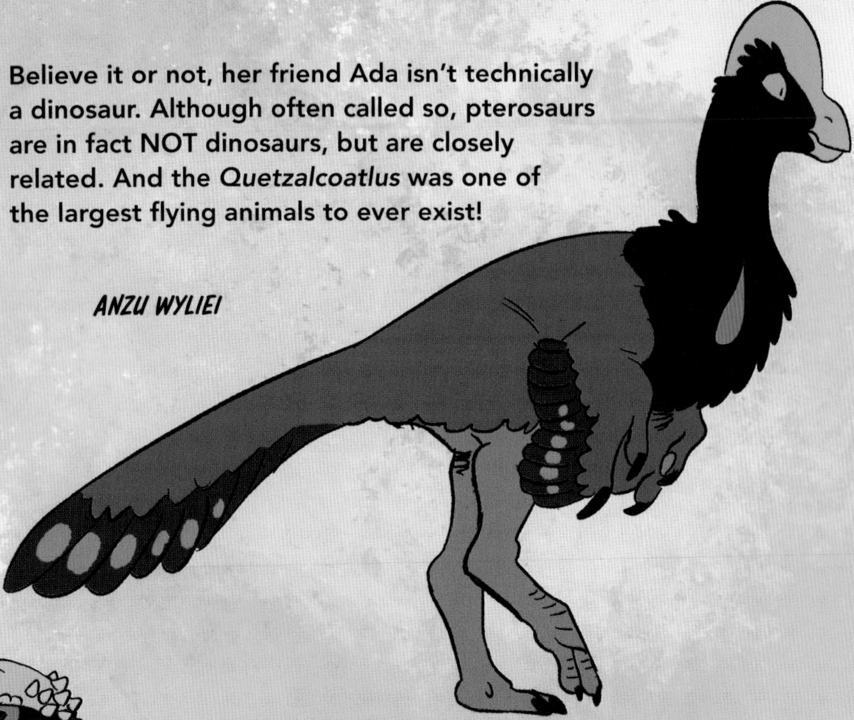

ANZU WYLIEI

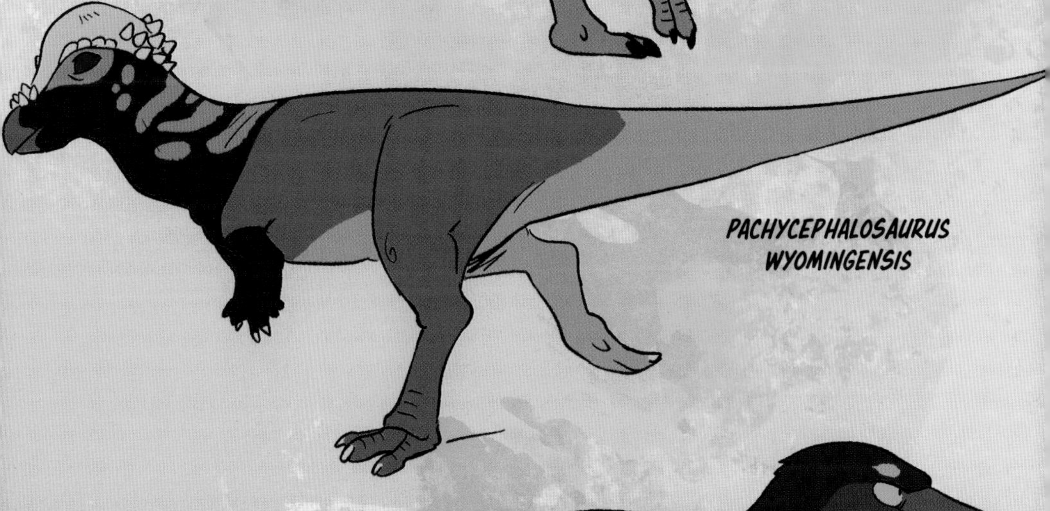

PACHYCEPHALOSAURUS WYOMINGENSIS

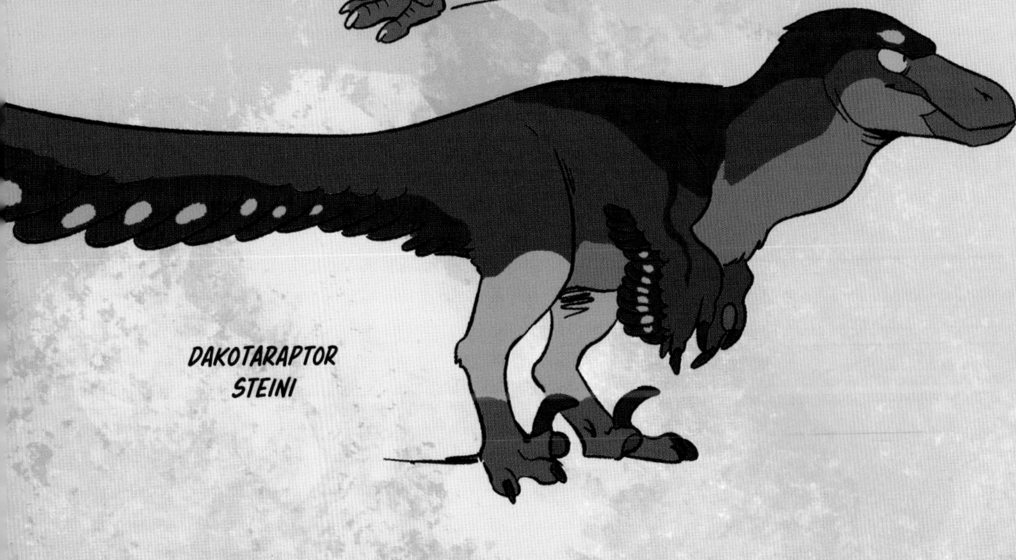

DAKOTARAPTOR STEINI

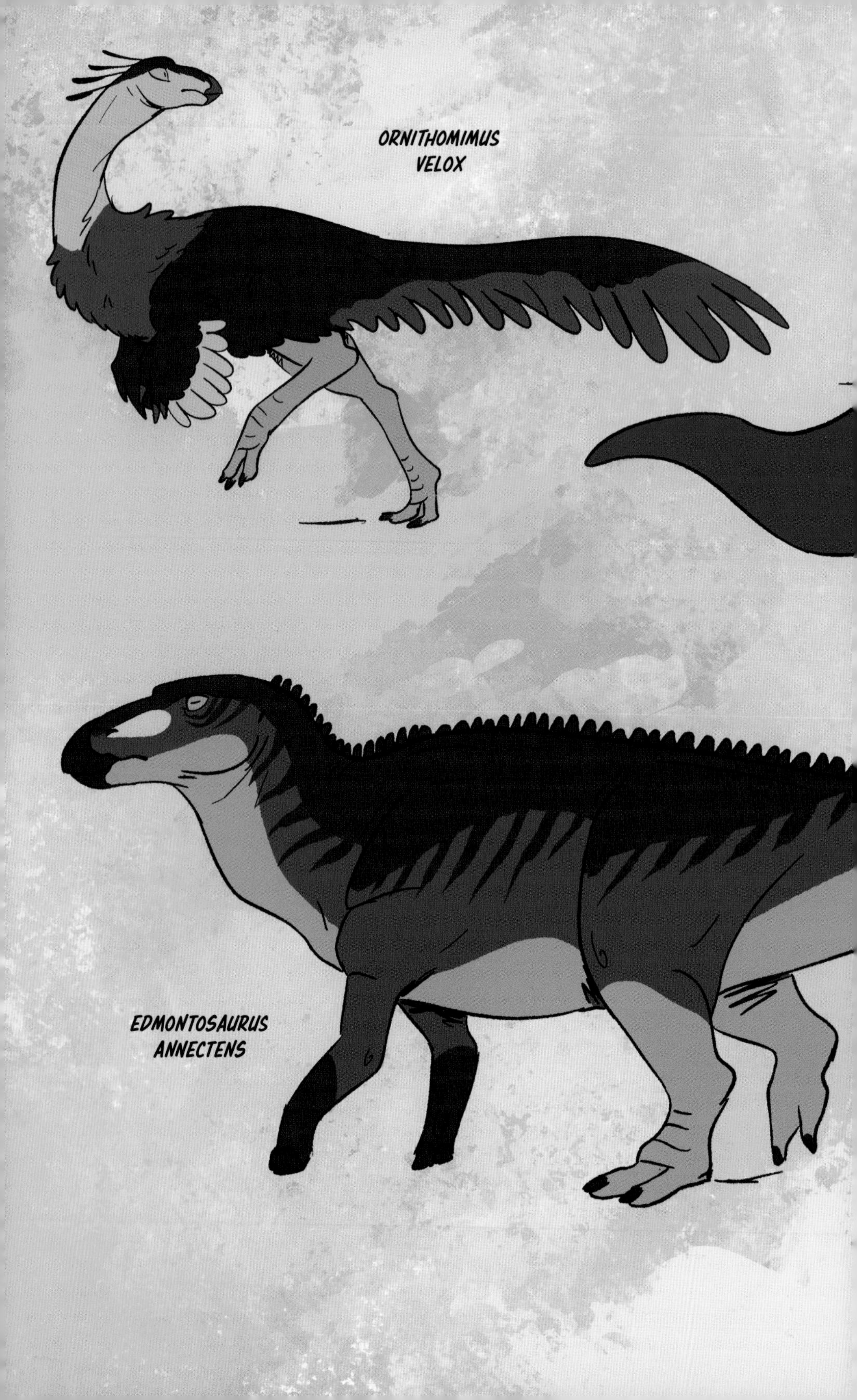
ORNITHOMIMUS VELOX
EDMONTOSAURUS ANNECTENS

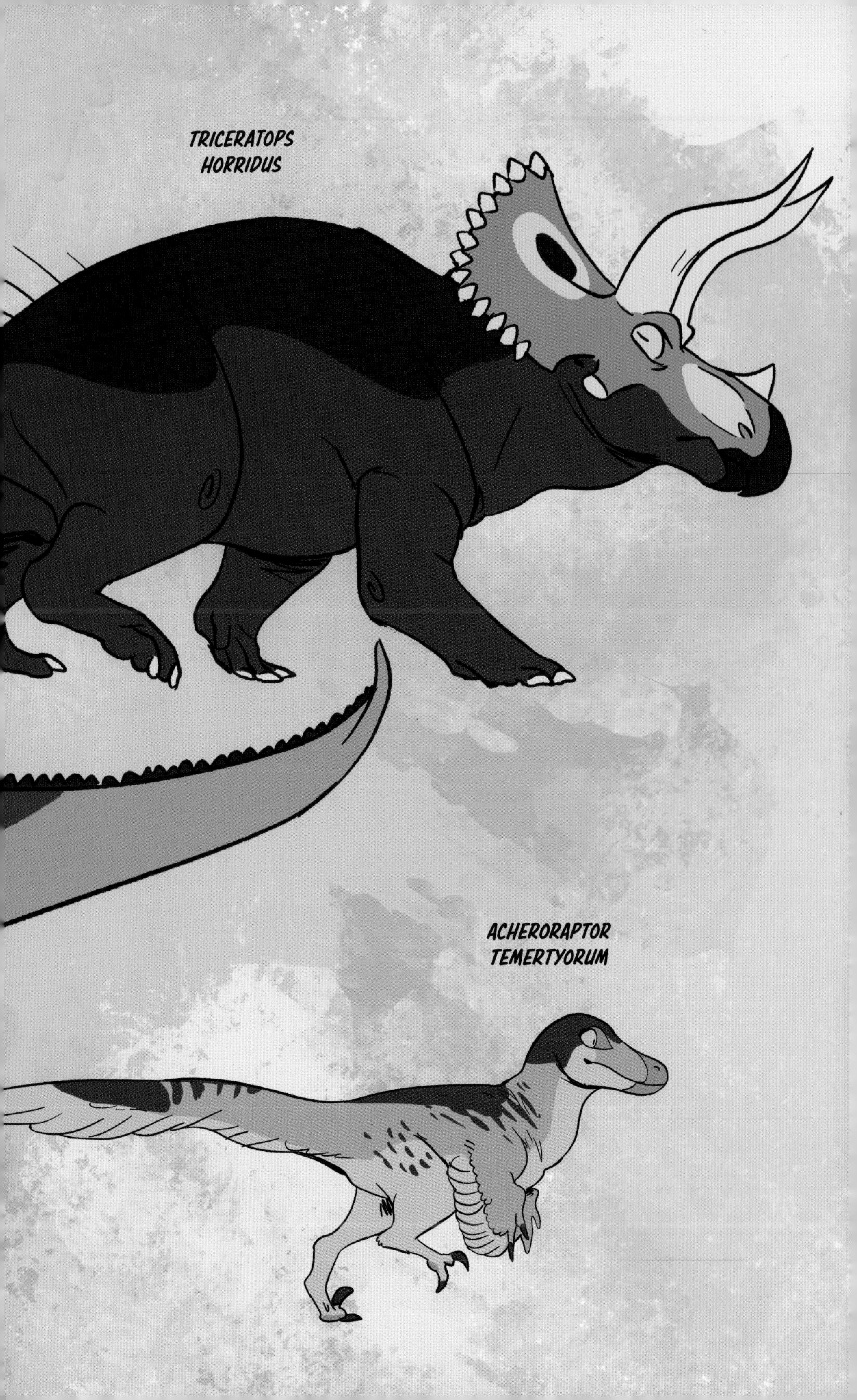
TRICERATOPS HORRIDUS
ACHERORAPTOR TEMERTYORUM

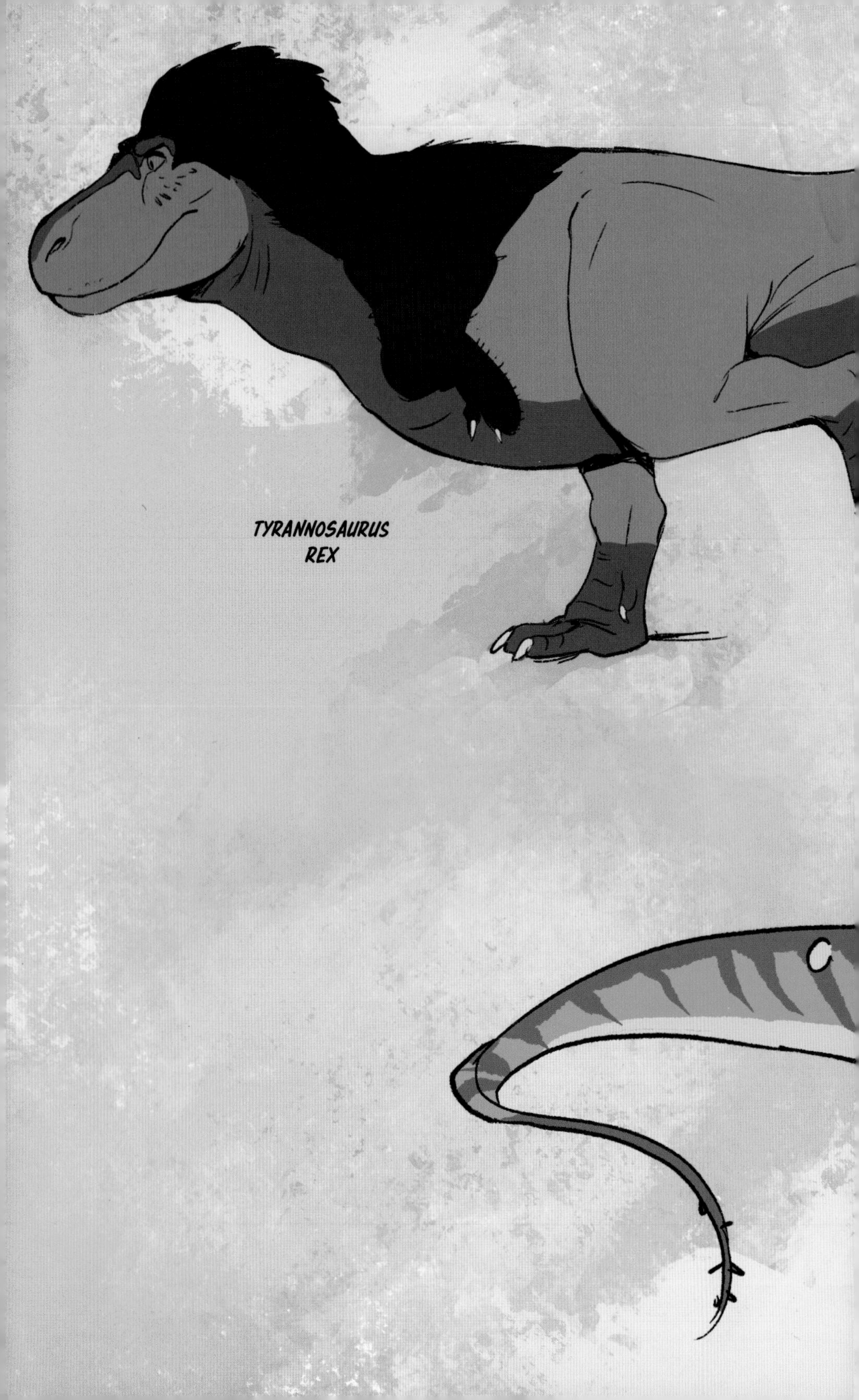
TYRANNOSAURUS
REX

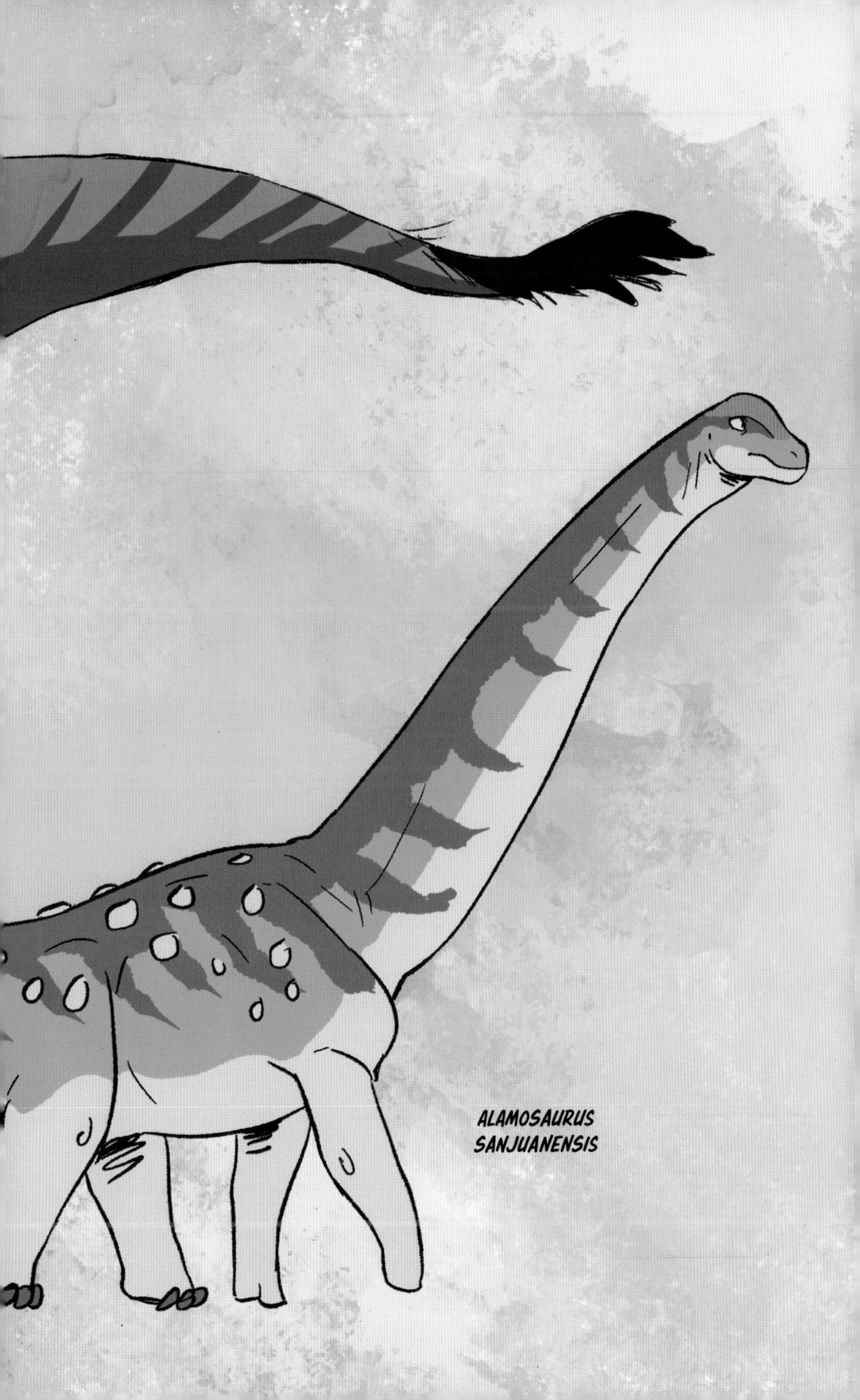
ALAMOSAURUS
SANJUANENSIS

Acknowledgments

Lost Time is a little story that's gone through so much work and love, ever since I first drew concepts for it in 2017. The fact that it's now a book in your hands was because of all the love and support I've had since those little sketches in 2017.

First, I want to thank my parents, particularly my mom, who has been with me all my life and has always, always fostered my creativity. She has been my cheerleader for everything I do, and that has always kept me going.

So much thanks also has to go to my partner in crime and in life, and the one who did all the beautiful inking in this book: Winter Kiakas. Not only did they help me so much in bringing this book to life, they were there to help me work through any plot problems, visualize elements better, and overall support me through this whole process. So much of this book belongs just as much to them.

Of course, I also want to extend my gratitude to my agent, Jen Azantian, for taking my pitch for this book so heartily and with so much love and enthusiasm. To my editor, Chris Hernandez, for immediately seeing my vision with this story and helping me the whole way to bring it out in the best ways. To Danielle Ceccolini, for putting this book together and helping bring it into existence. All of this work was essential to making this book a reality.

And finally, to all the wonderful online resources available for free to learn about the incredible discoveries of prehistory. Most notably to Mark Witton, with incredibly insightful blogs on the wonderfully bizarre animals that are pterosaurs, and Scott Hartman, with his beautifully detailed skeletal diagrams of dinosaurs. And, lastly, a shout-out to the Royal Tyrrell Museum, the museum I would visit every year in my childhood, which built this love for all things long dead.

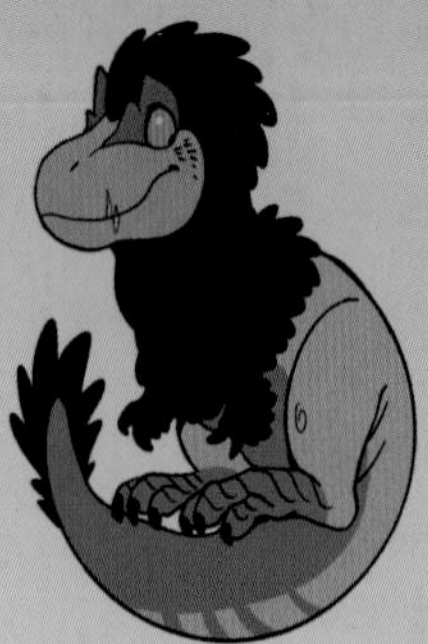

To all the lonely, weird kids.
You're not alone. Keep it up.
—Tas Mukanik

RAZORBILL
An imprint of Penguin Random House LLC, New York

First published in the United States of America by Razorbill,
an imprint of Penguin Random House LLC, 2023

Visit us online at penguinrandomhouse.com.

Library of Congress Cataloging-in-Publication Data is available.

ISBN: 9780593327050 (paperback)
1 3 5 7 9 10 8 6 4 2
ISBN: 9780593327036 (hardcover)
1 3 5 7 9 10 8 6 4 2

Manufactured in China

TOPL

Inks by Winter Jay Kiakas
Edited by Chris Hernandez
Design by Danielle Ceccolini